"Are you saying ... gether and that I am the father of your baby?" he demanded.

She stared wordlessly at him, hurt still crowding viciously into her chest. "Are you trying to say we didn't? That I imagined the weeks we spent together or that you left me without a word and never looked back?"

"I don't remember you," he said hoarsely. "I don't remember any of it. You. Us. That." He gestured toward her belly.

He trailed off and something about the bewilderment in his voice made her stop in her tracks. She crossed her arms protectively over her chest and swallowed.

"You don't remember."

He ran a hand through his hair and swore under his breath. "I had an…accident. Several months ago. I don't remember you. If what you're saying is true, we met during the part of my memory that is a complete blank."

Dear Reader,

This month marks the release of the first book in my new PREGNANCY & PASSION mini-series for Desire™! I'm so excited to bring you the stories of four very powerful men who are brought to their knees by four very special women.

In *Enticed By His Forgotten Lover*, Rafael de Luca makes a very painful discovery about his past actions. Actions that could very well drive away the woman he's fallen hard for.

Rafael and Bryony certainly don't have a smooth path to happily ever after, but it's all the more sweet because love is a very hard-fought victory for these two.

I hope you enjoy their story and that you'll join me for the stories of Rafael's closest friends, Ryan Beardsley, Devon Carter and Cameron Hollingsworth. Nothing about these men is easy, which makes their stories that much more endearing.

Until next time, happy reading!

Love,

Maya Banks

ENTICED BY HIS FORGOTTEN LOVER

BY
MAYA BANKS

Published in Great Britain 2012
by Mills & Boon, an imprint of Harlequin (UK) Limited,
Eton House, 18-24 Paradise Road, Richmond, Surrey TW9 1SR

2in1 ISBN: 978 0 263 89151 5

51-0412

Harlequin (UK) policy is to use papers that are natural, renewable and recyclable products and made from wood grown in sustainable forests. The logging and manufacturing processes conform to the legal environmental regulations of the country of origin.

Printed and bound in Spain
by Blackprint CPI, Barcelona

Maya Banks has loved romance novels from a very (very) early age, and almost from the start, she dreamed of writing them, as well. In her teens she filled countless notebooks with overdramatic stories of love and passion. Today her stories are only slightly less dramatic, but no less romantic.

She lives in Texas with her husband and three children and wouldn't contemplate living anywhere other than the South. When she's not writing, she's usually hunting, fishing or playing poker. She loves to hear from her readers, and she can be found on Facebook www.facebook.com/AuthorMayaBanks or you can follow her on Twitter @maya_banks. Her website, www.mayabanks.com is where you can find up-to-date information on all of Maya's current and forthcoming releases.

To Jane Litte because she loves this trope above all others ;)

To Charles Griemsman for all his words of encouragement and his never-ending patience

One

Rafael de Luca had been in worse situations before, and he'd no doubt be in worse in the future. He could handle it. These people would never make him sweat. They'd never know that he had absolutely no memory of any of them.

He surveyed the crowded ballroom with grim tolerance, sipping at the tasteless wine to cover the fact that he was uneasy. It was only by force of will that he'd managed to last this long. His head was pounding a vicious cadence that made it hard to down the swallow of wine without his stomach heaving it back up.

"Rafe, you can pack it in," Devon Carter murmured next to him. "You've put in enough time. No one suspects a thing."

Rafael swiveled to see his three friends—Devon, Ryan Beardsley and Cameron Hollingsworth—standing protectively at his back. There was significance there. Always at his back. Ever since they were freshmen in college, determined to make their mark on the business world.

They had come when he was lying in the hospital, a yawning black hole in his memory. They hadn't coddled him. Quite the opposite. They'd been complete bastards. He was still grateful for that.

"I've been told I never leave a party early," Rafe said as he tipped the wine toward his mouth again. As soon as the aroma wafted through his nostrils, he lowered the glass, changing his mind. What he wouldn't give for a bloody painkiller.

He'd refused any medication. He despised how out of control painkillers made him feel. But right now, he'd gladly take a few and pass out for several hours. Maybe then he'd wake up without the god-awful pain in his temples.

Cam's lips twisted in a half snarl. "Who gives a damn what you typically do? It's your party. Tell them all to—"

Ryan held up his hand. "They're important business associates, Cam. We want their money, remember?"

Cam scowled as he scanned the room.

"Who needs a security team with the three of you around?" Rafael drawled. He joked, but he was grateful for people he could trust. There was no one else he'd admit his memory loss to.

Devon leaned in quickly and said in a low voice, "The man approaching is Quenton Ramsey the third. His wife's name is Marcy. He's already confirmed for the Moon Island deal."

Rafael nodded and took a step away from the shelter of his friends and smiled warmly at the approaching couple. A lot rode on making sure their investors didn't get nervous. Rafael and his business partners had located a prime spot for their resort—a tiny island off the coast of Texas just across the bay from Galveston. The land was his. Now all they had to do was build the hotel and keep their investors happy.

"Quenton, Marcy, it's wonderful to see you both again. And may I say how lovely you look tonight, Marcy. Quenton is a very lucky man."

The older woman's cheeks flushed with pleasure as Rafael took her hand and brought it to his lips.

He nodded politely and pretended interest in the couple, but his nape was prickling again, and he squelched the urge to rub it. His head was lowered as if he were hanging on to every word, but his gaze rapidly took in the room, searching for the source of his unease.

At first his gaze flickered past her but he yanked his attention back to the woman standing across the room. Her stare bore holes through him. Unflinching and steady even when his eyes locked with hers.

It was hard for him to discern why he was so arrested by her. He knew he generally preferred tall, leggy blondes. He was a total sucker for baby blues and soft, pale skin.

This woman was petite, even in heels, and had a creamy olive complexion. A wealth of inky black curls cascaded over her shoulders and her eyes were equally dark.

She looked at him as if she'd already judged him and found him lacking. He'd never seen her before in his life. Or had he?

He cursed the gaping hole in his memory. He remembered nothing of the weeks before his accident four months ago and had gaps in his memory preceding the weeks that he remembered nothing of. It was all so…random. Selective amnesia. It was complete and utter bull. No one got amnesia except hysterical women in bad soap operas. His physician suggested that there was a psychological reason for the missing pieces of his memory. Rafael hadn't appreciated such a suggestion. He wasn't crazy. Who the hell *wanted* to lose their memory?

He remembered Dev, Cam and Ryan. Every moment of the past decade. Their years in college. Their success in business. He remembered most of the people who worked for him. Most. But not all, which caused him no end of stress in his offices.

Especially since he was trying to close a resort development deal that could make him and his partners millions.

Now he was stuck not remembering who half his investors were and he couldn't afford to lose anyone at this stage of the game.

The woman was still staring at him, but she'd made no move to approach him. Her eyes had grown colder the longer their gazes held, and her hand tightened perceptibly on her small clutch.

"Excuse me," he murmured to the Ramseys. With a smooth smile, he disengaged himself from the group who'd assembled around him and discreetly made his way in the direction of his mystery woman.

His security team followed at a short distance, but he ignored them. They didn't shadow him for fear of his safety as much as his partners feared it getting out that he'd lost his memory. The security team was an annoyance he was unused to, but they kept people at arm's length, which served him well at the moment.

The woman didn't pretend to be coy. She stared straight at him and as he approached, her chin thrust upward in a gesture of defiance that intrigued him.

For a moment he stood in front of her, studying the delicate lines of her face and wondering if in fact this was their first meeting. Surely he would have remembered.

"Excuse me, but have we met?" he asked in his smoothest voice, one that he knew to be particularly effective on women.

Likely she'd titter and then deny such a meeting. Or she'd blatantly lie and try to convince him that they'd spent a wonderful night in bed. Which he knew couldn't be true, because she wasn't his type.

His gaze settled over the generous swell of her breasts pushed up by the empire waist of her black cocktail dress. The rest of the dress fell in a swirl to her knees and twitched with sudden impatience.

She did none of the things he'd supposed. When he glanced back up at her face, he saw fury reflected in the dark pools of her eyes.

"*Met?* Have we *met?*" Her voice was barely above a whisper, but he felt each word like the crack of a whip. "You sorry bastard!"

Before he could process the shock of her outburst she nailed him with a right hook. He stumbled back, holding his nose.

"Son of a—"

Before he could demand to know if she'd lost her damn mind, one of his guards stepped between him and the woman, and in the confusion accidentally sent her reeling backward. She stumbled and went down on one knee, her hand automatically flying to the folds of her dress.

It was then, as she cupped her belly, that the realization hit him. The folds had hidden the gentle curve of her body. Had hidden her pregnancy and the evidence of a child.

His guard went to roughly haul her to her feet.

"No!" Rafael roared. "She's pregnant. Do not hurt her!"

His guard stepped back, his startled gaze going to Rafael. The woman wasted no time scrambling to her feet. Her eyes flashing, she turned and ran down the marble hallway, her heels tapping a loud staccato as she fled.

Rafael stared at her retreating figure, too stunned to do or say anything. The last time she'd looked at him, it wasn't fury he'd seen. It wasn't the fiery anger that prompted her to hit him. No, he'd seen tears and hurt. Somehow, he'd hurt this woman and damned if he knew how.

The vicious ache in his head forgotten, he hurried down the hallway after her. He burst from the hotel lobby, and when he reached the steps leading down to the busy streets, he saw two shoes sparkling in the moonlight, the silvery glitter twinkling at him. Mocking him.

He bent and picked up the strappy sandals and then he

frowned. A pregnant woman had no business wearing heels this high. What if she'd tripped and fallen? Why the devil had she run? It certainly seemed as if she wanted a confrontation with him, but at first opportunity, she'd fled.

At least she'd had the common sense to ditch them so she wasn't running down some street on a pair of toothpicks.

"What the hell is going on, Rafe?" Cam demanded as he hurried up behind him.

In fact, his entire security team, along with Cam, Ryan and Devon, had followed him from the hotel into the crisp autumn air. Now they gathered around him and they looked as though they were concerned. About him.

He blew out his breath in frustration and then shoved the pair of sparkly, ultra-feminine shoes at Ramon, his head of security.

"Find the woman who wore these shoes."

"What would you like me to do with her when I find her?" Ramon asked in a sober voice that told Rafael he'd definitely find the woman in short order. Ramon didn't typically fail in any task Rafael set him to.

Rafael shook his head. "You aren't to do anything. Report back to me. I'll handle the situation."

He was treated to a multitude of frowns.

"I don't like it, Rafe," Ryan said. "This screams setup. It's not impossible that your memory loss hasn't already been leaked to the press or even a few confidential sources who haven't yet gone wide with it. A woman could manipulate you in a thousand ways by using it against you."

"Yes, she could," Rafael said calmly. "There's something about this woman that bugs me, though."

Cam's brow lifted in that imperious way that intimidated so many people. "Do you recognize her? Is she someone you knew?"

Rafael frowned. "I don't know. Yet. But I'm going to find out."

* * *

Bryony Morgan stepped from the shower, wrapped a towel around her head and then pulled on a robe. Even a warm shower hadn't stopped the rapid thump of her pulse. Try as she might, she hadn't been able to let go of her rage.

Have we met?

His question replayed over and over until she wanted to throw something. Preferably at him.

How could she have been so stupid? She wasn't typically one to lose her mind over a good-looking man. She'd been immune to a good many with charm and wit.

But from the time Rafael de Luca had stepped onto her island, he'd been it for her. No fighting. No resisting. He was the entire package. Perfection in those uptight business suits he wore. Oh, she'd managed to get them off of him. By the time he left the island, his pilot hadn't even recognized him.

He'd gone from a sober, uptight, type A personality to laid-back, relaxed and well vacationed.

And in love.

She closed her eyes against the sudden surge of pain that swamped her.

He obviously hadn't been in love. Or anything else. He came. He saw. And he conquered. She was just too hopelessly naive and too in love herself to consider his true motives.

That may well have been the case, but it didn't mean he was going to get away scot-free with his lies and deception. She didn't care what she had to do, he wasn't going to develop the land she'd sold him into some ginormous tourist mecca and turn the entire island into some playground for bored, wealthy jet-setters.

It had taken all her courage to crash his party tonight, but once she'd learned the purpose—a gathering of his potential investors for the project he planned to ruin her land with—she'd been determined to confront him. Right there in their midst. Daring him to lie to her when the entire room knew of his plans.

She hadn't counted on him denying that he'd ever met her. But then how better to paint her as the village idiot? Or some crazy do-gooder granola bar out to halt "progress."

The force of just how wrong she'd been threatened to flatten her. She sighed heavily and shook her head. She had to calm down or her blood pressure was going to skyrocket.

Slowly she unclenched her jaw. Her teeth were ground together with enough force to break them.

Where was room service? She was starving. She rubbed her belly apologetically and made a conscious effort to let all the anger and stress flow out of her body. It couldn't be good for the baby to have her mother so pissed off all the time.

She gritted her teeth before she realized that she'd done so again. Forcing her jaw to relax once more, she performed the arduous task of combing out her hair and blow-drying it.

She was finishing up when a loud knock sounded at her door.

"Food. Finally," she murmured as she turned off the hair dryer.

She hurried to the door and swung it open. But there was no food cart or hotel employee. Rafael stood there, her abandoned shoes dangling from his fingertips.

She stepped back and tried to slam the door, but he stuck his foot in, preventing her from shutting it.

As indomitable as ever, he pushed his way in and stood in front of her. She hated how small and vulnerable she felt against him. Oh, she hadn't always hated it. She'd loved how protected and cherished he'd made her feel when she curled her much smaller body into his.

She bared her teeth into a snarl. "Get out or I'll call hotel security."

"You could," he said calmly. "But as I own this hotel, you might have a hard time having me thrown out."

Her eyes narrowed. Of course he'd own the hotel she'd chosen to stay in. What were the odds of that?

"I'll call the police then. I don't care who you are. You can't force yourself into my hotel room."

He raised an eyebrow. "I came to return your shoes. Does that make me a criminal?"

"Oh, come on, Rafael! Stop playing stupid games. It's beneath you. Or it should be. I get it. Believe me—I get it! I got it as soon as you looked right through me at the party. Though I have to say, the 'have we met?' line? That was priceless. Just priceless. Not to mention overkill."

It was all she could do not to hit him again, and maybe he realized just how badly she wanted to because he took a wary step back.

She advanced, not willing for a moment to allow him to control the situation. "You know what? I never took you for a coward. You played me. I get that. I was a monumental idiot. But for you to hide from the inevitable confrontation like you've done makes me physically ill."

She stuck a finger into his chest, ignoring the baffled look on his face. "Furthermore, you're not going to get away with your plans for *my* land. If it takes every cent I own, I'll fight you. We had a verbal agreement, and you'll stick to it."

He blinked, then looked as if he was about to say something.

She crossed her arms, so furious she wanted to kick him. If it wouldn't land her on her ass, she'd do it.

"What? Did you think you'd never see me again? That I'd hide away somewhere and sulk because I learned you don't really love me and slept with me to get me to agree to sell to you? You couldn't be more mistaken," she seethed.

Rafael reacted as though she'd hit him again. His face paled and his eyes became hard, cold points. If she weren't so angry, what she saw in his gaze would probably scare the bejesus out of her. But Mamaw had always said that common sense was the first thing to go when someone got all riled up. Boy, was that the truth.

"Are you trying to insinuate that you and I have slept together?" he asked in a dangerously low voice that—again—should have frightened her. But she was way beyond fear. "I don't even know your name."

It shouldn't have hurt her. She'd long since realized why Rafael had chosen her. Why he'd seduced her and why he'd told her the lies he told. He couldn't shoulder the entire blame. She'd been far too easy a conquest.

But still, that he'd stand there before her and categorically deny even knowing her name sliced a jagged line through her heart that was beyond repair.

"You should go," she said in a barely controlled tone. Damn the tears, but if he didn't leave now, she wasn't going to keep her composure for long.

His brow furrowed and he cocked his head to the side, studying her intently. Then to her dismay, he swept his hand out and smudged a tear from the corner of her eye with his thumb.

"You're upset."

Sweet mother of God, this man was an idiot. She could only pray their child inherited her brains and not his. She nearly laughed aloud but it came out as a strangled sob. How could she hope for the poor baby to inherit any intelligence whatsoever when it was clear that both his parents were flaming morons?

"Get. Out."

But instead he cupped her chin and tilted it upward so he could stare into her eyes. Then he wiped at the dampness on her cheek in a surprisingly gentle gesture.

"We can't have slept together. Besides the fact that you aren't my type, I can't imagine forgetting such an event."

Her mouth gaped open and any thoughts of tears fled. She

wrenched herself from his grasp and gave up trying to get the man out of her room. He could stay. She was going.

She gripped the lapels of her robe and stomped around him. She made it into the hall before his hand closed around her wrist and he pulled her up short.

Enough was enough. She opened her mouth to let out a shriek, but he yanked her against his hard body and covered her mouth.

"For God's sake, I'm not going to hurt you," he hissed.

He muscled her back into the hotel room, slammed the door and bolted it shut behind them. Then he turned and glared at her.

"You've already hurt me," she said through gritted teeth.

His eyes softened and grew cloudy with confusion.

"It's obvious you feel as though I've wronged you in some way. I'd apologize, but I'd have to remember you and what I supposedly did in order to offer restitution."

"Restitution?" She gaped at him, stunned by the difference in the Rafael de Luca she fell in love with and this man standing before her now. She yanked open her robe so that the small mound of her belly showed through the thin, satin nightgown underneath. "You make me fall in love with you. You seduce me. You tell me you love me and that you want us to be together. You get my signature on papers agreeing to sell you land that has been in my family for a century. You feed me complete lies about our relationship and your plans for the land. But that wasn't enough. No, you had to get me pregnant on top of it all!"

His face went white. Anger removed all the confusion from his features. He took a step toward her and for the first time, fear edged out her fury. She took a step back and braced her hand against the TV stand.

"Are you saying that we slept together and that I am the father of your baby?" he demanded.

She stared wordlessly at him, hurt still crowding viciously

into her chest. "Are you trying to say we didn't? That I imagined the weeks we spent together? Do you deny that you left me without a word and never looked back?"

Sarcasm crept into her voice but there was also deep pain that she wished wasn't so evident. It was enough that he'd betrayed her. She didn't want to be humiliated further.

He flinched and closed his eyes. Then he took a step back and for a moment she thought he was finally going to do as she'd demanded and leave.

"I don't remember you," he said hoarsely. "I don't remember any of it. You. Us. That." He gestured toward her belly.

He trailed off and something about the bewilderment in his voice made her stop in her tracks. She crossed her arms protectively over her chest and swallowed.

"You don't remember."

He ran a hand through his hair and swore under his breath. "I had an…accident. Several months ago. I don't remember you. If what you're saying is true, we met during the period where my memory is a complete blank."

Two

Rafael watched as all the color leeched from her face and she swayed unsteadily. With a curse, he reached to grasp her arms. This time she didn't fight him. She was limp in his hands and he felt the slight tremble beneath his fingers.

"Come, sit down, before you fall," he said grimly.

He led her to the bed and she sat, her hands going to the edge to brace herself.

She glanced up at him, her eyes haunted. "You expect me to believe you have *amnesia?* Is that the best you could come up with?"

He winced because he felt much the same about the idea of amnesia. If all she'd said was true and their positions were reversed, he'd laugh her out of the room.

"I don't ask this to make you angry, but what is your name? I feel at quite a disadvantage here."

She sighed and rubbed a hand wearily through her thick hair. "You're serious about this."

He made a sound of impatience and she pinched the bridge of her nose between her fingers.

"My name is Bryony Morgan," she said quietly.

She bowed her head and black curls fell forward, hiding her profile. Unable to resist, he ran his finger over her cheek and then pushed the hair back behind her ear.

"Well, Bryony, it would seem you and I have a lot to discuss. I have many, many questions as you can well imagine."

She turned her head to stare up at him. "Amnesia. You're seriously going to stick to this insane story?"

He tried to remember how skeptical he'd be in her shoes, but her outright disbelief was ticking him off. He wasn't used to having his word questioned by anyone.

"Do you think I like being punched in the face at a public gathering by a woman claiming to be pregnant with my child when to my knowledge it's the first time we've met? Put yourself in my shoes for a moment. If a man you'd never seen before or had no memory of walked up to you and said the things to you that you're saying to me, don't you think you'd be a little suspicious? Hell, you'd probably have already called the cops you keep threatening me with."

"This is crazy," she muttered.

"Look, I can prove what happened to me. I can show you my medical records and the doctor's diagnosis. I don't remember you, Bryony. I'm sorry if that hurts you, but it's a fact. I have only your word that we were ever anything to each other."

Her lips twisted. "Yeah, we can't forget I'm not your type."

He winced. Trust her to remember that remark.

"I'd like for you to tell me everything. Start from the beginning. Tell me when and where we met. Maybe something you say will jog my memory."

A knock sounded at the door and he scowled. "Are you expecting someone at this hour?" he asked when she rose to answer it.

"Room service. I'm starving. I haven't eaten all day."

"That can't be good for the baby."

She didn't look as though she appreciated the remark. Gathering her robe tighter around her, she went to the door and a few seconds later, a room service attendant wheeled in a cart bearing covered plates. She signed the bill and offered a halfhearted smile of thanks to the man.

When Rafael and Bryony were alone again she pushed the cart the rest of the way to the bed. "Sorry. Obviously I wasn't counting on company. I only ordered enough food for one."

He lifted a brow as she began uncovering the dishes. There was enough food to feed a small convention.

"Sit down and relax. We can talk while you're eating."

She settled in the armchair catty-corner to the bed and curled her feet underneath her. As she reached for one of the plates, he studied the face of the woman he'd forgotten.

She was beautiful. No denying that. Not the kind of woman he usually gravitated toward. She was entirely too outspoken for his liking. He preferred women who were gentle and, according to his close friends, submissive.

Quite frankly it made him sound like a jackass. But he couldn't deny he did like his women a bit more biddable. He found it fascinating that he'd supposedly met and fallen in love with Bryony Morgan, the antithesis of every woman he'd dated for the past five years.

Okay, so he bought that he'd been attracted to her. And yeah, he could buy sleeping with her. But falling in love? In a span of a few weeks?

That was a giant hole in the fairy tale she'd spun.

But she was also a woman, and women tended to be emotional creatures. It was possible she thought he was in love with her. Her hurt and betrayal certainly didn't seem feigned.

And then there was the fact she was pregnant with his child. It would probably make him seem even more of a bastard, but it would be stupid not to insist on paternity testing. It wasn't out of the realm of possibility that she'd made the entire thing up after learning of his memory loss.

He had the sudden urge to call his lawyer and have him tell him whose signature was on the real estate contract for the land he'd purchased sometime during the weeks he'd lost. He hadn't seen the paperwork since before his accident. He paid people to keep his business running and his affairs in order. Once he scored the deal, there was no reason to look back.

Until now.

Damn but this was a mess. And yeah, he was definitely calling his lawyer first thing in the morning.

"What are you thinking?" she asked bluntly.

"That this is a huge cluster f—"

"You're telling me," she muttered. "Only I don't see what's so bad from your perspective. You've got more money than God. You're not pregnant, and you didn't just sign away land that's been in your family for generations to a man who's going to destroy it to build some tourist trap."

The pain in her voice sent an uncomfortable sensation through his chest. Something remarkably like guilt ate at him, but what did he have to feel guilty about? None of this was his fault.

"How did we meet?" he asked. "I need to know everything."

She toyed with her fork, and her lips turned down into an unhappy frown.

"The first time I saw you, you were wearing an uptight suit, shoes that cost more than my house and you had on sunglasses. It annoyed me that I couldn't see your eyes, so I refused to speak to you until you took them off."

"And where was this?"

"Moon Island. You were asking about a stretch of beach-front property and who owned it. I, of course, was the owner, and I figured you were some guy from the city with big plans to develop the island and save all the locals from a life of poverty."

He frowned. "It wasn't for sale? I remember it being for sale before I ever went down there. I wouldn't have known about it otherwise."

She nodded. "It was. I…I needed to sell it. My grandmother and I could no longer afford the property taxes. But we agreed we wouldn't sell to a developer. It was bad enough that I was forced to sell land that's been in my family for generations."

She broke off, clearly uncomfortable with all she'd shared.

"Anyway, I figured you for another stiff suit, and so I sent you across the island on a wild-goose chase."

He sent a glare in her direction. For the first time, a smile flirted on the edge of her lips.

"You were so angry with me. You stormed back to my cottage and banged on my door. You demanded to know what the hell I was doing and said I didn't act like someone who desperately needed to sell a piece of land."

"That sounds like me," he acknowledged.

"I informed you that I wasn't interested in selling to you and you demanded to know why. When I told you of my promise to my grandmother that we'd only sell to someone willing to sign a guarantee that they wouldn't commercially develop the stretch of beach, you asked to meet her."

An uncomfortable prickle went up his nape. That didn't sound like him. He wasn't one to get personal. Everyone had their price. He would have simply upped his offer until he found theirs.

"The rest is pretty embarrassing," she said lightly. "I took you to meet Mamaw. The two of you got along famously. She invited you to stay for supper. Afterward we took a walk on the beach. You kissed me. I kissed you back. You walked me back to my cottage and told me you'd see me the next day."

"And did I?"

"Oh, yes," she whispered. "And the day after, and the day after. It took me three days to talk you out of that suit."

He lifted a brow and stared.

Her cheeks turned red and she clamped a hand over her mouth. "Oh, God, I didn't mean it like that. You wore that suit everywhere on the beach. You stuck out like a sore thumb. So I took you shopping. We bought you beachwear."

This was starting to sound like a nightmare. "Beachwear?"

Her head bobbed up and down. "Shorts. T-shirts. Flip-flops."

Maybe the doctor had been right. He lost his memory because he *wanted* to forget. Flip-flops? It was all he could do not to stare down at his very expensive leather loafers and imagine wearing flip-flops.

"And I wore this…beachwear."

She raised an eyebrow. "You did. We bought swim trunks, too. I don't know of anyone who goes to an island and doesn't pack something to swim in, so we got you some trunks and I took you to my favorite stretch of the beach."

So far her version of the weeks missing from his memory was so divergent from everything he knew of himself that it was like listening to a story about someone else. What could have possessed him to act so out of character?

"How long did this relationship you say we had go on?" he croaked.

"Four weeks," she said softly. "Four wonderful weeks. We were together every day. By the end of the first week, you gave up your hotel room and you stayed with me. In my bed. We'd make love with the windows open so we could listen to the ocean."

"I see."

Her eyes narrowed. "You don't believe me."

"Bryony," he said carefully. "This is very difficult for me. I'm missing a month of my life and what you're telling me sounds so fantastical, so utterly out of character for me, that I can't even wrap my head around it."

She pressed her lips together but he could still see them tremble. "Yeah, I get that this is difficult for you. But try to see things from my perspective for just a few moments. Imagine that the person you were in love with and thought was in love with you suddenly can't remember you. Imagine what kind of doubts you have when you discover that everything he told you was a lie and that he made you promises he didn't keep. How would you feel?"

He stared into her eyes, gutted by the sorrow he saw. "I'd be pretty damn upset."

"Yeah. That about covers it."

She stood and pushed the serving cart back so that she could step around it. Her hand crept around the back of her neck and she rubbed absently as she stood just a short distance from where he sat on the edge of the bed.

"Look, this is…pointless. I'm really tired. You should probably go now."

He shot to his feet. "You want me to go?" It was on the tip of his tongue to ask her if she was out of her damn mind, but that wouldn't win him any more points with her. "After dumping this story on me, after telling me I'm going to be a father, you expect me to just walk away?"

"It's what you did before," she said wearily.

"How the hell can you say that? How do you know what I did or didn't do when *I* don't even know? You said you loved me and that I loved you. I've just told you I can't remember any of it. How do you get that I walked away from you? That I somehow betrayed you? I was in an accident, Bryony. What was the last day you saw me? What did we do? Did I dump you? Did I tell you I was leaving you?"

Her face was white and her fingers were balled into tiny fists at her sides.

"It was the day after we closed on the land. You said you

had to go back to New York. It was some emergency you had to attend to personally. You said it wouldn't take more than a day or two. You told me you'd be back, that you couldn't wait to come back, and that once you'd returned, we'd discuss what we'd do with the land," she said painfully.

"What day was it? The date, Bryony. The exact date."

"June third."

"The day of my accident."

She looked stricken. Her hand flew to her mouth. She looked so unsteady that he thought she might fall. He reached out, snagged her wrist and pulled her down to sit beside him. She didn't fight. She just stared at him numbly.

"How? What happened?"

"My private jet went down over Kentucky," he said grimly. "I don't remember a lot. I woke up in a hospital and had no idea how I'd come to be there."

"And you remember nothing?" she asked hoarsely.

"Only those four weeks. I have some other gaps but it's mostly people I'm supposed to know or remember but don't. I didn't initially remember the circumstances surrounding my decision to fly down to Moon Island, but that's easy enough to figure out since I bought a piece of property while I was there."

"So you just forgot *me,*" she said with a forced laugh.

He sighed. "I know it's not easy to hear. Try to understand that I'm having the same difficulty believing all you've told me. I may not remember you, Bryony, but I'm not a complete bastard. It doesn't bring me any satisfaction to see how much this hurts you."

"I tried to call," she said bleakly. "At first I waited. I told myself all sorts of excuses. It was a bigger emergency. You're a really busy guy. But then I tried to call the number you'd given me. No one would let me speak to you. There were always excuses. You were in a meeting. You were out of town. You were at lunch."

"There was a pretty tight security net around me after the accident. We didn't want anyone to know of my memory loss. We were afraid it would make investors lose their confidence in me. Any sign of weakness will make many people pull out of a deal."

"It looked—and felt—like a brush-off, and it pissed me off the more time that passed because you didn't have the balls to tell me to my face."

"So why now? Why did you wait so long to come here and confront me?"

She stared warily at him as if determining whether he was suspicious of her motives. And maybe he was. It certainly made sense that if she'd been that angry—and pregnant—she wouldn't have waited four months to confront him.

"I didn't find out I was pregnant until I was nearly ten weeks along. And Mamaw was having health problems so I was spending a lot of time with her. I didn't want to upset her by telling her that I suspected you'd seduced me and lied to me—to us—about your plans for the land. It would have broken her heart. Not just about the land. She knew how much I loved you. She wanted me happy."

Well, damn. He felt about two inches tall.

He ran a hand through his hair and wondered how the hell someone's life could change so drastically in a single day.

"We have some decisions to make, Bryony."

She turned and tilted her head in his direction. "Decisions?"

He met her gaze. "You've told me that I was in love with you. That you were in love with me. You've also said that you're pregnant with my child. If you think I'm just going to walk out of your hotel room and not look back, you're insane. We have a hell of a lot to work out and it isn't going to be resolved in a single night. Or day. Or week even."

She nodded her agreement.

"I want you to come with me."

Her eyes widened. Her mouth parted and her tongue swept nervously over her bottom lip.

"Where exactly are we going?"

"If everything you say is true, then a hell of a lot of my life and future changed on that island. You and I are going to go back to where it all started."

She stared in bewilderment at him. Had she expected him to walk away? He wasn't sure if he was angry or resigned over that fact.

"We're going to relive those weeks, Bryony. Maybe being there will bring it all back."

"And if it doesn't?" she asked cautiously.

"Then we'll have spent a lot of time getting reacquainted."

Three

"Have you lost your mind?" Ryan demanded.

Rafael stopped pacing and leveled a stare at his friends, who'd gathered in his office.

"Let's not talk about who's lost their mind," Rafael said pointedly. "I'm not the one mounting a search for the woman who screwed me over with my brother."

Ryan glared at him then shoved his hands into his pockets and turned to stare out the window.

"Low blow," Devon murmured.

Rafael blew out his breath. Yeah, it had been. Whatever the reason for Ryan trying to track down his ex-fiancée, he didn't deserve Rafael acting like an ass.

"Sorry, man," Rafael offered.

Cam leaned back in Rafael's executive chair and placed his feet up on the desk. "I think you're both certifiable. No woman is worth this much trouble." He clasped his hands behind his head and leveled a stare in Rafael's direction. "And you. I don't even know what to say to your crazy idea of going back with her to Moon Island. What do you hope to accomplish?"

That was a damn good question. He wasn't entirely certain. He wanted his memory back. He wanted to know what had made him go off his rocker and supposedly fall in love with and impregnate a woman in a matter of weeks.

He was thirty-four years old, but from all accounts, he'd acted like a teenager faced with his first naked woman.

"She says we fell in love."

He nearly groaned. Just saying the words made him feel utterly ridiculous.

The three other men stared at him as if he'd just announced he was taking a vow of celibacy. Though at the moment, it didn't sound like a bad idea.

"She also claims the child she's pregnant with is yours," Devon pointed out. "That's a lot of things she's claiming."

"Have you talked to your lawyer?" Ryan asked. "This entire situation makes me nervous. She could do a lot of damage to this deal if she goes public. If she spills her tale of you being a complete bastard, knocking her up and hauling ass before the ink on the contracts was dry, it's not going to make any of us look good."

"No, I damn well haven't spoken to Mario yet," Rafael muttered. "When have I had time? I'm calling him next."

"So how long are you going to be gone on this soul-searching expedition?" Cam asked.

Rafael shoved his hands into his pockets and rocked back on his heels. "As long as it takes."

Devon glanced down at his watch. "As much as I'd love to stick around and be amused by all this, I have an appointment."

"Copeland?" Cam smirked.

Devon curled his lip in Cam's direction.

"The old man still adamant that you marry his daughter if you want the merger?" Ryan asked.

Devon sighed. “Yeah. She’s…flighty, and Copeland seems to think I’d settle her.”

Rafael winced and shot his friend a look of sympathy.

Cam shrugged. “So tell him the deal’s off.”

“She’s not that bad. She’s just young and…exuberant. There are worse women to marry.”

“In other words, she’d drive a stick-in-the-mud like you crazy,” Ryan said with a grin.

Devon made a rude gesture as he headed toward the door.

Cam swiveled in Rafael’s chair and let his feet hit the floor with a thud. “I’m off, too. Make damn sure you give us a heads-up before you head off to find yourself, Rafe.”

Rafael grunted and claimed his chair as Cam followed behind Devon. Ryan still stood at the window and he turned to Rafael once they were alone.

“Hey, I’m sorry for the crack about Kelly,” Rafael said before Ryan could speak. “Have you been able to find her yet?”

Ryan shook his head. “No. But I will.”

Rafael didn’t understand Ryan’s determination to hunt down his ex-fiancée. The whole fiasco had taken place during the four weeks Rafael had lost, but Devon and Cam had told him that Kelly had slept with Ryan’s brother. Ryan had tossed her out and had seemingly moved on. Only now Ryan had hired an investigator to find her.

“You don’t remember Bryony?” Ryan asked. “Nothing at all?”

Rafael slapped a pen against the edge of his desk. “No. Nothing. It’s like looking at a stranger.”

“And you don’t think that’s odd?”

Rafael made a sound of exasperation. “Well, of course it’s odd. Everything about this situation is odd.”

Ryan leaned back against the window and studied Rafael. “You’d think if you’d fallen head-over-ass for this woman, spent every waking moment for four weeks with her and managed to knock her up in the process that there would at least be some serious déjà vu."

Rafael tossed the pen down and spun in his chair until his foot caught on the trash can next to his desk. "I get where you're going with this, Ryan, and I appreciate your concern. Something happened on that island. I don't know what, but there is a gaping hole in my memory and she's at the center. I've got to go back, if for no other reason than to disprove her story."

"And if she's telling the truth?" Ryan asked.

"Then I've got a hell of a lot of catching up to do," Rafael muttered.

Bryony stood outside the high-rise office building and stared straight up. The sleek modern architecture glistened in the bright autumn sun. The sky provided a dramatic backdrop as the spire punched a hole in the vivid blue splash.

An orange leaf drifted lazily onto her face, brushing her nose before fluttering to the ground. It joined others on the sidewalk and skittered along the concrete until it was crunched beneath the feet of the many passersby.

She was jostled by someone shouldering past her and she heard a muttered "Tourist" as they hurried on by.

The city frightened and fascinated her in equal parts. Everyone was so busy here. No one stopped even for a moment. The city pulsed with people, cars, lights and noise. Constant noise.

How did anyone stand it?

And yet she'd been ready to embrace it. She'd known that if she were to have a life with Rafael, she'd have to grow used to city life. It was where he lived and worked. Where he thrived.

Now she stood in front of his office building feeling hesitant and insecure. There was a seed of doubt and it grew with each breath. She couldn't help but wonder if she wasn't being an even bigger fool this time.

"Fool me once, blah blah," she muttered. "I must be insane to trust him."

But if he were telling the truth. If his utterly bizarre and improbable story were true, then he hadn't betrayed her. He hadn't dumped her. He hadn't done any of the things she'd accused him of.

Part of her was relieved and the other part had no idea what to think or believe.

"Bryony, is it?"

She yanked her gaze downward, embarrassed that she was still standing in front of the building looking straight up like a moron, and saw two of the men she'd seen with Rafael at the party.

She took a wary step back. "I'm Bryony, yes."

They were both tall. One had medium brown hair, short and neat. He smiled at her. The other one had blond hair with varying shades of brown. It was longish and unruly. He frowned at her, and his blue eyes narrowed as though she were a nasty bug.

The smiling one stuck out his hand. "I'm Devon Carter, a friend of Rafael's. This is Cameron Hollingsworth."

Cameron continued to scrutinize her so she ignored him and focused on Devon, although she had no idea what to say.

"Nice to meet you," she murmured.

"Are you here to see Rafe?" Devon asked.

She nodded.

"We'll be happy to take you up."

She shook her head. "No, that's okay. I can make it. I mean I don't want to be a bother."

Cameron shot her a cool, assessing look that made her feel vastly inferior. Her chin automatically went up and her fingers balled into a fist at her side. She really wasn't a violent person. Truly. But in the past few days, she'd had her share of violent fantasies. Right now she visualized Cameron Hollingsworth picking himself up off the pavement.

"It's no bother," Devon said smoothly. "The least I can do is see you to the elevator."

She frowned. "You think I'm incapable of finding the elevator? Or are you just one of those really nosy friends?"

Devon's smile was lazy and unbothered. He looked at her as if he knew exactly how wound up she was and that her stomach was in knots. Maybe she had that beautiful look of a woman about to puke.

"Then I'll bid you a good day," Devon finally said.

She swallowed, wishing she hadn't been quite so rude. It was a fault of hers that she went on the offensive the minute she felt at a disadvantage. She wasn't going to win any friends acting like a bitch.

"Thank you. It was nice to meet you."

She injected enough sincerity into her tone that even she believed herself. Devon nodded but Cameron didn't look impressed. She forced herself not to scowl at him as the two men walked to the street and got into a waiting BMW.

Taking a deep breath, she headed to the revolving door and entered the building. The lobby was beautiful. A study in marble and exposed beams. The contrast between old and modern should have looked odd, but instead it looked opulent and rich.

There was a large fountain in the middle of the lobby and she paused to allow the sound of the water to soothe her. She missed the ocean. She didn't venture off the island often, and it made her anxious now, in the midst of so much hustle and bustle, to return to the peace and quiet of the small coastal island she'd grown up on.

Her throat tightened and pain squeezed at her chest. Because of her, her family's land was now in the hands of a man determined to build a resort, golf course and God knew what else. Not that those were bad things. She had nothing against progress. And she certainly wasn't opposed to free enterprise and capitalism. A buck was a buck. Everyone wanted to make a few. Not that Rafael seemed to have any problem in that area.

But Moon Island was special. It was still untouched by the heavy hand of development. The families that lived there had been there for generations. Everyone knew everyone else. Half the island fished or shrimped and the other half had retired to the island after working thirty years in cities like Houston or Dallas.

There was an unspoken agreement among the residents that they wanted the island to remain as it was. A quiet place of splendor. A haven for people wanting to get away from life in the fast lane. Things just moved slower there.

Now because of her, that would all change. Bulldozers and construction crews would move in, and slowly the outside world would creep in and change the way of life.

She bit her lip and turned in the direction of the elevator. It hurt to think how naive she'd been. And now that she had distance from the whirlwind relationship she'd jumped into with Rafael, she knew how stupid she'd been. But at the time… At the time she hadn't been thinking straight. She'd been powerless under his onslaught, his magnetism and the idea that he was as caught up as she was.

She angrily jabbed the button for the thirty-first floor then stepped back as others crowded in. It wasn't as if the thought hadn't occurred to her to add in a legal clause to the contract, but she'd imagined that it would seem as though she didn't trust him. Sort of like demanding a prenuptial agreement before marriage. Yeah, it was smart, but it was also awkward and brought up questions she hadn't wanted at the time.

He'd absolutely sold her on the idea that he wanted to buy the land for personal use. It hadn't been a corporation name on the closing documents. It had been his and only his. Rafael de Luca. And she'd believed him when he'd said he'd be back. That he loved her. That he wanted them to be together.

She was so deeply humiliated over her stupidity that she couldn't bear to think about it. Now, when she'd come to New York to confront Rafael over his lies, she was confronted by his extraordinary claim that he'd lost his memory. It was so damn convenient.

But she couldn't help whispering, "Please let him be telling the truth." Because if he was, then maybe the rest wasn't as bad as she thought. And that probably made her an even bigger moron than she'd already proved herself to be.

When she got off the elevator, there was a reception desk directly in front of her. As Bryony walked up, the receptionist smiled. "Do you have an appointment?"

An appointment? It took her a moment to collect herself and then she nodded. "Rafael is expecting me."

Her voice sounded too husky and too unsure, but the receptionist didn't seem to notice.

"Are you Miss Morgan?"

Bryony nodded.

"Right this way. Mr. de Luca asked that you be shown right in. Would you like some tea or coffee?" With a glance down at Bryony's belly, she added, "We have decaf if you prefer."

Bryony smiled. "Thank you, but I'm fine."

The receptionist opened a door, and Rafael looked up from his desk. "Mr. de Luca, Miss Morgan is here."

Rafael rose and strode forward. "Thank you, Tamara."

"Is there anything you'd like me to get for you?" Tamara inquired politely.

Rafael shook his head. "See that I'm not disturbed."

Tamara nodded and retreated, closing the door behind her.

Bryony stared at Rafael, such a short distance away. She could smell him he was so close. She was at a complete loss as to how to act around him now. She could no longer maintain the outraged, jilted-lover act because if he couldn't remember her, he couldn't very well be blamed for acting as though she didn't exist for the past months.

But neither could she just take up where they'd left off and throw herself into his arms.

The result was tension so thick and awkward that it made her want to fidget out of her shoes.

He stared at her. She stared at him. One would never guess that they'd made a child together.

Rafael sighed. "Before this goes any further, there is something I have to do."

Her brows came together and then lifted when he took a step toward her.

"What?" she asked.

He cupped her face and stepped forward again until their bodies were aligned and his heat—and scent—enveloped her.

"I have to kiss you."

Four

Bryony took a wary step back but Rafael was determined that she wouldn't escape him. He caught her shoulders and pulled her almost roughly against him, swallowing up her light gasp just before his lips found hers in a heated rush.

He wasn't entirely certain what he'd expected to happen. Fireworks? His memory miraculously restored? Images of those missing weeks to flash into his head like a slide show?

None of that happened, but what did shocked the hell out of him.

His body roared to life. Every muscle tensed in instant awareness. Desire and lust coiled tight in his belly and he became achingly hard.

And hell, but she was responsive. After her initial resistance, she melted into his chest and returned his kiss with equal fervor. She wrapped her arms around his neck and clung to him tightly, her lush curves molded perfectly to his body. A body that was screaming for him to pin her to the desk and slake his lust.

He pulled back as awareness returned. For the love of God, what was he thinking? She was pregnant with his child, he couldn't remember her and yet he was ready to tear both of their clothes off and damn the consequences.

Well, at least she couldn't get pregnant again….

He ran a hand through his hair and turned away, his heart thudding out of control and his breaths blowing in ragged spurts from his nose.

Not his type? He shook his head. He'd never met a woman in his life with whom he shared such combustible chemistry.

When he turned back around, Bryony stood there looking dazed, her lips swollen and her eyes soft and fuzzy. It was all he could do not to haul her back into his arms to finish what he'd started.

"I'm sorry," he began before breaking off. "I just had to know."

Her eyes sharpened and the haze lifted away. "Know what?"

She crossed her arms over her chest and tapped her foot in agitation as she stared him down.

"If I could remember anything," he muttered.

Her lip curled into a snarl, baring her teeth. He was reminded of a pissed-off cat, and remembering that she'd decked him the night before, he took a step back.

"And?"

He shook his head. "Nothing."

She threw him a disgusted look and then turned to stalk out of his office.

"Wait a damn minute," he called as he started after her.

She made it to the door before he caught her arm and turned her around to face him.

"What the hell is your problem?"

She gaped at him. "My problem? Gee, I don't know. Maybe I don't appreciate being mauled as some sort of experiment.

I get that this is difficult for you, Rafael, but you aren't the only one suffering here. You don't have to be such an ass."

"But—"

Before he could protest, she was gone again, and he watched her walk away. At least she was wearing sensible shoes she wouldn't trip in.

He stood there arguing with himself over whether to go after her, but what would he say when he caught up? He wasn't sorry he kissed her even if it hadn't been a magic cure-all. It had told him one important thing. He couldn't get close to her without erupting into flames, which meant the likelihood of her carrying his child…?

Pretty damn good.

He strode back to his desk and picked up the phone. A few seconds later, Ramon answered with a curt affirmative.

"Miss Morgan has just left my office. See that she gets back to her hotel safely."

Bryony got off the elevator and exited the office building, no longer caring whether she and Rafael had dinner plans. Her jaw ached from the tight set of her teeth and tears stung the corners of her eyes.

She'd hoped for any sign of the Rafael de Luca she'd fallen in love with. Maybe she had also hoped that their kiss would spark…something. Or that maybe he would embrace the possibility that he'd felt something for her…once.

But there had been no recognition in his eyes when he'd pulled away. Just lust. Lust that any man could feel. A man could have sex with any number of women, but it didn't mean he harbored any deeper feelings for her.

The crisp air ruffled her hair and she started down the sidewalk, no clear direction in mind. It seemed colder than before and she shivered as she walked. Around her, horns honked, people jostled as they passed, dusk was settling and streetlights had started to blink on.

There was still plenty of light for her to walk the few blocks back to her hotel and she needed to let off some steam. She was flushed from Rafe's kiss and she was furious that he'd been so cold and calculating about it.

She'd felt like…a plaything. Like she hadn't mattered. Like she was just a set of boobs for his amusement.

But then that's likely all she'd ever been from the start.

She couldn't afford to be stupid a second time. Not until she had his guarantee—his *written* guarantee—that he wouldn't develop the land would she allow herself to think that his intentions toward her had been sincere.

She hugged her arms to her chest and stopped at a pedestrian crossing. A man knocked into her and she turned with a startled "Hey!"

He mumbled an apology about the time the light turned and the crowd surged forward. With her attention diverted she didn't feel the tug at her other arm until it was too late.

Her purse strap fell and her arm was nearly yanked from its socket as the thief started to run.

Anger rocketed through her veins and, reacting on instinct, she grabbed ahold of the strap with her other hand and tugged back.

The man was close to her own unimpressive height and nearly as slight, but grim determination was etched into his grimy face. He slammed into her, sending her sprawling to the pavement. She hit with enough impact to jar her teeth, but the strap was wrapped around her wrist now.

He jerked again and this time dragged her a few feet before he let out a snarl of rage and backhanded her. Her grip loosened and out of the corner of her eye she saw a flash of silver.

Fear paralyzed her when she saw the knife coming toward her. But her attacker slashed at the strap, sending her flying backward as the tension was released. He was gone, melting into the crowd as she lay sprawled on the curb holding her eye.

It had only taken a few seconds. Under a minute, surely. She heard someone shout and then someone knelt next to her.

"Are you okay, lady?"

She turned, not recognizing the person who'd spoken, and she was too stunned to respond. Then she saw a sleek black car screech to a halt in front of her and a huge mountain of a man rushed out to hover protectively over her.

He moved with a grace that belied his enormous size and he knelt in front of her, his hand cupping her chin as he turned her this way and that to examine her eye.

He barked rapidly into his Bluetooth but she was too muddled to know what he said or to whom he had spoken. She hoped it was the police.

"Miss Morgan, are you all right?" he asked urgently.

"H-how do you know my name?"

"Mr. de Luca sent me."

"How would he know what happened?" she asked in a baffled tone.

"He wanted to make sure you made it to your hotel safely. I didn't catch you in time to give you a ride. I was looking for you when I saw what happened."

"Oh."

"Can you stand?" he asked.

She slowly nodded. She'd certainly try. As he gently helped her to her feet, she clutched at her belly, worried that her fall had hurt her child.

"Are you in pain?" the man demanded.

"I don't know," she said shakily. "Maybe. I'm just scared. The fall…"

"I'm taking you to the hospital at once. Mr. de Luca will meet us there."

She didn't protest when he ushered her into the backseat of the car. He got in beside her and issued a swift order for the driver to take off. They were away and into traffic in a matter of moments.

She sank back into the seat, her hands shaking so badly that she clenched them together in her lap to try and quell the movement.

The giant beside her took up most of the backseat. He leaned forward and rummaged in an ice bucket in the console and a moment later held an ice pack to her eye.

She winced and started to pull away, but he persisted and held it gently to her face.

"Are you feeling any pain anywhere else?" he queried.

"I don't think so. I'm just shaken up."

His expression was grim as he pulled away the ice pack to examine her eye.

"You're going to have one heck of a bruise. I think it's a good idea to have a doctor check you out so you can be sure the baby wasn't harmed."

She nodded and grimaced when he put the ice pack back into place.

"Thank you," she murmured. "For your help. Your timing was excellent."

His face twisted with anger. "No, it wasn't. If I had been there a moment earlier, he wouldn't have hurt you."

"Still, thanks. He had a knife."

She swallowed the knot of panic in her throat and drew in steadying breaths. She could still see the flash of the blade as it slashed out at her. A shiver stole up her spine and attacked her shoulders until she trembled with almost violent force.

"I don't even know your name," she said faintly.

He looked at her with worried eyes as if he thought his name was the last thing that should be on her mind.

"Ramon. I'm Mr. de Luca's head of security."

"I'm Bryony," she said, before realizing he already knew her name. He'd called her Miss Morgan earlier.

"We're almost there, Bryony," he said in a steady, reassuring voice.

Was she about to melt down on him? Was that why he was staring at her with such concern and speaking to her as if he was trying to talk her down from the ledge?

She leaned her head back against the seat and closed her eyes. He followed with the ice pack and soon it was smushed up against her face again.

A few seconds later, the car ground to a halt and the door immediately opened. She opened her eyes as Ramon removed the ice pack and hurriedly got out of the car. He reached back to help her out and they were met by an E.R. tech pushing a wheelchair.

Astonished by the quickness in which they got her back to an exam room, she stared with an open mouth as she was laid on one of the beds by two nurses and they immediately began an assessment of her condition.

Ramon hung by her bedside, watching the medical staff's every move. As if sensing Bryony's bewilderment, Ramon leaned down and murmured, "Mr. de Luca is a frequent contributor to this hospital. He called ahead to let them know you'd be arriving."

Well, that certainly made more sense.

"The on-call obstetrician will be in to see you shortly," one of the nurses said. "He'll want to make sure all is well with the baby."

Bryony nodded and murmured her thanks.

The nurse went over a series of questions as she did her assessment. Bryony was a little embarrassed over all the fuss. Near as she could tell, all she'd suffered was a black eye and a bruised behind. But she wouldn't turn down the opportunity to make sure all was well with her baby.

She'd leaned back to close her eyes when the door flew open and Rafael strode in, his expression dark and his gaze immediately seeking out Bryony.

He hurried to her bedside and took her hand in his. "Are you all right?" he demanded. "Are you hurt? Are you in any pain?" He took a breath and dragged a hand through his hair in agitation. "The…baby?"

Before she could respond, his gaze settled on her face and his eyes darkened with fury. He tentatively touched her cheek and then he turned to Ramon, his jaw clenched.

"What happened?"

"I'm fine," Bryony said in answer to the barrage of questions. But Rafael was no longer concentrating his efforts on her. He was interrogating his head of security.

"Rafael."

When he still didn't stop his tirade of questions, she tugged at his hand until finally he turned back to her.

"I'm okay. Really. Ramon showed up just in time. He took good care of me."

"I should not have let you leave my office," Rafael gritted out. "You were upset and in no condition to be out on the streets. I'd thought Ramon would give you a ride home."

She shrugged. "I walked. He didn't catch up with me until after…."

Rafael looked hastily around and then dragged a chair to her bedside. He perched on the edge and stared intently at her.

"Has the doctor been in yet? What has he said about the baby? Are you hurt anywhere else? Did the bastard hit you?"

She shook her head at the flurry of questions and blinked at the fierceness in his voice and expression. This wasn't a side of Rafael she'd ever seen before.

"The nurse said the on-call obstetrician would be in to see me shortly and that he would conduct an assessment to make sure all was well with the baby. And no, I'm not hurt anywhere else."

She raised her hand to her eye and winced when she pushed in on the already swelling area.

Rafael captured her hand and pulled it away from her eye. "It's unacceptable for you to be walking the streets of New York City alone. I don't even like you staying in that hotel alone."

She smiled in amusement. "But it's your hotel, Rafael. Are you suggesting it isn't safe?"

"I'd prefer you were with me, where I know you are safe," he said through gritted teeth.

Her brows came together as she studied him. "What are you saying?"

"Look, we were going to be leaving together for Moon Island in a few days anyway. It's only reasonable that you'd stay with me until we depart. It will give us additional time to…reacquaint ourselves with one another."

She stared hard into his eyes, looking for… She wasn't sure what she was looking for. What she saw, however, was burning determination and outrage that she'd been harmed.

He may not remember her, but his protective instincts had been riled, and whether he fully accepted that she carried his child, he was certainly concerned about both mother and baby.

Wasn't that a start?

"All right," she said softly. "I'll stay with you until we leave for the island."

Five

Rafael would have carried her into his penthouse if she'd allowed it. As it was he argued fiercely until she rolled her eyes and informed him that she was perfectly okay and that no one got carried around because of a black eye.

The reminder of her black eye just infuriated Rafael all the more. She was a tiny woman and the idea that some street thug had manhandled her—a pregnant woman—made his jaw clench. Even though the doctor had assured him that all was well with her pregnancy.

He wasn't sure what to do with himself. He was in new territory for sure. Bryony was the first woman he'd ever brought up to his penthouse and it felt as though his territory had been invaded.

"Would you like me to order in dinner?" he asked when he'd settled her on the couch. Surely it wasn't a good idea for her to go out and it was late.

"I'd like that, thanks," she said as she leaned her head back against the sofa.

He frowned when he saw the fatigue etched on her face. "You must be tired."

Her lips twisted ruefully and she nodded. "It's been an eventful couple of days."

Guilt crept up his nape until he was compelled to rub the back of his neck. He hadn't made things easier for her. She'd traveled a long way and then… Then things had gone all to hell.

He stood, irritated with himself. Why should he feel guilty about anything? He couldn't remember. God knew he'd tried. He went to bed frustrated every single night, hoping when he woke the next morning that everything would be restored and he could stop wondering about the holes. Stop wondering if he'd done something ridiculous like seduce and fall in love with a woman in the space of a few weeks.

It sounded so incredible that he couldn't wrap his head around it.

No, he shouldn't feel guilty. None of this had been his fault.

Except for the fact that he'd upset her and caused her to flee his office and she'd wound up being mugged as a result.

He studied her from across the room as he picked up the phone to call in their food order. She already looked as if she was asleep and he battled with whether to even bother waking her for dinner.

His gaze drifted to her belly and he swiftly decided against allowing her to sleep through the meal. It had likely been hours since she'd eaten anything.

He returned to her a moment later and settled on the chair next to the couch where she lay sprawled. "Would you like something to drink while we wait for the food?"

She stirred and regarded him lazily through half-lidded eyes. "Do you have juice? I feel a little light-headed."

He bolted to his feet. "Why didn't you say anything before now?"

She shrugged. "Quite frankly all I wanted was a comfortable place to sit and relax. Having all those people around me was making me crazy."

He strode to the kitchen and rummaged in the fridge for orange juice. After checking the date on the carton, he poured a glass and went back into the living room.

This time he sat on the couch next to her and handed her the glass. She drank thirstily until half the contents were gone and then handed him back the glass.

"Thanks. That should do the trick."

"Is this something that happens regularly or is it just the excitement of the day?" he asked suspiciously.

"I'm borderline hypoglycemic. My blood sugar gets too low every once in a while. Pregnancy sort of messes with that and I have to be careful to eat regularly or I risk passing out."

Rafael swore under his breath. "What if you were to pass out when you were alone?"

"Well, the point is to make sure I don't pass out."

He scowled and then checked his watch. Only five minutes had passed since he'd placed the order.

"I'll be fine, Rafe," she said softly. "My grandmother is a diabetic. I'm well acquainted with how to handle low or elevated blood sugar."

The shortened version of his name, only used by his closest friends, slipped from her lips as if she'd used it a thousand times before. Coming from her, it sounded…right. As if he'd heard it before or maybe even encouraged her to use it.

He put a hand to his nape and looked away. Why couldn't he remember? If he had truly been involved with this woman, and if, like she'd said, they'd formed some romantic attachment—he couldn't quite bring himself to say *love*—then why would he shove her as far from his memory as he could?

She kicked off her shoes and then curled her feet underneath her on the couch before grabbing one of the cushions to snuggle into. It occurred to him that if they were a real couple he would have sat beside her and…cuddled. Or maybe offered her a foot rub. Weren't pregnant women supposed to have swollen ankles or something?

Which further proved to him that the idea of him falling in love and spending four weeks wrapped up in one woman was just…ludicrous. He dated. He even had relationships, but they were on his terms, which meant that his female companions didn't come to his penthouse. If they had sleepovers, it was done in one of his hotels. He certainly didn't engage in cuddling or cutesy things that a man would do for the woman he loved.

But then she glanced up and their eyes met. There was something in her gaze that peeled back his skin and squeezed his chest in a manner he wasn't familiar with. She looked… tired and vulnerable. She looked as if she needed…comfort.

Hell.

"Rafe, he got away with my purse," she said quietly.

He nodded. The police had come to the hospital to take her statement but it was doubtful they'd find her attacker.

"I didn't think…I mean everything happened so fast, and then at the hospital…" She lifted her hand in a helpless gesture that only made his desire to comfort her stronger.

"What is worrying you, Bryony?"

"I need to cancel my credit cards. My bankcard. God, he's probably already emptied all my accounts. My driver's license was in it. How am I supposed to get back home? I can't fly without identification."

The more she spoke, the more agitated she became. He slid onto the couch beside her and awkwardly put his arms around her.

"There's no need to panic. Do you have the telephone numbers you need?"

She shook her head and then laid it on his shoulder, her hair brushing across his nose.

"I can look them up on the internet if you have a computer."

He snorted. "Do I have a computer… I'm never without an internet connection of any kind."

She lifted her head and stared into his eyes. "You were when you were on the island."

His brow crinkled. "That's impossible. I wouldn't have just dropped off the map like that. I have a business to run."

"Oh, you kept in touch," she said. "But you often made your calls or answered emails in the morning or late at night. During the day you left your BlackBerry at my house while we explored the island."

He sighed. "See this is why I have such a hard time with the story you tell. I would never do something like that. It isn't me."

Her lips turned down in a frown and she leaned away from him.

To cover the sudden awkwardness, he stood and went to his briefcase to pull out his laptop. He stood for a long moment with his back to her just so he could compose himself and keep from turning and apologizing. He didn't want to hurt her, damn it. But one of them was crazy, and he didn't want it to be him.

He finally went back to the couch, opened the laptop and set it on a cushion next to her.

"If you have any problems canceling your cards or ordering new ones, let me know. I've typed up my address so you can have them overnighted here."

"And my license?" she asked in a tight, frustrated voice. "How am I going to get home?" She dragged her fingers through her hair, which only drew attention to the dark bruise marring her creamy skin.

"I'll get you home, Bryony. I don't want you to worry. Can you call your grandmother to fax a copy of your birth certificate? It's my understanding you can fly with the birth certificate but you'll be subjected to closer scrutiny by security."

"Couldn't we take your jet? Oh, I guess… Sorry." She broke off, seemingly embarrassed at her slip.

"I have more than one," he said dryly.

She continued to stare at him. "Then why aren't we taking it? Wouldn't it be easier to fly without identification if we were on a private jet?"

He cleared his throat and then rubbed the back of his neck. "Let's just say I have a newly developed phobia of flying on small planes."

She frowned. "I must sound so insensitive. I'm just… This has been a rotten trip all the way around."

"Yes, I suppose it has been for you," he murmured.

He eased back onto the couch beside her as she tapped intently on the keys. He hated how unsure of himself he was around her. But it was himself he was angry at. Not her.

If she was to be believed, her life had been completely upended. By him.

More and more he had an uneasy feeling that she was telling the truth. No matter how bizarre and unlikely such a scenario seemed. And if she was telling the truth, then he had to figure out what the hell he was going to do with the woman he supposedly loved and the child she carried. His child.

Six

"This reminds me of the nights we spent at my house," Bryony said as she forked another bite of the seafood into her mouth.

He paused, fork halfway to his own mouth, resigned to hearing more about his uncharacteristic behavior. But she said nothing and resumed eating, her gaze downcast, almost as if she knew how ill at ease he was.

But his curiosity was also piqued because, damn it, *something* had happened between them and she was the only key he had to recover the missing pieces of his memory.

He forced himself to sound only mildly inquisitive. "What did we do?"

A faraway look entered her eyes and she stared toward the window at the night sky. "We used to sit cross-legged on the deck and eat the dinner I'd cooked. Then I'd lay my head in your lap and you'd stroke my hair while we listened to the ocean and watched the stars."

Her voice lowered, catching on a husky note. "Then we'd

go inside and make love. Sometimes we didn't make it to the bedroom. Sometimes we did."

The dreamy quality of her voice affected him fiercely. His body ached and he hardened at the images she provoked. It was suddenly very easy for him to see her spread out before him, his mouth on her skin, her fingers clinging to him as he brought them both pleasure.

He shook his head when he realized he was staring and that he was so tense that his muscles had locked. Part of him wanted to just get it over with. Take her to bed, have sex with her until they both forgot their names. His body was eager enough, but his mind was calling him a damn fool.

And she'd likely think it was some damn experiment after he'd basically admitted earlier that his kiss had been nothing more than that.

An experiment.

He wanted to laugh. Could he call desire so keen that his eyes had crossed when he'd looked at her an experiment?

Whether he wanted to admit it or not, they had compelling—uncontrollable—chemistry. Maybe he'd gotten so wrapped up in her that he'd lost all common sense. Maybe he'd made her rash promises in the heat of the moment. If her outrage was anything to go on, he at least hadn't been stupid enough to sign anything.

He needed her cooperation. He needed this deal. He had too many investors committed. Money had exchanged hands. Construction was on a tight deadline, and the last thing he needed was her making noises over him reneging on a deal.

She'd lifted her gaze and was now studying him so intently that he found her scrutiny uncomfortable. He studied her in return, finding himself mesmerized by her dark eyes. The delicate lines of her face called to him. He wanted to trace his fingers over her cheekbone and down to her jaw and then over the softness of her lips.

Had this been the way he'd felt when he'd first seen her?

Logic told him it had to have been. How could his reaction now have been any different than the first time he'd laid eyes on her?

"Why are you staring at me?" she asked in a low voice.

"Maybe I find you beautiful."

Her reaction wasn't what he expected. She lifted her nose in scorn and shook her head.

"I thought I wasn't your type."

"What I said was that you aren't my *normal* type."

Her lips twisted. "That isn't what you said. To quote you exactly, you said, 'You aren't my type.' That pretty much tells me you don't find me remotely appealing."

"I don't care what I said," he growled. "What I meant was that you aren't the type of woman I normally…date."

"Have sex with?" she asked mockingly. "Because we did, you know. We had lots and lots of sex. You were insatiable. In fact, unless you are the best damn actor in the world and can fake, not only an erection, but an orgasm as well, I'd say you're either lying now about me not being your type, or you're not terribly discerning when it comes to the women you sleep with."

He'd just been insulted but he was so distracted by the sparks shooting from her eyes and how damn gorgeous she looked when she got sassy that he couldn't formulate a response.

"See, the problem is, a woman can get away with faking sexual attraction," she continued. "We can pretend all manner of things. Men? It's kind of hard to pretend attraction to a woman if your penis isn't cooperating."

"Holy hell," he muttered. "I think we've established that it's pretty damn obvious I'm sexually attracted to you. Whatever I may have thought in the past about my preferences in women obviously doesn't apply to you."

"So then you're willing to concede that you slept with me and that the child I'm carrying is yours?"

"Yes," he said through gritted teeth. "I'm willing to concede it's possible, but I'm not stupid enough to believe it's absolutely true until either I regain my memory, or we have DNA testing done."

Her top lip curled a moment and it looked as if she wanted to light into him again, but instead, she took a calming breath. "As long as you're willing to accept the possibility, I can work with that," she muttered.

"Were you always this…charming with me when we spent all this time together?"

She lifted one eyebrow. "What's that supposed to mean?"

"Just that I tend to like my women a little more…"

"Stupid?" she challenged.

He scowled.

"Weak? Mousy? Unchallenging?" she continued. "Or maybe you prefer them to simply nod and say 'yes, sir' to your every whim."

She broke off in disgust and regarded him as if he were some annoying bug she was about to squash.

He finally decided remaining silent was his best option so he didn't dig his hole any deeper.

She laid down her fork and raised her haunted gaze to his. He was surprised to see tears shimmering in her eyes, and his throat knotted. Damn. He hadn't wanted to upset her again. He wasn't *that* big of a jerk.

"Do you have any idea how hard this is for me?" she asked in a quiet, strained voice. "Do you know how difficult it is for me to see you again and not touch you or hug you or kiss you? I came here expecting to confront a man who scammed me in the worst possible way. I had resigned myself to it and there was nothing I wanted more than to wash my hands of you. But then you tell me this story about losing your memory and what am I supposed to do then? Now I have to consider that maybe you didn't lie to me, but I'm scared to death of believing that and then being wrong. Again. I have to put everything on hold until you regain your memory, and that sucks because I just don't know how to feel anymore."

He stared at her, frozen, an uncomfortable sensation coiling in his chest.

"I can't exactly walk away. It's what I accused you of and there's a part of me that thinks, 'What if he's telling the truth? What if he regains his memory tomorrow and remembers he loves you? What if it's all some horrible misunderstanding and we have a chance to get back what we had on the island?'"

She shoved her plate away and looked down as she visibly tried to collect herself.

"But what if I was right?" she whispered. "What if me sticking around hoping makes me an even bigger fool than falling for your lies to begin with? I have a child to consider now."

Before he could think twice about what he should say or do, he found himself reaching for her. It was impossible not to want to touch her, to offer her comfort. The pain in her expression was too real. Her eyes were clouded with moisture and hurt shimmered in their depths.

He pulled her into his arms and leaned back against the couch. For a moment she lay there stiffly, so still that he wondered if she held her breath.

He inhaled the scent of her hair and felt keen disappointment that it stirred nothing to life in his memories. Wasn't smell supposed to be the most powerful memory trigger?

Gradually she relaxed against him, her fingers curling into his chest as her cheek rested on his shoulder.

He dropped his mouth to the top of her head and stopped himself a moment before brushing his lips across her hair. It seemed the most natural thing to do and yet he knew tenderness wasn't a usual characteristic. It seemed too personal. Too intimate.

But the need to show her a more gentle side of himself was a physical ache.

"I'm sorry," he said truthfully. He had no love for seeing this woman hurt. He didn't like to see anyone needlessly suffer. The fact that he was the source of her pain made him extremely uncomfortable.

"Just let me stay here a minute and pretend," she said. "Just don't say…anything."

He carefully laid his hand over her dark curls and did as she asked. He sat there, her head on his shoulder, one arm wrapped around her, his hand wrapped in her hair, and silence descended on them.

But the silence felt awkward to him, as if he should fill the gaps. Or ask questions. Something…

He glanced down at the soft curls splayed out over his chest. He could just feel the swell of her belly against his side.

Was this his reality? And if it was, why wasn't he running as hard as he could in the other direction?

It wasn't as if he was commitment-phobic. Okay, maybe a little, but it wasn't as if he'd endured some trauma in the past that made him leery of women. Nor was he some patsy who was afraid of allowing a woman to hurt him.

He hadn't ever committed because… Well, he wasn't entirely certain. Men in relationships lacked a certain amount of control. They could no longer make solo decisions, and Rafael was used to making decisions in a split second—without conferring with someone else.

It wasn't a fluke that he owned his own business, not to mention had a partnership with three of his friends. His work took a lot of time. Time he wouldn't have if he had to worry about being home every night for dinner.

He liked being able to jet off at a moment's notice. He looked forward to business meetings—considered them a challenge. While he didn't have a lot of downtime, he did enjoy taking it at his leisure. He met Ryan, Devon and Cam at least once a year for golf, lots of alcohol and other pursuits only available to men who were not otherwise involved in a relationship.

Simply put, he'd never met a woman who made him want to give up all that. He damn sure couldn't imagine meeting her and giving up his life in a matter of four weeks. That kind of decision would have to be made over the course of years. Maybe never.

But on the other hand.

There was always a *but.*

As he stared down at the woman curled trustingly in his arms, something pulled at him. Some desire he hadn't ever acknowledged, one that would normally have horrified him—*should* horrify him.

He found himself wishing he could remember all the things she'd described to him, because all of a sudden, they sounded appealing.

And if that didn't scare the hell out of him, he wasn't sure what would.

Seven

"Rafael! Rafael! Wake up! Hurry!"

Rafael came awake with a start, his arms flying out as he pushed himself up from his bed. Bryony stood at his bedside, fully dressed, hopping around like her feet were on fire.

He threw his feet over the side and leaned forward. "What is it? Is it the baby? Are you hurt?"

She frowned a moment, shook her head and then grinned like a maniac. He rubbed his eyes and ran his hand through his hair.

"Then what the hell are you shouting about?" He glanced over at his bedside clock. "For God's sake, it's early!"

"It's snowing!"

She grabbed at his hand and started to pull. The covers fell away from his hips and they both went still. Her gaze dropped about the time his did and it was then he remembered he hadn't worn anything to bed, and worse, his penis was making its presence known in a not very subtle way.

He yanked the covers back over him as she stepped hastily

back, pulling her sweater around her like a protective barrier. Hell, it wasn't as if he was bursting into *her* room trying to maul her.

"Sorry," she said. "I'll just go down by myself."

She turned and he scrambled out of bed, pulling the sheet with him.

"Wait a minute," he ordered. "What are you doing? Where are you going?"

Her eyes came alive again, brimming with excitement. The sparkle was infectious.

"Outside, of course! It's snowing!"

He glanced toward his window but he was too bleary-eyed to make sense of the weather. "Haven't you ever seen snow before?"

She shook her head.

"Are you serious?"

She nodded this time. "I live on an island off the Texas coast. We don't exactly get snow there, you know."

"But you've been off the island. Haven't you ever been anywhere it snowed before?"

She shrugged. "I don't leave much. Mamaw needs me. I go to Galveston to do our shopping, but I do a lot of it online."

He saw her cast sidelong glances at the window as if she were afraid the snow would disappear at any moment. Then he sighed. "Give me five minutes to get dressed and I'll go down with you."

Her smile lit up the entire room and he was left with the feeling that someone had just punched him in the stomach. She nearly danced from his bedroom and shut the door behind her.

Slowly he dropped the sheet to the floor and stared down at his groin. "Traitor," he muttered.

He went into the bathroom, splashed water on his face and surveyed his unshaven jaw with a grimace. He never left his apartment without looking his best. There wasn't time for even a shower. The lunatic was probably already outside dancing in the snow.

He brushed his teeth and then went to his closet to pull out a pair of slacks and a sweater. He realized that since she'd never seen snow, she'd hardly be dressed for it, so he pulled a scarf and a cap from the top shelf.

Any of his jackets or coats would swallow her whole so he'd simply have to limit her snow gazing to a short period of time.

After donning his overcoat, he walked out of his bedroom to find Bryony glued to the window in the living room. Big flakes spiraled downward and her smile was like a child's at Christmas.

"Here," he said gruffly. "If you're going to go out, you need warmer things."

She turned and stared at the scarf and cap he held out and then reached for them, but he waved her hand off and looped the scarf around her neck himself, pulling her closer.

"You probably don't even know how to put one on," he muttered.

After wrapping the scarf around her neck, he arranged the cap over her curls and stepped back. She looked…damn cute.

Before he could do something idiotic, he turned and gestured toward the door. "Your snow awaits."

Bryony walked into the small courtyard that adjoined the apartment building, surprised that it was empty. How could everyone just stay inside on such a beautiful day? As soon as one of the flakes landed on her nose, she turned her face up and laughed as more drifted onto her cheeks and clung to her lashes.

She held out her hands and turned in a circle. Oh, it was marvelous and so pretty. There was just a light dusting on the patio surface, but along the fence railing and the edges of the stone planters, there was enough accumulation for her to scoop into a ball.

She scraped her hands together until she had a sizeable amount of snow and then she turned to grin at Rafael. He regarded her warily and then held up his hand in warning.

"Don't even think…"

Before he could finish, she let fly and he barely had time to blink before the snowball exploded in his face.

"…about it," he finished as ice slid down his cheek.

He glared at her but she giggled and hastily formed another snowball.

"Oh, hell no," Rafael growled.

As she turned to hurl it in his direction, a snowball hit the side of her face and melting ice slid down her neck, eliciting a shiver.

"I see you couldn't resist," she said with a smirk.

"Resist what?"

"Playing. But who could resist snow?"

He scowled. "I wasn't playing. I was retaliating. Now come on. You've seen the snow. We should go back inside. It's cold out here."

"Well, duh. It *is* snowing," she said. "It's supposed to be cold."

Ignoring his look of exasperation, she hurled another snowball. He ducked and she ran for cover when she saw the gleam in his eyes. She hastily formed another snowball then peered around one of the hedges in time to get smacked by his. Right between the eyes.

"For someone who doesn't play in the snow, your snowball fighting is sure good," she muttered.

She waited until he went for more snow and she nailed him right in the ass. He spun around, wiping at his expensive slacks—but who wore slacks to play in the snow for Pete's sake?—and then lobbed another ball in her direction.

She easily dodged this one and nailed him with another on the shoulder.

"I hope you know this means war," he declared.

She rolled her eyes. “Yeah, yeah. I made you lose that stuffy attitude once. I’ll do it again.”

His eyes narrowed in confusion and she used his momentary inattention to plaster him in his face.

Wiping the slush from his eyes, he began to stalk toward her, determination twisting his lips.

“Uh-oh,” she murmured and began backtracking.

There wasn’t a whole lot of room for evasion in the small garden, and unless she wanted to run back inside, there wasn’t anywhere to go. Since it was probably his plan to herd her back indoors, she decided to meet him head-on and weather whatever attack he had in mind.

She began scooping and pelting him with a furious barrage of snow. He swore as he twisted and ducked and then he made a sound of resignation and began scooping snow from the stone benches and hurling it back at her as fast as he could.

Unfortunately for her, his aim was a lot better and after six direct hits in a row, she raised her hands and cried, “Uncle!”

“Now why don’t I believe you?” he asked as he stared cautiously at her, his hand cocked back to blast her with another snowball.

She gave him her best smile of innocence and raised her empty hands, palms up. “You win. I’m freezing.”

He dropped the snowball and then strode forward to grasp her shoulders. He swept that imperious gaze up and down her body, much like he’d done the first time they’d met. This time it didn’t rankle, for she knew that beneath that boring, straight-laced hauteur lay a fun-loving man just aching to get out. She just had to free him. Again.

She sighed at the unfairness of it all. It was like some sick joke being played on her by fate. Karma maybe. Though she was sure she’d done nothing so hideous as to have the love of her life and father of her child regard her as a complete stranger.

She shivered and Rafael frowned. “We should go inside

at once. You aren't dressed for the weather. Did you bring nothing at all to wear for colder weather?"

She shook her head ruefully.

"We'll need to go shopping then."

She shook her head again. "There isn't a point. We'll be leaving to go back to Moon Island and it's still quite warm there."

"And in the meantime you'll freeze," he said darkly.

She rolled her eyes.

"You at least need a coat. I'll send out for one. Do you have a preference? Fur? Leather?"

"Uh, just a coat. Nothing exotic."

He made a dismissive gesture with his hands as if deciding that consulting with her was pointless. "I'll have it arranged."

She shrugged. "Suit yourself." He always did.

"When the doorman told me you were out playing in the snow, I asked him if the real Rafael had been abducted by aliens."

Bryony and Rafael both swung around to see Devon Carter leaning against one of the light posts just outside the door leading back into the apartment building.

"Very funny," Rafael muttered. "What are you doing here?" He took Bryony's hand in his.

Devon raised one lazy brow. "Just checking in on you and Bryony. I heard there was some excitement yesterday."

Bryony grimaced and automatically put her other hand to the bruise she'd forgotten about until now.

"As you can see, she's fine," Rafael said. "Now if you'll excuse us, we're going up so she can change into some warmer clothing."

"Actually I was checking on you," Devon said with a grin. "Bryony strikes me as someone who can take care of herself."

Bryony cleared her throat as the moment grew more awkward. Devon wasn't worried about her. He was worried about Rafael in her clutches. Her face warm with embarrassment, she extricated her hand from Rafael's grasp.

"I'll just go up and leave you to, uh, talk. Did you leave the door unlocked?" Or whatever it was they did in these kinds of apartments. Rafael fished in his pocket and then held out a card. "You'll need this for the elevator."

She tucked it into her hand and hurried toward the door after a small wave in Devon's direction.

The two men watched her go and then Rafael turned to his friend with a frown. "What was that all about?"

Devon shrugged. "Just checking in on you, like I said. You've had a lot to digest over the past couple of days. Wanted to see how you were holding up and whether you'd remembered anything."

Rafael grimaced and then shoved Devon toward the door. "Let's at least go inside. It's cold out here."

The two men stopped in the coffee shop off the main lobby and Rafael requested the table by the fire.

"Things are fine," Rafael said after they were seated. "I don't want you worrying, nor do I want you plotting with Ryan and Cam to protect me for my own good."

Devon sighed. "Even if I think this idea of yours to jet off to this island is a damn foolish idea?"

"Especially then."

Devon sipped at his coffee and didn't even attempt to sugarcoat his question. But then that wasn't Devon. He was blunt, if anything. Cut and dried. Practical to a fault.

"Are you sure this is what you want to do, Rafe? Do you really think it's a good idea to go off with this woman who claims to be pregnant with your child? It seems to me, the smarter thing to do would be to call your lawyer, have paternity testing done and sit tight until you get the results."

Rafael's lips were tight as he stared back at Devon. "And what then?"

Devon blinked. “Well, that depends on the outcome of the tests.”

Rafael shook his head. “If it turns out that I’m the father, if everything she claims is true, then I will have effectively denied her for the entirety of the time I wait for the test results. If she’s telling the truth, I’ve already dealt her far too much hurt as it is. How can I expect to mend a rift if I have my lawyer sit on her while we wait to see if I’m going to be a father?”

Devon blew out his breath. “It sounds to me like you’ve already made up your mind that she’s telling the truth.”

Rafael dragged a hand through his hair. “I don’t know what the truth is. My head tells me that she couldn’t possibly be telling the truth. That the idea of me falling head-over-ass for her in a matter of weeks is absurd. It sounds so ludicrous that I can’t even wrap my head around it.”

“But…?”

“But my gut is screaming that there is definitely something between us,” Rafael grimly admitted. “When I get near her, when I touch her… It’s like I become someone else entirely. Someone I don’t know. I hear the conviction in her voice when she talks of us making love by the ocean and I believe her. More than that I *want* to believe her.”

Devon let out a whistle that sounded more like a crash-and-burn. “So you believe her then.”

Rafael sucked in his breath. “My head tells me she’s a liar.”

“But your gut?”

Rafael sighed because he knew what Dev was getting at. Rafael always went with his gut. Even when logic argued otherwise. And he’d never been wrong.

“My gut tells me she’s telling the truth.”

Eight

"Do you feel well enough to travel?" Rafael asked Bryony over dinner.

Bryony looked up from the sumptuous steak she was devouring to see Rafael studying the bruise on her face.

"Rafael, I'm fine."

"Perhaps you should see an obstetrician before we leave the city."

"If it makes you feel any better, I'll go see my doctor as soon as we get to the island, but I'm certainly capable of traveling. Unless you have matters to attend to here? I can go ahead of you if you can't get away yet."

Rafael frowned and put down his fork. "We'll go together. It's important we retrace all our steps and follow the same pattern we did when I was there before. Perhaps the familiarity will bring back my lost memories."

Bryony cut another piece of her steak, but paused after she speared it with her fork. "What does your doctor say?"

Rafael became visibly uncomfortable. Even though the

table they'd been seated at provided complete privacy from the other patrons, he glanced around as if the idea of anyone overhearing his personal business caused him no end of grief.

His lips pursed in distaste and then he finally said, "He thinks there's a psychological reason behind my memory loss. If I was so happy and in love then why would I want to forget? It makes no sense."

She was unable to control the flinch. Her fingers went numb as she realized how tightly she gripped the fork.

"I didn't say that to hurt you," he said in a low voice. "There's just so much I don't understand. I want to go back because I want to find the person I lost while I was there. The man you say you loved and who loved you is a stranger to me."

"Apparently we're both strangers to you," she said quietly. "Maybe that man doesn't exist. Maybe I imagined him."

Rafael's gaze dropped down her body to where her belly was hidden by the table. "But neither of us imagined a child. He or she is all too real, the one real thing in this whole situation."

She couldn't keep the sadness from her expression. The corners of her mouth drooped and she shoved her plate aside, her appetite gone.

"Our baby isn't the only real thing in our relationship. My love for you was real. I held nothing back from you. I guess we won't know whether you were real when you were with me. You deny that you could be that person. You deny it with your every breath. And I'm supposed to forget all of this denial if you suddenly remember you did and do love me."

She dropped her hands into her lap and wound her fingers tightly together as she leaned forward.

"Tell me, Rafael, which man would I believe? The man who tells me I'm not his type and that he couldn't possibly have loved me, or the lover who spent every night in my arms while we were on the island? No matter what you remember tomorrow, or the next day, I'll always know that a part of you rebels at the mere thought of being with me."

She could tell her words struck a chord with him. Discomfort darkened his features and regret simmered in his eyes. He splayed his hand out in an almost helpless gesture.

"Bryony, I…"

She gave a short, forceful shake of her head. "Don't, Rafael. Don't make it worse by saying you didn't mean it. We both know you did. At least you've been honest. You just need to remember that you're not the only victim in this."

"I'm sorry," he said, and she knew he meant it.

He reached across the table and slipped his hand over hers. For a moment he stroked his thumb across her knuckles and then he gently squeezed.

"I really am sorry. I'm being a selfish bastard. I know this has to hurt you and that none of this is easy for you. Forgive me."

Her heart squeezed at the sincerity in his eyes. It was all she could do not to throw herself into his arms and hold on for all she was worth. She wanted to whisper to him that she loved him. She wanted to beg him never to let her go. But all she could do was stare across the table in helpless frustration.

"What if you never remember?" she asked, voicing her greatest fear.

"I don't know," he said honestly. "I hope it doesn't come to that."

She leaned back in her seat, slipping her hand from underneath his. The heaviness in her chest was a physical ache, one that clogged her throat and made it hard to breathe.

"What have you packed?" she asked lightly, forcing a smile.

He looked confused by the abrupt shift in conversation. "I haven't yet."

She raised an eyebrow. "We leave in the morning and you

don't know how long you'll be gone. Aren't you leaving it to the last minute?"

He grimaced. "I wasn't sure what to pack. You mentioned things like swimwear and flip-flops."

She laughed as some of the tension in her chest eased. "Well, it's too cold to swim. The weather is still quite warm but the water is chilly. But we can buy you shorts and flip-flops like we did before. We can't have you wearing suits all the time, and your expensive loafers will just get ruined."

"I'm trusting you," he muttered. "Since you swear I did this before."

"And it didn't kill you," she teased. "When I was done with your makeover, you looked more relaxed and less like a stuffed shirt."

"You're implying I'm stuffy?" he asked in mock outrage.

"Oh, you were. Totally stuffy."

"I don't want to stand out this time. I'd like to keep my… problem…as private as possible."

"Of course," Bryony murmured.

He sat back in his chair and fiddled with his wineglass, though he didn't pick it up to drink. He turned in the direction of the band playing soft, mellow jazz and then back to her, his expression thoughtful.

"Tell me, Bryony. Did we ever dance?"

Caught off guard by the question, she shook her head mutely.

He stood and held his hand out to her. "Then dance with me now."

Mesmerized by the husk in his tone, she slipped her hand into his and allowed him to pull her to her feet. He led her onto the dance floor and slid his palm over her back as he pulled her into his embrace.

She closed her eyes and sighed as she melted against him. His warmth wrapped tantalizingly around her and his scent brushed over her nose. She inhaled deeply, holding his essence in the deepest part of her.

Oh, how she'd missed him. Even when she'd hated him, when she'd thought the absolute worst, she'd lain awake at night remembering the nights in her bed when they'd made love with the music of the ocean filling the sky.

She was acutely aware of him as they swayed in time to the sultry tones. He cupped her to him possessively, as if telling the world she belonged to him. It was nice to get lost in the moment and her daydreams.

As he turned her, she tilted her neck and gazed up at him as he tucked her hand between them, his thumb caressing the pulse at her wrist.

"You are an interesting dilemma, Bryony."

She raised her brows. "Dilemma?"

"Conundrum. Puzzle. One of the many things I can't seem to figure out lately."

She cocked her head to the side in question.

"I swear I have no memory of you. I look at you and draw a blank. But when you get close to me, when I touch you…" His voice dropped to a mere whisper and it sent a shiver racing down her spine. "I feel as though…"

"As though what?" she whispered.

He had a slightly bewildered look on his face as if he were searching for just the right word. Then finally he sighed and stared down at her, his gaze stroking over her skin.

"We fit," he said simply. "I have no explanation for it, but it just feels…right."

Her heart sped up. Hope pulsed in her veins, the first real hope she'd had since hearing his fantastic story. She didn't know whether to squeeze him or kiss him, so she stood there as they swayed with the music and smiled so brilliantly that her cheeks hurt.

"Amazing that such a simple thing could make you so happy," he murmured.

"We do fit," she said, her voice catching as her throat throbbed with a growing ache. She reached up to frame his face and then she leaned up on tiptoe to brush her lips across his.

She meant it to be a small gesture of affection. Maybe a reminder of what they'd once shared. Or maybe to just reaffirm the sensation to him that they fit. But he didn't allow her to stop there.

Cupping his hand to the back of her head, he wrapped his other arm around her waist and hauled her up until her lips were in line with his.

There was nothing tentative about his kiss. No hesitancy as he attempted to find his way back. It was as if they'd never been apart. He kissed her like he'd kissed her so many times before, only this time… There was something different she couldn't quite put her finger on. More depth. More emotion. It wasn't just sexy or passionate. It was…tender.

Like he was apologizing for all the hurt. For the separation and misunderstanding. For what he couldn't remember.

She sighed into his mouth, sadness and joy mixing and bubbling up in her heart until she was overwhelmed by it all. When he finally drew away, his eyes were dark, his body trembled against hers, and as he eased her down, his hand slid up her arms to cup her face.

"Part of me remembers you, Bryony. There's a part of me that feels like I've come home when I kiss you. That has to mean something."

She nodded, unable to speak as emotion clogged her throat. She swallowed several times and then finally found her voice.

"We'll find our way back, Rafe. I won't let you go so easily. When I thought you didn't want me, that you'd played me, it was easy to say never again. But now that I know what happened, I won't give up without a fight. Somehow I'll make you remember. It's not just your happiness at stake. It's mine, too."

He smiled and stroked a thumb over one cheekbone. "So fierce. You fascinate me, Bryony. I'm beginning to see how it could be true that I was so transfixed by you from the start."

Then he leaned down and kissed her again, the room around them forgotten. "I want to remember. Help me remember."

"You'll get it back," she said fiercely. "We'll get it back. Together."

Nine

The flight back to Houston was much better than her trip to New York. On the way she'd been squeezed between two men who she swore had to be football players. She hadn't been able to move and had spent the entire time being miserable.

She and Rafael occupied the first two seats in first class, and once they'd taken off, she'd reclined without guilt, since there was plenty of room between the rows.

By the time they landed in Houston, she actually felt rested and ready for the drive from the airport.

Apparently Rafael had ideas of having a driver take them to the island.

"My car is here. There's no reason for us not to take it," she insisted as they stood in baggage claim.

"We would both be more comfortable if you let me see to the travel arrangements."

"And what am I supposed to do without my car? We'll need it on the island. It's small but everything isn't in walking distance."

As their luggage piled up, Rafael sighed. "All right. We'll take your car. But it's senseless for you to drive when we've already been traveling half the day."

She rolled her eyes and bit her lip to keep from making a remark about spoiled men.

She grabbed a cart for their luggage and Rafael piled it up and pushed it as she led him to the parking garage.

"Where is the damn parking lot?" he demanded. "In Galveston?"

"It's a bit of a walk," she admitted. "But it's all indoors and then we'll take the elevator to the top level."

"Why did you park on the roof?"

She shrugged. "I just kept going around and around and then suddenly I was on the roof. It's the same as parking anywhere else."

He shook his head as they trudged down the long corridor. When they finally got to the elevator, Bryony breathed in relief. A few moments later, they were on the roof and she took out her keys to remotely unlock the car.

"What the…"

She cast him a puzzled look.

"That's your car?" he asked.

She looked toward the MINI Cooper and nodded. "Is something wrong?"

"You expect to fit me *and* the luggage in this tin can?"

"Quit being so grumpy," she said mildly. "We'll manage. It does have a luggage rack. I'm sure I have a bungee cord in the trunk."

"Who the hell carries around bungee cords?"

She laughed. "You never know when they'll come in handy."

They filled the trunk and then piled suitcases into the back until the bags were stacked to the roof of the car.

"There," she said triumphantly as she shut the door. "We didn't even have to use the bungee cords."

"Unfortunately we didn't push the passenger seat back before we stored all the luggage," he said dryly.

Bryony winced when she saw him fold his legs to get into the front seat. His knees were pushed up into the dash and he didn't look at all comfortable.

"Sorry," she mumbled as she got into the driver's seat. "I wasn't thinking. No one who ever rides in my car has such long legs."

"How do you plan to drive the baby around after he or she is born?"

Bryony reversed out of the parking space and then drove toward the exit. "In a car seat, of course."

"And where do you think the car seat will fit in here? Even if you crammed it in, if you got into a wreck, neither of you would likely survive. Someone could run right over you in this thing and probably not even realize it."

"It's what I have, Rafael. There's not a lot I can do about it. Now let's talk about something else."

"How far of a drive is it?"

She sighed. "An hour to Galveston from the airport. Then we take a ferry to Moon Island. It's about a half-hour ferry ride so we should be there in under two hours barring any traffic issues."

It was a bad thing to say. Thirty minutes later, they were completely stalled on I-45. Bryony cursed under her breath as Rafael fidgeted in his seat. Or at least tried to fidget. He couldn't move much and he looked as if he was ready to get out and walk. It would probably be faster since traffic hadn't moved so much as an inch in the past five minutes.

"I know what you're going to say," she said when she saw him turn toward her. "We should have left my car at the airport. Yeah, I know that now, but really, traffic jams are a fact of life in Houston."

A smile quirked at the corners of his mouth. "I was actually going to say it's a good thing I went to the bathroom before we left the airport."

She heaved a sigh. "Just be grateful you aren't pregnant."

He arched an eyebrow. "Want me to take over?"

She shook her head. "You'd never be able to drive with your knees jammed to your chin. Let's find something to talk about. Music would just irritate me right now."

He seemed to think for a moment and then he said, "Tell me what you do. I mean, do you work? You said you took care of your grandmother but I wasn't sure if that was a full-time task or not."

Bryony smiled. "No. Mamaw is still quite self-sufficient. I wouldn't say I take care of her as much as we take care of each other. She's been sicker lately, though. As for what I do, I'm sort of a Jill of all trades. I do a little bit of everything. I'm the go-to gal on the island for whatever needs doing."

He looked curiously at her.

"Basically I'm a consultant if you want a posh name for my job. I'm consulted on all manner of things, though nothing you'd probably think was legitimate," she added with a laugh.

"You have me curious now. Just what exactly are some of the things you do?"

"One day a week I take care of the mayor's correspondence. He's an older gentleman, and he's not fond of computers. Or the internet for that matter. He likes old-school things like actual newspapers, print magazines, watching the news on the local channel instead of surfing to CNN. That sort of thing. He doesn't even have cable if you can believe it."

"And this guy got elected?"

Bryony laughed. "I think you'll find that our island is pretty tolerant of being old-fashioned. It's a bit of a throwback. While you can certainly avail yourself of all the modern conveniences such as internet, cable TV and the like, a large percentage of our population is quite happy in their technology-challenged world."

Rafael shook his head. "I'm shuddering as you speak. How can anyone be happy living in the Dark Ages?"

"Oh, please. You enjoyed it well enough yourself once I finally weaned you off your BlackBerry and your laptop. You went a whole week without using either. A week!"

"Surely a record," he muttered.

"Oh, look, traffic is moving!"

She put the MINI Cooper into gear as cars began to crawl forward. She checked her watch to see that they'd already lost an hour; it would be close to dark by the time they arrived on the island.

Still, the delay couldn't dim her excitement. It was foolish of her to get her hopes up, but she wanted so badly to relive her time with Rafael on the island. Take him through all the steps they'd taken before.

She wanted him to remember. Because if he didn't, things would never be the same for them. He'd resisted the idea of being with her. Her only hope was for him to remember and then…

Then just as she'd told him the night before, she'd forever have to live with the fact that at least some part of him recoiled at the idea of them being lovers.

"Penny for your thoughts?"

She grimaced as she navigated her way down the interstate. "They aren't worth that much."

"Then don't think them."

To her surprise, he leaned over, curled his hand around her nape and massaged lightly, threading his fingers through her thick hair. It was tempting to close her eyes and lean her head all the way back but then they'd have a wreck and never get off this damn interstate.

"I'm nervous, Rafael," she admitted.

She bit her lip, wondering if she shouldn't just shut up, but she'd always had this habit of being completely honest. It wasn't in her makeup to shy away from the bald truth, no matter how uncomfortable. She always figured if people talked more about their issues then there wouldn't *be* so many issues.

Rafael—the old Rafael—hadn't minded her speaking her mind. They'd enjoyed long conversations and she'd always told him what was occupying her thoughts.

But now, she had a newfound reservation against being so forthright. She hated feeling so unsure of herself.

"Why are you nervous?" he asked softly.

"You. Me. Us. What if this doesn't work? I feel like this is my only chance and that if you don't remember, I've lost you."

"Regardless of whether I regain my memory, we still have a child to think about. I'm not going to disappear just because I can't remember the details of his conception."

"You sound like you've accepted that I'm carrying your child."

He shrugged. "I've embraced the very real possibility. Until I'm proven wrong, I choose to think of it as my child."

Her heart did a little squeeze in her chest. "Thank you for that. For now it's enough. Until we figure out everything else, it's enough that you accept our baby."

"And you."

She turned to glance quickly at him before returning her gaze to the highway.

He lowered his hand from her neck to cover her hand that rested on his leg. "There is definitely something between us. If I accept that we made a child together, surely I have to accept that we were lovers, that you meant something to me?"

"I hope I did," she said softly.

"Tell me, Bryony, do you still love me?"

There was a note of raw curiosity in his voice. Almost as if he wasn't sure how he wanted her to answer.

"That's unfair," she said in a low voice. "You can't expect

me to lay everything out when there's a real possibility we'll never be what we once were to each other. You can't expect me to admit to loving a man who thinks of me as a complete stranger."

"Not a stranger," he corrected. "I've already admitted that it's obvious we were something to each other."

"Something. Not everything," she said painfully. "Don't ask me, Rafael. Not until you remember me. Ask me then."

He reached up to touch her cheek. "All right. I'll ask you then."

Ten

After what seemed an interminable time, Bryony drove her little car onto the ferry and was immediately sandwiched by vehicles twice the size of hers.

Rafael had serious reservations about her driving around with a newborn in something only a little larger than a Matchbox car.

To his surprise, she opened her door and started to climb out.

"Where are you going?"

She ducked down to look at him through the window and flashed a wide smile. "Come on. It's a beautiful sunset. We can watch it from the railing."

Her exuberance shouldn't have surprised him by now. He'd gotten a taste of it in bits and pieces, but now that they'd left the city, she seemed to be even more excited, as if she couldn't wait to go back….

There was no doubt that he wanted to regain his memory. Having a gaping hole in his mind wasn't at all acceptable to someone like him, who was used to control in every aspect of his life. Now he was dependent on someone else to guide him and it made him extremely uncomfortable.

But in addition to knowing what happened during those lost weeks, he found himself hoping. Hoping that Bryony was right even if it meant a drastic change for him. He wasn't at all sure he was ready for fatherhood and a relationship. Love. If Bryony was to be believed… Love. It baffled him and intrigued him all at the same time.

He didn't want to hurt her. At this point he'd do anything to keep from hurting her and so he hoped that some miracle had occurred on this island and that he'd be able to find that same miracle again.

He climbed out of the car and stretched his aching legs. He inhaled deeply, enjoying the tang of the salty air. A breeze ruffled his hair, but he noted it was a warm breeze despite the coolness of the evening. The air was heavier here but… cleaner, if that made sense.

Bryony, in her impatience—which he was fast learning was an overriding component of her personality—grabbed his hand and tugged him toward the rail where others had gathered. Some had chosen to remain inside their vehicles, but others, like he and Bryony were leaning over the side and staring at the burst of gold on the horizon. Pink-and-purple hues mixed with the strands of gold, and spread out their fingers until the entire sky looked as if it were alive and breathing fire.

"It's beautiful, isn't it?"

He glanced down at Bryony and nodded. "Yes, it is."

"You don't see too many sunsets," she said smugly.

"What's that supposed to mean?"

She shrugged. "You mentioned before when we used to sit out on my deck that it wasn't something you ever had time to do. You usually worked late and were always in too big a hurry. So I was determined to show you as many as I could while you were here. Looks like I get to do it all over again. Oh, look! Dolphins!"

He looked to where she was pointing to see several sleek, gray bodies arc out of the water and then disappear below the surface.

"They follow the ferry quite a bit," she said. "I look for them every time I make the trip to Galveston."

He found himself caught up in the moment and before he knew it, he was pointing as they resurfaced. "There they are again!"

She smiled and hooked her arm through his, hugging him close. It seemed the most natural thing in the world to extricate his arm and then wrap it around her. They stood watching as the dolphins raced through the water, with her tucked up close to his side.

He shook his head at the absurdity of it all. Here he was without his phone or an internet connection. He'd left his BlackBerry in the car. He was on a ferry, of all things, watching dolphins play as he held the mother of his child.

Much was said about near-death experiences and how they changed a person. But it would appear that he'd begun his great transformation act *before* his accident.

It was little wonder Ryan, Dev and Cam were so worried about him. They were probably back in the city researching mental hospitals in preparation for his breakdown.

He rubbed his hand up and down Bryony's arm and then pressed a kiss to the top of her head. Then he sighed. He had to admit, he was actually looking forward to being on the island and spending time with Bryony and not just because he was anxious to recover his memory.

She wrapped her arms around his waist and squeezed. Her hug warmed him all the way through but not in a particularly sexual way. It was comforting. It was like holding a ray of sunshine.

As strange as it might sound, he felt comfortable around

her. A complete stranger. Someone, who before a few days ago, he hadn't remembered, and for all practical purposes had never laid eyes on.

Yeah, his statement the night before had been a little—okay, a *lot* corny—but it was absolutely true. They fit. She fit him. And he had absolutely no explanation for it, other than somehow, he'd lost his heart and soul on that island and then the entire event had been wiped from his mind.

Okay. He accepted it. Hell, he embraced it. He wasn't fighting it. He was ready for whatever lay ahead. So why couldn't he remember?

He held her tightly to him, his face buried in her fragrant, dark curls. Tentatively he slid his hand down to cup her belly, the first time he'd made an overt gesture to acknowledge the life inside her womb.

She stiffened momentarily and then slowly turned her face up so she could look at him.

He rubbed in a gentle back-and-forth motion, exploring the firmness of the swell. Something he could only define as magic tightened his chest and flooded his heart.

This was his child.

Somehow he knew it.

He was going to be a father.

The realization befuddled him and at the same time, he felt such a sense of awe. He hadn't planned on fatherhood. In fact, he'd always been extremely careful in his sexual relationships. Extremely careful. He'd bordered on phobic about an accidental pregnancy.

Had he purposely discarded protection with Bryony? Had he considered the fact that they could make a child? Had she entertained such a possibility?

He frowned as he remembered her outrage and anger that it hadn't been enough that he'd screwed her over, but that he'd made her pregnant, too. No, that didn't strike him as the reaction of a woman who'd embraced such a thing.

Evidently it hadn't been something either of them had planned, but it was also obvious he hadn't gone to great lengths to prevent it.

He kissed her upturned lips and she smiled as she snuggled closer to him. Then she sighed in regret and carefully pulled away.

"We're nearly there. We should go back to the car."

Bryony turned on her headlights as they rounded the sharp turn and began the drive north toward her cottage. She frowned when she saw several vehicles parked on the highway near her driveway.

Her heart began to pound as fear gripped her. Had something happened to Mamaw? She'd spoken to her grandmother just hours earlier when she and Rafael had landed in Houston. She'd sounded fine then and eager to see Bryony again.

She recognized one of the vehicles as belonging to Mayor Daniels. What would he be doing here?

She pulled into the gravel driveway and turned off the ignition. Her grandmother stepped out onto the front porch followed by Mayor Daniels, who wore a frown, and Sheriff Taylor, who didn't look any happier.

She opened her door and scrambled out. "Mamaw, is everything all right? Are you okay?"

"Oh, honey, I'm fine. Sorry if we worried you. The mayor and the sheriff had some questions." Her grandmother eyed Rafael as he got out of the passenger seat. "We all do."

Bryony frowned and looked over at Mayor Daniels. "It couldn't wait? We've been traveling all day and got stuck in a traffic jam on the interstate."

The mayor picked up his finger and began to shake it, as he did every time he was upset over something. The sheriff put a hand on his shoulder.

"Easy, Rupert, give her a chance to explain."

"Explain what?" Bryony demanded.

"Why a ferry full of construction equipment landed on our island yesterday and why they're set to start building some fancy new hotel on the land you sold to Tricorp Investment," the mayor said as he shook an accusing finger at Bryony.

She shook her head adamantly. "There must be some mistake, Mayor. I've been in New York City all week to straighten out this mess. Rafael would have told me if construction was already scheduled to begin. And I didn't sell to Tricorp. I sold to Rafael."

The sheriff grimaced. "There's no mistake, Bry. I questioned the men myself. Asked to see their permits. Everything is all legal. I even asked to see the plans. That whole stretch of the beach is going to be turned into a resort, complete with its own helicopter pad."

Her mouth dropped open and she turned to Rafael, dread and disappointment nearly choking her. "Rafael?"

Eleven

Rafael bit out a curse as he faced four accusing stares. Bryony's was confused, though, and a little dazed. Pain and bewilderment made their way across her face and the look in her eyes made him wince.

"Now see here," the mayor began as he stepped forward.

Rafael brought him up short with a jerk of his hand. He stared hard at the other man and the mayor took a hasty step back, nearly pulling the sheriff in front of him for protection.

"This is a matter between Bryony and myself," he said in an even voice. "As she said, we're tired. We've traveled all day, she's pregnant and she's dead on her feet. I won't stand here arguing with you in her driveway."

"But—" The mayor turned to the sheriff. "Silas? Are you going to let him get away with this?"

The sheriff sighed and adjusted his hat. "What he's doing isn't illegal, Rupert. It might be unethical, but it isn't illegal. He owns the land. He can do what he likes with it."

"Rafael? Did you approve this? Is it true they're starting construction?" Bryony asked in a strained voice.

Her grandmother stepped to her side and wrapped her arm around Bryony's waist. Her grandmother was a frail-looking woman and it irritated Rafael to no end that it was Bryony who looked the more fragile of the two at the moment.

"We'll discuss this in private," he said tightly.

"Do you want him here, Bry?" the sheriff asked.

Bryony raised a hand to her temple and rubbed as if she had no idea what to say to that question. Hurt crowded her eyes, and then deep fatigue, as if all her energy had been sapped in a single instant.

Knowing if he didn't take control of the situation, he'd likely be carted off to some second-rate jail cell, Rafael moved to Bryony's side and gently pried her away from her grandmother. He wrapped his arm around her waist and cupped his hand over her elbow.

"We'll talk inside," he murmured.

She stared up at him as if she searched for some shred of truth or maybe deceit. He couldn't be entirely sure what she was thinking.

Then she stiffened and looked toward the two men. "He's staying here, Silas. I appreciate your concern."

"And the construction?" Rupert asked in agitation. "What am I supposed to tell everyone? It wasn't me who sold the land to the outsider but it happened on my watch. I'll never win reelection if it becomes known that the island went to hell during my term."

"Rupert, shut up," Bryony's grandmother said sharply. "My granddaughter is upset enough without you yammering on about your political career."

"Come on, Rupert. Nothing good can come of us standing in her driveway at this hour. There'll be plenty of time to sort this out tomorrow," Silas said as he herded the older man toward his vehicle.

As he left, he tipped his hat to Bryony. "Let me know if you need anything, young lady."

Bryony gave him a tight smile and nodded her thanks. When the two men were gone, Bryony's grandmother hugged her.

"I'm glad you're home. I worry when you travel. Especially to a city like New York."

If Rafael had expected the older woman to turn on him in anger he was wrong. Instead she gently enfolded him in a hug and patted his cheek.

"Welcome back, young man. I'm glad you found your way back here."

With that, she walked down a narrow stone path in the grass that led to the adjoining yard.

"Will she be okay?" Rafael asked with a frown. "Should we take her home?"

Bryony sighed. "She lives next door. Just a few steps from my front door."

"Oh. Right. Sorry."

"Yeah, I know, you don't remember."

This time her tone lacked the patience and understanding she'd exhibited until now. There was an undercurrent of hurt that cut into him and pricked his conscience.

Hell. He'd once have argued that he didn't have a conscience when it came to business. Business was business. Nothing personal. Only now…it was definitely personal.

"Come on," she said. "We need to get all this luggage inside."

He put his hand on her arm. "You go in. I'll bring in the luggage. Don't argue. Go get something to drink or eat if you're hungry. I'll be in in just a moment."

She shrugged and walked to the steps leading onto the porch. A moment later, she disappeared into the house, leaving Rafael standing in the driveway staring at his surroundings with keen eyes.

So this is where he'd spent so many days and nights. This is where his life had supposedly undergone such a drastic change. He didn't feel anything other than that he was distinctly out of his comfort zone and in way over his head.

He carried the luggage in two trips to the front porch and then propped her door open and began lugging the bags into the living room.

As he stepped in, he stared around, absorbing the look and feel of the place Bryony called home. It reflected her personality to a T. Sunny, cheerful, a little cluttered, as if she were always in too much of a hurry to keep it spotless. It looked lived-in, nothing like his sterile apartment, which a cleaning lady made spotless every day regardless of whether he was in residence or not.

She stood with her back to him, staring out the French doors that led onto the deck. Her arms were wrapped protectively around her chest and when she turned, he could see the barricade she'd erected as surely as if it were a tangible shield.

"Did you know about the construction? Did you order it to begin?" she asked.

He sighed. "Do you want me to lie, Bryony? I won't. I've been nothing but truthful to you. Yes, I ordered construction to begin. I would have started much sooner but my accident delayed me significantly. My investors are anxious. They want to see progress in return for the money they've shelled out."

"You promised," she choked out.

He ran a hand through his hair and wished he could make this go away. At least until they had matters between them sorted out.

"You know I can't remember," he said. "As far as I knew, the land was bought, the deal closed, the property to do with as I liked. There was nothing in the contract that stipulated how I could use the land. I wouldn't have signed such a contract. The land is useless to me unless I develop it."

Damn it. Why couldn't he remember? Surely he wouldn't have made her such a promise. It defied all logic. Why on earth would he have bought the land and promised not to develop it?

He closed the distance between them and slid his hand over her shoulder. She flinched and lifted her shoulder away, but he kept his hand against her skin.

"Bryony, again, I'm not doing this to hurt you. I don't remember. You say I made you a promise, but I have no proof of that. What I do have is proof of sale. I have your signature on the closing documents as well as a copy of the bank draft issued to you from my bank."

She turned to face him again, her eyes red-rimmed. She looked to be fighting tears with every bit of her power.

"I made it clear from the start that I wouldn't sell to you unless you promised it wouldn't be developed on a large scale. Obviously I can't control what a new owner does with the land, but I'd hoped for something in keeping with the integrity of our community here. You looked me in the eye and you promised me that you had no such plans. That was a lie, Rafael. It's an obvious lie because clearly you had investors lined up, plans drawn, a schedule planned. You yourself just said that your accident delayed the groundbreaking significantly."

Rafael swore because one of them had to be lying and he didn't want it to be him. He didn't want it to be her.

"Damn it, Bryony, I refuse to feel guilt for something I can't remember."

"We should get some sleep," she said dully. "There's little point in arguing over this when we're both tired and I'm upset. I'll show you to the guest room. It has its own bathroom. There are towels and soap, everything you should need."

And just like that, she was dismissing him. She'd withdrawn and he was treated to the cold, angry woman she'd been the first night in New York when she'd confronted him at his event.

He drew in a breath, feeling like a fool for what he was about to say, but it rushed out before he could think better of it, before he could question his sanity.

"I'll put a temporary halt to construction. Tomorrow. I'll go to the site myself. Until we sort things out between us and I regain my memory, I'll halt the groundbreaking."

She blinked in surprise, her mouth forming a silent O. From all appearances it was the last thing she'd expected him to say, and he was suddenly glad of it. Fiercely glad that he'd caught her off guard.

"Really?"

He nodded. "I'd go tonight but no one will be at the site and I have no idea where they're staying, but if I'm there at dawn in the morning, I'll make sure nothing is done until I give the okay to begin."

Once again she surprised him by launching herself into his arms and hugging him so tight he struggled to breathe. For such a small woman, she possessed amazing strength.

"Every time I think you've let me down, you do something to completely change my mind," she whispered fiercely. "Every time I think I've lost the Rafael I fell in love with, you do something to make me realize he's still there and I just have to find him again."

He wasn't sure he liked the sound of that. As if he was some sort of Dr. Jekyll and Mr. Hyde. Hell, maybe he *was* crazy. It was the only explanation behind the past few months of his life.

Most men bought a flashy sports car, had an affair or hooked up with a girl barely out of school in their midlife crisis. Apparently he did bizarre things like fall in love and throw away a multimillion-dollar deal.

Ryan, Dev and Cam were going to kill him.

Twelve

"You did *what?*"

Rafael held the phone away from his ear and winced at the string of expletives that flooded the airways.

"I'm coming down there. We all are," Devon said. "This is precisely what I was afraid of happening. You get down there and she has you by the balls. Make me the bad guy. I don't care, but construction has to begin immediately. We're already months behind schedule."

Rafael paced back and forth over the slight bluff overlooking the beach while Bryony waited in the car. The crew hadn't been happy that they were being asked to stand down, until Rafael informed them they'd be paid full wages during the temporary layoff. He'd stressed *temporary* and hoped like hell that he would have this resolved in a few days' time.

He didn't offer that little tidbit to Devon. Devon would really lose his composure if he knew Rafael was footing the bill for a crew of construction workers to sit around and enjoy beach life for the next few days.

"You stay your ass in New York," Rafael said. "I don't need you and Cam and Ryan to babysit me. It's the right thing to do, Devon. Until I know what the hell I promised or didn't promise or whatever else happened while I was down here the first time, the right thing to do is wait."

"Since when have you ever been concerned with doing the right thing?" Devon asked incredulously. "We're talking about the king of get-it-done, it's business, not personal, whatever it takes, score the deal. Are you getting soft in your old age or has she messed with your head so much that you no longer know up from down?"

Rafael scowled. "You make me sound like a complete bastard."

"Yeah, well, you are. Why should that bother you now? It's what's made you so successful. Don't go growing a conscience on me now."

Rafael frowned even harder. "What do you know about this deal, Devon? What aren't you telling me?"

There was a long silence. And then his friend said, "Look, I don't know what happened down there. What I do know is that before you left New York, you said quite clearly that you'd come back with a signed bill of sale and you didn't give a damn what you had to do to achieve it."

"Son of a bitch," Rafael muttered. "That's not helping my case here."

"Why do you want it to help your case? You've got the land. You've got our investors on board. The only thing standing in our way right now is you."

Rafael stared back at the car to see that Bryony had gotten out and leaned against the door. Her hair blew in the morning breeze and it was a little chilly. She hadn't worn a sweater.

"Yeah, well, for now I'm not moving," he said quietly. "I'll accept full responsibility for this."

"Damn right you will," Devon said in disgust. "We've all made sacrifices, Rafael. We're on the verge of being huge.

With this resort deal and the merger with Copeland hotels, we'll be the largest luxury resort business in the world. Don't screw it up for all of us."

Rafael sighed. Yeah, he knew they'd made sacrifices. Devon was even marrying Copeland's daughter to cement this deal. They were close to having everything they'd ever wanted. Success beyond their wildest imaginations.

And he'd never felt worse or more unsure of himself in his life.

"Trust me on this, Dev. Give me some time, okay? I'll make it right. I've never not come through before. But this is my future we're talking about here."

Rafael heard the weary sigh through the phone. "One week, Rafe. One week and if ground isn't broken, I'm coming down there and I'm bringing Ryan and Cam with me."

Rafael ended the call and shoved the phone into his pocket. One week. It seemed a ridiculous amount of time to decide the fate of his entire future. And Bryony's future. The future of his child.

He blew out his breath and walked away from the beach toward Bryony's car. She was probably tired. He'd bet that neither of them had slept much the night before. He'd seen dark circles under her eyes when they'd left her cottage before sunup to drive to the construction site.

With a week's reprieve, it was time to concentrate on the most important issue at hand—regaining his memory and figuring out his relationship with Bryony Morgan.

As Rafael strode back toward the car, Bryony regarded him warily. He looked angry and determined. Whatever phone call he'd made, it hadn't been pleasant. She could hear his raised voice all the way inside the car, though she couldn't make out what it was he said.

True to his word, he'd given the order to suspend groundbreaking. It hadn't taken long for her cell phone to start ringing. Rupert had been first, congratulating her on keeping

Rafael de Luca in line. Bryony had rolled her eyes and bitten her tongue. As if anyone could leash Rafael de Luca. No, whatever reason he had for agreeing to postpone construction, it hadn't been because she'd asked him to.

Her pride had already taken enough of a beating. She wasn't going to beg him.

Then Silas had called to confirm that construction had indeed been halted and then expressed his concern that the workers were now on the island with nothing to do for the next however many days. He worried about the implications. As if Bryony had any experience with enforcing the law.

Still, she had to remember that a lot of people counted on her to keep things running smoothly. It was what she did. Never mind that her life was in shambles. She didn't offer any guarantees about keeping her own affairs straight.

When Rafael arrived, he didn't say anything. He took the keys from her and guided her around to the passenger side.

When he got in, she eyed him sideways. "Everything okay?"

"Fine."

He started the engine and drove over the bumpy dirt path back to the main road and then accelerated.

"Feel like some breakfast?"

It sounded like he grunted in return, but she couldn't be sure. Still, he hadn't said no, so she took it as an affirmative.

"I'll make your favorite."

He glanced sideways at her. "My favorite?"

"Eggs Benedict."

"Yeah, it is," he mumbled. "I guess I told you that before."

"Uh-huh."

Clearly he wasn't in a talkative mood. He looked downright surly. She was more of a morning person, but Mamaw wasn't, and she often told Bryony she was too cheerful for her own good before noon. Mamaw didn't have any compunction about telling her to shut up and go away, but Bryony guessed Rafael was too polite to do the same.

Funny, but she hadn't noticed him being particularly grumpy in the mornings before, but then more often than not, they'd slept late after a night of making love.

Just the memory of them waking in bed, wrapped around each other, had her cheeks warming and a tingle snaking through her body.

She missed those nights. And the mornings. Most of the time she'd cooked for them both, but at least twice, Rafael had risen while she still slept and brought her breakfast in bed.

So instead of saying anything further, she reached over and took his hand, squeezing it before lacing her fingers through his.

He looked surprised by the gesture, but he didn't make any effort to extricate his hand from hers.

"Thank you."

He cocked his head.

"For doing that. It means a lot not just to me, but also to the people on this island."

He looked uncomfortable. "You need to understand that this is only a temporary solution. I can't suspend operations indefinitely. There are a lot of people counting on me. They've trusted me with their money. My partners are heavily invested with me. This is… This is huge for us."

"But you understand I would have never sold you the land if you hadn't given me your promise," she said. "The result would be the same. It's not as though I sold you the land under false pretenses."

Rafael sighed but then squeezed her hand. "For now let's not talk about it. There's no simple solution to all this whether I regain my memory or not."

For the first time she weighed his position in the matter.

If all he'd said were true, then it couldn't have been easy for him to call off the operation.

Regardless of whether he'd lied to her before, he'd done the honorable thing now and it was costing him dearly.

She leaned over and brushed her lips across his cheek. "I realize this isn't easy, but we all appreciate it. I've already gotten calls from the mayor and the sheriff. I'm sure there will be more before the day is out. You can expect to be courted by the locals while you're here. They'll want to present their case."

"Are they angry with you?" he asked. "The mayor didn't seem pleased with you last night. Do they all blame you?"

She blew out her breath. "They think I'm young and gullible. Some of them blame that and not me directly. They're too busy feeling sorry for me for being taken by a suave, debonair man. Others put the blame solely on my shoulders, as they should."

Rafael's face grew stormy. "It's your land. You can't allow others to guilt you into keeping it just because they don't want their way of life to change."

She shrugged. "I grew up here. They consider me a part of their family. Family doesn't turn their backs on each other. A lot of them think I did just that. Maybe I did. I knew that if you and I were going to be together that I wouldn't stay here. I knew I'd have to make the move because your business is based in the city. At the time I didn't care."

He slowed to pull into her driveway and stopped the car. For a long moment he stared out the windshield before finally turning to face her.

"So you were willing to give up everything to be with me."

"Yes," she said simply. Throwing his words back at him, she continued. "I don't say that to hurt you. It's simply the truth and we've both been honest and blunt. I'm not trying to make you feel guilty."

"I don't know what to say."

She smiled. “Let’s not say anything. Let’s go eat instead. I’m starving. After breakfast we’ll go buy you the things you need for your stay and then maybe we’ll sit on the deck. Enjoy the day.”

Strangely enough, it sounded blissful.

Suddenly, after a not-so-great start to the day, he found himself quite looking forward to the rest.

Thirteen

Bryony tugged Rafael from shop to shop in the town square where she made him try on more casual clothing. Jeans. Lord but the man looked divine in jeans. They cupped his behind in all the right places and molded to his muscular legs.

And a T-shirt. Such an unremarkable item of clothing but on him… A simple white T-shirt displayed his lean, taut body to perfection.

He looked uncomfortable when he came out of the dressing room. He had on the jeans and the shirt she'd picked out and he was barefooted. Barefooted.

She was standing there drooling over a barefooted man in jeans. And she wasn't the only one.

"Oh, my," Stella Jones breathed. "Honey, that is one fine specimen you've got there. He looks hot in the *GQ* stuff, don't get me wrong, but he fills out a pair of jeans like nobody's business."

Bryony shot the saleswoman a glare but had to admit she was right.

"Will this make you happy?" Rafael asked wryly as he turned, hands up.

"Oh, yeah," Bryony murmured. "Me and every other female on this island."

Stella chuckled. "Shall I bag up a few more pair like that one?"

"And T-shirts. Lots of T-shirts. I'm thinking white and maybe a red one."

"Green wouldn't be bad with those dark eyes and hair," Stella advised.

Rafael rolled his eyes. "I'm going back in to change while you ladies sort it out."

"No! No!" Bryony said in a rush. "Just let me pull off the stickers. No reason to change out of them. Stella will ring them up. You'll be more comfortable."

"And so will the rest of us," Stella said over her shoulder as she sashayed off to get the rest of the clothing.

Rafael grinned and sauntered toward Bryony. "So you like me in jeans?"

"I think *like* is perhaps too mild a word," Bryony muttered.

Although Bryony had been openly affectionate with Rafael the entire day, taking his hand, hugging him or twining her arm through his, he hadn't made any overt gestures of his own. But now he slid his arms around her and pulled her into his embrace.

He rested his hands loosely at the small of her back and then slid his fingers into her back pockets, pulling her closer until she was pressed against his chest.

"I like you in jeans, too," he said with a sly grin.

Her heart fluttered as she curled her arms around his shoulders.

"Yeah, but I'm wearing baggy jeans with an elastic maternity waist."

"They fit your behind just fine."

To emphasize his point he moved his fingers to where they were snug in her back pockets.

"We'll have the whole island talking," she murmured.

He snorted. "As if they aren't already? I think everyone who lives here has been out to either look at us or tell me what a wonderful thing I did by stopping the construction. And I think it's a widely known fact that it's my child you're carrying. What else could they possibly talk about beyond that?"

"Okay, you have a point," she said wryly.

He leaned down and kissed her softly. "Why don't we take our jeans-clad selves back to your cottage and I'll fix us some lunch."

She raised her eyebrows. "What have you got in mind?"

"I don't know. It depends on what you have in your pantry. You cooked breakfast for us and you've taken me around town all morning. The least I can do is pamper you awhile. Are your feet tired?"

She laughed even as her heart squeezed at the concern in his voice.

"My feet are fine, but I wouldn't turn down a massage if you're offering."

He gave her a smile filled with genuine warmth. "I think that could be arranged."

She flung her arms around him and buried her face in his chest. "Oh, Rafael. Today has been perfect. Just perfect. Thank you."

When she pulled away, he had a befuddled expression on his face as if he didn't know quite how to respond to her outburst.

"I had no idea shopping for jeans made you so happy," he teased.

She flashed him a cheeky grin. "Only when I get to see you wear them."

He patted her affectionately on the behind and then gestured for her to go ahead of him. "Let's go then. All this shopping has worked up my appetite."

She laced her fingers with his, delighting in the sense of closeness that had quickly built between them. Whether he remembered or not, the moment they'd arrived, Bryony had sensed a change in Rafael. He'd reverted to the more relaxed, easygoing man with whom she'd fallen in love.

He may not see himself as someone who would get away from the stress of the business world, or someone who would leave his cell phone off or his computer put away for a period of days, but Moon Island had changed him. She'd like to think that his relationship with her had changed his priorities. Maybe it was fanciful and naive for her to think such things, but it didn't stop her from hoping that he'd rediscover the island—and her.

They drove back to the cottage but Bryony directed him to pull into her grandmother's driveway instead of her own.

"I want to check in with her and see how she's doing. I've only talked to her on the phone for the last week. I don't often leave her for long periods of time."

Rafael nodded. "Of course. Would you prefer I go ahead to your cottage and begin lunch?"

"Only if you want to. I don't mind if you come unless you're uncomfortable. I'm only going to talk to her a minute or two. Make sure everything's okay."

"Then I'll go with you," Rafael said. "I'd like to get reacquainted. You two seem to be very close. Did I spend a lot of time with her before?"

Bryony smiled. "You got along famously. You'd drop in on her every other day or so whether I was with you or not. You spoiled her by bringing her favorite flowers and a box of goodies from the bakery."

"I sounded…nice," he said, as though the idea were ridiculous.

She paused in the act of opening her car door and turned

her head so she looked directly at him. "You say that as if you aren't…nice."

He shrugged. "*Bastard* has been used on more than one occasion to describe me. This morning being the most recent. I've been called a lot of things. Ruthless. Driven. Ambitious. Son of a bitch. You name it. But nice? I can't say that being thoughtful was ever a priority. It's not that I intended to be a jerk, but I was never really concerned about it."

"Well, you were wonderful to my grandmother and I loved you for it," she said. "You were wonderful to me, too. Maybe you don't associate with the right people."

He laughed at that. "Maybe you're right. I guess we'll see, won't we?"

Bryony's grandmother appeared on the front porch and waved for them to come in. Bryony reached over and squeezed Rafael's hand. "Stop worrying so much about what you were or weren't. No one says you have to stay the same forever. Maybe you were ready for a change. Here you could be whoever you wanted because no one knew you before. You got to have a fresh start."

He raised her hand and pressed a kiss to her palm. "What I think is that you're a special woman, Bryony Morgan."

She smiled again and opened her car door. As she got out, she waved at her grandmother. "We're coming!"

Mamaw smiled and waved, then waited with the screen door open while Rafael and Bryony made their way up the steps.

"Good afternoon to you," Mamaw said cheerfully.

She pulled Bryony into a hug and then did the same with Rafael, who looked a little dumbstruck by the reception.

"Come in, come in, you two. I just sweetened a pitcher of tea and it's ready to pour. I'll get us some glasses. Have a seat on the back porch if you like. It's a beautiful day and the water is gorgeous."

Bryony tugged Rafael to the glass doors leading onto a

deck that was similar in build to her own. The wood was older and more worn but it added character. The railings were dotted with potted plants and flowers. Colorful knickknacks and decorative garden figurines were scattered here and there, giving the deck an eclectic feel.

Bryony often thought it resembled a rummage sale, but it so fit her grandmother's personality that it never failed to bring a smile to Bryony's face.

Mamaw didn't much believe in throwing things away. She wasn't a hoarder and she *would* part with stuff after a while, but she liked to collect items she said made her house more homey.

"It's beautiful out here," Rafael said. "It's so quiet and peaceful. There aren't many stretches of private beach like this. It must be amazing to have this all to yourself."

Bryony settled into one of the padded deck chairs and angled her head up to catch the full sun on her face. "It is," she said, her eyes closed. "The whole island is like this. It's why we're so resistant to the idea of commercially developing parts of it. Once the first bit of 'progress' creeps in, it's like a snowball. Soon the island would just be another tourist stop with cheesy T-shirts and cheap trinkets."

"What I purchased was just a drop in the bucket for an island this size. Surely you don't begrudge any development. You could have the best of both worlds. The majority of the island would remain unspoiled, a quiet oasis, while a very small section would be developed so that others could be exposed to your paradise."

She dropped her head back down, opening her eyes to look at him. "You sound just like a salesman. The truth is, the whole sharing-our-paradise-with-others spiel is precisely what we don't want to do. Call us selfish but there are numerous other islands that tourists can go to if they want sun and sand. We just want to be left alone. Many of the people who live here retired to this island precisely because it was private and unspoiled. Others have made their whole lives here and to change it now seems grossly unfair."

"Having one resort wouldn't ruin the integrity of the island and it would boost the economy and bring in an influx of cash from those tourists you all despise."

She smiled patiently, unwilling to become angry and frustrated and ruin a perfect day. Besides, biting his head off didn't serve her purpose.

"We don't need an influx of cash into our economy," she said gently.

He arched a disbelieving eyebrow. "Everyone can always use a boost in capital."

She shook her head. "No, the thing is, many of the people who retired here left high-paying corporate jobs. Hell, some of them were CEOs who sold their companies or left the management to their sons and daughters and came to Moon Island to escape their high-pressure jobs. They have more money than they'll ever spend."

"And the rest? The ones who've lived here all their lives?"

She shrugged. "They're happy. We have shrimpers who are third- and fourth-generation fishermen. We have local shop owners, restaurant workers, grocery store clerks. Basically everyone's job fulfills a need on the island. Selling souvenirs to tourists isn't a need. Neither is providing them entertainment. We have a comfortable living here. Some of us don't have much but we make it and we're happy."

"There is a certain weirdness to this whole place," Rafael said with an amused tone. "Like stepping into a time warp. I'm shocked that you have internet access, cable and cellular towers."

"We keep up," she said. "We just don't particularly care about getting ahead. There is a certain je ne sais quoi about our lifestyle, our people and our island. In a lot of ways it can't be described, only experienced. As you did for those weeks you were here."

"And yet you were going to walk away from your life here. For me."

She went still. "Yes, I've already said so. I mean I assumed I would have to make changes. You run a business. You have a home in New York. I could hardly expect you to give all that up and live here. I expected it to be an adjustment but I thought it—you—would be worth it."

"Given your passion for this island and the people here, I'm a little awed that you thought I was worth that kind of sacrifice."

"You sell yourself short, Rafael. Don't you think you're worth it? That someone could and should love you enough to give up important things to be with you?"

He averted his gaze, staring out over the water as if he had no answer. His body language had changed and he held himself stiffly. His jaw tightened and then he made an effort to relax.

"Maybe I've never met anyone who thought that much of me," he finally said.

"Again, you're associating with the wrong people. And you've definitely been dating the wrong women."

The mischievous tone in her voice wrung a smile out of him.

"Why do I get the feeling that I probably tried like hell to keep you at arm's length and you were having none of that?"

She frowned. "Not at all. You seemed…" Her expression grew more thoughtful. "You were definitely open to what happened between us. You certainly did your share of pursuing. Put it this way. I didn't have to try very hard to get past that stuffy exterior of yours."

He shook his head. "I'm beginning to think I have a double running around impersonating me. I know I keep saying this, but the man you describe is so far out of my realm of understanding that he seems a complete and utter stranger. If

I didn't know better, I'd say I suffered the head injury before I arrived here. Not after."

"Does it appall you that much?"

He jerked his gaze to her. "No, that's not what I'm saying at all. It's not that I'm shamed or angry. It's hard to explain. I mean think for a moment of things you would never do. Think of something so not in line with your personality. Then imagine someone telling you that you did all those things but you can't remember them. You'd think they'd lost their mind, not that you'd lost yours."

"Okay, I can understand that. So it's not that you can't accept the person you were."

"I just don't understand him," Rafael mused. "Or why."

"Maybe you took one look at me and decided you had to have me or die," she said impishly.

He leaned sideways until their mouths were hovering just a breath apart. "Now that I can understand because I find I feel that way around you with increasing frequency."

She closed the remaining distance between them and found his lips in a gentle kiss. He kissed the bow of her mouth and then each corner in a playful, teasing manner, and every time she felt a thrill down to her toes.

"I have tea, but I can see you're not that interested," Mamaw said with a laugh.

Bryony pulled back and turned to see her grandmother standing outside the glass doors holding two tea glasses. "Of course I want your tea. It's the best in the south."

"Do I like it?" Rafael asked, a hint of a smile on his face.

Mamaw walked over and handed him a glass. "You sure do, young man. Said it was better than any of that fancy wine you drink in the city."

He gave her a smile that would have made most women melt on the spot. "Well, then if I said it I must have meant it." He took the glass and took a cautious sip.

Bryony took her own glass and sent Rafael an amused

look. "It isn't spiked. I promise. You're looking at it like you expect it to be poisoned."

He took another sip. "It's good."

Mamaw beamed at him as if it were the first time she'd heard the compliment.

"Have a seat, Mamaw. We came to see you, not to be alone."

Her grandmother pulled up a chair and sat across from Bryony and Rafael. "Bryony tells me you were in a plane crash. That must have been traumatic for you."

Rafael nodded. "I don't remember much about the crash. I do have a few memories. Mostly of the aftermath and feeling relief that I was alive. But the rest is a blur. Including the weeks before the crash as I'm sure Bryony has told you."

Mamaw nodded. "It's a shame. Bryony was so upset. She was sure you'd pulled a fast one on her and left her alone and pregnant."

Heat crept up Bryony's neck. "Mamaw, don't."

"No, it's fine," Rafael said to Bryony. "I'm sure she has anger toward me just like you did. There's no need for her to pretend differently."

Mamaw nodded. "I like a man who's honest and straightforward. Now that you're back and are trying to work things out with my granddaughter, I think we'll get along just fine."

He smiled. "I hope so, Ms...." He stopped in midsentence and looked to Bryony for help. "What do I call her? I don't remember you telling me her name."

Bryony laughed. "That's because to everyone she's just Mamaw."

Mamaw reached forward and patted Rafael's leg. "There now, if that makes you uncomfortable, you can call me Laura. Hardly anyone does. Just the mayor because he thinks it's unseemly for a man of his position to be so familiar with one of his constituents. His malarkey, not mine. He's a bit of an odd duck, but he's a decent enough mayor."

"Laura. It suits you. Pretty name for an equally pretty lady."

To Bryony's amusement, her grandmother's cheeks bloomed with color and for once she didn't have a ready comeback. She just beamed at Rafael like he'd hung the moon.

"Are things okay with you, Mamaw?" Bryony asked. "How have you been feeling and do you need us to get you anything while we're out?"

"Oh, no, child, I'm good. Silas came by while you were gone and took my grocery list to his nephew. He's got a job delivering groceries now. Just got his driver's license and he's excited to get to be driving everywhere. I keep expecting to hear of him getting into an accident with the way he zips around these roads but so far nothing's happened and not one of my eggs was broken, so I guess he's got it under control."

"You're taking your medicine every day like you're supposed to?"

Mamaw rolled her eyes and then looked toward Rafael. "One would think she was the grandmother and I was the ditzy young granddaughter. Mind you, it wasn't me who got herself pregnant. I know how to take *my* pills."

"Mamaw!"

She shrugged. "Well, it's true."

"Oh, God," Bryony groaned. "You're on fire today, aren't you. I should have just gone home."

Rafael chuckled and then broke into steady laughter. Bryony and her grandmother stared as he laughed so hard he was wiping at his eyes.

"You two are hilarious."

"Easy for you to say. She wasn't taking you to task for not using a condom," Bryony said sourly.

"It was next on my list," Mamaw said airily.

Rafael shook his head. "At least I can claim I have no memory of the event."

"It broke," Bryony said tightly.

"Now see, if you were taking your pills like you were supposed to, a broken condom wouldn't be an issue," Mamaw said.

Bryony stood and tugged at Rafael's arm. "Okay, I've had enough of let's embarrass the hell out of Bryony today. It's obvious Mamaw is feeling her usual sassy self, so let's go home. I'm starving."

Rafael laughed again and climbed out of his chair. He bent down to kiss Mamaw on the cheek. "It was a pleasure to reacquaint myself with you."

Fourteen

"Comfortable?" Rafael asked as he plumped a pillow behind Bryony's back.

Bryony reclined on the wicker patio lounger. She smiled up at Rafael and sighed. It was an absolutely beautiful day as only a fall day could be on the island. Still quite warm but without the oppressive heat and humidity of summer. The skies were brilliant blue, unmarred by a single cloud, and the salt-scented air danced on her nose as the soft music of the distant waves hummed in her ears.

"You're spoiling me," she said. "But by all means keep on. I'm not opposed in the least."

He sat at the opposite end of the lounger and pulled her feet into his lap. He toyed with the ankle bracelet and then traced a finger over the arch of her foot.

"You have beautiful feet."

She shot him a skeptical look. "You think my feet are beautiful?"

"Well, yes, and you draw attention to them and your ankles

with this piece of jewelry. I like it. You have great legs, too. A complete package."

"I don't think I've ever had my feet propped on a gorgeous guy's lap while he does an analysis of my legs and ankles before. It makes me feel all queenly."

He began to press his thumb into her arch with just enough force to make her moan.

"Isn't that how a man should make the mother of his child feel? Like a queen?"

"Oh, God, you're killing me. Sure, in theory, but how many guys really do? Of course, I've never been pregnant before so how would I know?"

He laughed. "I think you're supposed to pick up on the fact that I'm embracing this child as our child. Our creation. Together. I know it seems I've ignored his or her presence. We haven't discussed your pregnancy much, but I've thought of little else since I found out. It's kept me up at night. I lay there thinking how ill-prepared I am to be a father and yet I have this eager anticipation that eats at me. I start to wonder who the baby will look like. Whether it will be a son or a daughter."

Tears crowded her eyes and she felt like an idiot. But there was no doubt the longing in his voice hit her right in the heart and softened it into mush.

"Why do you think you're ill-prepared to be a father?" she asked softly.

He closed both hands around her foot and rubbed his thumbs up and down the bottom, pressing and massaging the sole, then moving up to her arch and on to the pads below her toes.

"I work to the exclusion of all else. I never go anywhere that I don't bring work with me. Most of my social events are work-related. There are times I sleep at my office. Just as many times I sleep on a plane en route to a meeting or to scope out a location for a new development. A child needs the attention of his parent. He needs their love and support. All I can really do is provide financially."

"I said this once already but you don't have to stay the same person just because that's who you've always been. Parents make changes for their children all the time. I'm not any more prepared for parenthood than you are. I always imagined I'd wait until I was older."

He arched a brow. "Just how old are you? You make it sound like you're some teenager."

She laughed. "I'm twenty-five. Plenty old to have children but since until a few months ago I haven't had a serious relationship, and by serious I mean thinking of marriage and commitment, et cetera. I knew that having children was still some years away."

"It would seem we're both going to be handed parenthood before we thought we were ready."

"But would we really ever say we were ready? I mean who just announces one day, 'Okay, I'm ready for children'? I think even people who plan their pregnancies still have to be a little unprepared for the changes that occur with the arrival of a child."

"You're probably right. I think you'd make a great mother, though."

She cocked her head, flushed with pleasure at the compliment. "That means a lot that you'd say that, Rafael, but what makes you think so? I haven't exactly shown a lot of responsibility to this point."

"You are a loving and affectionate woman. Warm, spontaneous. Loyal and generous. And you're direct. You had no qualms about taking me on when you thought I'd wronged you. I can only imagine how fierce you would be in protection of our child."

"Do you know why I think you'd make a great father?"

His hands stilled on her foot and he glanced up at her.

"Because you admit your shortcomings," she said gently.

"You know your faults. You acknowledge them. You're well aware of the areas where you'd need to change. Most people aren't that self-aware. I have no doubt that you'd be sensitive to your child's needs and make adjustments. There's nothing you can say to convince me that you wouldn't absolutely put your child first in your priorities."

He slid one hand up her leg to snag her fingers and then he squeezed. "Thank you for that."

"I still love you, Rafael."

The words slipped out. They were an ache in her heart that she had to let loose. Here in this moment, it was more than she could take, even though she'd sworn she wouldn't make herself vulnerable again until they had resolved his memory loss and their relationship. She simply had to tell him how she felt.

His eyes darkened. His hands were no longer gentle as he roughly pulled her up and toward him. She sprawled indelicately across his lap as he framed her face in his grasp. For a long moment, he stroked her cheek as he stared into her eyes.

Then he leaned his forehead against hers in a surprisingly tender gesture as he gathered her hand in his, trapped it between their chests.

"I had no idea how I'd feel when I asked you if you still love me yesterday. It was an idle curiosity. I had no idea the impact those words would make. I can't even explain it. How can I?"

"I had to tell you," she whispered. "I've been honest. I don't want to hold anything back. It's hard for me. I'm unused to being reserved. You deserve to know the truth. You're here. You're making the effort. The least I can do is meet you halfway. It was my pride that held me back before. I didn't want to humble myself or make myself vulnerable to you again, but holding back the words doesn't change anything."

He lowered his head and kissed her, forgoing his earlier

gentle and playful smooches. His lips moved heatedly over hers, dragging breath from her then returning it, demanding it.

He tasted of the lemonade he'd served with the lunch he'd prepared. Tart and sweet and so hot. He licked over the seam of her mouth then plunged inward again as if determined to taste every part of her.

Always before, his lovemaking had seemed practiced and deliberate. Smooth and seductive. Now there was a desperation to his every caress and kiss, like he couldn't wait to touch her or to have her. Even as the differences plagued her, she gave herself over to this seemingly new man. It felt different. He was different.

"I want to make love to you, Bryony, but I want it to be for the right reasons. I want you to know I want you for the right reasons. Right now I couldn't care less about the past or what I do or don't remember. What I know is that right here, right now, I want to touch you and kiss you more than I want anything else."

As gracefully as she could manage when her legs and hands were shaking, she got off his lap to stand before him. Then she reached down for his hand and slid her fingers through his.

"I want you, too," she said simply. "I've missed you so much, Rafe."

He rose unsteadily, his eyes dark and vibrant with desire. His usually calm composure seemed shaken and he raised a trembling hand to her cheek.

"Be sure of this, Bryony. Whatever happens today, whatever has happened in the past, what I remember or don't remember—it's not going to matter if you give yourself to me again. Now. If we do this now, we're starting over. New page. Fresh beginning."

She rubbed her cheek over his hand and closed her eyes. "I'd like that. No past. Just today. Here and now. You and me."

He wrapped an arm around her and urged her toward the door. They stumbled inside the cottage and she guided him toward her bedroom. Past the guest room where he'd slept the night before. Back to the place where they'd spent so many hours making love in the past.

He closed the door and she stood in front of him, suddenly shy and unsure. Though she'd made love with him countless times before, it seemed new. He seemed different. Maybe she herself was even different.

And then she laughed.

Her laughter startled him. He looked up and cocked his head to the side. "What's so funny?"

She closed her eyes and shook her head ruefully. "I was standing here thinking that this felt like the first time and I'm so terribly nervous but then I thought how ridiculous that was when I'm pregnant with your child, a testament to the fact that it's far from the first time for us."

His expression softened and he pulled her gently into his arms. "In a lot of ways this is our first time. I think we should treat it as such. I know I plan to reacquaint myself with your body. I want to touch and see every part of you. There'll be no rushing. I want to savor every moment and draw it out until we're both crazy."

She swayed toward him, feeling light-headed, as if she were a little drunk. He caught her to him and carefully walked her back until she met with the edge of the bed.

Silently he began to unbutton her shirt, taking his time as he worked down her body. When he was done, he carefully parted the lapels and pushed back and over her shoulders so that the material fell away and she stood in her jeans and bra.

"Pretty and delicate," he said as he fingered the lace that cupped the swell of her breast. "A lot like you. It suits you. I like you in pink."

"You don't fancy a siren in red or black?" she asked with a grin.

"No. Not at all. I like the softness of pink and how feminine it looks on you. Very girly."

He lowered his head to kiss the bare expanse of skin that peeked above the cup and then nuzzled lower, pushing down the lace ever so slightly until he was just a breath from her taut nipple.

Then he drew away. "I like girly."

"You are a tease," she said in a strained voice.

He reached down to unbutton her pants, loosening them and then pulling them down just enough to bare the swell of her belly.

To her utter shock, he went to his knees and molded her stomach with both hands. He gently caressed the bump and then pressed a kiss to her flesh.

It was an exquisitely tender moment and an image she'd never forget as long as she lived. This proud, arrogant man on his knees in front of her, lavishing attention on their baby—and her.

She gazed down, lovingly running her fingers through his dark hair. He stared up at her and the look in his eyes made her catch her breath.

Then he tugged at her jeans and slowly rolled them over her hips and down her legs. When they pooled at her feet, he lifted one leg, his hands sliding up and down in a sensual caress. He tugged the material free and then lifted her other foot to completely remove the jeans.

"Matching lacy pink," he said just before pressing a kiss to the V of her underwear. "I like it. I like it a lot."

Her legs trembled and butterflies fluttered through her veins, around her chest and up into her throat.

She wasn't self-conscious about her pregnant body as many women were. In fact, she liked the newfound lushness of her curves. In a lot of ways she'd never looked better. Her skin glowed with a healthy sheen. Her breasts had grown larger and she was fascinated by the shape of her expanding abdomen.

She hadn't really considered being worried over Rafael's reaction to the changes in her body. If she had, she would have worried in vain because he seemed entranced. Nothing in his actions told her he found her anything but desirable.

"You're beautiful," he said in a raw voice, almost as if he'd been privy to her thoughts.

Slowly he rose, sliding his hands up her body as he straightened to stand in front of her. Then he tangled his fingers in her hair and fit his mouth to hers.

She struggled for air but wouldn't retreat long enough to take a breath. She took every bit as much as he did, demanding more in return.

There was something markedly different between them. Their lovemaking had always been casual. Fun, a little flirty and laid-back. The Rafael who stood before her now was… different. It was in the way he looked at her, so dark and forbidding, as if he were set to devour her. As if he wanted her more than he'd ever wanted another woman.

Fanciful but there was definitely nothing casual about the way he touched and kissed her.

She liked the new Rafael. He was commanding and yet gentle and loving. Reverent.

He cupped one hand around her nape, his fingers pressing possessively on her neck as he pulled her into another bone-melting kiss. Then he nibbled a path down her jaw to her ear and sucked the lobe into his mouth. Each tug sent pulsating waves of desire low into her pelvis. Her muscles clenched and she tensed as a whispery sigh floated from her lips.

His mouth never leaving the sensitive column of her throat, he slipped his arms underneath hers and hoisted her upward so he could lift her onto the bed. He lowered her then hovered over her, his denim-clad knee sliding between her thighs.

He kissed her again, then reached up to brush the hair from

her forehead, his touch so light and caressing that it sent a thrill coursing through her veins.

Once more he brushed his mouth across hers as if he hated to leave her even for the time it would take him to undress. But he stepped back and the fact that his hands shook as he pulled at his T-shirt endeared him to her all the more.

He stripped the shirt off, the muscles rippling across his chest and shoulders. He tossed it aside and then began undoing the fly of his jeans. She nearly moaned when he pulled both jeans and underwear down in one impatient shove.

The man was sexy. Cut like a flawless gem. Toned. Fit. Lean but not too lean. He had enough bulk that told of his workout regimen.

Her gaze drifted downward to his groin and she sighed her appreciation as his erection jutted upward. Impatient for him to return to her, she shifted and leaned up on her elbows so she could better see him.

But then he was crawling back onto the bed, straddling her body. He put the flat of his palm on her chest and gently pushed her down onto the mattress. Then he carefully slipped the straps of her bra off her shoulders, nudging until the cups released her breasts.

He lifted her just enough that he could fit one hand underneath to unhook her bra and then he pulled it away and tossed it onto the floor.

For a long moment he stared down at her, his gaze drifting up and down her body then focusing on her, their eyes catching and holding.

"I'm burning the image of you into my memory," he said in a husky voice. "I don't want to ever forget again. I can't imagine how I ever did to begin with. What man when presented with such beauty could possibly let such a memory of it escape?"

Her heart went all fluttery again. It was hard to breathe around him. When he wasn't sending shivers of delight over her flesh with his touch, he sent ripples of pleasure through her heart with his words.

"Kiss me," she begged softly.

"Just as soon as I've taken the last of your pink girly underwear off," he said with a smile.

His fingers danced down her sides and hooked into the lacy band of her panties and he tugged, moving backward as he pulled them down her legs.

This time he moved up the side of her and curled his arms around her, pulling her against him so her naked flesh met his. It was a shock. A delicious, decadent thrill. His hardness was cupped intimately in the V of her legs and her breasts pressed against the slightly hair-roughened surface of his chest.

As he kissed her, his hand roamed possessively down her back and over the swell of her buttocks and then around to cup her belly before drifting lower into the damp, sensitive flesh between her legs.

She moaned and arched forward as his fingers found her most sensitive points. His erection slid between her slightly parted legs, burning, rigid, branding her flesh.

She wanted him inside her, a part of her, after being so long without him. She stirred restlessly, clinging to him, spreading her legs wider to encourage him to take her.

He smiled against her mouth. "So impatient. I'm not nearly finished yet, little love. I want to make you crazy with pleasure before I make you mine again. So crazy that you'll scream my name when I slide into your warmth."

"I want you," she whispered. "So much, Rafe. I missed you. Missed holding you like this. Missed having you touch me."

He drew away and regarded her, his expression so serious that it touched something deep inside her. "I think somehow that I've missed you, too, Bryony. A part of me has. I don't think I could be so happy so quickly with you if we hadn't known each other before, if we hadn't been…close. Lovers.

You feel so perfect next to me. I feel like I've opened the door into someone else's life because this feels nothing like mine and yet I want it so badly I can taste it. I can feel it."

She reached up and tugged him down into a kiss, so moved by his words that her heart felt near to bursting.

"I don't want to wait. I need you now, Rafe. Please. Be inside me. Let me feel you."

He leaned over her body, pressing into her, his heat enveloping her. She savored the sensation of being mushed beneath him, of inhaling his scent so deeply that she could almost taste him.

"Are you sure you're ready, Bryony?"

Even as he spoke, he slid one finger inside her and rolled his thumb across her clitoris. She closed her eyes and gripped his arms until her fingers felt bloodless.

"Please," she whispered again.

He positioned himself and pushed the tiniest bit forward until he was barely inside.

"Open your eyes. Look at me, Bryony. Let me see you."

Her eyelids fluttered open and she met his gaze, so dark and sensual.

He slid forward again, just a bit, stroking her insides with fire. He seemed determined to draw out their reunion, to make it last.

She let her hands wander down his sides and she caressed up and down, encouraging him to complete the act.

He leaned down until their noses brushed and then he angled his mouth over hers just as he slid the rest of the way inside her welcoming body.

Tears burned her eyes. The knot in her throat was such that she couldn't speak. She didn't have words anyway to describe the sensation of being back with the man she loved after having thought she'd lost him.

He withdrew and thrust again, his mouth never leaving

hers. He breathed her. She breathed him. Their tongues tangled, stroked and coaxed.

He let his body descend on her and planted his forearms into the mattress so that she wasn't completely bearing his weight as his hips rocked against hers.

It was much like the ocean waves, rolling forward then receding. Gentle and yet building in intensity. He was patient, much more patient than he'd ever been.

"Tell me if I hurt you," he said against her mouth. "Or if I'm too heavy for you."

In answer she wrapped both arms around him and hugged him tight. She slid one hand down to cup his firm buttocks as he undulated his hips against her.

"Tell me what you need," he whispered. "Tell me how to please you, Bryony."

Her hands ran up his back to his shoulders and then one slid to his nape, her fingers thrusting upward into his hair.

"You're doing just fine," she said dreamily. "I feel like I'm floating."

He dropped his head to suck lightly at her neck and then he nibbled to the curve of her shoulder and sucked again, harder this time until she was sure he'd leave a mark.

She hadn't had such a mark since she was a teenager, but strangely it thrilled her that she would have a reminder of his possession.

He groaned. "I'm sorry, Bryony. I can't— Damn it." He issued several more muffled curses that ended in a long moan as he increased his pace.

As soon as the intensity changed, the orgasm that had begun as a lazy, slow build escalated into a sharp coiling burn low in her abdomen. It rose and spread until she gasped at the tension.

She dug her fingers into his back, not knowing how else to handle the mounting pressure. She arched her buttocks off the bed, pushing him deeper inside her. He tensed and shuddered against her, reaching fulfillment while she was still reaching blindly for her own.

He pulled from her body, rolled to the side and slid his hand between her legs, caressing and stroking her taut flesh. He lowered his head to her breast and sucked her nipple into his mouth, laving it with his tongue as he pressed another finger inside.

His thumb rolled over her clitoris, his fingers worked deep and his mouth tugged relentlessly at her breast. Her surroundings blurred and the coiling tension suddenly snapped, unraveling at super speed.

"Rafael!"

Her back came off the mattress and her hand went to his hair, gripping, her fingers curling into his nape as she went rigid underneath him.

Her release was sharp. It was sweet. It was intense. It was one of the most shattering experiences of her life. She was left clinging to him, saying his name over and over incoherently as she came down.

He continued to stroke her, more gently than before, sweetly and comfortingly as she settled beneath him, her body quivering and shaking like she'd experienced a great shock.

Her mind couldn't quite put it all together yet. All she knew was that it had never been this way between them before. She was…shattered. There was no other way to put it. And completely and utterly vulnerable before him. Bare. Stripped.

He gathered her close, holding her tightly as they both fought for breath. His hands seemed to be everywhere. Caressing. Touching. Soothing. He kissed her hair, her temple, her cheek and even her eyelids.

The one thing that seemed to penetrate the haze that surrounded her was that however undone she was, he'd been equally affected.

She wrapped herself around him as tightly as he was

wound around her, snuggled her face into the hollow of his neck and drifted into a fuzzy sleep, so sated that she couldn't have moved if she wanted to.

Fifteen

Bryony woke to warm kisses along her shoulder and hands possessively stroking her body.

"Mmm," she murmured as she lazily stretched.

"Oh, good, you're awake. I'd hate to think I was taking advantage of a sleeping woman."

She laughed. "Oh, I bet."

"I have a lot to make up for," he said.

He slid his mouth down the midline of her chest and then over the swell of one breast.

"You do?"

He traced the puckered crest of her nipple with his tongue and then sucked gently. He let go and looked up to meet her gaze. In the soft glow of her bedside lamp, she could see regret simmering in his eyes.

"Evidently I have no control when it comes to you. I wanted to make it good for you. I wanted it to last. I didn't take care of you very well. I guess it goes along with my selfish-bastard ways."

She rolled her eyes and lifted her palm to caress the side of his face. “If I had been any more satisfied I think I would have died. I like that I drove you a little wild.”

He arched one eyebrow. “A little? I’m not sure that accurately describes the mind-numbing experience I had. I don’t ever remember losing it like that with any other woman. Was it like that between us before?”

“No,” she said softly. “Not like that.”

“Better?”

“Definitely better.”

“Ah, good then. I was starting to feel threatened by the self I couldn’t remember.”

She laughed and then so did he. It felt good for once to joke about an event that had altered the courses of both their lives.

“I’m hungry.”

He lowered his mouth to her breast again. “So am I.”

Laughing, she smacked his shoulder. “For food! It’s been… What time is it anyway?”

He shrugged underneath her palm that had stilled on his shoulder. “Sometime in the wee hours of the morning. We slept a long time. You wore me out.”

“Let’s eat in bed and then…”

He arched an eyebrow as he stared lazily back up at her. “Then what?”

She smiled wickedly. “Then I’m going to have dessert.”

“In that case—” he scrambled up, covers flying “—you stay here. I’ll get us something to eat and be back in a minute.”

She pulled the covers to her chin and snuggled into the pillows, smiling as he strode naked out of the bedroom. He didn’t look at all abashed by his nudity. Confidence in a man was so sexy. She sighed and stretched, a dreamy smile spreading across her face.

Fifteen minutes later, Rafael returned with a tray holding

two saucers. Piled on each was two grilled-cheese sandwiches. There were two glasses of leftover lemonade from lunch.

She sat up as he placed the tray over her lap and her mouth watered at the smell of the buttery grilled bread and melted cheese.

"Oh, this is perfect."

"Glad you approve. It was all I could think of that would be done this quickly," Rafael said as he climbed onto the bed. He sat cross-legged in front of her and reached for one of the sandwiches.

They ate, stealing glances, their gazes meeting and then ducking away. She was mesmerized by this unguarded side of Rafael. If possible she was more in love now—after only a few days—than she'd been before. It seemed like he was freer with her now.

She left half of one of the sandwiches and drank the lemonade down then waited patiently for him to finish his own food.

When he would have gotten up to remove the tray, she leaned forward and wrapped her hands around his wrists, holding him motionless. Then she shoved the tray off the bed. It landed with a clatter, the saucers and glasses rolling this way and that.

She kissed him. Not a sweet, nice-girl kiss. She gave him the naughty version that said *I'm about to have my wicked way with you.*

"Oh, hell," he groaned.

"Oh, yes," she purred just before she gave him a shove.

He fell back, sprawled on the bed, his eyes glowing with fierce excitement as she threw one leg over his knees and straddled him.

She reached down and wrapped her fingers around his straining erection and smiled. "I think it's time for dessert."

"Oh, damn…"

She lowered her mouth and ran her tongue around the tip

of his penis. His breath hissed out, the sound explosive in the silence. His fingers tangled in her hair and he arched his hips.

"Bryony," he whispered.

She took him hard, loving and licking every inch of him. She wanted to give him as much pleasure as he'd given her. She wanted to show him her love—her heart.

She settled between his legs, her hair drifting down over his hips. His fingers gentled against her scalp and stroked lovingly as she continued making love to him.

He made low sounds of appreciation and of pleasure and he began thrusting upward, seeking more of her mouth. Finally it seemed to be too much for him to bear.

He grasped her shoulders and hauled her up his body until she straddled him.

She scooted up until his erection was against her belly and she carefully wrappped her fingers around his length. Instinctively she glanced back up, seeking direction. He held out his hands for her to grab and when she did, he pulled her toward him.

"Take me," he whispered. "I made you mine again. Now make me yours."

Oh, how seductive his husky words were. Prickles of anticipation licked over her skin like flames to dry wood. She rose up, using his hands to brace herself with. Their fingers slid together, twining, symbolic of their joining. She arched over him and he let one of her hands go long enough to position himself at her opening.

As soon as she began the delicious slide downward, he laced their fingers back again and she began the delicate mating dance of a woman reclaiming her man.

Before she'd never felt bold enough to take the initiative in their lovemaking. Rafael had always been the one to take control, had always seen to her pleasure before his own. And yet she preferred this man who wanted her so badly that he found his release before her, who was so lost in passion that he couldn't control his response. This man seemed more... real.

Now she delighted in teasing him, pleasuring him, taking control and driving him crazy with desire.

It was a heady, intoxicating feeling that only heightened as she watched him through half-lidded eyes.

He squeezed her hands and then took his away from hers. He caressed her hips then slid his palms up her sides to cup her breasts, toying and teasing her nipples as she undulated atop him.

His eyes glittering and his mouth tight, he lowered one hand, splayed it over her pelvis and dipped his thumb between their bodies to rub gently over her clitoris.

She flexed and spasmed around him and they both gasped. He stroked harder, finding a rhythm she responded to, and with his other hand, he caressed and plucked at her nipples, alternating until she was nearly mindless.

How quickly he'd turned the tables. Though she was on top, taking him in and out of her body at her leisure, his hands worked magic, finding all her sweet spots.

"Come for me, Bryony," he said. "I want to feel your heat around me as you come apart."

Her head fell back. Her entire body trembled. Her knees shook where they dug into the mattress. Beautiful, intense, vicious tension coiled low in her belly, spread to the spots he so expertly stroked and then it gathered and burst in all directions.

The force of her orgasm was staggering. She fell forward, but he was there to catch her. She braced her hands on his chest, not wanting to leave him, not wanting to stop until he found his own release, but she couldn't be still.

She writhed uncontrollably. All the while he held her and stroked his hands over her body as he whispered her name over and over in her ear.

She heard a sob, an exclamation of pleasure and knew it was herself, but it sounded so distant that it seemed impossible it could have come from her.

When her strength sagged from her, he simply held her hips and took over, thrusting upward into her still quivering body until he went tense underneath her.

Then he wrapped his arms around her, pulling her down until there was no space separating them. He thrust one last time and then they both went limp on the bed.

She was sprawled atop him. She probably resembled a dishrag, but she couldn't muster the energy to care.

He rubbed his hand up and down her back, down over her buttocks and then back up to tangle in her hair. He kissed her forehead and then ran his fingers through her hair again.

"That was incredible."

"Mmm-hmm," she agreed.

He stroked her arm in a lazy pattern. "What happened here, Bryony? It sure as hell wasn't just sex. I've had just sex before. This doesn't qualify."

"No," she said in a low voice. "It wasn't just sex."

"Then what was it?"

She raised her head and stared down into his eyes. "It was making love, Rafael. I love you. You loved me. I'd like to think that didn't just go away. Some things the heart knows even if the mind hasn't accepted it or has blocked it out."

"It scares the hell out of me that something this huge could be forgotten. I haven't loved anyone before."

"Never?"

He shook his head. "I'm sure I loved my parents in the beginning. I don't hate them now. I just don't think about them, the same way they don't think about me. I was an inconvenience. They were merely the people who gave me my DNA. It sounds cold, but it is what it is. I'm not saying that because I'm harboring some horrible psychological defect because my mommy doesn't love me. I'm merely saying that

I've never deeply loved anyone and now that I supposedly have, I forgot it? It and nothing else?"

"Maybe finally falling in love was so traumatic for you that you blocked it out," she teased.

"I can't believe you can joke about this," he grumbled.

"Well, it's either laugh or cry and crying gives me a headache. Besides, you'll remember. I think you're already starting to. A lot of things are instinctive to you. You don't treat me like a stranger even though for all practical purposes I am. If you really thought I was unknown to you would you be in my bed sharing your deep, dark secrets?"

"Probably not," he admitted.

She leaned down to kiss him and then rested her head on his shoulder again. "One day at a time, Rafe. It's all we can do and hope that each day brings us closer to the time you remember us."

He tightened his arm around her and kissed her forehead. "I'm not sure I deserve your sweetness or your patience, but I'm damn grateful for both."

Sixteen

When his BlackBerry rang first thing the next morning, Rafael knew by the ring tone who it was and he ignored it. Devon had called Cam in. Cam was calling to curse and yell at him that he was a moron who was thinking with his dick.

Cam was predictable if nothing else.

When his phone immediately began to ring again, Rafael cursed and leaned down as far as he could without loosening his hold on Bryony. He managed to drag his pants closer and fish the BlackBerry out. He hit the ignore button first and then hit the power button second.

His business could run without him for a couple of days. He paid many people very good money to think on their feet and be able to handle any situation that arose. It was time to give them the freedom to do what he'd hired them to do.

Oddly, in the past such an idea would make the control freak in him break out in hives. Now, he reasoned that he parted with good money so that he could occasionally enjoy a break.

Maybe Bryony was right. He didn't have to be the person he'd always been. Furthermore, she was right in that he would make sacrifices for his son or daughter.

He didn't want to be an absentee father. He didn't want to be like his own father, who thought being a provider was his only obligation to his family.

There was a hell of a lot more to parenthood than providing all the material necessities. Rafael wanted to be there for all the school plays, the soccer games. He wanted to be the one to put money under his kid's pillow when he lost a tooth and pretend that it was the tooth fairy.

He wanted to be a father. The best father he could be.

He gazed down at Bryony, whose head was pillowed on his shoulder. The morning sun shone on her skin, giving it a translucent, angelic glow. She looked at peace. She looked content. She looked…loved.

Then his mind kicked in with a screaming *whoa*.

No way was he falling for this woman after only a few days.

But had it been just a few days? Or was he responding to the weeks they'd spent together before?

It could be she was right. On some level he remembered her, recognized her as the woman he'd chosen. But the woman he'd fallen in love with?

He'd always considered that love was like being struck by lightning. This odd sort of contentment didn't match with what he considered falling in love might feel like. He damn sure hadn't thought it could be so…easy.

Easy. Yeah. Love was complicated, wasn't it? No one managed to pull it off in a few days. It was the good sex talking.

But, no. Bryony had been right about one thing. It wasn't just sex. Calling it that cheapened it on some level. Reduced it to the level of flirtatious, sex-only relationships he'd had in the past. A quick romp in bed, send the woman on her way. Move on to the next.

Nothing about his past experiences came even close to the way he felt about Bryony or the way he felt about making love to her.

Last night had felt like something he'd been anticipating forever. A sense of homecoming that was so keen, it had nearly flattened him. He'd been ridiculously emotional, like he wanted to go around blurting out how he felt and crap. The mere idea should have humiliated the hell out of him, but it didn't.

Being forthright with Bryony just felt natural. She'd played it completely straight with him. He'd played it straight with her even when it had meant admitting or saying something that had hurt her.

It was weird being this honest and open with a woman—hell, with anyone. He trusted Ryan, Dev and Cam, but he never talked about intensely personal issues with them. Not that they wouldn't listen, but that wasn't the nature of their relationship.

His thoughts flickered back to the woman in his arms. Yeah, she did odd things to him. Made him want to do stuff, different stuff. Stuff that should have him running the other direction.

He sighed. This was a woman a man kept. Maybe he'd known that when he met her. Maybe it was true that a man just knew when he'd met the woman who would change everything for him.

Bryony was the marrying kind. Not the bed-'em-and-leave-'em-with-a-smile kind of woman. She had permanent written all over her sweet face.

She was…his. And hell if he was going to let her go. He didn't care if he ever remembered. He had enough pieces of the puzzle to know that she belonged with him. They had a lot to work out—what new couple didn't? They'd jumped ahead a few steps in the relationship with her being pregnant, but it wasn't anything they couldn't work out.

The more he settled the matter in his mind, the more convinced he became that this was right. She was right. Bryony. Their baby. Him. A family. He could have it all.

The resort.

He grimaced. It hung over him like a dark cloud. It was the one thing standing between him and Bryony. She swore he had promised her he wouldn't develop the land, which made absolutely no sense. Why buy it at all? He certainly didn't have need of a private expanse of beach for personal use.

A hell of a lot rode on this deal.

There had to be some way to convince her and the rest of the people on the island that one resort wouldn't change their way of life.

It was either that or he had to go back to his partners—and friends—and investors and pull the plug on the entire thing. He would lose a hell of a lot of money, but worse than that, he'd lose credibility, future backing and his standing in the business community.

All because of a promise he couldn't remember making.

Bryony stirred in his arms and his grip tightened possessively around her. Before she could open her eyes, he pulled her close and kissed her lingeringly.

She sighed as her eyelashes fluttered, then her warm brown eyes found his and she smiled. "That's a nice way to wake up."

"I was thinking the same thing," he murmured.

"What time is it?"

"Seven."

She yawned and snuggled closer to him. "Plenty of time."

"Plenty of time for what?"

"To do whatever we want or nothing at all."

He chuckled. "I like your attitude."

"Any idea what you'd like to do today?"

"Yeah, actually. I thought you could take me around the island. Private tour. Show me what makes it so special to everyone who lives here. I can't remember the last time I went to a beach just to see and enjoy the sights and sounds."

She leaned her head back and frowned. "You work entirely too hard. Maybe your accident was a blessing in disguise. If it causes you to slow down and reevaluate then it's a good thing."

"I wouldn't have put it that way exactly. I'm not sure nearly dying is the kind of wake-up call anyone wants," he said dryly.

She touched his cheek. "But would you be thinking the way you're thinking now if it hadn't happened?"

He sighed. "Maybe not. Maybe you're the reason for my reevaluation. Ever think of that?"

She smiled and leaned up to kiss him. "I'll take that explanation. I prefer it over thinking about you dying anyway."

"You and me both," he muttered.

"Tell you what. You hit the shower. I'll cook breakfast. Then I'll take my bath and we'll head out. The weather is supposed to be gorgeous all week. We can pack a picnic and eat out on the beach."

"I've got a better idea. How about we shower together then I'll help you cook breakfast. I cook a mean piece of bacon."

She laughed and he sucked in his breath at the love shining in her eyes as she stared up at him. No one had ever looked at him like that.

Then her expression grew serious as she stroked her palm over his unshaven jaw. "I love you, Rafe. I don't want to make you uncomfortable. I don't expect anything in return. But now that I've told you I can't not keep saying it. I look at you and it just bursts out."

He captured her hand and pulled it to his mouth, his heart thudding against the wall of his chest. "I like you saying it," he said hoarsely. "It means… It means everything to me right now."

She pulled away, joy lighting her eyes. Eyes he could drown in. Her eyes were so expressive. They reflected her mood so perfectly. Sad, angry, happy. You only had to look into her eyes to know exactly what she was thinking.

She crawled over him, giving him a good view and feel of her soft curves. It was all he could do not to haul her back and make love to her all over again.

When her feet hit the floor, she turned back and held out her hand. “How about that shower?”

He stared at her profile for a long moment, committing to memory just how she looked bathed in morning sunlight, her gently rounded abdomen, the swell of her breasts and the wild curls that spilled down her back.

This was his. His woman. His child.

“Do you have any idea how beautiful you are?”

She flushed, her face grew pink, but her eyes lit up until they were as bright as the sunlight pouring into her room.

“I do now.”

He grinned at her cheeky response. “Let’s go hit the shower.”

Seventeen

"You've done a good thing, Mr. de Luca," Silas Taylor said as they stood on the patio of Laura's house.

Bryony's grandmother had invited everyone over for tea and lemonade and for some of her famous peanut butter cookies. And by everyone, she meant whomever happened to wander by.

Such a thing baffled Rafael, who was used to strict guest lists and checking invitations at the door. Laura didn't seem to mind. In fact, the more guests that meandered through, the more delighted she seemed to be.

There was no entertainment. Conversation drifted from one mundane topic to the next or people just stood around, enjoying the day and inquiring as to the health of yet another islander who was either family, friend or both.

"My investors probably wouldn't agree," Rafael said dryly as he turned his attention back to the sheriff.

Silas shrugged. "They'll find something else to invest in. Those kind always do. People are always looking for places to put their money and there are always people willing to take it. Seems to me it wouldn't be that hard to figure it out."

Rafael wanted to laugh. Or shake his head. Months of financial analysis, blueprints being drawn up, investors courted, endless planning on his and Ryan, Devon and Cam's parts all reduced to a few words so casually tossed out.

"That may be so, but I lose credibility and respect in the process," Rafael said evenly. "Next time I want their backing, they won't be so willing to give it."

"And what will you gain?" Silas asked as he looked in Bryony's direction. Bryony, who stood in a small group of people looking so damn beautiful that it made Rafael's teeth ache. "Seems to me you gain far more than you lose." With that, Silas slapped him on the shoulder.

"Something to think about, my boy."

Then he walked away, leaving Rafael to shake his head again. Boy. He wanted to laugh. Granted the sheriff was at least thirty years older than Rafael, but no one had called him a boy since he'd been a boy.

Time was running out. His BlackBerry was full of voice-mail notifications and missed calls, and his inbox was bursting. His week would soon be up, and Dev would come down with Ryan and Cam to kick Rafael's ass.

For the past several days, Rafael had willfully ignored everything but Bryony and their time together. They'd spent every waking moment walking the beach, cooking together, laughing together, talking of nothing and everything.

They made love, they ate, they made love some more. There was an urgency he couldn't explain, almost as if he wanted to cram a lifetime into as few days as possible because he feared it would all slip away from him.

Tomorrow decisions had to be made. He couldn't hold them off any longer. He still had no idea what he would do, but he couldn't—wouldn't—lose Bryony over a resort. Over money.

"Can I get you something, Rafael?"

Rafael turned to see Bryony's grandmother smiling at him. He smiled back and shook his head. "No, I'm okay. Don't let me keep you from your guests."

"Oh, they're fine. Besides, you're a guest, too. How are you liking your stay so far?"

Again Rafael's gaze found Bryony. This time she lifted her head as if sensing that he watched her and her face lit up with a gorgeous smile.

"I'm enjoying it very much. I'm only sorry I can't remember when I was here before."

Laura stared thoughtfully at him for a long moment and then put her hand on his shoulder. "Maybe it's better that you don't."

She patted him and after offering those cryptic words, she turned to talk to another group of people.

Rafael shoved his hands in his pockets and turned to stare out over the water. He hadn't ever been someone who practiced avoidance, but he knew that was precisely what he was doing. Here, it was as if he existed in a bubble. Nothing could intrude or interfere, but the outside world was still there, just waiting. The longer he put off the inevitable, the more he dreaded it.

"Rafael, is something wrong?"

Bryony's soft voice slid over him at the same time her hand slipped through his arm and she hugged herself up to his side.

He disentangled his arm from her grasp just long enough to wrap it around her waist and then pulled her in close again.

"No, just thinking."

"About?"

"What has to be done."

Instead of pressing him for answers as he thought she might, she said, "Why don't we take off, go for a long walk?

Mamaw won't mind. She's having fun being the center of attention. She won't even notice we've gone."

Unable to resist, he leaned down to kiss her brow. She was so in tune with his moods. It shouldn't have surprised him that she could read him so easily. He'd found that he could pick up on the nuances of her moods just as quickly. He anticipated her reactions much like she did his own.

It was something he imagined a couple doing after years of marriage.

When he drew away, she took his hand and tugged him toward the stone path leading through the garden and down the dune onto the sand.

Sand slid over his toes but he found he didn't mind as much as he had when he first started wearing these ridiculous flip-flops.

They ventured closer to the water that foamed over the sand. Soon the cool waves washed over their feet, and Bryony smiled her delight as they danced back to avoid a larger one from getting them too wet.

Soon Laura's and Bryony's cottages were distant points behind them as they approached the land that he'd purchased from her.

"My father used to bring me here," she said. "He used to tell me that there was nothing greater than owning a piece of heaven. I feel like I've let him down by selling it."

Rafael grimaced feeling even guiltier over his part in the whole thing. It didn't matter that if it hadn't been him it would have been someone else. She could no longer afford the taxes and if someone hadn't bought it, eventually the land would have been seized for taxes owed. Either way it would no longer belong to her.

But you have the power to give it back to her.

The thought crept through his mind, whispering to him. It was true. He owned the land. Not his company. Not his partners. He'd purchased the land outright. The building of the resort and development of the land was what he'd brought investors in for.

"I love you," she said as she squeezed his hand.

He looked curiously at her, startled by her sudden affection.

She smiled. "You just looked like you needed that today."

He stopped and pulled her into his arms, brushing a thick strand of her hair from her eyes as the wind blew off the water. "I did need that. I shouldn't be surprised that you always know just what to say." He took in a deep breath. "I love you, too, Bryony."

Her eyes went wide with shock and then filled with tears. Her body trembled against him. "You remember?" she whispered.

He shook his head. "No, but it doesn't matter. You said I loved you then. I know I love you now. Isn't now all that matters?"

Wordlessly she nodded.

"The whole story doesn't seem so crazy anymore," he admitted. "I couldn't accept that I fell in love with you in a matter of weeks and yet here I am in love with you after only a few days."

"Are you sure?"

He smiled but his heart clenched at the hope and fear in her eyes. She seemed so worried that he'd change his mind or that he wasn't really sure of himself or his feelings.

He tipped her chin up and leaned down to brush a kiss across her lips. "I've handled this whole thing so clumsily. I don't have any experience with telling a woman I love her. I imagine there were more romantic ways of doing it but I simply couldn't *not* say it any longer."

"Oh, Rafe," she said, her eyes bright with love and joy. "You've made me so happy today. I've been so afraid and unsure. I hate being uncertain more than anything else. The not knowing just eats at you until you're a nervous wreck."

"I'm sorry. I don't want you to worry. I love you."

She wrapped her arms around his neck and hugged him to her. "I love you, too."

He slowly pulled her arms away until he held her in front of him. She looked a little worried at the sudden seriousness of his expression and he tried to soften his features to reassure her. But he couldn't really offer her any reassurance. Not yet.

"I need to leave tomorrow," he said grimly.

Her expression went blank and her mouth opened but nothing came out. "Wh-why?" she finally stammered out.

"I need to go back and work things out with my partners and our investors. I've avoided it for as long as I can. I can't do so any longer. I wanted you to know how I felt before I leave. I don't want you to have any doubts that I'll come back this time."

Uncertainty flickered across her face and her eyes went dim. He could tell she didn't entirely trust him and he couldn't blame her. Not after what had happened last time.

"You could come with me," he said. He was grasping at straws, anything to allay her fears. "We wouldn't have to be gone long. A few days at most. I know you don't like to be away from…here."

She reached for him, her hands clutching at his arms as she looked up at him, her eyes so earnest. "I don't like to be away from *you,* Rafe. You. Not here. Or there. Or anywhere."

"Then come with me. I won't lie to you, Bryony. I don't know if I can fix this. All I can do is promise to try."

She let her hands slide down to grip his, so tight that her knuckles went white. "I believe in you."

He crushed her to him and buried his face in her hair. She made him want to be the man she was so convinced he already was.

"You'll come with me?"

"Yes, Rafe. I'll come with you."

She pulled away and he laced their fingers together, holding their hands between them.

"No matter what happens, Bryony, I love you and I want this to work out between us. I need for you to trust in that."

"I do trust you. You'll fix this, Rafe. I know you will."

He smiled then, feeling some of the anxiety lift away. He could breathe easier. The idea of expressing his feelings had given him a sense of uneasiness, but now that he'd done it, he realized it had been harder not to tell her what was in his heart even if his head still screamed that this was all wrong.

He'd spent a lifetime of listening to his head and being ultra-practical. Maybe it was time he threw a little caution to the wind and let his heart lead for once.

Eighteen

Bryony's phone rang in the middle of the night. She pried herself from Rafael's arms and reached blindly for the phone on her bedside table.

"Hello?"

"Bry, it's Silas. You need to come to the hospital. It's your grandmother."

Bryony scrambled up, shaking the fuzz of sleep from her eyes. "Mamaw? What happened?"

"She had one of her spells. Blood sugar dropped. She called me and I couldn't understand a word she was saying so I rushed over and took her to the hospital."

Dear Lord, and she and Rafael had slept through it all.

"Why didn't someone come over and tell me?" she demanded.

"There wasn't a need to alarm you if it turned out to be nothing. I still think it's nothing but the nurse insisted I contact you so you could come down and sign some paperwork. They just want the insurance stuff squared away. You know these damn hospitals. Always wanting their money," Silas grumbled.

"Of course, I'll be right there."

Bryony hung up to see Rafael sitting up in bed, a look of concern on his face.

"Is Laura all right?"

Bryony grimaced. "I don't know. She's a diabetic and she doesn't always take care of herself. Sometimes she doesn't always take her insulin and at other times she doesn't eat when she should. I never know if she's in insulin shock or on the verge of diabetic coma."

"I'll go with you," he said as he hurried from the bed.

Twenty minutes later, they strode into the small community hospital. Silas met them in the main hallway.

"How is she?" Bryony asked anxiously.

"Oh, you know your grandmother. She's as mad as a wet hen at having to stay overnight. She didn't even want to go to the hospital. I made her drink some orange juice at the house and she came right around but I thought she ought to be checked out anyway. She's not speaking to me as a result."

Bryony sighed. "Where is she now?"

"They moved her out of the emergency room to observation. They won't release her until they know for sure they have someone to watch over her for the next twenty-four hours."

"Take us to her," Bryony said.

As Silas predicted, Mamaw was in a fit of temper and ready to go home. The doctor was attempting to lecture her on the importance of not missing a meal and Mamaw's lips were stretched tight in irritation.

She brightened considerably when Bryony and Rafael walked through the door but glowered in Silas's direction.

Bryony went to the bed and kissed her grandmother's cheek. "Mamaw, you scared me."

Mamaw rolled her eyes. "I'm fine. Any fool can see that. I'm ready to go home. Now that you're here, they should let me go. They seem to think I need a babysitter for the next little while."

"Glad to see you're all right, Laura," Rafael said as he bent to kiss her cheek.

Mamaw smiled and patted Rafael's cheek. "Thank you, young man. Sorry to drag you and my granddaughter out of bed at this hour. Pregnant women need their rest, but no one but me seems to be concerned with that little tidbit."

"Is she okay to go home, Doctor?" Bryony asked, directing her attention to the physician standing to the side.

The doctor nodded. "She knows what she did wrong. I doubt it'll do any good to tell her not to do it again, but she's fine otherwise. You'll need to keep an eye on her for the next twenty-four hours and check her blood sugar every hour. Make sure she eats properly and takes her insulin as directed."

"Don't worry. I will," Bryony said firmly. "Can we take her home now or does she need to stay?"

"No, as long as she goes home with someone, she's free to leave as soon as we get her discharged. That'll take a few minutes so make yourself comfortable."

Mamaw shooed the doctor away with a scowl and then stared pointedly at Silas, who still stood by the door. With a sigh, Silas nodded in Bryony's direction and walked out.

Bryony shook her head in exasperation. "When are you going to stop being such a twit to him, Mamaw? He's crazy about you and you know darn well you're just as crazy about him."

"Maybe when he stops treating me like I'm incapable of taking care of myself," she grumbled.

Bryony threw up her hands. "Maybe he'll stop when you prove that you can. You know better than to skip meals, especially after taking your insulin."

Rafael picked up Mamaw's hand and gave her a smooth smile. "You cannot fault a man for wanting to ensure the safety of the woman he loves. It's a worry we never get over. We always want to protect her and see to her well-being."

Mamaw looked a little gob-smacked. "Yes, well, I suppose…" She cleared her throat and glanced at Bryony again. "I thought you two were leaving in the morning."

"Rafael will have to go without me," Bryony said brightly. "You come first, Mamaw. I'm not leaving you alone after promising the doctor I'd look after you."

Rafael slid his hand over Bryony's shoulder. "Of course, you should stay. Hopefully my business in the city won't take long and I'll be back to see my two favorite women again."

"You have a smooth tongue, young man," Mamaw said sharply. Then she smiled. "I like it. I like it a damn lot. If Silas were that smooth, I'd probably have already said yes to his marriage proposal."

Bryony's mouth popped open. "Mamaw! You never told me Silas has asked you to marry him. Why haven't you said yes?"

Mamaw smiled. "Because, child, at my age I'm entitled to a few privileges. Making my man stew a little is one of them. If I said yes too quickly he'd take for granted my affection for him. A man should never take his woman for granted. I aim to make sure he always knows how lucky he is to have me."

Rafael broke into laughter. "You are a very wise woman, Laura. But do me a favor. Let Silas off the hook soon. The poor guy is probably miserable."

"Oh, I will," Mamaw said airily. "At my age I can't afford to wait too long."

Bryony squeezed her grandmother's hand. "I'll stay over with you at your house. I know you don't like to be away from your home for very long."

Mamaw's expression became troubled. "I don't want to interfere in your plans. You two have had enough problems without me adding to them."

Rafael put a finger to his lips to shush her. "You're no burden, Laura. I'll be back before either of you know it and then Bryony and I can plan our future together."

Bryony's heart pounded a little harder. It was the first time he'd spoken of their future—as in a life—together. He'd told her he loved her. She believed him. But she'd been greatly unsure of where that put them. There were still a lot of obstacles to overcome.

The fact that he seemed committed to them being together long-term sent relief through her veins.

Just then a nurse walked in with discharge papers and began the task of taking Mamaw's IV out and discussing the doctor's orders with her.

A half an hour later, they had Mamaw bundled into the car and were on their way back to her cottage.

Once Bryony got her grandmother into bed, she walked back into the living room where Rafael waited. She went into his arms and savored the hug he gave her.

"Crazy night, huh?" he said.

She drew away. "Yeah. Sorry I won't be able to go with you. I don't think I should leave Mamaw even if she says she's fine."

"No, of course you shouldn't," he agreed. "I'll call you from New York and let you know how things are going. Hopefully I can be back in a few days. I have motivation to get this done."

She arched a brow. "Oh?"

He smiled. "Yeah, a certain pregnant lady will be waiting for me to return. I'd say that's pretty powerful incentive to get everything wrapped up so I can get my butt back on a plane."

"Yeah, well, Rafael? This time don't get into an accident. I'd really like not to have to wait months to see you again."

He tweaked her nose. "Smart-ass. If it's all the same, I have no desire to ever crash again. Once was enough. I know how lucky I am to be alive. I plan to stay that way for a long time to come."

She leaned into him and wrapped her arms around him. "Good. Because I have plans for you that are going to take a very, very long time to fulfill."

He gave her a questioning look. "Just how long are we talking about?"

"As long as you can keep up with me," she murmured.

"In that case, it's going to be a very long time indeed."

She kissed him and then reluctantly pulled away. "You should probably go back home so you can shower and get packed. It'll be light soon and you'll need to be down to catch the ferry. Rush-hour traffic going into Houston is a bitch and you're going to be hitting it at a bad time."

"You sure you're okay with me driving your car?"

She laughed. "The question should be whether it's going to hurt your pride to drive my MINI. I could always have Silas drive you to Galveston and you could get a car service to the airport."

He shook his head. "Your car is fine. Right now my only concern is that it gets me there so I can hurry up and return to you."

She rested her forehead on his chest. "I'll miss you, Rafe. I won't lie, the idea of you leaving panics me because I keep thinking of the last time I said goodbye to you thinking I'd see you again in a few days."

He cupped her face and tilted her head back so she looked up at him. "I'm coming back, Bryony. A plane crash and the loss of my memory didn't keep us apart last time."

"I love you."

He kissed her. "I love you, too. Now go get some rest. I'll call you when I land in New York."

Nineteen

"It's about damn time you got your ass up here," Cam said grimly as he got out of his car in passenger pickup at LaGuardia and strode around to help Rafael with his bags. "Devon's been in a snit ever since you left. Your delaying the groundbreaking just pissed him off even more. Copeland has got him over a barrel with this whole marrying-his-daughter thing. Ryan has been stewing over private investigator reports. I swear no one's head is where it should be right now. Except mine. It's obvious that any time a woman's involved disaster follows," he said sourly.

"Cam?" Rafe said mildly as he opened the door to the passenger side.

Cam yanked his gaze up and stopped before climbing into the driver's seat. "What?"

"Shut the hell up."

Cam got into the car grumbling about flaky friends and vowing all the while never to mix business and friendship again. Rafael rolled his eyes at his friend's consternation, considering that the four had always done business together.

"So what the hell is going on, Rafael? Dev says you've gotten cold feet."

"I don't have cold feet," Rafael growled. "I just think there has to be another way of making this deal go through that doesn't involve using the property on Moon Island."

Cam swore again. He went silent as traffic got snarled and he expertly weaved in and out, making Rafael white-knuckle his grip on the door handle.

Anyone riding with Cam deserved hazard pay. Not that he drove often. Cam almost always had a driver and it wasn't because he was too good to drive himself. Quite simply he was so busy that he utilized every moment of his time to conduct his business affairs and if he had a driver, he had that much more time to work.

Rafael figured Dev must have leaned on him pretty hard to get him to drive himself to the airport to pick up Rafael.

"So you still don't remember anything?" Cam asked when they'd cleared one particularly nasty snarl.

"No. Nothing."

"And yet you believe her? Have you even started the process for paternity testing yet?"

"It doesn't matter what happened before. I love her now," Rafael said quietly.

There was dead silence in the car. Only the sounds of traffic and car horns penetrated the thick silence inside the car.

"And the resort deal?" Cam finally asked.

"There has to be something we can work out. It's why I'm here. We have to fix this, Cam. My future depends on it."

"How nice of you to be so concerned about your future," Cam muttered. "Nothing about the rest of ours, though."

"Low blow, man," Rafael bit out. "If I didn't give a damn about you and Ryan and Dev, I wouldn't be here. I would have just called off the whole damn thing and told all the investors to go to hell."

Cam shook his head. "And you wonder why I've sworn off women."

"Planning to play for the other team?" Rafael asked for a grin.

Cam shot him the bird and glowered. "You know damn well what I mean. Women are good for sex. Anything more and a man might as well neuter himself and be done with it."

Rafael chuckled. "You know I look forward to the day that I get to shove those words down your throat. Even better, I can't wait to meet the woman who does it for you."

"Look, I just don't understand what's changed. Four months ago you were on top of the world. You got what you wanted. And now suddenly it's not what you want."

They pulled to a stop in front of Rafael's apartment building. Rafael turned to Cam. "Maybe what I want has changed. And how the hell would you know that I got what I wanted four months ago? I didn't see you until I woke up in a hospital bed after the plane crash."

Cam shook his head. "You called me the day before you left. You were all but crowing. Said you'd closed the land deal that day and that next you were going to be on a plane back to New York. I asked if you'd had a good vacation since you'd been gone for four damn weeks. You told me that some things were worth the sacrifice."

Rafe went still. Suddenly it was hard to get air into his lungs. His chest squeezed painfully as pain thudded relentlessly in his head.

"Rafael? You okay, man?"

Still images flashed through his head like photos. The pieces of his lost memory shot out of a cannon. Random. Out of order. It all hurled at him at supersonic speed until he was dizzy and disoriented.

"Rafe, talk to me," Cam insisted.

Rafael managed to open the car door and stumble out onto the curb. He put a hand back toward Cam when his friend would have gotten out, too.

"I'm fine. Leave me. I'll call you later."

He hauled his luggage out of the trunk and then walked mechanically toward the entrance. His doorman swung open the glass doors and offered a cheerful greeting.

Like a zombie, Rafael got into the elevator, clumsily inserted his card and nearly fell when the elevator began its ascent.

Memories of the first time he saw Bryony. Making love—no, having sex with her. The day at the closing agent's office when Bryony had signed over her land and he'd given her the check. Of the day he'd told her goodbye.

It all came back so fast his head spun trying to catch up.

He was going to be sick.

The elevator doors opened and it took him a full minute to force himself inside his apartment. Leaving his luggage inside the doorway, he staggered toward one of the couches in the living room, so sick, so devastated that he wanted to die.

He slumped onto the sofa and lowered his head to his hands.

Oh, God, Bryony would never forgive him for this.

He couldn't forgive himself.

"Mamaw, would it really be so terrible if they built a resort here?" Bryony asked quietly as the two women sat on Mamaw's deck.

Mamaw glanced over at Bryony, her eyes soft with love. "You're taking on too much, Bryony. You have to decide what's best for you. It's not your responsibility to make the entire island happy. If this resort is coming between you and Rafael, you have to decide what is the most important to you. Is it making everyone here happy? Or is it being happy yourself?"

Bryony frowned. "Am I being unreasonable to hold him to a promise he made? It seemed so simple then, but apparently he has business partners—close friends of his—and investors counting on him. This is how he makes his living. And I'm asking him to give all that up because we're all afraid that our lives will change."

Mamaw nodded. "Well, that's something only you can answer. We've been lucky for a lot of years. We've been overlooked. Galveston gets all the tourists. We stay over here and no one ever comes calling. But we can't expect that to last forever. If Rafael doesn't build his resort, someone else will eventually. We'd probably be better off if Rafael builds it because he at least has met the people here and he knows where they're coming from. If some outsider comes in, he won't give a damn about you or me or anyone else here."

"I don't want everyone to hate me," Bryony said miserably.

"Everyone won't hate you," Mamaw said gently. "Rafael loves you. I love you. Who else do you want to love you?"

Suddenly she felt incredibly foolish. She closed her eyes and slapped her head to her forehead. "You know what? You're right, Mamaw. It's my land. Or it was. Only I should have the right to decide who I sell it to and what they do with it. If the other people here wanted things to remain the way it was so badly then they could have banded together to buy the land. It was okay when they didn't have to foot the tax bill. They were more than happy to tell me what I could or couldn't do with my own land."

Mamaw chuckled. "That's the spirit. Get angry. Tell them to piss off."

"Mamaw!"

Her grandmother laughed again at Bryony's horrified expression.

"You've tied yourself in knots for too long, honey. First

you were upset that he left. Then you were convinced he left you for good. Then you found out you were pregnant and you grieved for him all over again. Then he came back and you were happy. Don't give it up this time. This time you can do something about it."

Bryony leaned forward and hugged her grandmother. "I love you so much."

"I love you, too, my baby."

"Don't think I'm not going to turn these words back on you about Silas."

Her grandmother laughed and pulled away. "You leave Silas to me. He knows I'll come around sooner or later and he seems content to wait until I decide to quit making him miserable. I'm old. Don't begrudge me my fun."

"I don't want to be away from you. I want you to see your great-grandchild when he's born."

Mamaw sighed in exasperation. "You act like we'd never see each other anymore. Your Rafael is as rich as a man can get. If he can't afford to fly you to see me, then what good is he? You should ask for a jet as a wedding present. Then you can go where you want and when you want."

Bryony shook her head. "You're such a mess. But you're right. I'm just being difficult because I hate change."

Mamaw squeezed her hand. "Change is good for all of us. Never think it isn't. It's what keeps us young and vibrant. Change is exciting. It keeps life from getting stale and predictable."

"I suppose I should call Rafael and tell him to go ahead with the resort. It'll be such a load off him I'm sure."

"Better yet, why don't you get on a plane and go see him," Mamaw said gently. "Some things are better said in person."

"I can't leave you. I promised the doctor—"

"Oh, for heaven's sake. I'll be fine. I'll call Silas over to drive you to the airport. If it makes you feel any better, I'll have Gladys come over and stay with me until Silas comes back."

"Promise?"

"I promise," Mamaw said in exasperation. "Now get on the internet and figure out when the first available flight is to New York."

Twenty

Bryony got into the cab and read off the address to the driver. She was nervous. More nervous than she'd ever been in her life. How ridiculous was it that she had to get Rafael's address from the papers from the sale of the land. She hadn't known. It hadn't been covered in ordinary conversation.

She was truly flying solo because Rafael hadn't answered his cell phone or his apartment phone. A dreaded sense of déjà vu had taken hold but she forced herself not to descend into paranoia. He had every reason the first time not to answer her calls given that he was in the hospital recovering from serious injuries.

Still, old feelings of helplessness and abandonment were hard to get rid of and the more times she tried to call with no response, the more anxious she became.

The ride was long and streetlights blinked on in the deepening of dusk. The city took on a whole different look at night. It seemed so ordinary and horribly busy during the day. People everywhere. Cars everywhere. Not that there wasn't an abundance of both at night, but the twinkling lights on every building lit up the sky and gave the skyline a beautiful look.

When the cab pulled up in front of Rafael's building she got out, paid the fare and then stood staring at the entrance. She shivered. Of course she'd forgotten a coat. It still hadn't been ingrained in her that while it was warm where she lived, it was cold in other places. And she'd been in such a hurry to get to Rafael, she hadn't bothered with more than an overnight bag and a few necessities.

She started toward the door when a man brushed by her. She frowned. He looked familiar. Ryan? One of Rafael's friends. Ryan Beardsley. Maybe he could at least get her inside since Rafe wasn't answering his phone.

"Mr. Beardsley," she called as she hurried to catch him before he disappeared inside.

Ryan stopped and turned, a frown on his face. When he saw her, the frown disappeared but neither did he smile.

"I don't know if you remember me," she began.

"Of course I remember you," he said shortly. "What are you doing here? And for God's sake, why aren't you wearing a coat?"

"It was warm when I left Texas," she said ruefully. "I came to see Rafael. It's important. He hasn't been answering his phone. I need to see him. It's about the resort. I wanted to tell him it was okay. I don't care anymore. Maybe I never should have. But I don't want him to mess things up for you or his investors or his other friends."

Ryan looked at her like she was nuts. "You came here to tell him all that?"

She nodded. "Do you know if he's home? Have you heard from him? I know he's busy. Probably more so now than ever, but if I could just see him for a minute."

"I'll do you one better," Ryan muttered. "Come on. I'll

take you up to his apartment. Devon should already be here. We haven't heard from him since he arrived."

Bryony's eyes widened in alarm.

"Now don't go looking like that," Ryan soothed. "Cam dropped him off and he was fine. He's probably just busy trying to dig himself out of this mess he's gotten himself into."

He took Bryony's arm and tugged her toward the door.

"What the hell have you done to yourself?" Devon asked in disgust.

Rafael opened one eye and squinted, then made a shooing gesture with his hand. "Get the hell out of my apartment."

"You're shit-faced."

"I always said you were the smart one in this partnership."

"Mind telling me what prompted you to tie one on when you should be salvaging a business deal you seem determined to flush down the toilet?"

"I don't give a damn about the resort. Or you. Or anyone else. Get lost."

Rafael closed his eye again and reached for the bottle he'd left on the floor by the couch. Damn thing was empty. His mouth felt like he'd ingested a bag of cotton balls and his head ached like a son of a bitch.

Suddenly he was jerked off the couch, hauled across the floor and slammed into one of the armchairs. He opened his eyes again to see Devon's snarling face just inches from his own.

"You're going to tell me what the hell is going on here," Devon demanded. "Cam said everything was fine when he picked you up. Then suddenly you go radio silent and I come up here to check on your ass and you're so liquored up you can't see straight."

Pain splintered Rafael's chest, and worse, shame crowded

in from every direction. He'd never been so ashamed in his life.

"I'm a bastard," he said hoarsely.

Devon snorted. "Yeah, well, what else is new? It never bothered you before."

Rafael lunged to his feet, gathered Devon's shirt in his fists and got into Devon's face. "Maybe it bothers me *now.* Damn it, Devon, I remember everything, okay? Every single detail and it makes me so sick I can't even think about it."

Devon's eyes narrowed but he made no move to remove Rafael's hands from his shirt. "What the hell are you talking about? What do you remember that's so bad?"

"I used her," Rafael said quietly. "I went down there with the sole intention of doing whatever it took to get the land. And I did. God, I did. I seduced her. I told her I loved her. I promised her whatever she wanted to hear. All so I could make this deal happen. And it was all a lie. I left there with the intention of never going back. I had what I wanted. The sale was closed. The paperwork was filed. I had won."

A wounded cry from the doorway made Rafael jerk his head around. He went numb from head to toe when he saw Bryony standing there, white as a sheet, Ryan right beside her, supporting her with an arm when she'd stumbled back.

It was a nightmare. His worst nightmare come to life. What was she doing here? Why now?

He let go of Devon's shirt and started toward her. "Bryony." Her name spilled from his lips, a tortured sound that reflected all the shame and guilt that crowded his soul.

She took a hasty step back, shaking off Ryan's arm. She was so pale that he worried she'd fall right over.

"Bryony, please, just listen to me."

She shook her head, tears filling her beautiful eyes. It was a sight that staggered him.

"Please, just leave me alone," she begged softly. "Don't

say anything else. There isn't a need. I heard it all. Leave me with some of my pride at least."

She turned and fled into the elevator, the sound of her quiet sobs echoing through his apartment.

Rafael stood, feeling dead on the inside as he watched the elevator close. "Go after her," he croaked out to Ryan. "Please, for me. Make sure she's okay. She doesn't know anyone here in the city. I don't want anything to happen to her."

With a curse, Ryan turned and jammed his finger over the call button. Behind Rafael, Devon got on the phone and called down to the doorman with muttered instructions to stall Bryony until Ryan arrived.

"Why aren't you going after her yourself?" Devon asked after Ryan got into the returning elevator.

Rafael dropped back into the armchair and cupped his head between both hands. "What am I supposed to say to her? I lied to her. I played her. I used her. Everything she feared I had done, I absolutely did."

Devon sat on the edge of the couch and eyed his friend. "And now?"

"I love her. And knowing what I did to her, what I felt while I was doing it, sickens me. I'm so ashamed of the person I was that I can't even think about it without wanting to puke."

"No one says you have to be that person now," Devon said quietly.

Rafael closed his eyes and shook his head. "Do you know she's been telling me that all along? She kept saying that I didn't have to be the person I always was and that just because something has always been didn't mean it always had to be."

"Sounds like a smart woman."

"Oh, God, Devon, I messed this up. How could I have done what I did? How could I have done something like that to her? She's the most beautiful, loving and generous woman I've ever met. She's everything I've ever wanted. Her and our child. I want us to be a family. But how can she ever forgive me for this? How can I ever forgive myself?"

"I don't have the answers," Devon admitted. "But you won't find them here. You're going to have to fight for her if you love her and want her. If you give up, that just tells her that you are the man you used to be and that you haven't changed."

Rafael raised his head, his chest so heavy that it was a physical ache. "I can't let her go. I have no idea how I'm going to make her understand, but I can't let her go. No matter what I did then, no matter how big of a bastard I was then, that's not who I am now. I love her. I want another chance. God, if she'll just give me another chance, I'll never give her reason to doubt me again."

"You're convincing the wrong person," Devon said. "I'm on your side, man. Even if you are the biggest jackass in North America. And hey, whatever happens with this resort deal, I'm behind you one-hundred percent, okay? We'll figure something out. Now go get your girl."

Twenty-One

Bryony walked off the elevator in shock. Her limbs were numb. Her hands were like ice. She was on autopilot, her mind barely functioning.

Rafael's harsh words played over and over in her mind.

I used her.

I seduced her.

She flinched and wobbled toward the door, where the doorman stepped in front of her and put a hand on her arm. "Miss Morgan, if you would wait here, please."

She looked up at the man in confusion. "Why?"

"Just wait, please."

She shook her head and started to walk out the door only to have him take her arm and steer her back into the lobby again.

Anger was slowly replacing her numb shock. She yanked her arm away from the older man and retreated. "Don't touch me." She backed right into another person; she turned to excuse herself but found herself looking up at the mountain who worked as Rafael's head of security.

"Miss Morgan, I had no idea you were in the city." He frowned. "You should have let Mr. de Luca know so I could have met you at the airport. Did you come with no escort?"

The doorman looked relieved that Ramon was there and he hastily resumed his position by the door, leaving her to stand by the security man.

"I'm not staying," she said tightly. "In fact, I'm on my way back to the airport now."

Ramon looked puzzled, and then Ryan Beardsley was there, inserting himself between her and Ramon.

"That will be all, Ramon. I'll take Miss Morgan where she needs to go."

"The hell you will," Bryony muttered. She turned and stalked toward the door.

Ryan caught up to her as soon as she stepped outside. He took her arm, but his hold was gentle. So was the look on his face. The sympathy burning in his eyes made her want to cry.

"Let me give you a ride," he offered gently. "It's cold and you really shouldn't take a cab if you have no idea where you're going. You probably don't even have a hotel, am I right?"

She shook her head. "I was planning to stay with Rafael." She broke off as tears brimmed in her eyes.

"Come on," he said. "I'll take you to my place. It's not far. I have a spare bedroom."

"I want to go back to the airport," she said. "There's no point in staying here."

He hesitated and then cupped her elbow to lead her out of the building. "All right. I'll take you back to the airport. But I'm not leaving you until you get on a plane. You probably haven't even eaten anything, have you?"

She looked at him, utterly confused by how nice he was being to her.

"Why are you doing this?" she asked.

He stared at her for a long moment, brief pain flickering in his own eyes. "Because I know what it's like to have the rug completely pulled out from under you. I know what it's like to find out something about someone you cared about. I know what it's like to be lied to."

Her shoulders sagged and she wiped a shaking hand through her hair. "I'm just going to cry all over you."

His smile was brief but he turned her and motioned to a distant car. "You can cry all you want to. From what I heard, you're entitled."

"You can go now," Bryony said in a low voice, as Ryan hoisted her only bag onto the scale at the airline check-in desk.

"You've got a little time. Let's go get something to eat. You're pale and you're shaking still."

"I don't think I can." She placed her hand on her stomach and tried to will the queasiness away.

"Then a drink. Some juice. I'll make sure you get back to security in enough time to catch your flight."

She sighed her acceptance. It was much easier to just cede to Ryan's determination, though for the life of her she couldn't figure it out. In a few moments he had her seated at a little round table outside a tiny bistro, a tall glass of orange juice in front of her.

Her eyes watered as she stared sightlessly at it. Her fingers trembled as she touched the cool surface.

"Ah, hell, you aren't going to cry again, are you?"

She sucked in steadying breaths. "I'm sorry. You've been nothing but kind. You don't deserve to have me fall apart all over you."

"It's okay. I understand how you feel."

"Oh?" she asked in a shaky voice. "You said you knew what it felt like. Who screwed you over?"

"The woman I was supposed to marry."

She winced. “Ouch. Yeah, it sucks, doesn’t it? At least Rafael never promised to marry me. He certainly hinted about it but he never went that far in his deception. So what happened?”

Ryan’s mouth twisted and for a moment, Bryony thought he’d say nothing.

“She slept with my brother just weeks after we became engaged.”

“That’ll do it,” she said wearily. “I’m sorry that happened to you. Sucks when people you put all your faith into gut you in return.”

“That about sums up my feelings on the subject,” Ryan said with an amused chuckle.

She drained the juice and set the glass back down on the table.

“Let me get you something to eat. Can you keep it down now?”

Ryan’s concern was endearing and she offered a half-hearted smile. “Thanks. I don’t feel hungry, but you’re right. I should probably eat.”

He got up and a few minutes later returned with a selection of deli sandwiches and another glass of orange juice. As soon as she took the first bite, she realized just how hungry she was.

Ryan studied her for a long moment, sympathy bright in his eyes. “What will you do now?”

She paused midchew and then continued before swallowing. She took a sip of the juice and then set the glass back down.

“Go home. Have a baby. Try to forget. Move on with my life. I have my grandmother and the people on the island. I’ll be fine.”

“I wonder if that’s what Kelly did,” he mused aloud. “Went on with her life.”

“Is that her name? Kelly? Your ex-fiancée?”

He nodded.

"So she didn't hang around? With your brother I mean? I suppose that would be awkward at family get-togethers."

"No, she didn't hang around. I have no idea where she went."

"Probably just as well. If she was the kind of person who'd sleep with the brother of the man she's going to marry, she isn't worth your idle curiosity."

"Maybe," he said quietly.

Silence fell and Bryony picked at her food, getting down what she could. She kept hearing Rafael's damning words over and over in her head. No matter what she did, she couldn't turn it off, couldn't make it go away.

She was humiliated. She was angry. But more than anything, she was destroyed. Twice she'd allowed him to manipulate her and to make her love him. Worse, she'd fallen even deeper in love the second time around. She'd been ready to capitulate and give him what he'd wanted all along. What he didn't even *need* from her because he had no intention of ever honoring his promise to her.

She was twice a fool for believing him and for not being smart enough to get the agreement in writing.

She was an even bigger fool for loving him.

A tear slid down her cheek and she hastily wiped it away but to her dismay another fell in its place.

"I'm sorry, Bryony. You didn't deserve this," Ryan said quietly. "Rafael is my friend, but he went too far. I'm sorry you got caught in the middle of this deal."

She wiped away more tears and bowed her head. "I'm sorry, too. I wanted so much for it all to be real even when my head knew that something wasn't right. I should have never come to New York to confront him. I should have trusted my first instinct. He used me to get what he wanted. I knew that and I couldn't leave it alone. If I had just stayed home, I'd be over it by now and I would have never gotten involved with him a second time."

"Would you be over it?" Ryan asked gently.

"I don't know. Maybe… I definitely wouldn't be sitting here crying my eyes out, thousands of miles from home."

"True," Ryan conceded. He checked his watch and grimaced. "We should get you to security. Your flight leaves soon." His phone rang, and he looked down then frowned. He hesitated a moment and then punched a button to silence the ring. Then he looked back up. "You ready?"

She nodded. "Thank you, Ryan. Really. You didn't have to be this nice. I appreciate it."

Ryan smiled as he took her arm and they began the walk toward the security line. When they reached the end, she turned and blew out a deep breath. "Okay, well, this is it."

Ryan touched her cheek and then to her surprise pulled her into his arms for a tight hug.

"You take care of yourself and that baby," he said gruffly.

She pulled away and smiled up at him. "Thanks."

Squaring her shoulders, she eased into the security line. In a few hours she'd be back home.

Twenty-Two

Rafael dragged himself into the shower, washed the remnants of his alcohol binge from his fuzzy brain and proceeded to punish himself with fifteen minutes of ice-cold water. He'd been trying to call Ryan to find out where the hell Bryony was, but Ryan wasn't answering. He had to get his act together and prepare to plead his case to her. This was the most important deal of his life. Not the resort. Not the potential merger with Copeland Hotels. Not his partnership with his friends.

Bryony and their child were more important than any of that. He was furious that he could have been such a cold, calculating bastard with her before. But if she'd listen to him, if she'd just give him another chance, he'd prove to her that nothing in this world was more important to him than her.

By the time he got out, his mind was clear, he was freezing his ass off and he had only one clear purpose. Get Bryony back.

He dressed and strode into the living room, surprised to see Devon and Cam both sprawled in the armchairs.

"You two look like hell," he commented on his way to the kitchen.

Cam snorted. "You're one to talk, alcohol boy. When was the last time you went on a bender like that? Weren't we in college? Hasn't anyone told you we're too old for stuff like that now? It's a good way to poison yourself."

"Tell me something I don't know," Rafael muttered.

"So what's the plan?" Devon drawled.

"I've got to get her back," Rafael said. "Screw the deal. Screw the resort. This is my life. The woman I love. My child. I can't give them up over some ridiculous development deal."

"You're serious," Cam said.

"Of course I'm serious," Rafael snarled. "I'm not the same bastard who would do anything at all to close a deal. I don't *want* to be that man any longer. I don't know how you stood him for as long as you did."

Cam grinned. "Well, okay then. Don't get pissy about it."

"Have either of you heard from Ryan? I sent him after her, but the son of a bitch won't answer his phone."

Devon shook his head. "I'll try him. Maybe he's just not answering *your* calls."

Like that was supposed to make Rafael feel any better. But at this point, he didn't care how he had to get to Bryony. Just as long as he did.

Just as Devon put the phone to his ear, the elevator doors chimed and Rafael jerked around, holding his breath that by some miracle Bryony had come back. He let it all out when he saw Ryan stride in.

Rafael strode forward to meet him. "Where the hell is Bryony? I've been calling you for the last couple of hours. Where have you been?"

Ryan glared back. There was condemnation in his eyes. And anger. "I just spent the past couple of hours listening to Bryony cry because you broke her heart. I hope to hell you're happy now that you've destroyed the best thing that's ever happened to you."

"Whoa, back off," Devon said as he stood. "This isn't any of our business, Ryan. He's already beaten himself up enough without you piling on."

"Yeah, well, you didn't have to listen to her cry."

"Where is she?" Rafael demanded when he found his voice. The image of Bryony crying sent staggering pain through his chest. "I need to see her, Ryan. Where did you take her?"

"To the airport."

Rafael's heart dropped. "The airport? Has she already left? Do I have time to catch her?"

Ryan shook his head. "She's probably already in the air."

Rafael cursed. Then he turned and slammed his fist into the wall. He leaned his forehead against the cabinet and fought the rage that billowed inside him.

When he looked up, an odd sort of peace settled over him. He looked at his friends—his business partners—and knew that this could very well be the end of their relationship.

"I have to go after her," he said.

Devon nodded. "Yeah, you do."

"I'm canceling the deal. I'm pulling the plug. I don't give a damn how much it costs me or if it costs me *everything.* It already has. I'm going to give back that damn land. Bryony will never believe that I love her as long as it stands between us. I have to get rid of it and make it a nonissue."

Slowly Cam nodded. "I agree. It's the only way you're going to get her to believe that you love her now."

To his surprise, all three of his friends nodded their agreement.

"You're not pissed? We had a lot riding on this."

"How about you let us deal with the resort plans," Devon said. "You go after your woman. Settle down. Have babies. Be nauseatingly happy. I'm going to see what I can do to salvage the resort proposal. Maybe we can find another location."

"I'm not even going to ask," Rafael said. "Tell me about it later. I owe you. I owe you big."

"Yeah, well, don't think I won't collect. Later. After you've kissed and made up with Bryony," Devon said with a grin.

"Need a ride to the airport?" Ryan asked. "My driver's still outside. I told him I wouldn't be long."

"Yeah. Just let me get my wallet."

"Not going to pack a bag?" Cam asked.

"Hell, no. Bryony can buy me more jeans and flip-flops when I get down there."

"After she kicks your ass you mean?" Devon asked.

"I'll let her do whatever she wants just as long as she takes me back," Rafael said.

"Good God," Cam said in disgust. "Could you sound any more pathetic?"

Devon laughed and slapped Cam on the back. "Apparently that's what falling in love does to a guy. Take my advice. Marry for money and connections, like I am."

"I think the best idea is to never marry," Cam pointed out. "Less expensive that way. No costly divorces."

Rafael shook his head. "And you all called me the bastard. Come on, Ryan. I've got a plane to catch."

"Bryony!"

Bryony turned to see her grandmother waving to her from her deck. Silas stood beside her, watching as Bryony stood close to the water's edge.

She'd been there for a couple of hours, just watching the water, alone with her thoughts. She knew her grandmother and Silas were both worried. She'd given them an abbreviated version of everything that had happened. No sense in them knowing the extent of Bryony's stupidity.

They knew enough that Rafael had made a fool of her and would develop the land, but then Bryony had been prepared to give up that fight. So the outcome would be the same, only Bryony wouldn't have the man she loved.

Bryony waved but turned back to the water, not ready to deal with them yet. Mamaw and Silas had both fussed over her ever since she'd gotten back home. She was exhausted and what she really wanted was to go to sleep for about twenty-four hours, but every time she closed her eyes, she heard Rafael's words. They wouldn't go away, she couldn't make herself stop hearing them no matter how hard she tried.

And she was damn tired of crying. Her head ached so badly from all the tears she'd shed that it was ready to explode.

Her cell phone rang in her pocket and she picked it up, just as she'd done the other twenty times that Rafael had tried to call her. She hit the ignore button and a few seconds later, heard the ding signaling that she had a voice mail. One of the many he'd left her.

What else was there left for him to say? He was sorry? He hadn't meant to deceive her? Was she supposed to forgive him just because he forgot what a jerk he had been? How could she be sure he hadn't made it all up just to get her to shut up and not make noises that would scare off his precious investors?

If he kept her quiet enough for long enough then the deal would be sealed.

She didn't like how cynical she'd grown. It would never occur to her before that anyone would be so devious, but Rafael had taught her a lot about the world of business and the lengths that some people would go for money.

She hoped he made a ton off his precious resort and she hoped it kept him warm at night. She hoped it made up for all the sweet baby kisses he'd miss.

The thought depressed her. Money was just paper. But a child was something so very precious. Love was precious. And she'd offered it to Rafael freely and without reservation.

She felt like the worst sort of naive fool.

Finally her feet got cold enough from the surf that she

could no longer feel her toes, so she turned to trudge back up to her grandmother's deck. She'd say her goodbyes, assure Mamaw that she'd be just fine and then she'd go home and hopefully sleep for the next day.

As she got close, she saw Rafael standing on the deck and Mamaw and Silas were nowhere to be found. How the hell had he gotten down here so fast? Why would he even bother? She didn't react to his presence. She wouldn't give him the satisfaction.

She walked up the steps, past him to collect her sweater and then she started down the walkway that led to her own cottage.

"Bryony," he called after her. "Wait, please. We have to talk."

She picked up her pace. She knew he followed her because she could hear his footsteps behind her, but she blindly went on. When she reached to open her door, his hand closed around her wrist and gently pulled her away.

"Please listen to me," he begged softly. "I know I don't deserve anything from you. But please listen. I love you."

She went rigid and closed her eyes as pain crashed over her all over again. When she reopened them she was grateful that no tears spilled over her cheeks. Maybe she'd finally cried herself out.

"You don't know how to love," she said in a low voice. "You have to possess a heart and a soul, and you have neither."

He winced but didn't let go of her wrist. "I'm not going to lie to you, Bryony. Neither am I going to sugarcoat what I did."

"Well, good for you," she said bitterly. "Does that ease your conscience? Just leave me alone, Rafael. You got what you wanted. You don't have to deal with me anymore. Just make this easier on both of us. If you're wanting absolution, see a priest. I can't offer you any. You should be happy. You got the land. You'll build your resort. Everyone gets what they want."

"Not you," he said painfully. "And not me."

"Please, Rafael," she begged. "I'm tired. I'm worn completely out. I just want to sleep before I fall over. Please, just go. I can't do this with you right now."

He looked so much like he wanted to argue, but concern darkened his eyes and slowly he eased his fingers from her wrist.

"I love you, Bryony. That's not going to change. I don't want it to change. Go get some sleep. Take care of yourself. But this isn't finished. I'm not letting you go. You think I'm ruthless? You haven't seen anything yet."

He touched her cheek and then let it slide down her face before falling away. Then he turned and walked back down the path to her grandmother's house.

She closed her eyes as pain swelled in her chest and splintered in a thousand different directions. She wanted to scream. She wanted to cry. But all she could do was stand there numbly while the man she'd given everything to walked away.

Twenty-Three

"It's been a week," Rafael said in frustration. "A week and she still won't acknowledge me, much less talk to me. As much as I loathe the man I used to be, at least he would have no qualms about forcing the issue."

Rafael stood on Laura's back deck having a beer with Silas and brooded over the fact that Bryony still refused to see him. He was about to go crazy.

Silas chuckled. "You've got stamina, son. I have to give that to you. Most men would have tucked tail and left by now. I'm still amazed that you managed to talk Laura down from killing you and actually got her to side with you. I can't figure out if you're the dumbest man alive or just the luckiest."

Bryony had holed up in her cottage and while Laura went over daily to check in on her, Bryony hadn't ventured out except to walk on the beach. The one time Rafael had confronted her on the sand, she'd retreated inside. He hadn't bothered her since because he wanted her to have that time outside without worrying that she'd encounter him.

"I'm not leaving," Rafael said. "I don't care how long it takes. I love her. I believe she still loves me, but she's hurting. I can't even blame her for that. I was a complete and utter bastard. I don't deserve her but she's the one who kept telling me I didn't have to be the same man. Well, damn it, I'm choosing to be different. I want her to see that."

Silas put his hand on Rafael's shoulder. "Around here we have a saying. Go big or go home. I'm thinking you need to go big. Really big."

Rafael frowned and turned to the other man. "What did you have in mind?"

"It's not what I have in mind. It's what you ought to be thinking about. You've already promised me and Laura that you have no intention of developing that land, but does she know that? Does the rest of the island know that? Seems to me you're missing an opportunity to make a grand gesture and prove once and for all you're a changed man."

"Okay, I'm with you," Rafael said slowly.

"No, I don't think you are. Call a town meeting. I'll let it leak out that you have a big announcement about the resort. Folks will show up because they'll want to launch their objections and nothing gets people out to a town meeting more than getting to air their grievances. Trust me, after twenty years of being the sheriff here, I know what I'm talking about."

"That doesn't help me when Bryony refuses to leave her cottage," Rafael pointed out.

"Oh, Laura and I will make sure she's there. You just worry about how you're going to humble yourself before everyone," Silas said with a grin.

Rafael sighed. He had the feeling this wasn't going to be one of his better moments. He might have no desire to be the unfeeling bastard he'd been before but it didn't mean he wanted to air his personal life in front of a few hundred witnesses.

But if it would get him in front of Bryony so she'd be forced to listen, he'd swallow his pride and do it.

"Are you crazy?" Bryony sputtered out. "Why would I want to go listen to his spiel about his plans for the resort?"

"Now, Bry, I didn't imagine you for a coward," Silas said in exasperation. "By now everyone knows what happened. They don't blame you."

"I don't care what they think," Bryony said in a low voice. "I was prepared to be the brunt of their censure when I went to New York to tell Rafael to go ahead with the plans, that I wouldn't fight him."

"Then what's the problem?" Mamaw asked.

"I don't want to see him. Why can't either of you understand that? Do you have any idea how much it hurts to even look at him?"

"The best thing you can do is show up with your head held high. The sooner you get it over with, the sooner you can start coming out of that cottage of yours. It's just like a bandage. Better to rip it off and have it done with than to delay the inevitable."

Bryony sighed. "Okay, I'll go. If I do, then will you please leave me alone and let me deal with this my own way? I know you're worried but this isn't easy for me."

Mamaw squeezed her into a big hug. "I think things will be a lot better after today. You'll see."

Bryony wasn't as convinced but she allowed Silas and Mamaw to drag her to the municipal building where the meeting would be held. It took everything she had not to run back out the door when Silas led her to a front-row seat.

Talk about being a masochist. She'd have a front-row seat in which to listen to the man she loved announce his plans for a resort made possible by her stupidity.

She sighed and sank into one of the folding chairs. Mamaw and Silas took the spots on either side of her. Several people stopped by to talk to Silas. Some even shot sympathetic looks in her direction.

Yep, it was clear everyone knew what a naive fool she'd been.

At least no one was yelling at her for allowing the outsider to come in and develop the island. Yet.

Rupert strode in a minute later, an uncharacteristic smile plastered on his face. It wasn't his politician smile. It was a genuine one filled with delight. He looked, for lack of a better word, giddy.

He held up his hands for quiet and then frowned when the din didn't diminish. He cleared his throat and scowled harder. He was forever complaining to Bryony that he wasn't given enough respect by his constituents.

Finally Silas stood, held up his hands and hollered, "Quiet, people. The mayor wants your attention."

Rupert sent Silas a disgruntled look when everyone hushed. Then he looked over the audience and smiled. "Today we have Rafael de Luca of Tricorp Investment Opportunities, who is going to talk about the piece of property he recently acquired here on the island. Give him your undivided attention, please."

It took all of Bryony's self-restraint not to swivel in her seat to see if he was here. Many of the assembled people began to murmur, and then Bryony heard footsteps coming up the aisle.

Rafael stepped to the podium and Bryony was shocked by his appearance. First, he was wearing jeans. And a T-shirt. He looked tired and haggard. His hair was unkempt and it didn't look like he'd shaved that morning.

There were hollows under his eyes and a gray pallor to his skin that hadn't been present before.

He cleared his throat and glanced over the audience before his gaze finally came to rest on her.

He looked…nervous. It didn't seem possible that this ultra-confident businessman was nervous. But he seemed uneasy and on edge.

She watched in astonishment as he fiddled with something on the podium and when he looked up again, there was a rawness to his eyes that made her chest tighten.

"I came to this island for one thing and one thing only. I wanted to buy property that Bryony Morgan had put up for sale."

Several muttered insults filtered around the room, but Rafael continued on, undaunted.

"When it became clear that she would attach stipulations to the sale of the land, I conspired to seduce my way into her heart. Basically I was willing to do whatever necessary to convince her I'd do as she asked without having to commit her conditions onto paper."

Bryony would have bolted to her feet, but Mamaw gripped her arm with surprising strength.

"Sit. You need to listen to this, Bryony. Let him finish."

Rafael held up his hands to quiet the angry murmurs of the crowd. Then his gaze found Bryony's again. She slowly slid back into her seat, caught by the intensity in his stare.

"I'm not proud of what I did. But it was part and parcel of the kind of man I was. I left here, never intending to return until it was time for groundbreaking. But my plane crashed. It took weeks to recover and I lost all memory of the time I was here. I'm so grateful for that accident. It changed my life."

The room went completely silent on the heels of his last statement. Everyone seemed to lean forward in anticipation of what he'd say next.

"I came back here with Bryony to try to regain my memory. What I did was fall in love with this island and with Bryony. For real this time. She's told me on multiple occasions that I don't have to always stay the person I was, that I can change and be whoever I want to be. She's right. I don't want to be the person I was any longer. I want to be someone I can be proud of, someone *she* can be proud of. I want to be the man Bryony Morgan loves."

Tears crowded Bryony's eyes and her fingers curled into tight little fists in her lap. Mamaw reached over to take one of her hands and rubbed it reassuringly.

"I'm giving Bryony back the land I bought from her. It's hers to do as she likes. If she wishes, she can make it a gift and deed it to the town. Turn it into a park. Make it a private sanctuary. I don't care. Because all I want is her. And our child."

He stopped speaking and seemed to be battling to keep his composure. His fingers curled around the edges of the podium, but she could see that they still shook.

Then he walked around the podium, down the single step that elevated the stage. He came to a stop in front of her and then dropped to one knee. He reached for her hand and gently pried her fingers open and then he laced them with his, something he'd done a hundred times before.

"I love you, Bryony. Forgive me. Marry me. Say you'll make me a better man than I was. I'll spend the rest of my life *being* that man for you and our children."

A sob exploded from her throat at the same moment she launched herself from her seat and threw her arms around him. She buried her face in his neck and sobbed huge, noisy sobs.

He gripped her tight, holding one hand to the back of her head. He shook against her, almost as if he were dangerously close to breaking down himself.

He kissed her ear, her temple, her forehead, the top of her head. Then he pulled back, framing her face in his hands before peppering the rest of it with kisses.

Around them there were sighs and exclamations, even a smattering of applause, but Bryony tuned them all out as she held on to the one thing she needed most in this world.

Rafael.

"Give me your answer, please, baby," he murmured in her ear. "Don't torture me any longer. Tell me I haven't lost you for good. I can be the man you want, Bryony. Just give me the chance."

She kissed him and stroked her hands over his face, feeling the stubble on his jaw and drinking in the haggardness of his appearance. He looked as bad as she'd felt over the past week.

"You already are the man I want, Rafael. I love you. Yes, I'll marry you."

He shot to his feet and lifted her up, twirling her round and round with a whoop. "She said yes!"

The crowd burst into cheers. Mamaw sniffed indelicately and when Silas handed her a handkerchief, she blew her nose loudly and then sniffed some more.

Slowly he allowed her to slide down his body until her feet touched the floor, but he kept his arms tight around her as if he didn't want to let her go even for a moment.

"I'm sorry, Bryony," he said sincerely. "I'm sorry I lied to you, that I hurt you. If I could go back and change it all I would."

"I'm glad you can't," she said. "As I sat here and listened to everything you said, I realized that if things hadn't happened exactly as they had, you wouldn't be here now. What's important is that you love me now. Today. And tomorrow."

"I'll love you through lots of tomorrows," he vowed.

Bryony glanced around as the townspeople began filtering out of the building. Mamaw and Silas had discreetly made their exit, leaving Bryony and Rafael alone at the front of the room.

"What are we going to do, Rafe? What are you going to do? I came to New York because I was going to tell you that you should go ahead with the resort deal. But if you don't go through with it, what will it mean for your business?"

Rafael sighed. "Ryan, Devon and Cam support me. You

support me. That's all I need. When I left, they were trying to work out a way to salvage the deal. I'm guessing they'll look for an alternative location. I really don't care. I told them I wasn't going to lose you and my child over money. You and our baby mean more to me than anything else in the world. I mean that."

"After the spectacle you just made of yourself, I believe you," she teased.

"I'm tired," he admitted. "And so are you. Why don't we go back to your cottage, climb into bed and get some rest. I can't think of anything better than having you back in my arms."

She leaned into his embrace, wrapped her arms around him and closed her eyes as the sweetness of the moment floated gently through her veins.

Then she tilted her head back and smiled up at him, feeling the weight and grief wash away. For the first time in days, the thick blanket of sadness lifted, leaving her feeling light and gloriously happy.

She took his hand and tugged him down the aisle to the doorway leading to the outside. As they stepped out, sunlight poured over them, washing the darkness away.

For a brief moment, she paused and tipped her face into the sun, allowing the warmth to brush over her cheeks.

She looked up at Rafael, who was staring intently at her. His love was there for the entire world to see, shining in his eyes with brightness that rivaled the sun.

It was a look she'd never grow tired of in a hundred years and beyond.

"Let's go home," she said.

Rafael smiled, took her hand and pulled her toward the waiting car.

* * * * *

"Tell me, Hattie. What do you want?"

She lifted her chin. She was tall for a woman, and he could see the shades of chocolate and cognac in her pupils. She licked her lips. Their long separation vanished like mist, and suddenly he was assaulted with a barrage of memories, both good and bad.

The soft, quick kiss he brushed across her cheek surprised them both. He was so close, he could smell cherry lipgloss. Some things never changed. "Hattie?"

She closed her eyes when he kissed her, but her lashes lifted and her cloudy gaze cleared. Astonishment flashed across her expressive features, followed by chagrin and what appeared to be resignation.

After a long, silent pause, she wrinkled her nose and sighed. "I need you to marry me."

Dear Reader,

I am married to a man who much prefers the mountains to the beach but who also loves Key West! We have made several trips down to the jewel-like islands that make up the tip of Florida, sometimes flying straight in and sometimes landing in Ft. Lauderdale and renting a car to drive down the Keys.

When I began to think of a fun destination that met certain requirements for Luc and Hattie's unconventional honeymoon, I knew that Key West would be a perfect locale. It has everything—fabulous weather, a colourful, original ambience, loads of history (everything from pirates to Hemingway), and undoubtedly—romance!

Two people who have joined forces for the sake of a child may try fooling themselves into thinking the marriage is in name only. But beneath a tropical moon, surrounded by scented breezes and centuries of swashbuckling adventure, Luc and Hattie can't resist revisiting the love they once shared.

Happy reading,

Janice

THE BILLIONAIRE'S BORROWED BABY

BY

JANICE MAYNARD

Published in Great Britain 2012
by Mills & Boon, an imprint of Harlequin (UK) Limited,
Eton House, 18-24 Paradise Road, Richmond, Surrey TW9 1SR

2in1 ISBN: 978 0 263 89151 5

51-0412

Harlequin (UK) policy is to use papers that are natural, renewable and recyclable products and made from wood grown in sustainable forests. The logging and manufacturing processes conform to the legal environmental regulations of the country of origin.

Printed and bound in Spain
by Blackprint CPI, Barcelona

Janice Maynard came to writing early in life. When her short story *The Princess and the Robbers* won a red ribbon in her primary school arts fair, Janice was hooked. She holds a BA from Emory and Henry College and an MA from East Tennessee State University. In 2002 Janice left a fifteen-year career as an elementary teacher to pursue writing full-time. Her first love is creating sexy, character-driven, contemporary romance. She has written for Kensington and NAL, and now is so very happy to also be part of the Harlequin family—a lifelong dream, by the way!

Janice and her husband live in beautiful east Tennessee in the shadow of the Great Smoky Mountains. She loves to travel and enjoys using those experiences as settings for books.

Hearing from readers is one of the best perks of the job! Visit her website at www.janicemaynard.com or e-mail her at jesm13@aol.com. And of course, don't forget Facebook, www.facebook.com/JaniceMaynardReaderPage. Find her on Twitter @janicemaynard.

For the next generation: Anastasia, Ainsley, Allie,
Sydney, Olivia, Dakota and Samuel Ellis.

One

It was a hot, beautiful Georgia morning, but all Hattie Parker noticed was the taste of desperation and panic.

"I need to speak to Mr. Cavallo, please. Mr. *Luc* Cavallo," she clarified quickly. "It's urgent."

The thirtysomething administrative assistant with the ice-blue suit and matching pale, chilly eyes looked down her perfect nose. "Do you have an appointment?"

Hattie clenched her teeth. The woman had an expensive leather date book open in front of her. Clearly, she knew Hattie was an interloper and clearly she was doing her best to be intimidating.

Hattie juggled the baby on her hip and managed a smile. "Tell him it's Hattie Parker. I don't have an appointment, but I'm sure Luc will see me if you let him know I'm here."

Actually, that was a bald-faced lie. She had no clue if Luc would see her or not. At one time in her life he had been Prince Charming, willing and eager to do anything she wanted, to give her everything she desired.

Today, he might very well show her the door, but she was

hoping he would remember some of the good times and at least hear her out. They hadn't parted on the best of terms. But since every other option she had considered, legal or not, had gone bust, it was Luc or no one. And she wasn't leaving without a fight.

The woman's expression didn't change. She was sheer perfection from her ash-blond chignon to her exquisitely made-up face to her expensive French manicure. With disdain, she examined Hattie's disheveled blond hair, discount store khaki skirt and pink cotton blouse. Even without the drool marks at the shoulder, the outfit wasn't going to win any fashion awards. It was hard to maintain a neat appearance when the little one grabbed handfuls of hair at regular intervals.

Hattie's legs felt like spaghetti. The stoic security guard in the lobby had insisted that she park her stroller before entering the elevator. Seven-month-old Deedee weighed a ton, and Hattie was scared and exhausted, at the end of her rope. The last six weeks had been hell.

She took a deep breath. "Either you let me see Mr. Cavallo, or I'm going to pitch the biggest hissy fit Atlanta has seen since Scarlett O'Hara swished her skirts through the red Georgia dust." Hattie's chin trembled right at the end, but she refused to let this supercilious woman defeat her.

Scary lady blinked. Just once, but it was enough to let Hattie know that the balance of power had shifted. The other woman stood up with a pained sigh. "Wait here." She disappeared down a hallway.

Hattie nuzzled the baby's sweet-smelling head with its little tufts of golden hair. "Don't worry, my love. I won't let anyone take you, I swear." Deedee smiled, revealing her two new bottom teeth, her only teeth. She was starting to babble nonsense syllables, and Hattie fell more in love with her every day.

The wait seemed like an eternity, but when Luc's assistant finally returned, the clock on the wall showed that less than five minutes had elapsed. The woman was definitely disgruntled. "Mr. Cavallo will see you now. But he's a very busy man, and he has many other important commitments this morning."

Hattie resisted the childish urge to stick out her tongue at the woman's back as they traversed the hallway carpeted in thick, crimson plush. At the second doorway, the woman paused. "You may go in." The words nearly stuck in ice woman's throat, you could tell.

Hattie took a deep breath, no longer concentrating on her would-be nemesis. She kissed the baby's cheek for luck. "Showtime, kiddo." With far more confidence than she felt, she knocked briefly, opened the door and stepped into the room.

Luc ran a multimillion-dollar business. He was accustomed to dealing with crises on a daily basis. The ability to think on his feet was a gift he'd honed in the fires of corporate America.

So he wasn't easily thrown off balance. But when Hattie Parker appeared in his office, the first time he'd seen her in over a decade, his heart lodged in his throat, his muscles tensed and he momentarily forgot how to breathe.

She was as beautiful now as she had been at twenty. Sun-kissed porcelain skin, dark brown eyes that held hints of amber. And legs that went on forever. Her silky blond hair barely brushed her shoulders, much shorter than he remembered. He kept the width of his broad mahogany desk between them. It seemed safer that way.

As he struggled with shock, he was stunned to realize the woman he had once loved was holding an infant. Jealousy stabbed sharp and deep. Damn. Hattie was a mother. Which meant there was a man somewhere in the picture.

The sick feeling in his gut stunned him. He'd moved on a long, long time ago. So why was his chest tight and his pulse jumping like a jackrabbit?

He remained standing, his hands shoved in his pockets. "Hello, Hattie." He was proud of the even timbre of his voice.

"Hello, Luc."

She was visibly nervous. He indicated the chair closest to him and motioned for her to sit. For a brief moment, Luc caught a glimpse of sexy legs as Hattie's skirt rode up her thighs. The baby clung to her neck, and Hattie wriggled in the chair until she was modestly covered.

He examined her face, deliberately letting the silence accumulate in tense layers. Hattie Parker was the girl next door, a natural, appealing beauty who didn't need enhancement. Even dressed as she was in fairly unflattering garments, she would stand out in a room full of lovely women.

At one time, she had been his whole world.

And it irked him that the memories still stung. "Why are you here, Hattie? The last time we had sex was a lifetime ago. Surely you're not going to try and convince me that baby is mine."

The mockery and sarcasm made her pale. He felt the pinch of remorse, but a guy needed to wield what weapons he could. The man he was today would not be vulnerable. Not ever again.

She cleared her throat. "I need your help."

He lifted a brow. "I'd have thought I would be the last person on your go-to list."

"To be honest, you were. But it's serious, Luc. I'm in big trouble."

He rocked on his heels. "What's her name?"

The non sequitur made Hattie frown. "This is Deedee."

Luc studied the baby. He didn't see much of Hattie in the child. Maybe the kid took after her dad.

Luc leaned over and punched the intercom. "Marilyn… can you come in here, please?"

It was a toss-up as to which of the two women was more horrified when Luc phrased his next request. When Marilyn appeared, he motioned to the baby. "Will you please take the little one for a few minutes? Her name is Deedee. Ms. Parker and I need to have a serious conversation, and I don't have much time."

Hattie wanted to protest, he could tell. But she reluctantly handed the baby over to Luc's assistant. "Here's a bottle. She's getting hungry. And you'll need this bib and burp cloth. You don't want to let her ruin your nice suit."

Luc knew his assistant would be fine. She might be a cold fish, but she was relentlessly efficient.

When the door closed, Luc sat down in his leather office chair. It had been specially ordered to fit his long, lanky frame. He steepled his hands under his chin and leaned back. "So spill it, Hattie. What's going on in your life to make you seek me out? As I recall, it was *you* who dumped *me* and not the other way around."

She flushed and twisted her hands in her lap. "I don't think we need to go there. That was a long time ago."

He shrugged. "All right then. We'll concentrate on the present. Why are you here?"

When she bit her lip, he shifted in his chair uneasily. Why in God's name did he still have such vivid memories of kissing that bow-shaped mouth? Running his hands through that silky, wavy hair. Touching every inch of her soft, warm skin. He swallowed hard.

Hattie met his gaze hesitantly. "Do you remember my older sister, Angela?"

He frowned. "Barely. As I recall, the two of you didn't get along."

"We grew closer after our parents died."

"I didn't know, Hattie. I'm sorry."

For a moment, tears made her eyes shiny, but she blinked them back. "Thank you. My father died a few years after I graduated. Lung cancer. He was a two-pack-a-day man and it caught up with him."

"And your mother?"

"She didn't do well without Daddy. He did everything for her, and without him, the world was overwhelming to her. She finally had a nervous breakdown and had to be admitted to a facility. Unfortunately, she was never able to go back to her home. Angela and I sold the house we grew up in…everything Mom and Dad had, but it wasn't enough. I practically bankrupted myself paying for her care."

"Angela didn't help?"

"She told me I should back off and let the state look after Mother…especially when Mom retreated totally into an alternate reality where she didn't even recognize us."

"Some people would think your sister made sense."

"Not me. I couldn't abandon my mother."

"When did you lose her?"

"Last winter."

He looked at her left hand, but it was bare. Where was her husband in all this? Was the guy a jerk who bailed on Hattie rather than help with the mom? And what about the baby?

Suddenly, it became clear. Hattie needed to borrow money. She was proud and independent, and things must be really bad if she had humbled her pride enough to come to him.

He leaned forward, his elbows on the desk. No one who knew their history would blame him if he kicked her out. But though his memories of her were bitter, he didn't have it in him to be deliberately cruel, especially if a child was involved. And though it might be petty, he rather liked the idea of having Hattie in his debt…a kind of poetic justice.

"You've had a rough time," he said quietly. "I'll be happy to loan you however much money you need, interest free, no questions asked. For old time's sake."

Hattie's face went blank and she cocked her head. "Excuse me?"

"That's why you're here, isn't it? To ask if you can borrow some money? I'm fine with that. It's no big deal. What good is all that cash in the bank if I can't use it to help an old friend?"

Her jaw dropped and her cheeks went red with mortification. "No, no, no," she said, leaping to her feet and pacing. "I don't need your money, Luc. That's not it at all."

It was his turn to rise. He rounded the desk and faced her, close enough now to inhale her scent and realize with pained remembrance that she still wore the same perfume. He put his hands gently on her shoulders, feeling the tremors she couldn't disguise.

They were practically nose to nose. "Then tell me, Hattie. What do you need from me? What do you want?"

She lifted her chin. She was tall for a woman, and he could see the shades of chocolate and cognac in her irises. Her breathing was ragged, a pulse beating at the base of her throat.

He shook her gently. "Spit it out. Tell me."

She licked her lips. He could see the tracery of blue veins at her temples. Their long separation vanished like mist, and suddenly he was assaulted with a barrage of memories, both good and bad.

The soft, quick kiss he brushed across her cheek surprised them both. He was so close, he could smell cherry lip gloss. Some things never changed. "Hattie?"

She had closed her eyes when he kissed her, but her lashes lifted and her cloudy gaze cleared. Astonishment flashed across her expressive features, followed by chagrin and what appeared to be resignation.

After a long, silent pause, she wrinkled her nose and sighed. "I need you to marry me."

Luc dropped his hands from her shoulders with unflattering haste. Though his expression remained guarded, for a split second some strong emotion flashed in his eyes and then disappeared as quickly as it had come. Most men would be shocked by Hattie's proposal.

Most men weren't Luc Cavallo.

He lifted a shoulder clad in an expensive suit. The Cavallo textile empire, started by their grandfather in Italy and now headquartered in Atlanta, had made Luc and his brother wealthy men. She had no doubt that the soft, finely woven wool fabric was the product of a family mill. His mouth twisted, faint disdain in his expression. "Is this a joke? Should I look for hidden cameras?"

She felt her face go even hotter. Confronting her past was more difficult than she had expected, and without the baby to run interference, Hattie felt uncomfortably vulnerable. "It's not a joke. I'm dead serious. I need you to marry me to keep Deedee safe."

He scowled. "Good Lord, Hattie. Is the father threatening you? Has he hurt you? Tell me."

His intensity made her shiver. If she really had an abusive husband, there was no doubt in her mind that Luc Cavallo would hunt him down and destroy him. She was making a hash of this explanation. "It's complicated," she said helplessly. "But no, nothing like that."

He ran two hands through his hair, mussing the dark, glossy strands. The reminder function on his BlackBerry beeped just then, and Luc glanced down at it with a harried expression. "I have an appointment," he said, his voice betraying frustration. "Obviously we're not going to resolve this in fifteen minutes. Can you get a sitter for tonight?"

"I'd rather not. Deedee has been through a lot of trauma recently. She clings to me. I don't want to change her routine any more than necessary." And the thought of being alone with Luc Cavallo scared Hattie. This brief meeting had revealed an unpalatable truth. The Hattie who had been madly in love with Luc was still lurking somewhere inside a heart that clung to silly dreams from the past.

He straightened his tie and strode to the other side of his desk. "Then I'll send a car for you." As she opened her mouth to protest, he added, "With an infant seat. We'll have dinner at my home and my housekeeper can play with the child while we talk."

There was nothing ominous in his words, but Hattie felt her throat constrict. Was she really going to try to convince Luc to marry her? Who was she kidding? He had no reason at all to humor her. Other than perhaps sheer curiosity. Why hadn't he shown her the door immediately? Why was he allowing her to play out this odd reunion?

She should be glad, relieved, down on her knees thanking the good lord that Luc wasn't already married.

But at the moment, her exact emotions were far more complicated and far less sensible.

She was still fascinated by this man who had once promised her the moon.

Two

What did one wear to a marriage proposal? While the baby was napping, Hattie rummaged through the tiny closet in her matching tiny apartment, knowing that she was not going to find a dress to wow Luc Cavallo. The only garment remotely suitable was a black, polished cotton sheath that she had worn to each of her parent's funerals. Perhaps with some accessories it would do the trick.

In a jewelry box she'd had since she was a girl, her hand hovered over the one piece inside that wasn't an inexpensive bauble. The delicate platinum chain was still as bright as the day Luc had given it to her. She picked it up and fastened it around her neck, adjusting the single pearl flanked by small diamonds.

Though there had been many days when the wolf was at the door, she had not been able to bring herself to sell this one lovely reminder of what might have been. She stroked the pearl, imagining that it was warm beneath her fingers.…

They had skipped their afternoon classes at Emory and escaped to Piedmont Park with a blanket and a picnic basket.

She was a scholarship student...his family had endowed the Fine Arts Center.

As they sprawled in the hot spring sunshine, feeling alive and free and deliciously truant, Luc leaned over her on one elbow, kissing her with teasing brushes of his lips that made her restless for more. He grinned down at her, his eyes alight with happiness. "I have an anniversary present for you."

"Anniversary?" They'd been dating for a while, but she hadn't kept track.

He caressed her cheek. "I met you six months ago today. You were buying a miniature pumpkin at Stanger's Market. I offered to carve it for you. You laughed. And that's when I knew."

"Knew what?"

"That you were the one."

Her smile faded. "College guys are supposed to be counting notches on their bedposts, not spouting romantic nonsense."

A shadow dimmed the good humor in his gaze. "I come from a long line of Italians. Romance is in our blood." His whimsical shrug made her regret tarnishing the moment. Lord knew she wanted it to be true, but her mother had drummed into her head that men only wanted one thing. And Hattie had given that up without a qualm.

Being Luc Cavallo's lover was the best thing that had ever happened to her. He was her first, and she loved him so much it hurt. But she was careful to protect herself. She had a degree to finish, grades to keep up. A woman had to stand on her own two feet. Depending on a man led to heartbreak.

Luc reached into the pocket of his jeans and withdrew a small turquoise box. He handed it to her without speaking.

If she had been able to think of a polite refusal, she would have handed it back unopened. But he looked at her with such naked anticipation that she swallowed her misgivings and removed the lid. Nestled inside the leather box was a necklace, an exquisite, expensive necklace.

Hattie knew about Tiffany's, of course. In fact, back in the fall she'd been in the store at Phipps Plaza with one of her girlfriends who was in search of a wedding gift. But even on that day, Hattie had felt the sting of being out of place. She couldn't afford a key chain in those swanky glass cases, much less anything else.

And now this.

Luc ignored her silence. He took the necklace from the box and fastened it around her neck. She was wearing a pink tank top, and the pearl nestled in her modest cleavage. He kissed her forehead. "It suits you."

But it didn't. She was not that woman he wanted her to be. Luc would take his place one day with the glitterati. And Hattie, with or without the necklace, would wish him well. But she wasn't "the one"...and she never would be.

A car backfired out on the street, the loud sound dragging Hattie back to the present. With a mutinous scowl at her own reflection, she closed the jewelry box with a defiant click. Luc probably didn't even remember the silly necklace. He'd no doubt bought pricey bling for a dozen women in the intervening years.

The afternoon dragged by, the baby fussy with teething... Hattie nervous and uncertain. It was almost a relief when a nicely dressed chauffeur knocked at the door promptly at six-thirty.

The pleasant older man took Hattie's purse and the diaper bag while she tucked Deedee into the top-of-the-line car seat. It was brand-new and not smeared with crusty Cheerios and spit-up. The baby was charmed by the novelty of having Hattie sit across from her. A game of peekaboo helped distract them both as the car wound its way from the slightly run-down neighborhood where Hattie lived to an upscale part of town.

Though it had been ten years since Hattie and Luc's college breakup, they had never crossed paths after graduation. It was a big city, and they moved in far different spheres.

West Paces Ferry was one of the premier addresses in Atlanta. Decades-old homes sat side by side with new construction created to resemble historic architecture. Even the governor's mansion called the narrow, winding avenue home. Luc had recently purchased an entire estate complete with acreage. Hattie had seen the renovation written up in a local magazine.

The article, accompanied by photos of Luc, had no doubt been responsible for this crazy decision to throw herself on Luc's mercy. Seeing his smiling face after so many years had resurrected feelings she believed to be long dead.

Perhaps it was a sign....

The old home was amazing. Azaleas and forsythia bloomed in profusion on the grounds. A lengthy driveway culminated in a cobblestone apron leading to the imposing double front doors. Luc stepped out to meet them almost before the engine noise had died. His dark hair and eyes betrayed his Mediterranean heritage.

He held out a hand. "Welcome, Hattie."

She felt him squeeze her fingers, and her skin heated. "Your home is beautiful."

He stepped back as she extracted Deedee. "It's a work in progress. I'll be glad when the last of it is finished."

Despite his disclaimer, and despite the small area of scaffolding at the side of the house where workmen had been repairing stonework, the interior of the house was breathtaking. A sweeping staircase led up and to the right. The foyer floor was Italian marble, and above a walnut chair rail, the walls were papered in what appeared to be the original silk fabric, a muted shade of celadon. A priceless chandelier showered them in shards of warm light, and on a console beneath an antique mirror on the left wall, a massive bouquet of flowers scented the air.

Hattie turned around in a circle, the baby in her arms quiet for once, as if she, too, was awed. "It's stunning, Luc."

His smile reflected quiet satisfaction. "It's starting to feel like home. The couple who lived here bought it in the 1920s. They're both gone now, but I inherited Ana and Sherman. He wears many hats…driver is only one of them."

"He was very sweet. I felt pampered. And Ana?"

"His wife. You'll meet her in a moment. She's the housekeeper, chef, gardener…you name it. I tried to get them both to retire with a pension, but I think they love this house more than I do. I get the distinct feeling that I'm on probation as the new owner."

As promised, Ana entertained Deedee during dinner while Luc and Hattie enjoyed the fruits of the housekeeper's labors—lightly breaded rainbow trout, baby asparagus and fruit salad accompanied by rolls so fluffy they seemed to melt in the mouth.

Luc served Hattie and himself, with nothing to disturb the intimacy of their meal. Surprisingly, Hattie forgot to be self-conscious. Luc was a fascinating man, highly intelligent, well-read, and he possessed of a sneaky sense of humor. As the evening progressed, sharp regret stabbed her heart. She was overwhelmed with a painful recognition of what she had lost because of her own immaturity and cowardice.

He refilled her wineglass one more time. "I suppose you're not nursing the baby."

She choked on a sip of chardonnay. An image of Luc in her bed, watching her feed a baby at her breast, flashed through her brain with the force of a runaway train. Her face was so hot she hoped he would blame it on the wine. She set the glass down gently, her hand trembling. Unwittingly, he had given her the perfect opening.

"The baby's not mine," she said softly. "My sister Angela was her mother."

"Was?"

Hattie swallowed, the grief still fresh and raw. "She was killed in a car crash six weeks ago. My brother-in-law, Eddie, was driving…drunk and drugged out of his mind. He got out and left the scene when he hit a car head-on. Both people in the other vehicle died. Angela lingered for a few hours…long enough to tell me that she wanted me to take Deedee. I was babysitting that night, and I've had the baby ever since."

"What happened to the baby's father?"

"Eddie spent a few days behind bars. He's out on bail awaiting trial. But I guarantee you he won't do any time. His family has connections everywhere. I don't know if we have the Mob in Georgia, but I wouldn't be surprised. Eddie's family is full of cold, mean-spirited people. Frankly, they scare me."

"I can tell."

"At first, none of them showed any sign of acknowledging Deedee's existence. But about two weeks ago, I was summoned to the family compound in Conyers."

"Eddie wanted to see his child?"

She laughed bitterly. "You'd think so, wouldn't you? But no. He was there when I arrived with her. A lot of them were there. But not one single person in that entire twisted family even looked at her, much less asked to hold her. They kept referring to her as 'the kid' and talked about how she was one of theirs and so should be raised by them."

"That doesn't make any sense given their lack of enthusiasm for the baby."

"It does when you realize that Eddie thinks Deedee will be his ace in the hole with the judge. He wants to portray the grieving husband and penitent dad. Having Deedee in the courtroom will soften him, make him more sympathetic to the jury."

"Ah. I take it you didn't go along with their plan?"

"Of course not. I told them Angela wanted me to raise her daughter and that I would be adopting Deedee."

"How did that go?"

She shivered. "Eddie's father said that no custody court would give a baby to a single woman with few financial means when the father wanted the child and had the resources to provide for her future."

"And you said…?"

She bit her lip. "I told them I was engaged to my college sweetheart and that you had a boatload of money and you loved Deedee like your own. And then I hightailed it out of there."

Luc actually had the gall to laugh.

"It's not funny," she wailed, leaping to her feet. "This is serious."

He topped off her wineglass once again. "Relax, Hattie. I have more lawyers than a dog has fleas. Deedee is safe. I give you my word."

Her legs went weak and she plopped into her chair. "Really? You mean that?" Suspicion reared its ugly head. "Why?"

He leaned back, studying her with a laserlike gaze that made her want to hide. He saw too much. "My motivation shouldn't matter…right, Hattie? If I really am your last resort?" Something in his bland words made her shiver.

She licked her lips, feeling as if she was making a bargain with the devil. "Are you sure you're willing to do this?"

"I never say anything I don't mean. You should know that. We'll make your lie a reality. I have the best legal counsel in Atlanta. Angela's wishes will prevail."

"I'll sign a prenup," she said. "I don't want your money."

His gaze iced over. "You made that clear a decade ago, Hattie. No need to flog a dead horse."

Her stomach clenched. Why was it that he could make her feel so small with one look?

When she remained silent, he stood up with visible impatience. "I know you need to get the little one in bed before it gets any later. I'll have my team draw up some documents, and then in a few days, you and I can go over the details."

"Details?" she asked weakly.

His grin was feral. "Surely you know I'll have a few stipulations of my own."

Her throat tightened and she took one last swallow of wine. It burned going down like it was whiskey. "Of course. You have to protect your interests. That makes sense." For some reason she couldn't quite fathom, the specter of sex had unexpectedly entered the room. Her mouth was so dry she could barely speak.

Surely lawyers didn't use legalese to dictate sex…did they?

Suddenly an unpalatable thought struck her. "Um…Luc…I should have asked. Is there anyone who will… I mean…who is…um…"

He cocked his head, one broad shoulder propped against the door frame. His face was serious, but humor danced in his eyes. "Are you asking if I'm seeing anyone, Hattie? Isn't it a bit late to worry about that…now that you've told everyone I'm your fiancé?"

Mortified didn't begin to describe how she felt. "Not everyone," she muttered.

"Just the Mob?" He chuckled out loud, enjoying her discomfiture a little too much. Finally, he sobered. "You let me worry about my personal life, Hattie. Your job is to take care of yourself and that little girl—" He stopped abruptly. "Speaking of jobs…what happened? Why aren't you teaching?" She had majored in math at Emory and had gone directly from college to a high school faculty position.

"I had to take a leave of absence for the rest of the year when the accident happened."

He sobered completely now, stepping close enough to run a hand over her hair. She'd worn it loose tonight. "You've been through a hell of a lot," he said softly, their bodies almost touching. "But things will get better."

She smiled wistfully. "Somedays it seems as if nothing will ever be the same."

"I didn't say it would be the same."

For some reason, the words struck her as a threat. She looked up at him, their breath mingling. "What do you get out of this? Why did you agree to back up an impulsive lie by a woman you haven't seen in ten years?"

"Are you trying to talk me out of it?"

"Tell me why you agreed. I was ninety percent sure you'd throw me out of your office on my fanny."

"I can be kind on occasion." The sarcasm was impossible to miss.

She searched his face. It hurt knowing that it was as familiar to her as if they had parted yesterday. "There's something more," she said slowly. "I can see it in your eyes."

His expression shuttered. "Let's just say I have my reasons." His tone was gruff and said more loudly than words that he was done with the conversation.

He was shutting her out. And it stung. But they were little more than strangers now. Strangers who had once made love with passionate abandon, but strangers nevertheless.

"I have to go."

He didn't argue. He ushered her in front of him until they entered a pleasant room outfitted as a den. Ana, despite her years, was down on an Oriental rug playing with a sleepy Deedee.

Hattie rushed forward to scoop up the drowsy baby and nuzzle her sweet-smelling neck. “Did she nap for you at all?”

Ana stood with dignity and straightened the skirt of her floral cotton housedress. “She slept about forty-five minutes…enough to keep her awake until you can get her home and in bed. Your daughter is precious, Ms. Parker, an absolute angel.”

“She’s not my daughter, she’s my niece…but thank you.” Did the housekeeper think Luc had brought his love child home for a visit?

Her host grew impatient with the female chitchat. “I’ll walk you out, Hattie.”

Sherman waited respectfully by the car door, making any sort of personal conversation awkward. Luc surprised Hattie by taking Deedee without ceremony and tucking her expertly into the small seat.

She lifted an eyebrow. “You did that well.”

He touched the baby’s cheek and stepped aside so Hattie could enter the limo. “It’s not rocket science.” He braced an arm on the top of the car and leaned in. “I’ll look forward to seeing you both again soon.”

“You’ll call me?”

“I’ll get Marilyn to contact you and set up a meeting. It will probably only take a couple of days. You need to go ahead and start packing.”

“Packing?” She was starting to sound like a slightly dense parrot. What had she gotten herself into? Luc was helping her, but with strings attached. She had known his every thought at one time. Now he was an enigma.

His half smile made her think of a predator anticipating his prey. “You and Deedee will be moving in here as soon as the wedding is over.”

Three

Two days later, Luc tapped briefly at his brother's office door and entered. Leo, his senior by little more than a year, was almost hidden behind piles of paperwork and books. A genius by any measure, Leo masterminded the financial empire, while Luc handled R & D. Luc enjoyed the challenge of developing new products, finding the next creative venture.

Leo was the one who made them all rich.

It was a full thirty seconds before his brother looked up from what he was doing. "Luc. Didn't expect to see you today."

The brothers met formally twice a month, and it wasn't unusual for them to lunch together a few times a week, but Luc rarely dropped by his brother's sanctum unannounced. Their offices were on different floors of the building, and more often than not, their customary mode of communication was texting.

Luc ignored the comfortable, overstuffed easy chair that flanked Leo's desk and instead, chose to cross the room and stand by the window. He never tired of gazing at Atlanta's distinctive skyline.

He rolled his shoulders, unaware until that moment that his neck was tight. He turned and smiled. "What are you doing on May 14?"

Leo tapped a key and glanced at his computer screen. "Looks clear. What's up?"

"I thought you might like to be my best man."

Now Luc had Leo's full attention. His older sibling, though still a couple inches shorter than Luc's six-three, was an imposing man. Built like a mountain, he looked more like a lumberjack than a numbers whiz.

He escaped the confines of his desk and cleared a front corner to lean on his hip and stare at his brother. "You're pulling my chain, right?"

"Why would you say that?"

"Three weeks ago I suggested you bring a date to Carole Ann's party, and you told me you weren't seeing anyone."

Luc shrugged. "Things happen."

Leo scowled, a black expression that had been known to make underlings quake in terror. "I can read you like a book. You're up to something. The last time I saw that exact look on your face, you were trying to convince Dad to let you take the Maserati for a weekend trip to Daytona."

"I have my own sports cars. I'm not trying to pull anything."

"You know what I mean." He changed tack. "Do I know her?"

Luc shrugged. "You've met."

"How long have *you* known her? It's not like you to go all misty-eyed over a one-night stand."

"I can assure you that I've known her for a very long time."

"But you've just now realized you're in love."

"A man doesn't have to be in love to want a woman."

"So it's lust."

"I think we've gotten off track. I asked if you would be my best man. A simple yes or no will do."

"Damn it, Luc. Quit being so mysterious. Who is she? Will I get to see her anytime soon?"

"I haven't decided. We've been concentrating on each other. I don't want to spoil things. Just promise me you'll show up when and where I say on the fourteenth. In a tux."

The silence was deafening. Finally, Leo stood up and stretched. "I don't like the sound of this. When it all goes to hell, don't come crying to me. Your libido is a piss-poor businessman. Be smart, baby brother. Women are generally not worth the bother."

Luc understood his brother's caution. They had both been burned by love at a tender age, but thankfully had wised up pretty fast. What Leo didn't know, though, was that Luc had a plan. *Revenge* was a strong word for what he had in mind. He didn't hate Hattie Parker. Quite the contrary. All he wanted was for her to understand that while he might still find her sexually attractive, he was completely immune to any emotional connection. No hearts and flowers. No protestations of undying devotion.

He was no longer a kid yearning for a pretty girl. This time *he* had the power. *He* would be calling all the shots. Hattie needed him, and her vulnerability meant that Luc would have her in his house…in his bed…under his control. Perhaps *revenge was* too strong a word. But when all was said and done, Hattie Parker would be out of his system… for good.

Hattie was ready to scream. Moving anytime was a huge chore, but add a baby to the mix, and the process was darned near impossible. She'd finally gotten Deedee down for a nap and was wrapping breakables in the kitchen when her cell phone rang. She jerked it up and snarled, "What?"

The long silence at the other end was embarrassing.

"Sorry," she said, her throat tight with tears of frustration.

Luc's distinctive tones were laced with humor. "I don't think I've ever heard you lose your temper. I kind of like it."

"Don't be silly," she said, shoving a lock of damp hair from her forehead. "What do you want?"

"Nothing in particular. I was checking in to see if you needed anything."

"A trio of muscular guys would be nice."

Another silence. "Kinky," he said, his voice amused but perhaps a tad hoarse.

Her face flamed, though he couldn't see her. "To help with moving," she muttered. "I wouldn't know what else to do with them. This mothering thing is hard work."

"Why, Hattie Parker. Are you hinting for help?"

"Maybe." Deedee was a good baby, but being a single parent was difficult. Hattie no longer felt as panicked as she had in the beginning. Much of the daily routine of dealing with an infant seemed easier now. But Deedee had been restless the three nights since Hattie had dined with Luc. Perhaps the baby was picking up on Hattie's unsettled emotions. And to make matters worse, Eddie had begun sending a harassing string of vague emails and texts. Clearly to keep Hattie on edge. And it was working.

Luc sighed audibly. "I would have hired a moving crew already, but you're always so damned independent, I thought you would pitch a fit and insist on doing it yourself."

"I've grown up, Luc. Some battles simply aren't worth fighting. I know when I'm in over my head."

"I'm sorry. I made a stupid assumption. It won't happen again."

The conversation lagged once more. She looked at the chaos in her kitchen and sighed. "Do you know yet when we're going to sit down and go over the finer points of our marriage agreement?"

"I thought perhaps tomorrow evening. When does Deedee go down for the night?"

"Usually by eight…if I'm lucky."

"What if I come over to your place then, so she won't have to be displaced. I'll bring food."

"That would be great."

"Have you heard any more from your brother-in-law?"

"Nothing specific." No need at the moment to involve Luc in Eddie's bluster. "He likes to throw his weight around. Right now, he's got the perfect setup. I'm babysitting for him, but when he's ready, he'll grab Deedee."

"I hope you don't mean that literally."

"He's not that stupid. At least, I don't think he is."

"Try not to worry, Hattie. Everything is going to fall into place."

For once, it seemed as if Luc was right. Deedee went to sleep the following evening without a whimper. Hattie found an unworn blouse in the back of her closet with the tags still attached. She'd snagged it from a clearance rack at Bloomingdale's last January, and the thin, silky fabric, a pale peach floral, was the perfect weight for a spring evening.

Paired with soft, well-worn jeans, the top made her look nice but casual…not like she was trying too hard to impress. Unfortunately, Luc showed up ten minutes early, and she was forced to open the door in her bare feet.

His eyes flashed with masculine appreciation when he saw her. "You don't look frazzled to me, Hattie."

She stepped back to let him in. "Thanks. Today was much calmer, maybe because the moving company you hired promised to be here first thing in the morning. And I was able to actually take a shower, because the baby took a two-hour morning nap."

As she closed the door, he surveyed her apartment. "No offense, but I don't see any point in storing most of this stuff. Let the movers take the bulk of it to charity, and bring only the things that are personal or sentimental with you."

She bit her lip. It had occurred to her that this subject would have to be broached, but she hadn't anticipated it would come so soon. "The thing is…"

"What are you trying to say?" He tossed the duffel bag he'd been carrying in a chair and deposited two cloth grocery bags in the kitchen. Then he turned to face her. "Is there a problem?"

She shifted from one foot to the other. Luc was wearing a suit and tie, and she felt like Daisy Duke facing off with Daddy Warbucks. "This union won't last forever. After all the money you're spending to help Deedee and me, you shouldn't have to finance the next phase of my life, as well. I thought it might be prudent to have something to fall back on in the future."

He nudged a corner of her navy plaid futon/chair with the toe of his highly polished wing tip, giving the sad, misshapen piece a dismissive glance. "When that happens, I won't cast off you and the child to live with cheap, secondhand furniture. I have a reputation to uphold in this town. Image is everything. You're going to have to face the truth, Hattie. You're marrying a rich man—whether you like it or not."

The mockery in his words and on his face was not veiled this time. He was lashing out at her for what she'd done in the past. Fair enough. Back then she had made a big deal about their stations in life. Luc's money gave him power, and Hattie had been taught at her mother's knee never to let a man have control.

The man Hattie called "daddy" was really her stepfather.

As a nineteen-year-old, her mother had been that most naive of clichés…the secretary who had an affair with her boss. When Hattie's mom told her lover she was pregnant, he tossed her aside and never looked back.

Hattie lifted her chin. "It was never about the money," she insisted. "Or not *only* the money. Look at what your life has become, Luc. You're the CEO of a Fortune 500 company. I'm a public school teacher. I clip coupons and drive a ten-year-old car. Even before I began helping with my mother's finances, I lived a very simple lifestyle."

He curled a lip. "Is this where I cue the violins?"

"Oh, forget it," she huffed. "This is an old argument. What's the point?"

He shrugged. "What's the point indeed?" He picked up the duffel bag. "Dinner will keep a few minutes. Do you mind if I change clothes? I came straight from the office."

"The baby is asleep in my room, but the bathroom's all yours. I'll set out the food."

She had rummaged in the bags only long enough to see that Luc's largesse was nothing as common as pizza, when a loud knock sounded at the door. She glanced through the peephole and drew in a breath. Eddie. Good grief. Reluctantly, she opened the door.

He reeked of alcohol and swayed slightly on his feet. "Where's my baby girl? I want to see her."

She shushed him with a quick glance over her shoulder. "She's in bed. Babies sleep at this hour of night. Why don't you call me in the morning, and we'll agree on a time for you to come by?"

He stuck a foot in the doorway, effectively keeping her from closing him out. "Or why don't I call the police and tell them you've kidnapped my kid?"

It was an idle threat. They both knew it. Hattie had already consulted a lawyer, and a nurse at the hospital had heard

Angela's dying request. Nevertheless, Eddie's bluster curled Hattie's stomach. She didn't want to be in the middle of a fight with Deedee as the prize.

"Go away, Eddie," she said forcefully, her voice low. "This isn't a good time. We'll talk tomorrow."

Without warning, he grabbed her shoulders and manhandled her backward into the apartment. "Like hell." He shoved her so hard, she stumbled into the wall. Her head hit with a muffled thud, and she saw little yellow spots.

He lunged for her again, but before his meaty fists could make contact, Luc exploded down the hallway, grabbed the intruder by the neck and put a chokehold on him. Eddie's face turned an alarming shade of purple before Hattie could catch her breath.

Luc was steely-eyed. "Call the cops."

"But I don't want..."

His expression gentled. "It's the right thing to do. Don't worry. I'm not leaving you to deal with this alone."

The response to the 911 call was gratifying. Just before the two uniformed officers arrived, Luc stuck his face nose to nose with Eddie's. "If I ever see you near my fiancée again, I'll tear you apart. Got it?"

Eddie was drunk enough to be reckless. "Fiancée? Yeah, right. If she was telling my daddy the truth about you and her, then where's the fancy diamond ring?"

"I had to order it," Luc responded smoothly. "It happens to be in my pocket even as we speak. But some jackass has ruined our romantic evening."

The conversation ended abruptly as Hattie opened the door to the police. They took Luc's statement, handcuffed Eddie and were gone in under twenty minutes.

In the sudden silence, Hattie dropped into a chair, her legs boneless and weak in the aftermath of adrenaline. Thank God the baby hadn't been awakened by all the commotion.

Luc crouched beside her, his eyes filled with concern. "Let me see your head." He parted her hair gently, exclaiming when he saw the goose egg that had popped up.

She moved restlessly. "I'm fine. Really. All I need is some Tylenol. And a good night's sleep."

Luc cursed under his breath. "Don't move." After bringing her medicine and water with which to wash down the tablets, he created a makeshift ice bag with a dish towel and pressed it to the side of her head. "Hold this." He lifted her in his arms and laid her gently on the ugly sofa. "Rest. I'll fix us a couple of plates."

He was back in no time. The smells alone made Hattie want to whimper with longing. Her stomach growled loudly.

He put a hand on her shoulder. "No need to get up yet. I'll feed you."

"Don't be ridiculous." But when she tried to sit upright, her skull pounded.

He eased her back down. "You don't have to fight me over every damn thing. Open your mouth." He fed her small manageable bites of chicken piccata and wild rice. While she chewed and swallowed, he dug into his own portion.

Hattie muttered in frustration when one of her mouthfuls landed on the sofa cushion. "See what you made me do…"

"Don't worry," he deadpanned. "A few stains could only help this monstrosity."

She eyed him, openmouthed, and then they both burst into laughter. Hattie felt tears sting the backs of her eyes. She told herself it was nothing more than delayed reaction. But in truth, it was Luc. When he forgot to be on his guard with her, she saw a glimpse of the young man she had loved so desperately.

She wondered with no small measure of guilt if her long-ago defection had transformed the boy she once knew so well into the hard-edged, sardonic Luc. A million times over the years she had second-guessed her decision. It had been gratifying to establish a career and to stand on her own two feet. Her mother had been proud of Hattie's independence and success in her chosen field.

But at what cost?

When the last of the food was consumed, the mood grew awkward. Luc gathered their empty plates. "Stay where you are. You have to deal with Deedee in the morning, so you might as well rest while you can."

She lay there quietly, wondering bleakly how her life had unraveled so quickly. Two months ago she'd been an ordinary single woman with a circle of friends, a good job and a pleasant social life. Now she was a substitute parent facing a custody battle and trying to combat a tsunami of feelings for the man who had once upon a time been her other half, her soul mate. Was it any wonder she felt overwhelmed?

A trickle of water from melting ice slid down her cheek. She sat up and sucked in a breath when a hammer thudded inside her skull. The food she had eaten rolled unpleasantly in her stomach.

Luc frowned as he rejoined her, pausing only to take the wet dish towel and toss it on a kitchen counter. "We probably should make a trip to the E.R. to make sure you don't have a concussion."

"I'll be fine." She knew her voice lacked conviction, but it was hard to be stoic with the mother of all headaches.

Luc put his hands on his hips, his navy polo shirt stretching taut over broad shoulders and a hard chest. "I'll stay the night."

Four

Hattie gaped. “Oh, no. Not necessary.”

“We have the baby to think of, too. You probably won’t rest very well tonight, and you’ll likely need an extra hand in the morning. I’ll sleep on the couch. It may be ugly as sin, but it’s long and fairly comfortable. I’ll be fine.”

Hattie was torn. Having Luc in her small apartment was unsettling, but the encounter with Eddie had shaken her emotionally as well as physically, and she was dead on her feet.

She shrugged, conceding defeat. “I’ll get you towels and bedding.” She brushed by him, inhaling for a brief instant the tang of citrusy aftershave and the scent of warm male.

When she returned moments later, he was on the phone with Ana, letting her know he wouldn’t be home that evening. It touched her that he would be so considerate of people who were in his employ. He was a grown man. He had no obligation to let anyone know his schedule or his whereabouts.

But wasn’t that what had drawn her to him in the beginning?

His kindness and his humor? Sadly, his personality had an edge now, a remoteness that had not existed before.

She began making up the sofa, but he stopped her as soon as he hung up. “Go to bed, Hattie. I’m not a guest. I don’t need you waiting on me. I can fend for myself.”

She nodded stiffly. “Good night, then.”

He lifted a shoulder, looking diffident for a moment. “May I see her?”

“The baby?” Well, duh. Who else could he mean?

“Yes.”

“Of course.”

He followed her down the short hallway into the bedroom. A small night-light illuminated the crib. Luc put his hands on the railing and stared down at the infant sleeping so peacefully. Hattie hung back. Her chest was tight with confused emotions. Had things gone differently in the past, this scene might have played out in reality.

A couple, she and Luc, putting their own daughter to bed before retiring for the night.

Luc reached out a hand, hovered briefly, then lightly stroked Deedee’s hair. She never stirred. He spoke softly, his back still toward Hattie. “She doesn’t deserve what has happened to her.”

Hattie shook her head, eyes stinging. “No. She doesn’t. I can’t let Eddie take her. She’s so innocent, so perfect.”

Luc turned, his strong, masculine features shadowed in the half-light. His somber gaze met her wary one, some intangible link between them shrouding the moment in significance. “We’ll keep her safe, Hattie. You have my word.”

Quietly, he left the room.

Hattie changed into a gown and robe. Ordinarily, she slept in a T-shirt and panties, but with Luc in the house, she needed extra armor.

She folded the comforter and turned back the covers before

heading for the bathroom. Well, shoot. She'd forgotten to give Luc even the basics. Taking a new toothbrush from the cabinet, she returned to the living room. "Sorry. I meant to give you this. There's toothpaste on the counter, and if you want to shave in the morning—"

She stopped dead, her pulse jumping. Luc stood before her wearing nothing but a pair of gray knit boxers, which left little to the imagination. Every inch of his body was fit and tight. His skin was naturally olive-toned, and the dusting of fine black hair on his chest made her want to stroke it to see if it was as soft as she remembered.

Long muscular thighs led upward to… She gulped. As she watched in fascination, his erection grew and flexed. She literally couldn't move. Luc didn't seem at all embarrassed, despite the fact that her face was hot enough to fry an egg.

"Thank you for the toothbrush." A half smile lifted one corner of his mouth.

She extended the cellophane-wrapped package gingerly, making sure her fingers didn't touch his. "You're welcome."

And still she didn't leave. The years rolled away. She remembered with painful clarity what it was like to be held tightly to that magnificent chest, to feel those strong arms pull her close, to experience the hard evidence of his arousal thrusting against her abdomen.

His gaze was hooded, the line of his mouth now almost grim. "Like what you see?"

The mockery was deliberate, she had no doubt…as if to say *you were so foolish back then. Look what you gave up.*

Heat flooded her body. The robe stifled her. She wanted to tear it off, to fling herself at Luc. But her limbs couldn't move. She was paralyzed, caught between bitter memories of the past and the sure knowledge that Luc Cavallo was still the man who could make her soar with pleasure.

"Answer me, Hattie," he said roughly. "If you're going

to look at me like that, I'm damn sure going to take the invitation."

Her lips parted. No sound came out.

The color on his cheekbones darkened and his eyes flared with heat. "Come here."

No soft preliminaries. No tentative approach.

Luc was confident, controlled. He touched only her face, sliding his hands beneath her hair and holding her still so his mouth could ravage hers. His tongue thrust between her lips—invading, dominant, taking and not giving. She was shaking all over, barely able to stand. He kissed her harder still, muttering something to himself she didn't quite catch.

She felt the push of his hips. Suddenly, her body came to life with painful tingles of heat. Her arms went around his waist, and she kissed him back. But when his fingers accidentally brushed the painful knot on her skull, she flinched.

Instantly, he cursed and thrust her away, his gaze a cross between anger and incredulity. "Damn you. Go to bed, Hattie."

If she had been a Victorian heroine, she might have swooned at this very moment. But she was made of sterner stuff. She marshaled her defenses, muttered a strangled good-night and fled.

Aeons later it seemed, she rolled over and flung an arm over her face. Bright sunshine peeked in through a crack between the curtains. She had slept like the dead, deeply, dreamlessly. A glance at the clock stopped her heart. It was nine o'clock. Deedee. Dear heaven. The baby was always up by six-thirty.

She leaped from the bed, almost taking a nosedive when the covers tangled around her feet. The crib was empty. She sucked in a panicked breath, and then her sleep-fuddled brain began to function.

Luc. Memories of his kiss tightened her nipples and made her thighs clench with longing. She touched her lips as the hot sting of tears made her blink and sniff. Ten years was a lifetime to wait for something that was at once so terrible and so wonderful.

She opened her bedroom door and simultaneously heard the sound of childish gurgles and smelled the heavenly aroma of frying bacon. Luc stood by the stove. Deedee was tucked safely in her high chair nearby.

He glanced up, his features impassive. "Good morning."

The baby squealed in delight and lurched toward Hattie. Luc unfastened the tray and handed her off. "I fed her a bottle and half a jar of peaches. I didn't want to give her anything else until I checked with you." The words were gruff, as if he'd had to force them from his throat.

Hattie cuddled the baby, stunned that Luc had taken over with such relaxed competence. Not that she didn't think he was capable. But she had never witnessed him with children, and she was shocked to see him so calm and in control, especially when Hattie herself had experienced a few rough moments in the last six weeks.

He started cracking eggs into a bowl. "This will be ready in five, and the movers will be showing up shortly. You might want to get dressed. I can handle Deedee."

Hattie held the baby close, realizing with chagrin that she had jumped out of bed and never actually donned her robe. The sheer fabric of her nightie revealed far too much. "She'll be fine with me." Suddenly she noticed the sheaf of legal papers on the nearby coffee table. "Luc…I'm so sorry. With everything that happened, we never did get around to dealing with the marriage stuff."

He popped two slices of bread into her toaster. "No worries. We'll have time later today."

She hesitated, eager to leave the room, but feeling oddly abashed that he had watched her sleeping…without her knowledge. Though they had made love many times when they were together, only once or twice had they enjoyed the luxury of spending the night together.

She cleared her throat. "Thank you for getting up with the baby. I can't believe I didn't hear her."

He shrugged. "I'm an early riser. I enjoyed spending time with her. She's a charming child."

"You haven't seen her throw a temper tantrum yet," she joked. "Batten down the hatches. She has a great set of lungs."

He paused his efficient preparations, the spatula in midair. "You're doing a great job. She's lucky to have you as her mother." His eyes and his voice were serious.

"Thanks." Despite the task he had undertaken, nothing about the setting made Luc look at all domestic: quite the opposite. Luc Cavallo was the kind of man you'd want by your side during a forced jungle march. He possessed a self-confidence that was absolute.

But that resolute belief in his own ability to direct the universe to his liking made Hattie uneasy. In asking for his help, she had unwittingly given him the very power she had refused to allow in their previous relationship. Even if she had second thoughts now, the situation was already beyond her control.

The contents of the small apartment were packed, boxes loaded and rooms emptied by 12:30. Luc had already paid out the remainder of Hattie's lease. All that was left for her to do was turn in her keys to the super and follow Luc out to the car where Sherman was waiting. But there she balked. "I'll follow you in my car."

Luc frowned. "I thought we had this discussion."

"I like my car. I'm sentimentally attached to my car. I'm not giving it away."

The standoff lasted only a few seconds. Luc shrugged, his expression resigned. "I'll see you at the house."

It was a small victory, but it made Hattie feel better. Luc had a habit of taking charge in ways that ostensibly made perfect sense, but left Hattie feeling like a helpless damsel in distress. She had *asked* for his help, but that didn't mean she'd let him walk all over her.

She strapped Deedee into the old, shabby car seat and slid into the front, turning the key in the ignition and praying the car would start. That would be the final indignity.

As their little caravan pulled away from the curb, Hattie glanced in the rearview mirror for one last look at her old life slipping away. Her emotions were not easy to define. Relief. Sadness. Anticipation. Had she sold her soul to the devil? Only time would tell.

Luc experienced a sharp but distinct jolt of satisfaction when Hattie stepped over his threshold. Something primitive in him exulted. She was coming to him of her own free will. She'd be under his roof…wearing his ring. Ten years ago he'd let his pride keep him from trying to get her back. That, and his misguided belief that he had to respect her wishes. But everything was different this time around. *He* was calling the shots.

The attraction was still there. He felt it, and he knew she did, as well. Soon she would turn to him out of sheer gratitude, or unfulfilled desire or loneliness. And then she would be his. He'd waited a long time for this. And no one could fault him. He was giving Hattie and her baby a home and security.

If he extracted his pound of flesh in the process, it was only fair. She owed him that much.

He left them to get settled in, with Sherman and Ana hovering eagerly. After changing clothes, he drove to the office and threw himself into the pile of work that had accumulated during his unaccustomed morning off.

But for once, his concentration was shot. He found himself wishing he was back at the house, watching Hattie...playing with the baby...anticipating the night to come.

He called home on the drive back. It wasn't late, only six-thirty. Hattie answered her cell.

"Hello, Luc."

He returned the greeting and said, "Ana has offered to look after Deedee this evening. I thought we might go out for a quiet dinner and discuss business."

Business? He winced. Did he really mean to sound so cavalier?

Hattie's response was cool. "I don't want to take advantage of Ana's good nature."

"You're not, I swear. It was her idea. Little Deedee has a way of making people fall in love with her. I'll be there to pick you up in twenty minutes."

It was only dinner. With a woman who had already rejected him once. Why was his heart beating faster?

Unfortunately for Hattie, the black dress had to do duty again. This time she had no inclination to wear Luc's necklace. Not for a *business* dinner. She tied a narrow tangerine scarf around her neck and inserted plain gold hoops in her ears.

She was ready and waiting in the foyer when he walked in the front door.

Luc seemed disappointed. "Where's the baby?"

Hattie grimaced, her nerves jumping. "She's taking an early evening nap. I couldn't get her to sleep much at all this afternoon…the uncertainty of a new place, I think. She was cranky and exhausted."

"Too bad. Well, in that case, I guess we can get going."

The restaurant was lovely—very elegant, and yet not so pretentious that Hattie felt uncomfortable. The sommelier chatted briefly with Luc and then produced a zinfandel that met with Luc's approval.

Hattie was persuaded to try a glass. "It's really good," she said. "Fruity but not too sweet."

He leaned back in his chair. "I thought you'd like it."

They enjoyed a quiet dinner, sticking to innocuous topics, and then afterward, Luc reached into a slim leather folder and extracted a sheaf of papers. "My lawyers have drawn up all the necessary documents. If you wish, you're welcome to have a third-party lawyer go over them with you. I know from experience that legalese is hard to wade through at times."

She took the documents and eyed them cautiously. "I have someone who has been helping me with the custody issues," she said, already skimming the lines of print. "I'll get her to take a look." Most of it was self-explanatory. When she reached page three of the prenup, her eyebrows raised. "It says here that if and when the marriage dissolves, I'll be entitled to a lump sum payment of $500,000."

He drummed the fingers of one hand on the table. His skin was dark against the snowy-white cloth. "You don't think that's fair?"

"I think it's outrageous. You don't owe me anything. You're doing me a huge favor. I don't plan to walk away with half a million dollars. Put something aside for Deedee's education if you want to, but we need to strike that line."

His jaw tightened. "The line stays. That's a deal breaker."

She studied his face, puzzled and upset. "I don't understand."

He scowled at her, his posture combative. "You've thrown

my wealth in my face the entire time I've known you, Hattie. And now you're using it to protect someone you love. I don't have a problem with that. But I'll be damned when that day comes if I'll let anyone say I threw you out on the street destitute."

Her lip trembled, and she bit down on it…hard. Luc was a proud man. Perhaps until now she had never really understood just how proud he was. She was sure his heart had healed after she broke up with him. But maybe the dent to his pride was not so easily repaired.

She owed him a sign of faith. It was the least she could do after treating him so shabbily in the past. He was an honorable man. That much hadn't changed. She reached into her purse for a pen and turned to the first yellow sticky tab. With a flourish, she signed her name.

He put a hand over hers. "Are you sure you don't want someone to look over this with you?"

She shivered inwardly at his touch. "I'm sure," she said, her words ragged.

He released her and watched intently as she signed one page after another. When it was all done, she handed the documents back to him. "Is that it?"

Luc tucked the paperwork away. "I have a couple of other things I think we need to discuss, but it requires a private setting. We'll be more comfortable at home."

"Oh." Her scintillating response didn't faze him. He seemed perfectly calm. He summoned their waiter, paid the check and stood to pull out her chair. As they exited the restaurant, she was hyperaware of his warm hand resting in the small of her back.

Hattie was silent on the drive back. Her skin was hot, her stomach pitchy. What on earth could he mean? Sex? It seemed the obvious topic, but she had assumed they might work up to that gradually…after they were married. She hadn't anticipated talking about it so bluntly or openly. They had been as close as two people could be once upon a time. But that was long, long ago.

Was she willing to go to his bed? To be his wife in every sense of the word? He was well within his rights as a husband to insist.

Did she expect him to be faithful in the context of a sham marriage? And if Luc no longer wanted to be intimate with Hattie, was it fair to deny him physical satisfaction?

She wouldn't lie to herself. She wanted Luc.

Dear Lord, what was she going to say?

In a cowardly play for more time, she stalled when they got back to the house. "I'd like to check on the baby and change clothes. Is that okay? It won't take me long."

Luc dropped his keys into the exquisite Baccarat dish on the table in the foyer. "Take your time. I'll meet you in the den when you're ready."

Five

Wearing ancient jeans and a faded Emory T-shirt, Luc sprawled on the leather sofa and stared moodily at the blank television screen. Was he insane? *Power.* A nice fantasy. Clearly he was fooling himself. What man was ever really in control when his brain ceded authority to a less rational part of his body?

Just being close to Hattie these last few days had caused him to resort to cold showers. He told himself that his physical response to her was nothing more than a knee-jerk reaction to memories…to sensual images of the way he and Hattie had burned up the sheets.

She'd been a virgin when they met, a shy, reserved girl with big eyes and a wary take on the world. As if she was never quite sure someone wasn't going to pull the rug out from under her feet.

He'd been embarrassed to tell her how many girls he'd been with before meeting her. A horny teenager with unlimited money at his disposal was a dangerous combination. In high school, he'd been too concerned about keeping his body in shape for sports to dabble in drugs. And even drinking, a rite of passage for adolescent boys, didn't hold much allure. Perhaps because he had grown up in a house where alcohol was freely available and handled wisely.

But sex…hell, he'd had a lot of sex. Money equals power… even sixteen-year-old girls could figure that out. So Luc was never without female companionship, unless he chose to hang with his buddies.

When Hattie came into his life, everything changed. She was different. She liked him, but his money didn't interest her. At first, he thought her attitude might be a ploy to snag his attention. But as they got to know each other, he realized that she really didn't give a damn that he was loaded.

She expected thoughtfulness from him, attention to her likes and dislikes. She wanted him to *know* her. And that was something money couldn't buy.

It was only much, much later that he realized his money was actually a stumbling block.

A faint noise made him turn his head. Hattie hovered in the doorway, her sun-streaked blond hair pulled back into a short ponytail, her feet bare. She was dressed as casually as he was.

He patted the seat beside him. "Would you like more wine?" The upcoming conversation might flow more easily if she relaxed.

She shook her head as she perched gingerly on the far end of the couch, tucking her legs beneath her. "No, thanks. Water would be nice." Her toenails were painted pale pink. The sight of them did odd things to his gut.

He went to the fridge behind the bar, extracted two Perriers and handed her one. As he sat back down, he allowed the careful distance she had created to remain between them. It meant she was nervous, and that gave him an edge. He handed her a slim white envelope. "We'll start with this." Inside were three credit cards with her soon-to-be name, Hattie Parker Cavallo, already imprinted.

She extracted them with patent reluctance. "What are these?"

He stretched an arm along the back of the sofa. "As my wife, you'll need a large wardrobe. I entertain frequently, and I also travel often. When it's feasible, I'd like you and Deedee to accompany me. In addition, I want you to outfit the nursery upstairs. I've put a selection of baby furniture catalogs in the desk drawer in your bedroom. Ana will show you the suite I picked out for Deedee. If it doesn't meet with your approval, we'll decide on another."

She paled, her eyes dark and haunted.

He ground his teeth. "What's wrong?"

She shrugged helplessly. "I…I feel like you're taking over my life. Like I've lost all control."

His fists clenched instinctively, and he had to force himself to relax. "I understood there was some sense of urgency to the situation…that we needed to back up your lie quickly."

"There is…and we do…but…"

"But what? Do you disagree with any of the arrangements I've made thus far?"

"No, of course not."

"Then I don't understand the problem."

She jumped to her feet and paced. With her back to him, he could see the way the soft, worn jeans cupped her butt. It was a very nice butt. With an effort, he dragged his attention back to the current crisis.

She whirled to face him. "I'm used to taking care of myself." The words were almost a shout.

Something inside him went still…crouched like a tiger in waiting. He feigned a disinterest he didn't feel. "We don't have to get married at all, Hattie. My team of lawyers loves going for the kill. Custody situations aren't their usual fare, but with Eddie in self-destruct mode, it shouldn't be too hard to convince a judge that you're the obvious choice to raise Deedee." He paused, risking everything on a gamble, a single toss of the dice. "Is that what you want?"

Hattie pressed two fingers to the center of the forehead, clearly in pain. Her entire body language projected misery. "I want my sister back," she said…and as he watched, tears spilled down her wan cheeks.

He tried to leave her alone, he really did. But her heartbreak twisted something inside his chest. She didn't protest when he took her in his arms, when he pulled the elastic band from her ponytail and stroked her hair, careful not to further hurt her injury.

She felt fragile in his embrace, but he knew better. Her backbone was steel, her moral compass a straight arrow.

The quiet sobs didn't last long. He felt and sensed the moment she pulled herself together. She stiffened in his embrace. Though it went against his every inclination, he released her and returned to his seat on the sofa. He took a swig of sparkling water and waited her out.

She studied a painting on the wall. It was a Vermeer he'd picked up at an auction in New York last year. The obscure work immortalized a young woman in her tiny boudoir as she bent at the waist to fasten her small shoe. The play of light on the girl's graceful frame fascinated Luc. He'd bought it on a whim, but it had quickly become one of his favorite pieces. Impulse drove him at times—witness the way he'd agreed so quickly to this sham marriage.

But in the end, his impulses usually served him well.

He grew impatient. "I asked you a question, Hattie. Do you want this marriage? Tell me."

She turned at last, her fists clenched at her sides. "If I don't go through with this, Eddie's family will know I lied. And they'll use it against me. I don't have a choice."

Her fatalistic attitude nicked his pride. His heart hardened, words tumbling out like cold stones. "Then we'll do this my way. You can't run out on me this time, Hattie. I love irony, don't you?"

His sarcasm scraped her nerves. She was being so unfair. Luc had done everything she had asked of him and more. He didn't deserve her angst and criticism. She owed him more than she could ever calculate.

The fact that her body still ached for his only complicated matters.

Swallowing her aversion to the feeling that she was being bought and paid for, she sat back down and summoned a faint smile. "Giving a woman that much plastic is dangerous. Should we discuss a budget?"

His expression was inscrutable. "I know you pretty well, Hattie Parker. I doubt seriously if you'll bankrupt me." He reached in his pocket and pulled out a small velvet box, laying it on the cushion between them. "This is next on the agenda. I thought it was customary to make such things a surprise, but given your current mood, perhaps I should return it and let you choose your own."

She picked up the box and flipped back the lid. *This* was a flawless diamond solitaire. Clearly he understood her style, because the setting was simple in the extreme. But the rectangular stone that flashed and sparkled was easily four carats.

She bit her lip. "It's lovely," she said, squeezing the words from a tight throat. He made no attempt to take her hand and do the honors. She told herself she was glad. When she slid the ring onto her left hand, the brilliant stone seemed to take on a life of its own.

"So you don't want to exchange it? I wouldn't want to be accused of controlling your life."

His tone was bland, but she felt shame, nevertheless. "I love it, Luc. Thank you."

It was his turn to get up and pace. "I've made some preliminary wedding inquiries. Do you need or want a church wedding?"

Disappointment made her stomach leaden. Like most girls she had dreamed of her wedding day. "No. That's not necessary."

"Our family owns a small private island off the coast, near Savannah. If you're agreeable, we can have the ceremony there. The location precludes the possibility of Eddie or any of his relatives showing up to make a scene. Do you have someone you'd like to stand up with you?"

She picked at a stray thread on the knee of her jeans, her mind in a whirl of conflicting thoughts. "My best friend, Jodi, would have been my choice, but her husband is in the military, and they were transferred to Japan two months ago. With Angela gone, well, I..."

"I'm sure Ana would be honored to help us out."

It was a good choice, and a logical one given the circumstances. "I'll ask her tomorrow."

"A honeymoon will be important," he said, bending to turn on the gas logs in the fireplace. The spring evening had turned cool and damp.

"I'm not sure what you mean."

He turned to face her, his expression blank. "We can't risk any accusation that our marriage isn't real. I know you'll protest, but I really think we should go away for at least a week. Ana's niece is a college student working on her early childhood certification. I've already spoken to her, and she's willing to stay here at the house with Ana and Sherman while we're gone, to help with the baby."

Hattie gnawed her bottom lip. He'd neatly cut the ground from beneath her feet. Every argument anticipated and countered. It all made perfect sense. And it scared the heck out of her. "You seem to have thought of everything."

He shrugged. "It's what I do. As far as the wedding dress and the ceremony itself, I'll leave that to you. I have a good friend who is a justice of the peace. He's prepared to fly down with us and officiate."

"Who's going to be your best man?"

"Leo."

"Does he know about me…about Deedee?"

"I told him I was marrying someone he knew, but I left it at that. Leo will be there. But as far as he is concerned right now, this is a normal marriage. You and I will be the only people who will know the truth."

"You'd lie to your own brother?"

"I'll tell him the situation later…when it's a done deal."

"And your grandfather?"

"He's flying over for his big birthday party in the fall. I won't encourage him to come this time."

"I wonder if Leo will even remember me."

Luc chuckled. "My brother never forgets a beautiful woman. We'll get together with him for dinner when we come back from our honeymoon, and you can reminisce."

Hattie winced inwardly. Leo probably thought she was the worst kind of tease. Leading Luc on back in college and then dumping him. Leo would side with his brother, of course. Just one more thing to look forward to in her new, surreal life.

She took a deep breath. "When are we going to do this?"

"May 14 works for my schedule. I've cleared the week following for our honeymoon. Is there anywhere in particular you'd like to go? The company has a top-notch travel agent."

She smiled faintly. "Since I've never really *been* anywhere, I'll let you choose."

"I thought Key West might be nice…a luxurious villa on a quiet street. A private pool."

Her mouth dried. "Um, sure. Sounds lovely." Why did she suddenly have a vision of the two of them naked and… cavorting in the moonlight? *Dear heaven.* May 14 was two and a half weeks away. This was happening. This was real.

She couldn't wait any longer to address the elephant in the room. Or perhaps she was the only one who was worrying about it. Luc was a guy. Sex came as naturally to him as breathing. He probably thought nature would take its course.

But she needed to have things spelled out. "Luc?"

He rejoined her on the sofa, this time sitting so close to her that their hips nearly touched. Deliberately, he lifted her hand nearest him and linked their fingers. "What, Hattie? Permission to speak freely."

His light humor did nothing to alleviate her nerves. She squeezed his hand briefly and stood up again, unable to bear being so close to him when she was on edge. "I had a feeling earlier this evening…at dinner…that one of the things you wanted to discuss in private was sex. It makes sense…to talk about it, I mean. You're a virile man, and I assume you'll be faithful to our wedding vows. So no one can question the validity of our marriage. For the baby's sake."

His face darkened. "For the baby's sake…right. Because I assume that otherwise you could care less if I went to another woman for satisfaction."

He was angry, and she wasn't sure why. She picked up the elastic band he'd removed from her hair. With swift, jerky movements she put her ponytail back in place. She didn't want to think about how it felt to have his fingers combing through her hair, his hard, warm palms caressing her back.

"I'm trying to explain, Luc, that I'm okay with it."

"Okay with what?"

His black scowl terrified her. If she handled this wrong, he might back out entirely. "I understand that it makes sense for us to be intimate…while we're together. A man and a woman living in the same house…married. I'm willing.… That's all I wanted to say."

His lip curled. His dark eyes were impenetrable. "Well, you were right about one thing."

"I was?"

"I did want to talk about sex."

"I thought so."

"But while I am deeply touched by your desire to throw yourself on the sacrificial altar, I don't need your penance."

"I don't understand."

His legs were outstretched, propped on the coffee table. He feigned relaxation, but his entire body vibrated with intense emotion. "It's simple, Hattie. All I wanted to say was that it seems somewhat degrading to both of us to exchange *physical pleasure* for money."

The way he drawled the words *physical pleasure* made her belly tighten. "You're confusing me."

"Sex has nothing to do with this marriage agreement. Is that clear enough? If we end up in bed together, it will be because we both want it. I'm attracted to you, Hattie…just as I would be to any beautiful woman. And I have a normal man's needs. I'll welcome you to my bed anytime. But you'll have to come to me. Your body is not on the bargaining table."

He was being deliberately cruel. Perhaps she deserved it. But humiliation swept through her in burning waves. She had offered herself up in all sincerity, and he had reduced the possibility of marital intimacy to scratching an itch.

Dimly, apprehensively, she began to understand what Luc was going to get out of this marriage. He was going to make her dance to his tune. He was going to make her beg.

And what scared her even more than being totally at his mercy was the inescapable knowledge that she would be the one to crack. And she might not make it through the honeymoon.

Six

The days before the wedding flew by. Hattie was consumed with setting up the nursery and shopping for an appropriate dress in which to become Mrs. Luc Cavallo.

After the embarrassing scene with Luc in the den, Hattie saw little of him. He spent four days in Milan at a conference, and when he returned to Atlanta, he worked long days, ostensibly getting caught up so he could be away for a week's vacation. No one at his office knew anything about a wedding.

Deedee was thriving. There had been no further word from Eddie, and on the surface, life seemed normal.… Or at least as normal as it could be given the current situation.

Sherman and Ana adored Deedee and spoiled her with toys and other gifts. Hattie relished being part of that circle. She had never known her own grandparents, and the new relationships she was building helped fill the emotional hole in her soul. Things might become awkward when the marriage ended, but she would worry about that when the time came.

The wedding was only four days away when trouble

showed up. Not Eddie this time. A loud knock sounded at the front door midday, and Hattie answered it. Sherman was out back washing the cars, and Ana was making dinner preparations.

The man standing on the doorstep was familiar. "Leo," she said, her heart sinking. "Please come in."

"Well, isn't this nice," he sneered. "Playing lady of the manor, are we?"

She ignored his sarcasm. Clearly, he *did* remember her… and not fondly. "Luc's not home."

Leo folded his arms across his broad chest. "I came to see you." He was a physically intimidating man, and his brains more than equaled his brawn. Back in college he had played at flirting with her. Not seriously, just to get his brother's goat. But the look on his face at the moment said he'd just as soon toss her in the river as look at her.

"How did you know I was here?"

"I didn't. But I knew *something* was going on. My brother's been acting damn strangely. And now I know why."

Ana appeared, wiping her hands on a dish cloth. "Mr. Leo. How nice to see you." She turned to Hattie. "If you would like to step out back to the patio, I'd be happy to bring you a snack."

Leo smiled at the housekeeper, a warm, I'm-really-a-nice-guy smile. "Sounds wonderful, Ana. I've been running all day and missed lunch." He eyed Hattie blandly. "What a treat."

Hattie felt Leo's eyes boring into her back as they made their way through the house. She hadn't expected a warm welcome from Luc's brother, but she also hadn't anticipated this degree of antipathy from him. They sat down in wrought-iron chairs, and moments later Ana brought out a tray of oatmeal cookies and fresh coffee.

The older woman poured two cups and stepped back. "I'll

put the monitor in the kitchen, Hattie, so I'll be able to hear the baby if she wakes up."

Leo paled. As soon as the housekeeper was out of earshot, he swallowed half a cup of coffee and glared at Hattie over the rim of a bone china cup. His big hand dwarfed it. "Luc's a daddy?"

"No, of course not. Or not in the way you're thinking. Has he told you anything about my situation?" It was difficult to believe that Luc would cling to his intent of keeping Leo uninformed.

"Luc didn't tell me diddly squat. All he mentioned was that I should show up on the fourteenth wearing my tux when and where he said."

"Oh."

"Perhaps you'd like to fill me in." It wasn't a request.

"I'm sorry he's been keeping secrets from you. It's my fault." She quickly gave him the shortened version of the last two months. "I think that until the lawyers get a handle on this custody thing, Luc thinks the less said the better."

Leo ate two more cookies, eyeing her with a laserlike stare as he chewed slowly. "That's not why he didn't tell me. Luc knows I can keep my mouth shut. But he knew I would try to talk him out of this ridiculous sham of a marriage."

Hattie's heart sank. The two brothers were close. Could Leo, even now, derail what Luc and Hattie had set in motion?

She set down her cup so he wouldn't see her hand shaking. "Why would you do that? If you're worried about the money, or the company…you needn't be. I've already signed a prenup."

Leo snorted. "You may be a lot of things, Hattie, but even I know you're not a gold digger."

"Then why is this any of your business?" She heard the snap in her own voice and didn't care. What did Leo Cavallo have to gain by sticking his big Roman nose into her affairs?

He pulled his chair closer to the table, his knees almost touching hers beneath the glass. His accusatory mood made her want to run, but she refused to give him the satisfaction. He spoke softly, with menace. "Ten years ago, you almost destroyed my brother. You let him fall in love with you, encouraged it even. And then when he proposed, the first and only time he's ever done that by the way, you shut him down. A man has his pride, Hattie. You let things go too far. If you weren't going to love him back, why in the hell did you sleep with him? Why did you let him think you were his girl, his future?"

She bent her head, staring down at the crumbs on her plate. "That's just it, Leo. I did love him. I was sick with loving him."

"That's bull." He lifted her chin, his gaze boring into hers. "Women in love don't do what you did to Luc."

"That's not true," she cried. "We never would have worked out in the long term. I wasn't the right person to be his wife. I did the right thing by breaking it off. You know I did."

He let go of her and sat back, brooding, surly. "Then how do you explain this?" He waved a hand. "You damn sure appear to be enjoying the fancy house and the hired help."

"Don't be hateful."

"Not hateful, honey. Just stating the facts."

"This is all temporary."

"Does Luc know that?"

"Of course he does. When enough time has passed to make our marriage appear to be the real thing, we'll separate quietly. And I'll raise Deedee on my own."

"And what happens when my softhearted baby brother falls in love with the little girl sleeping upstairs? Will you tear his heart out again by taking her away?"

Hattie closed her eyes, regret raking her with sharp claws. "That won't happen," she said weakly.

"How do you know?" Leo asked quietly. "And how do you know he won't fall in love with *you* again?"

She laughed without amusement. "I can assure you *that* is not a possibility. Luc's helping me because he's a good man. But he's made it very clear that this is strictly business."

"And you believe him?"

"Why would he lie?"

"To protect himself perhaps?"

"From what?"

"The correct answer is *from whom.* You, Hattie. A man never forgets his first love. Why else would he turn his entire life upside down in a matter of days?"

"I think he's hoping for some payback, if you want to know the truth. I know I hurt him. I'm not stupid. This is his chance to be in control. To make me fall in line, not in love."

"How so?"

"He made it very clear that he has no feelings for me anymore."

Leo shook his head. "You don't know anything at all about men, sweetheart. If that's what he said, he's kidding himself. He sounds like a man who knows his own limits and is covering his ass."

Hattie mulled over Leo's words, torn between embarrassment and hope.

She was on the bed playing with Deedee when the master of the house came home. It surprised her that he sought her out. They had barely spoken a dozen words in the last week.

He looked tired. Not for the first time, she pondered the unfairness of what she had asked him to do. But what choice did she have? On her own, Eddie's family would have eaten her alive. And Luc had jumped at the opportunity to throw his weight around. So why did she feel guilty?

He sat down on the corner of the bed and grinned at

Deedee. She wriggled her way across the mattress toward him in a sort of commando crawl. He scooped her up and held her toward the ceiling. "Hey, kiddo. What mischief have you been up to today?"

Deedee squealed with laughter, her round cheeks pink with exertion. Luc nuzzled her tummy and lowered her to blow raspberries against her belly button.

Hattie watched them, her heart warmed by the budding connection man and infant shared. "She really likes you."

Luc glanced at Hattie. "The feeling is mutual."

His obvious enjoyment of something as simple as playing with a baby brought Leo's words rushing back. In all the time Hattie had thought about what would happen when the marriage ended, she had never considered the toll on Luc and her niece. Deedee would still be young. She wouldn't even remember Luc after a few months. But would Luc grieve?

Damn Leo for planting doubts.

Luc let the baby loose to roam the mattress again. Hattie had surrounded the edge with pillows, so Deedee couldn't go far. When the child latched on to one of her favorite toys, Luc finally spoke directly to Hattie. "How was your day?"

The prosaic question surprised her somehow. She leaned back on her elbows. "They delivered the nursery furniture early this morning. Deedee has already napped twice in the new bed and pronounced it quite satisfactory."

"Good." Long awkward silence. "Are you ready for the weekend? Do you need anything?"

She sat up. "I'm pretty much packed. Ana has been helping me."

"And the dress?"

"I finally found what I wanted yesterday. I hope it will be appropriate."

"I'm sure it's fine."

Hattie sighed inwardly. Next thing you know, they'd be

discussing the weather. She grabbed Deedee's ankle and pulled her toward the center of the bed. "Leo came by today."

That got Luc's attention. His eyes narrowed. "What did he want?"

"Well, apparently you neglected to mention that you were marrying me…or that I came with a baby. He wasn't happy."

Luc shrugged, his expression dangerous. "I don't make decisions based on Leo's likes and dislikes. If he doesn't want to come to the wedding, Sherman can do the honors."

"Don't be so pigheaded. Leo loves you."

"Leo believes his fourteen-month head start gives him the obligation to run my life."

"I think you should call him."

Luc's face went blank, wiped clean of all emotion. "I'll see him soon enough."

"Fine. Be an arrogant jerk. See if I care."

Luc stood up, gazing down at Hattie with an odd expression. "Sherman and Ana have the night off."

"I know. Did you want me to fix you something for dinner?"

"I thought we could take the baby on a picnic."

"It's kind of late."

"It won't hurt her to stay up just this once. Will it?"

"I guess not. I'll need to change, though."

He eyed her snug yellow T-shirt and khaki shorts. "You're fine. Let's go. I'm starving."

Luc had a garage full of expensive cars for every occasion. They took one of the more sedate sedans, a sporty Cadillac, and Luc moved the car seat. On the way, he dialed his favorite Chinese restaurant for takeout. Ten minutes later a helpful employee ran three bags out to the curb. The young man smiled hugely when Luc handed over a hundred and told the kid to keep the change.

Hattie wasn't prepared for their destination. Atlanta had

many lovely spots for al fresco dining, but Piedmont Park brought back too many memories. Had Luc chosen the location on purpose?

As Hattie freed Deedee from her seat, Luc gathered the food, a blanket from the trunk, a bottle of chilled wine and a corkscrew he'd added before they left the house. It was a perfect spring evening. The park was crowded, but after a few minutes' walk, they found a quiet spot away from Frisbees and footballs.

Deedee had eaten earlier, so Hattie buckled her into a small, portable seat with a tray and fed her Cheerios while Luc opened containers. The smells made Hattie's stomach growl.

She snagged an egg roll. "This looks heavenly. I'm probably going to make a pig of myself."

Luc ran his gaze from her long legs all the way up past her waist to her modest breasts. "A few extra pounds wouldn't do you any harm."

The intimacy in his voice caught her off guard. What kind of game was he playing?

They ate leisurely, rarely speaking, content to watch the action all around them. Hattie remembered their college days with wistfulness. Back then, Luc would already have had his head in her lap. She'd be stroking his hair, touching his chest.

She trembled inwardly as arousal made her weak with longing. Deedee was no help. Her little head slumped to the side as she succumbed to sleep. Hattie unbuckled her and lifted her free. Luc moved the seat, and together they tucked the baby between them.

Luc reclined on his side facing Hattie. "I heard from the lawyers today. They've spoken to their counterparts, and it seems that Eddie's trying to claim it was really your sister at the wheel that night. That he was confused by the impact and that was why he left the scene."

Hattie clenched her fists. "Please tell me that won't fly."

He propped up one knee. "The police report is pretty clear. But that doesn't mean the case won't drag on. I don't know what they're getting paid, but my guys said the other team doesn't seem to have trouble with Eddie committing perjury if it will get him off."

Hattie was stunned. Since when could a man literally murder other people by driving under the influence and not end up in prison?

Luc was attuned to her distress. He stroked the sleeping infant's back. "Try not to worry. I'm only keeping you informed. But I don't want you to obsess about this. Our bottom line is keeping Eddie away from Deedee. Some judges side with a biological parent automatically, but if it comes to a hearing—and it may not—we'll show proof that Eddie would be a danger to his own child."

Hattie shivered. "I hope you're right. Judges can be bought."

Luc's grin was feral. "Good thing I have deep pockets."

Moments later he surprised the heck out of her by falling asleep. As Hattie looked at man and baby, she realized an unpalatable truth. It would be dangerously easy to fall in love with Luc Cavallo again. The few men she had dated seriously in the last decade were shadows when held up against Luc's vibrant personality.

Hesitantly, she reached out and barely touched his hair. It was soft and thick and springy with the waviness he hated. Usually, he kept his cut conservatively short, but perhaps he'd been too busy for his customary barber visit, because she could see the beginnings of a curl at the back of his ear.

Something hot and urgent twisted in her belly. She wanted to lie down beside him, whisper in his ear, pull him on top of her and feel his powerful body mate with hers. Her hand shook as she pulled it back. She would go to him eventually. It was inevitable. And he would have the satisfaction of knowing that she had made a mistake in leaving him. He would taste her regret and know the scales had been evened.

Luc held all the power. She was helpless to stem the tide of the burgeoning desire she felt. It had only been lying dormant, waiting to be resurrected.

And no matter how much pain she would have to endure when the marriage ended, she would not be able to walk away from the temptation to once again be Luc Cavallo's lover.

Seven

The morning of May 14 dawned bright and clear. The entire household was up at first light. Ana brought Hattie breakfast in bed, toast and jam and half a grapefruit.

Hattie, who had been awake for some time, sat up, shoving the hair from her eyes. "You didn't have to do this."

Ana sat down on the edge of the bed. "A bride deserves special treatment on her wedding day. Sherman and Mr. Leo have taken Deedee outside for a walk in the stroller. All you need to do is relax and let the rest of us pamper you."

Hattie took a bite of toast and had trouble swallowing. Even the freshly brewed hot tea didn't help. Fear choked her. Panic hovered just offstage. She wiped her hands on a soft damask napkin and looked at Ana. "Am I doing the right thing?"

A few nights ago, Luc and Hattie had decided the older couple needed to know the truth. Luc had hired round-the-clock security to be in place during the honeymoon, but it wasn't fair to leave Deedee's caregivers out of the loop.

Ana smoothed the embroidered bedspread absently.

"Did I tell you that Mr. Luc offered Sherman and me an embarrassing amount of money if we wanted to retire?"

It seemed an odd answer to Hattie's question.

"I knew he gave you the option. But he told me you loved the house and didn't want to leave."

"As it was, he almost doubled our salaries. We're taking our first cruise this fall, nothing too fancy, but it will be a change of pace."

"Sounds like fun."

"The thing is, Hattie, I've worked my whole life. I wouldn't know what to do if I had to sit around all day. The previous owners of this grand old property were both in their nineties when they passed. They never had a family, and Sherman and I weren't able to have children, either. This is a big, wonderful house with all kinds of interesting history. But until you and Deedee moved in, it was missing something." She paused and smiled softly. "Mr. Luc wants to help you and that precious baby. What could be wrong with that?"

"But it isn't a real marriage. We're not a family."

Ana shrugged. "That may be true at the moment, but things happen for a reason. I've seen it too many times in my life not to believe that. Take it a day at a time. You'll be fine, Hattie dear. Now eat your breakfast and get in the shower. Mr. Luc's not one for running late."

Luc had chartered a private plane, and at ten-thirty sharp, it was wheels up. The short flight from Atlanta to the southeast coast of the state was a source of constant fascination for Deedee. She sat with Ana and Sherman, stuck her nose to the window and was uncustomarily still as she watched the clouds drift by.

Leo and Luc huddled together in the front row talking business and who knows what else. Luc's friend, who was to do the ceremony, sat with them. Hattie was left to chat with

Ana's niece, Patti. The young woman's eyes were almost as big as Deedee's.

She took a Coke from the flight attendant and turned to Hattie with a grin. "I've never been on a plane before, and especially not one like this. I could get used to the lifestyle. Did you know the bathroom has *real* hand towels…not paper?"

Hattie smiled at the girl's enthusiasm. "I can't thank you enough for helping out while we're gone on our honeymoon."

Patti wrinkled her nose. "Well, I love kids, and when Mr. Cavallo offered to pay my fall tuition in exchange for the week, I wasn't about to say no. My aunt and uncle and I will take such good care of Deedee. You won't have to worry about a thing."

Hattie gulped inwardly. Her debts to Luc were piling up more quickly than she could calculate.

Before Hattie could catch her breath and gird herself for what was to come, the plane landed smoothly on a small strip of tarmac. Three large SUVs sat waiting for the wedding party. Once in the cars, they were all whisked away to a nearby dock where they boarded a sleek black cabin cruiser.

At first, Luc's island was nothing more than a speck against the horizon, but as the boat cut through the choppy waves, land came into view. Down at the water's edge, a large wooden pier had been festooned with white ribbons. Uniformed staff secured a metal ramp and soon everyone stood on dry land.

Hattie looked around with wonder. They were too far north in latitude for the island to have a tropical flavor, but it was enchanting in other ways. Ancient trees graced the windswept contours of the land, and birds of every color and size nested in limbs overhead and left dainty footprints in the wet sand.

Luc appeared at her side. "What do you think?"

She smiled up at him. "It's amazing…so peaceful. I love it, Luc. It's perfect."

"We're trying to get the state to designate it as a wildlife refuge. Leo and I have no plans to develop this place. But one day, when we're gone, we want it to be protected." He took her arm. "Let's go. There's more to see."

Hattie's skin tingled where he touched her. Their hands were linked…perhaps he didn't notice. But the intimacy, intentional or not, was poignant to Hattie.

Dune buggies took the group up and over a crest to the far side of the island where a weathered but genteel guesthouse stood, built to blend into the landscape.

Luc helped her out of the fiberglass vehicle. "There's plenty of room inside for everyone to change. Will thirty minutes give you long enough? There's no real rush." He paused, and stared down at her, his expression pensive. "This is your day, Hattie. I know the circumstances aren't ideal, but you're doing a wonderful thing for Deedee."

For one brief moment, wistfulness crushed her chest as she wondered what it would have been like to marry Luc when she was twenty-one. Determinedly, she thrust aside regret. This was not the same situation at all. She lifted a hand and cupped his cheek. "Thank you, Luc. I don't know what I would have done if you had turned me away."

The space around them was ionized suddenly, the hot, sticky air heavy with unspoken emotions. She went up on her tiptoes and found his mouth with hers. Someone groaned. Maybe both of them. He tasted like all her memories combined, hot and sweet and dangerous.

But they were not alone.

Luc took a step backward, and her hand fell away. Something akin to pain flashed across his face. "We both want what's best for the baby," he said, his voice gruff. "That's the important thing."

* * *

Sherman and Patti tended to Deedee while Ana helped Hattie get dressed. Hattie disappeared into a well-appointed bathroom to freshen up and slip into an ivory bustier and matching silk panties. Ana stepped in briefly to help with buttons and then tactfully left Hattie alone.

The day was warm and humid, and Hattie was glad she had decided to wear her hair up. She tweaked the lace trim at her breasts, adjusted the deliberately casual knot of hair at the back of her head and looked into the mirror. Too bad Luc wouldn't get a chance to see her in the delicate garments. They made her feel feminine and desirable, and she had charged them to one of the new credit cards without a qualm.

Ana waited in the bedroom, the wedding dress draped over her arms. In a small exclusive boutique in Buckhead, Hattie had found exactly what she wanted. The off-white dress was made of watered silk fabric and chiffon. The halter neckline flattered her bust and the fitted drop waist fluffed out into several filmy layers that ended in handkerchief points. The ecru kid slippers she'd bought to match were trimmed in satin ribbons that laced at her ankles.

Both women blinked away tears when Ana zipped up the dress and turned Hattie to face the mirror. It was fairy-tale perfect for a beach wedding—definitely bridal, but spritely and whimsical. Truth be told, it was not really a "Hattie" sort of dress. But it was her wedding day, damn it, and she wanted to be beautiful for Luc.

Ana picked up the narrow tiara and pinned it carefully to the top of Hattie's head. It was the appropriate finishing touch.

The older woman fluffed the skirt and stepped back. "You look like an angel." Her expression sobered. "I'm so sorry your mother and sister aren't here with you."

Hattie hiccupped a sob. "Me, too."

Ana looked alarmed. “No crying, for heaven’s sake. My fault. Shouldn’t have said anything. Let’s touch up your makeup and get outside. I’ll bet good money you have an eager groom waiting for you.”

Ana left to take her place, and for a moment, Hattie was alone with her thoughts. She couldn’t say in all honesty that she had no doubts. But perhaps a lot of brides felt this way. Scared and hopeful.

There was a brief knock at the door. When Hattie opened it, Leo’s large frame took up the entrance. He looked her over, head to toe. A tiny smile lifted a corner of his mouth. “You’ll do, Parker.” He handed her a beautiful bouquet of lilies and eucalyptus. “These are from my brother. He’s impatient.”

He held out his arm, and she put her hand on it, her palm damp. “I care about him, Leo…a lot.”

“I know you do…which is the only reason I’m here. But God help me, Hattie…if you hurt him again, I’ll make you pay.”

Not exactly auspicious words to start a new life.

Leo escorted her to the corner of the house, just out of sight of the water’s edge where the ceremony would take place. He bent and kissed her cheek, then stepped back. Perhaps he saw the sheer panic in her eyes, because he smiled again, a real smile this time. “Break a leg, princess.” And then he was gone.

Hattie’s cue was to be the opening notes of "Pachelbel’s Canon.” A sturdy boardwalk led from the porch of the house out over a small dune to the temporary platform and the wooden latticed archway where she and Luc would stand.

The music started. She clenched her fists and then deliberately relaxed them. One huge breath. Several small prayers. One foot in front of the other.

Afterward, she could not remember the exact details of her solitary journey to the altar. In keeping with the unorthodox nature of the marriage and the ceremony, she had decided to walk to Luc on her own. This was her decision, her gamble.

When she first caught sight of the groom, her breath lodged in her throat and she stumbled slightly. Though there were three other people framed against the vibrant blue-green of the ocean, she only had eyes for Luc. He was wearing a black tux…a formal morning coat and tails over a crisp white shirt and a gray vest.

His gaze locked on hers and stayed there as she traversed the final fifty feet. As she stepped beneath the arch and took her place by his side, she saw something hot and predatory flash in his dark eyes before he turned to face the justice of the peace.

Without looking at Hattie again, Luc reached out and took her right hand, squeezing it tightly. The officiant smiled at both of them. "We are gathered here today to witness the union of Luc Cavallo and Hattie Parker. Marriage is a…"

Hattie tried to listen…she really did. But her thoughts scattered in a million directions. Too many stimuli. The feel of Luc's hard, warm fingers twined with hers. The familiar tang of his aftershave, mingling with the scent of her bouquet. The muted roar of the nearby surf as waves tumbled onto shore.

If she had the power, she would freeze this moment. To take out later in the quiet of her bedroom and savor everything she missed the first time around.

Out of the corner of her eye, she could see the giant live oaks that cast shade and respite on this hot, windy day. Sherman and Patti stood guard over the stroller, which was draped in mosquito netting. Apparently, Deedee had decided to cooperate and sleep through it all.

Closer to hand, Ana smiled, her cheeks damp. She was wearing a moss-green designer suit that flattered her stocky frame and shaved ten years off her age. Hattie had no doubt that Luc had financed the expensive wedding finery.

For a split second Hattie caught Leo's eye. The resemblance between the two brothers was striking, but where Luc was classically handsome, quieter and more reserved, Leo was larger than life. He winked at her deliberately, and she blushed, turning her attention back to the words that would make her Luc's wife.

"May I have the rings?"

Ana commandeered the bouquet, Hattie and Leo complied, and moments later, Hattie slid a plain gold band onto Luc's left hand. He returned the favor, placing a narrow circlet of platinum beside the beautiful engagement ring to which Hattie had yet to grow accustomed.

More words, a pronouncement and then the moment she had unconsciously been waiting for. "You may kiss the bride."

In unison, she and Luc turned. The breeze ruffled his hair. His expression was solemn, though his eyes danced. He took Hattie's hands in his. Time stood still.

Ten years…ten long years since she had been free to kiss him whenever she wanted.

He bent his head. His mouth brushed hers, lingered, pressed more insistently. His tongue coaxed. His arms tightened around her as her skirt tangled capriciously with his pant legs.

Her heart lodged in her throat, tears stung her eyes, and she moved her mouth against his.

Aeons later it seemed, a chorus of unison laughter broke them apart. Luc appeared as dazed as Hattie felt.

Suddenly, hugs and congratulations separated them, but every moment, Luc's eyes followed her.

They led their small parade back to the house. Hattie had only seen one of the bedrooms, but now they all entered the great room on the opposite side of the building. The ambience was rustic but elegant. Exposed beams of warmly-hued wood were strung with tiny white lights. Dozens of blush-pink roses in crystal vases decorated every available surface.

A single table covered in pale pink linen was set with exquisite china, crystal and silver. When they were all seated, with Luc and Hattie at the head, Leo stood up.

As a waiter deftly poured champagne for everyone, Leo raised his glass. "Luc here, my baby brother, is and will always be my best friend. When Mom and Dad drowned, out on that damned boat they loved so much, Luc and I were shipped off to Italy to live for three years with a grandfather we barely knew. The language was strange, we were a mess, but we had each other."

He paused, and Hattie saw the muscles in his throat work with emotion. He moved to stand between and behind the bride and groom, laying a hand on each of their shoulders. "To Luc and his beautiful bride. May they always be as happy as they are today."

Applause and cheers filled the room, and moments later, the unobtrusive waitstaff began serving lunch.

Hattie knew the food was delicious. And wine flowed like water. But she couldn't taste any of it.

She was married to Luc. For some undefined period of time in order to protect the baby she had grown to love. But at what price?

When Luc put his arm around her bare shoulders, her heartbeat wobbled and sped up. He leaned over to whisper in her ear. "Are you doing okay, Mrs. Cavallo?" Gently, he tucked a wayward wisp of her hair into place.

She nodded mutely.

Luc laughed beneath his breath. "It might help if you quit looking like a scared rabbit."

She shrugged helplessly. "I'm in over my head," she admitted quietly. "What have we done, Luc?"

He stroked her back as he answered a cheerful question from across the table. "Forget reality," he murmured. "Pretend we're on Fantasy Island. Maybe this is all a dream."

Beneath the table, his hand played with hers.

The silly, childish game restored her equilibrium. Moments later their intimate circle was broken as Deedee demanded, in a loud string of nonsense syllables, to be recognized.

Luc chuckled as he stood to take the baby from Sherman and handed her to Hattie. Immediately, Deedee reached for the tiara. She yanked on it before Luc could stop her, and soon Hattie's hair was askew.

Amidst shrieks of infant temper, the tiara was rescued, the baby given one of her toys and the two at the head table became three. Luc tickled one chubby thigh, making Deedee chortle with laughter. He growled at her playfully and reached to take her in his arms.

Deedee's eyes went wide. She clung to Hattie's neck, burying her little face. And in a soft, childish, unmistakably clear voice, she said, *"Mama."*

Eight

Luc had known Hattie for a very long time. And he saw the mix of feelings that showed so clearly on her face. Shock. Fierce pride. Joy. Sorrow. Almost too much for one woman to bear, particularly on a day already filled with strong emotion.

He stood and addressed the small group. "Hattie and I are going to slip away for a few moments to spend some time with Deedee before we have to say goodbye. We'll cut the cake when we return. In the meantime, please relax and enjoy the rest of your meal."

He coaxed Hattie out of her seat, witnessing the way she held the baby so tightly to her chest. A crisis was brewing.

In the bedroom where Hattie had changed clothes, his brand-new bride faced him mutinously. "I can't leave her. It's cruel. We'll have to change our plans."

At that moment, Deedee spotted a carry-all stuffed with her favorite toys on the floor in a corner. She wiggled and squirmed and insisted on being put down. Hattie did so with patent reluctance.

Luc tugged Hattie toward the bed and sat her down. "Deedee will be fine. You know it in your heart. Aside from the fact that we need to make our marriage look absolutely real, you need a break, Hattie. Badly. This past year has been one crisis after another. You desperately need to rest and recharge your batteries."

Hattie looked up at him, her lips trembling, her big, brown eyes suspiciously shiny. "She called me *Mama*."

"She certainly did." Luc smoothed her hair where the baby had disheveled it. "And that's what you are."

Hattie bit her lip, not seeming to notice that he was touching her. "I feel guilty," she whispered.

"Why on earth would you say that?"

"I'm happy that Deedee is growing closer to me. I know that's a good thing in the long run. But does that make me disloyal to Angela? How can I be so thrilled that the baby called me *Mama* when she won't even remember Angela, her real mother..."

Luc struggled for wisdom, though he didn't have a good track record when it came to Hattie. "As Deedee grows older you'll show her pictures of your sister.... And later still, you'll explain what happened, when the time is right. Angela will live in your heart, and by your actions, in Deedee's."

"And what about Eddie? What do I tell her about him?"

Luc ground his teeth, unused to feeling helpless in any situation. Did he want to replace Eddie as the baby's father? The temptation was there—he felt it. But he had no desire to be a family man, and Hattie had made it painfully clear that his help was only needed on a temporary basis.

He tried to swallow his frustration. "None of us knows how that situation will work out, but I doubt seriously if Eddie has any interest in being a father. That truth will be hurtful when she's old enough to understand it. But if you've filled her life with love and happiness, Deedee will get through it."

"I hope so," she said softly, her gaze pensive.

He reached out with one hand and touched her bare shoulder, resisting the urge to stroke the satiny skin. "You look beautiful today." The words felt like razor blades in his throat.

Finally, he regained her attention.

A pale pink blush stained her cheeks, and she lowered her head. Her long eyelashes hid her thoughts. "Thank you. I thought this was a better choice than a traditional wedding dress."

Something in her voice made him frown. "Do you regret missing out on a church wedding?"

She shrugged. "I thought I would. It's what many women dream about. But today was…"

"Was what?" he prompted.

She touched his hand briefly, not linking their fingers… more of a butterfly brush. "It was…meaningful."

Her answer disappointed him. He'd hoped for more enthusiasm, more feminine effusiveness. But it hadn't escaped his notice that she'd been careful with the wording of the ceremony. He'd left that portion of the day in her capable hands. The printed order of service she'd handed over on the plane had notably omitted any reference to "till death do us part" or even the more modern "as long as we both shall live."

He turned his attention toward the baby, trying not to notice the way Hattie's rounded breasts filled the bodice of her gown. She hadn't worn the pearl necklace today, and the omission hurt him, though he'd chew glass before he'd admit it. The only reason he cared was because it was an outward symbol of the fact that she belonged to him. She relied on him. She needed him. No other reason.

He bent and picked up Deedee. "We'd better get back to our guests. They'll be waiting for cake."

* * *

Though the day and the room were plenty warm, Luc realized that Hattie's fingers were cold when he put his hand over hers and pressed down firmly with the knife. Hattie had insisted, in private, that having a photographer document their faux wedding was unnecessary. So at the official cake cutting, only Sherman's digital camera was available to record the moment.

Hattie's smile toward Luc was apologetic as she picked up a small square and pressed it into his mouth. He wasn't sure which he wanted to eat more: the almond-flavored dessert, or her slender, frosting-covered fingertips.

He returned the favor, being careful not to mess up Hattie's makeup or dress. He fed her a tiny piece of cake and then deliberately lifted her hand and licked each of her fingers clean. The guests and servers signaled their approval with a cheer, and Hattie's red-faced embarrassment was worth every penny Luc had spent to make his bride's day special.

Ana stepped forward with a smile. "Shall I help you change clothes, *Mrs. Cavallo?*"

Luc put an arm around Hattie's waist, drawing her closer. He kissed her cheek. "I think we can handle that," he said, his voice low and suggestive.

Once in the bedroom, an irate Hattie rounded on him. "What was that show about? Ana and Sherman know the truth. You embarrassed me."

He shrugged, his hands in his pockets to keep from stripping the deliberately tantalizing dress from her in short order. "The waitstaff and the drivers are outsiders. They may talk, and if they do…I want them to believe that you and I are so much in love we can't keep our hands off each other. Any gossip will help us, not hurt us if they think we're a normal bride and groom."

Hattie stood in the middle of the room, her expression troubled.

He lost his temper. "Oh, for God's sake. I'm not going to jump you when your back is turned. Take off that damned dress and put some clothes on."

She blanched. He felt like a heel. Sexual frustration was riding him hard, and he wondered with bleak mirth what in hell had possessed him to insist on a honeymoon. If his brand-new bride didn't soon admit she wanted him the way he wanted her, he'd be a raving, slobbering lunatic by the time they got back home.

But he couldn't let her think he was affected by the day and the ceremony. The softer, gentler Luc she had known back in college was a phantom. The real Luc was cynical to a fault. What he was feeling was lust, pure and simple. Hattie would be in his bed. Soon. But he wouldn't be weak. Never again. He had his emotions on lockdown.

He turned his back on her and looked out the window blindly, the ocean nothing but a blur. All of his senses were attuned to Hattie's movements. Even when he heard the bathroom door shut, he remained where he was. It was impossible not to imagine her nudity as she stepped out of her bridal attire.

His hands were clammy, and his gut churned.

The bathroom door opened again, and he sighed inwardly. But still he didn't turn around. It was only when Hattie appeared at his elbow that he finally spoke. "Are you ready to go?"

He turned and inhaled sharply. The tiara was gone, her hair was down, but she was still dressed.

She raised a shoulder, her face rueful. "I'm sorry. I can't unzip it. Will you help me?"

God in heaven. She turned her back to him with innocent trust. His hands shook. Inch by inch, as he lowered the zipper, the dress gaped, revealing a sexy piece of fantasy-fueling lingerie. He cleared his throat. "Do you…uh…"

Hattie nodded. "Yeah. The bustier, too."

A million tiny buttons held the confection in place. God knows how long it took him, but he finally succeeded in revealing the pale skin and delicate spine he remembered with such painful clarity. He also remembered running his tongue down that very spine, not stopping until he reached the curve of her ass. And sometimes not even then.

The exercise in torture lasted for what seemed like hours rather than minutes. At last he was finished.

Hattie held the dress to her front with a death grip.

He made himself step back. "All done," he croaked.

She nodded jerkily and scooted toward safety. But just as she reached the bathroom, her toe caught on a scatter rug, she stumbled, and Luc grabbed for her instinctively. His arms went around her from behind and his hands landed in dangerous territory.

Lush, soft breasts. Pert nipples begging to be stroked. He sucked in a breath, sucker punched by the slug of hunger. Hattie froze on the spot like an animal hoping not to be noticed by a hunter.

He nuzzled the nape of her neck. "Your skin is so soft," he muttered. He squeezed gently, cupping the mounds of flesh that he remembered in his dreams.

Her head fell back against his shoulder. "Luc…"

That was all. Just his name. But the single word fraught with what he hoped like hell was longing made him hard as stone and ready for action. He tugged the dress and undergarment from her deathlike grasp and tossed them aside. He couldn't see her face, and he didn't want to.

He continued to play with her breasts slowly. "Tell me you want me, Hattie."

"I want you, Luc…but…"

The last word made him frown. He slid one hand down her belly, between her legs. Hattie gasped audibly.

He bit gently at her earlobe. "But?"

"I don't think we're ready." Her whispered protest barely registered on his consciousness.

He pressed his aching erection against her, her beautiful round butt covered in less than nothing. "Oh, I'm ready, Hattie. Trust me."

The choked laugh she managed made him smile.

At that precise moment, when he felt paradise within his grasp, a loud shout of nearby laughter shattered the moment. They weren't alone. And they had guests waiting.

He cursed in frustration and released her abruptly, wanting to howl at the moon. His timing sucked. "Damn it.… I'm sorry."

Hattie didn't even turn around. He suspected her face was one huge blush. He reached for the discarded clothing and handed it to her. "Go," he said curtly. "We'll deal with this later."

Hattie huddled in the bathroom, her blood running hot and cold in dizzying, equal measure. She had come within inches of shoving her new husband onto the bed and pouncing on him. Feeling his hands on her bare skin had been more arousing than anything she had experienced in the last ten years.

She hadn't been celibate. But still…*holy cow.*

It took her three tries to button her lavender silk blouse. The cream linen trousers she stepped into were part of the outrageously expensive new wardrobe that now filled two large Louis Vuitton suitcases and a garment bag.

She looked in the mirror, wincing at her crazy tousled hair. Nothing to do but to put it up again. Ana had promised to collect the wedding finery and make sure it got back to the house. So all that was left for Hattie to do was to slip into low-heeled, gold leather sandals and wash her face.

She added fresh lip gloss, took the shine off her nose with a dash of powder, and spritzed her favorite perfume at her throat. What had Luc been thinking as he undressed her? Did he have any feelings left for her at all? Or was it only sex? What if she had turned in his arms and kissed him? Would she have been able to read his face?

He might feel the tug of attraction, but he was no green kid unable to control his body. Hell would probably freeze over before Luc would ever think about having a real relationship with Hattie, whether he saw her naked or not. He liked having her at his mercy. She had invited that with her artless marriage proposal. But Luc was thinking about sex…not a wistful reunion of lovers.

Luc had gained a heck of a lot of sexual experience since they parted. Hattie was old news.

Thinking of the women Luc had probably invited into his bed over the years was a bad thing to do on her wedding day. It only increased her misery. She'd had her chance. And being with Luc again made her rethink her youthful decision for the umpteenth time. Luc's money gave him power. No doubt about it. But from the perspective of ten years down the road, she admitted ruefully that he wouldn't have used the inequality in their bank accounts to control her, no matter what her mother said.

Her mother's take on life had always been hard-edged. Early disappointments had made her suspicious of people and their motives. Hattie had tried not to follow suit. But perhaps unconsciously that inherent attitude of distrust had been largely to blame for Hattie's breakup with Luc.

When she could procrastinate no longer, she slowly opened the bathroom door. Luc looked up and stared. Something arced across the room between them.

He cleared his throat. "I'll go change now. Why don't you play with the baby? I won't be long."

Before she could respond, he was gone.

Twenty minutes later, amidst the chaos of getting everything and everyone packed up for the return trip, she finally saw her husband again. He was wearing dark slacks and a pale blue dress shirt with the sleeves rolled up. His casual, masculine elegance took her breath away.

It shocked her to realize that she and Luc were not returning on the plane with the rest of the group. And Luc didn't take the time to explain, leaving Hattie to build scenarios in her head, each more unlikely than the next.

Ana stood by as Hattie said one last goodbye to the baby who had become so dear. When Angela was still alive, Hattie had been extremely fond of her tiny niece…as any doting aunt would. But now…now that Hattie played the role of mother, the bond was fierce and unbreakable. She couldn't pinpoint a single instant when it had happened. But the connection was substantial. As much as she was looking forward to spending time with Luc, it pained her to say goodbye to Deedee.

So much was still uncertain. And the baby was so helpless.

Ana patted Hattie's shoulder. "Don't worry…please. We'll watch over her as if she were our own."

Hattie handed over the sleepy child and forced a smile. "I know you will. She adores you and Sherman already. I wouldn't trust her with anyone else." The captain signaled Luc, and Luc began ushering everyone toward the boat.

Leo lingered to speak to Hattie. "I hope you know what you're doing."

She smiled wryly. "Do any of us ever really know what we're doing? I'm trying my best, Leo. It's all I can do."

He hesitated. "Call me if you need anything," he said gruffly. "And be good to my brother."

Before she could respond, he loped toward the end of the dock and boarded the cabin cruiser.

A mournful toot of the horn heralded departure. Luc rejoined Hattie, and they both watched and waved as the vessel moved away from the pilings, picked up speed and slowly skimmed out of sight.

Hattie shifted her feet restlessly. The sun was lower in the sky now, and a breeze had picked up, alleviating some of the heat. "Why didn't we go with them?"

Luc took her arm, leading her back toward the house. "It's been a long, stressful day. I thought it might be nice to relax here for the night. I've ordered a helicopter to pick us up at ten in the morning. He'll take us to the Atlanta airport, and we'll catch our flight to Key West from there."

"Oh."

He must have misread her quiet syllable as lack of enthusiasm, because he frowned. "I'm sorry I'm not taking you somewhere more exotic…like Paris, or St. Moritz. But with Eddie still a loose cannon, I thought it would be wiser to stay where we could get home quickly if need be."

"I think you're right."

Conversation evaporated as they neared the house. Hattie's heart was pounding in her breast. Two people alone on the proverbial deserted island. What happened next?

The truth was anticlimactic. Luc paused on the porch, running a hand through his hair, and for the first time that day, looking uncertain. "Are you hungry at all? We have leftovers."

Hattie had been too nervous earlier to eat much at their wedding meal. "Well, I…"

"It might be nice to sit out on the beach and watch the water while we eat."

Was that a note of coaxing in his voice? She indicated her clothes. "I dressed to travel. Do you mind if I change?"

"Roll up your pants legs. We'll go barefoot and pretend we're teenagers again."

This time there was definitely self-mockery in his words, but she was easily persuaded. They raided the kitchen, and in short order cobbled together a light meal. Luc found a large-handled tote, and they loaded it. Leaving Hattie to carry nothing but two bottles of water, Luc scooped up an old, faded tarp and swung the bag over his shoulder.

She laughed when he kicked off his shoes and rolled his trousers to his knees before they left the house. Following suit, she joined him outside, smiling when she felt the still warm boards beneath her feet.

It was her wedding day. Perhaps an unorthodox one at best, but still deserving of at least a jot of ceremony.

What had happened earlier lingered between them… unspoken, unacknowledged. But it was there, filling her veins with heady anticipation.

Luc managed to spread the ground cloth with her help, though the stiff wind made it necessary to quickly secure the corners with food containers. They sat down side by side. With no baby to act as a shield between them, either literally or figuratively, the mood was much different than it had been during the evening at the park.

Here, on an island far from land, removed from any other humans, it was more difficult to ignore the past.

Luc leaned back on his elbows, his expression pensive. "I wondered about you over the years…what you were doing… if you were happy." He turned his head suddenly and looked straight at her. "Were you?"

"Happy, you mean?"

He nodded.

"It's hard to pin down happiness, isn't it? I had a job that I liked. Friends. Family. So yes, I guess I was happy."

He frowned slightly. "I was an idiot back then. When we

were in college. Confusing lust with love. I'm not sure love exists."

Her chest hurt. "How can you not believe in love?"

His gaze returned to the sea. "I understand loving a child, a parent. Those emotions are real. But between men and women?" His lips twisted. "Mostly hormones, I think. Makes the world go round."

The deliberate cynicism scraped at her guilt. Was that his intention? She curled her legs beneath her, poking at a small crab scurrying in the nearby sand. "You've never come close to marrying before now?"

He smiled faintly. "You mean after the debacle with you? No. Once was enough."

"I'm sorry."

"Don't be. It was a lesson well learned."

She hated his current mood. He was spoiling whatever pleasure she had managed to squeeze from today's events.

Her temper sizzled. Abruptly, she stood up. "I can only apologize so many times. You hate me. I get it. But I can't change the past."

Nine

Luc cursed beneath his breath as Hattie ran from him. Had that been his subconscious intent? To make her angry? So there would be no question of appeasing the ache in his groin?

To say he was conflicted was an understatement. He wanted Hattie with a raw intensity that only increased day by day. But he wasn't willing to give up his position of power. He wouldn't let her see him as a supplicant. It was up to her to come to him. God help him.

He reached into the food bag and found a block of aged cheddar. Not bothering with a knife, he ripped off a hunk and bit into it. The cheese tasted bitter in his mouth. And since he knew all the food at the wedding was top-notch, the problem must be him.

He tossed the uneaten portion back in the bag and went to stand at the water's edge.

Until now, he hadn't allowed himself to think about the men who had shared her life in the intervening years. His fists curled, and he wished violently that he was at the gym so he could beat the crap out of a punching bag.

A swim in the rough surf might appease the beast inside him, but he couldn't take the chance. He wasn't worried about his own safety, but leaving Hattie alone if something happened to him would be the ultimate mark of irresponsibility.

And he was nothing if not responsible.

Damn it. He took off in his bare feet, running full-out, dragging air into his lungs, ignoring the shell fragments that pierced his skin. He kept up the brutal pace, rounding the point and covering mile after mile until he came full circle to where the uneaten picnic lay.

With his chest burning, his feet aching and his skin windburned, he stopped suddenly, bent at the waist and rested his hands on his knees. He was used up, worn-out, ready to stop.

But still he wanted Hattie.

Inquisitive gulls had found the bag of food. Much of it would have to be tossed. He waved them away and packed up what he and Hattie had brought to the beach.

The house was quiet and dark when he slipped through the door. He dumped everything in the kitchen and went to his own bedroom, acutely aware that Hattie's was only a few yards away. It was only nine o'clock, but he couldn't see any light from beneath her door.

He stripped off his clothes and took a blisteringly hot shower. The water felt good on his tight, salty skin, but if he had been hoping for a soothing experience, he was out of luck.

His recalcitrant imagination brought Hattie into the glass stall with him. Her generous breasts glistened with soapy water as he washed her from head to toe. His erection was painful. As he stroked himself, he imagined lifting her and filling her, wrapping her long legs around his hips.

Ah.... He came with a muffled groan, slumping at last to sit on the narrow seat and catch his breath. He ran his hands through his wet hair, massaging the pain in his temples.

He was ninety-nine percent sure that Hattie was still sexually attracted to him. And he wanted her in his bed again. But on his terms. She had nearly destroyed him once upon a time. He'd be a fool to let it happen twice. So he'd be on his guard.

Sleep was elusive. Though he'd been up before dawn, he tossed and turned until he finally gave up the pretense of reading and turned out the light. He left the window open, relishing the humid night air. It suited his mood.

The nocturnal sounds were vastly different from back home. Birds and other wildlife filled the night with muted chirps and rustles and clicks. The sea created a hushed backdrop.

At 2:00 a.m. he tossed the tangled covers aside and padded to the kitchen in his boxers to get a drink. The house was dark and silent. He might as well have been the only person on the planet.

He drained the tumbler of water and stepped outside, tempted to run on the beach again. As he moved forward on the boardwalk, his heart stopped. A slender figure in white stood silhouetted against the dark horizon. Hattie. As he closed the distance between them, unconsciously treading as silently as possible, he saw that her back was to him. Her head was lifted to the stars. Her hair danced in the breeze. That same wind plastered her satin nightgown to her shapely body, leaving little to the imagination.

He should have turned back. It was the wise choice. But retreat had never been an option for him. Jump in the deep end, full steam ahead, onward and upward. Pick your cliché—that was how he lived his life. Perhaps if he had handled things differently a decade ago, he might never have lost her.

Something in her posture screamed sadness. And loneliness. An artist would have painted her and titled the canvas *Melancholy*. Seeing Hattie like this cracked something inside him. It hurt.

She didn't flinch when he joined her. Was she as attuned to him as he was to her?

He stood beside her, their shoulders almost touching. Her freshly washed hair was a tangle of damp waves, the light scent of shampoo mingling with the faint fragrance of her perfume.

"Are you okay, Hattie?"

Her chin lowered a bit, her gaze now on the water. She shrugged, not answering in words.

"I was being an ass earlier. I'm sorry."

Her lips twisted. "I should be the one apologizing. I was painfully young and immature back then. I know I hurt you, and I regret it more than you realize. I should have done things differently."

He winced inwardly. She wasn't apologizing for the breakup…only for the way she did it. The distinction was telling.

"I think we're going to have to agree to leave the past where it belongs. We're different people now."

"Leo remembers."

"Leo?"

"He threatened to tear me limb from limb if I hurt his baby brother again. He's very loyal."

Luc snorted. "Leo's a pain in the butt when he wants to be. Forget anything he said to you. I don't need his protection. And he's hardly in a position to be giving relationship advice."

"Maybe not, but he loves you very much."

They fell silent. Luc tried to steady his breathing, but the longer he stood beside her, so close that her warmth radiated to him, the more he became aroused.

"You're sad," he accused softly. "Tell me why."

She shifted restlessly from one foot to the other. "It's not exactly the wedding night I dreamed of."

Dangerous territory. "I'm sorry, Hattie. But, hey." He forced a dry chuckle from his throat. "At least there's moonlight, a romantic beach, a million stars. Could be worse."

"Could be raining." She shot back with the famous line from *Young Frankenstein,* and they both burst into laughter.

He couldn't help himself. He touched her. It was a matter of utmost urgency to find out which was softer—the satin, or her skin. At first, all he did was take her chin in his hand. He turned her so that they were face-to-face, their pose and position mimicking that of the wedding ceremony.

Hattie moved restlessly and he dropped his hand. He sighed. "I take it you couldn't sleep?"

"No."

"Me, either. I've never had a wedding night before. Turns out this stuff is pretty stressful."

That coaxed a small smile from her. "At least you didn't have to contend with a receiving line and five hundred guests."

"Why do people do that? Sounds exhausting."

"I imagine they want to share their happiness with as many people as possible, and they want to express their appreciation to those who made the effort to show up."

"You apparently have given this some thought."

"It's a typical teenage girl fantasy."

"I wish you could have had your dream wedding."

"Can we talk about something else?" The hint of fatigued petulance made him smile. It was so unlike her.

"I could tell you that when I first looked out here, I thought I was seeing a ghost."

She touched his cheek, making him tremble. "I suppose this must seem like a bad dream to you, your whole world turned upside down. And no end in sight. I owe you, Luc."

He put his hand on hers, keeping the connection. "Perhaps I could collect an installment right now." He'd be kidding himself if he didn't admit that this had been his intent all along. Otherwise, he'd have stayed in the house. But he wouldn't force her. "I'm not the groom you would have chosen, and this sure as hell isn't what you expected from a wedding day. But at least we deserve a kiss…don't we?"

His free hand settled at her waist, caressing the satin-covered curve that led to her hip. As far as he could tell, she was bare beneath the seductive piece of lingerie.

Her eyes searched his, and she moved her hand away. Now both of his palms cupped her hips, inexorably pulling her closer. Her breasts brushed his bare chest. Someone moaned. Was it him?

He leaned his forehead on hers. "Do you want me to stop?"

Small white teeth mutilated her bottom lip. "What I want and what is wise are two different things."

He pushed his hips against hers, letting her feel the evidence of his arousal. He was going to pay like hell for this, but he couldn't stop. "I don't really give a damn about what's wise right at this moment."

They were pressed together now, and they might as well have been naked for all the modesty their thin garments afforded. Every hill and plane of her body fit with his like the most exquisite puzzle. Yin to yang. Positive to negative. Male to female.

She slid her arms around his neck.

He shuddered, struggling to keep a rein on his passion. Sexual attraction. That's all it was. Natural male urgency after a stretch of celibacy.

At first, their lips barely met, hardly touched. Some innate caution they both recognized pretended to slow the dance. But the cataclysm was building and nothing could hold it back.

When her small tongue hesitantly traced his bottom lip,

he growled and lifted her off her feet. Their mouths dueled, fumbled, smashed together again in reckless, breathless pleasure.

He had never forgotten her taste…sweet, but with a tart bite like an October apple. The month they first met. The time he'd fallen hard.

And speaking of hard. He rubbed his shaft against her soft belly, making her whimper. That sound of feminine longing went straight to his gut, destroying all semblance of sanity.

Again and again he kissed her…throat, cheeks, eyelids, and back to her soft, puffy-lipped mouth. He dropped to his knees and tongued her navel, wetting the fabric and gripping her hips so tightly he feared bruising her.

Her hands fisted in his hair. But she was holding him close, not pushing him away.

The tsunami crashed over him, an unimagined, unexpected wave of yearning so endless, his eyes stung.

But the aftermath was devastation.

He stumbled to his feet when Hattie tore herself from his embrace, her hair wild, her eyes dark and wide.

She held out a hand when he would have taken her in his arms again. "You've got to give me time," she whispered, her voice hoarse. "It's not just me anymore. I have the baby to think about. I can't afford to make another mistake."

"A mistake." He repeated it dumbly, his control in shreds. His soul froze with a whoosh of unbearable coldness. He shrugged, the studied nonchalance taking every ounce of acting skill he possessed. "You'll have to forgive me. I got carried away by the ambience. But you're right. We're both adults. We should be using our heads, not succumbing to moonlight madness. Let's chalk this up to a long day and leave it at that."

Her arms wrapped around her waist. For a moment he could swear she was going to say something of import.

But she didn't. And for the second time that day, she left him.

If Hattie slept at all, it was only in bits and snatches. Her eyes were gritty when the alarm went off at eight-thirty. And the fact that she had set an alarm for the first morning of her honeymoon made her want to laugh hysterically. She bit down on the macabre humor, afraid that if she let loose of the tight hold she had on her emotions that she would dissolve into a total mess.

She was dressed, packed and sitting on the bed by nine-fifteen. There was plenty of food in the kitchen, but the prospect of eating made her nauseous. Her stomach was tightly knotted, her mouth dry with despair.

When Luc knocked on her door just before ten, she opened it with pseudo calm. "Good morning."

He didn't return her greeting, but merely held out a cup of coffee. It was black and lightly sweet, just the way she liked it. Luc's expression was shuttered, dark smudges beneath his eyes emphasizing his lack of sleep.

As he picked up two of her bags, he spoke quietly. "I can hear the chopper. The pilot and I will load the luggage. Why don't you wait on the porch until we're ready?"

It was all accomplished in minutes. The man flying the helicopter was polite and deferential as he handed Hattie up into the large doorway. Luc followed. They buckled in, the rotors roared to life and moments later they were airborne.

Hattie gazed down at the island and had to blink back tears. It had been a fairy-tale wedding. Too bad she knew that fairy tales were nothing more than pleasant fiction.

The noise in the chopper made conversation impossible. Which was fine by Hattie. She kept her nose glued to the glass and watched the shoreline recede as they cruised across central Georgia. Ignoring Luc at the moment equaled self-preservation.

Landing at Atlanta's enormous airport was frantic. Chaos reigned in controlled waves. Luc gave her a sardonic look as they made their way into the terminal followed by their luggage. "We're flying commercial today," he said, scanning the departure board for their gate. "I know your Puritan soul would have balked if I had chartered a jet for just the two of us."

The security lines were long and slow. But finally, they were able to board. Hattie had never flown first-class. The width of the seat was generous, but still dangerously close to Luc's. She closed her eyes and pretended to sleep as the jet gathered speed and took off.

Pretense became reality. She woke up only when they touched down in Miami. Luc must have slept, as well, because his usual sartorial perfection was definitely rumpled.

Their connecting flight to Key West was a small plane with only two seats on either side of a narrow aisle. Now she and Luc were wedged hip to hip. After her long nap, it was hard to fake sleep again. So she pretended an intense interest in watching the commotion outside her window.

When they were airborne for the short flight, Luc pulled out a business magazine and buried his head in it.

Hattie and her new groom had barely spoken the entire day.

She was travel-weary, depressed and missing Deedee.

The Key West airport was as tiny as Atlanta's was huge. Nothing more than a handful of plastic chairs and a few car rental counters. Luc had taken care of every detail. Their leased vehicle, a bright, cherry-red convertible, was waiting for them.

The first humorous moment of the day arrived when they

struggled to fit their luggage into the car's small trunk. A disgruntled Luc finally conceded defeat and went inside to swap the car for a roomier sedan.

While he was gone, Hattie made a decision. They couldn't ignore each other forever. Last night was a bad mistake. He knew it, and she knew it. So it was best to start over and go from here.

She managed a smile when he returned with the new set of keys. "Sorry that didn't work out. I liked the convertible."

He thrust the last bag into the backseat and motioned for her to get in. "I'd buy you one, but it's not a great car for a mom."

His casual generosity was one thing, but hearing herself called a "mom" shocked her. It was true. She was a mother. The knowledge still had a hard time sinking into her befuddled brain.

Luc had apparently been here before or had at least memorized the route, because he drove with confidence, not bothering to consult the navigation system. When they pulled up in front of a charming two-story structure that looked like a sea captain's home from the nineteenth century, Hattie was surprised and delighted. This was so much better than an impersonal hotel.

The wooden building was painted mint-green with white trim. Neatly trimmed bougainvillea, and other flowers Hattie couldn't name, bloomed in profusion, emphasizing the tropical ambience.

Luc and Hattie had barely stepped from the car when a distinguished gentleman, perhaps in his early sixties, came out to meet them. He extended a hand to each of them. "Welcome to Flamingo's Rest. I'm the innkeeper, Marcel. We have the honeymoon suite all ready for you."

Marcel opened the weathered oak door and ushered them inside.

He grinned at Hattie, clearly happy to be welcoming guests. "You've come at a beautiful time of year."

Marcel led them up carpeted stairs and flung open the door to an apartment that took up half of the second floor. Before Hattie could do more than glance inside, their host smiled broadly. "Key West is the perfect spot for a romantic getaway. Let me know if you need anything at all."

Ten

In the wake of the innkeeper's departure, Hattie watched as Luc prowled the elegant quarters. The bedroom boasted an enormous four-poster king-size bed. Just looking at it through the doorway made Hattie tremble.

At the moment, she was ensconced in less volatile territory. The living area was furnished luxuriously, including a sofa and several chairs, a flat-screen TV, a wet bar and plush carpet underfoot.

Hattie curled up in one of the leather chairs. "This is very nice," she said, her words carefully neutral.

A brief knock at the door heralded the arrival of their luggage. Marcel and a younger employee stowed everything in the generous closets, accepted Luc's tip with pleased smiles and exited quietly.

In the subsequent silence, awkwardness grew.

Hattie waved a hand, doing her best to seem unconcerned. "I'll sleep out here. The couch is big and comfortable. I'll be fine." She tried changing the subject. "I'm going to call Ana now and see if I can talk to Deedee." She stopped and grinned wryly. "Well, you know what I mean. Do you want to say anything?"

Luc grabbed a beer from the fridge, his movements jerky. "Not right now. I have some business calls I need to make. I'll be in the bedroom if you need me."

Hattie choked on a sound that wasn't quite a giggle. She couldn't help it. After last night, his careless comment struck her as darkly funny.

Luc grimaced, his gaze flinty. "Give Ana and Sherman my regards."

Hattie sighed as he disappeared. Luc was definitely disgruntled. She didn't really blame him. Men didn't do well with sexual frustration, and Hattie herself was feeling out of sorts. What would it take to coax him back into a less confrontational mood?

Deedee chortled and babbled when Ana held the phone to the baby's ear. But Hattie couldn't really tell if Deedee recognized her voice. When the call ended, she had to wipe her eyes, but she knew that this separation wouldn't harm her niece. It was Hattie who was having a hard time.

The sitting room actually had its own bathroom, so Hattie decided to freshen up. Fortunately, she had kept her personal bag with her, so she didn't have to invade the bedroom. Knowing how airlines could lose luggage, she'd packed a pair of khaki walking shorts and a teal blouse in her carry-on. She changed out of her dress into the more casual clothes, breathing a sigh of relief.

Being Luc Cavallo's wife was going to take some adjustment. Hattie was accustomed to traveling in jeans and sneakers, not haute couture.

Her shoes were in one of the big suitcases, so she padded barefoot to the window and looked out into the courtyard. Two small pools, one behind the other, glowed like jewels in the late afternoon sun. It struck her as she glanced at her watch that she had been married an entire day already.

It was a full hour before Luc reappeared. He, too, had changed, but only into a fresh dress shirt. He had his briefcase in hand and a jacket slung over his shoulder.

Hattie's eyes widened. "What's going on?"

"I have to leave." He didn't quite manage to meet her gaze as he fiddled with his watch strap. "There's a crisis in the Miami office, and I'm the closest man on the ground. Our VP there is supposed to be signing a hot new Latin designer, and apparently things aren't going well."

"You're going to Miami?" She was stunned.

He shrugged into his jacket. "I'll talk to Marcel on the way out. Everyone understands business emergencies. He'll look out for you while I'm gone. Shouldn't be more than twenty-four hours at the most, not enough time for anyone to question our marriage. You'll enjoy the shopping here. And order dinner in if you don't feel like getting out tonight."

"You're leaving me on our honeymoon?" The reality was sinking in. She couldn't decide if she was more angry or hurt.

Luc strode to the door, opened it and looked back, his eyes empty of any emotion. "My life didn't suddenly stop when you came back, Hattie. I've done everything you asked. Deedee is safe. We both know this marriage is temporary. You'll have to make some allowances. I sure the hell am."

She curled up on the massive bed and cried for an hour. Insulting, that's what it was. So what if this wasn't a real marriage? Didn't she deserve at least a *pretend* honeymoon?

And did Luc care so little for her feelings that he could simply desert her after last night?

Her eyes were red and puffy, but she was calm when her cell phone rang at nine o'clock. She didn't recognize the number, though she knew it was an Atlanta area code.

Leo's deep voice echoed on the other end. "I need to talk to my brother. He's not answering his damn phone."

Hattie tucked a strand of hair behind her ear and scooted up on the down pillows. "He's not here, Leo."

"What do you mean he's not there?"

"He left. He's gone. Kaput. Some commotion in the Miami office about a new designer and an important contract."

"What the hell?"

Hattie winced. "I don't know what to say, Leo. He's not here."

Muffled profanity on the other end of the line was followed by Leo's long, audible sigh. "I'm sorry, Hattie. I should have gone to Miami. But I've been tied up with another deal."

"It's not your fault. I'm pretty sure this is his way of showing me he's the boss. Or maybe he's dishing out a bit of payback. He still harbors a lot of anger toward me. And I can't really blame him."

"I'm sure the Miami crisis is real."

"It probably is," she said, her voice dull. "But how many brides do you know who would put up with this? Me? I don't have a choice. He holds all the cards. Good night, Leo."

Luc stood on his balcony, staring out at the ocean and cursing his own stubbornness. He'd handled the business crisis in record time and had been ready to speed back to his lovely wife. But at the last moment he decided to stay gone overnight. It was important that Hattie understand he wouldn't be swayed by his lust.

They were going to have sex…and soon. But he wasn't a slave to his libido. And he wasn't going to fall at her knees and beg.

The irony didn't escape him. He'd been on his knees on his wedding night. But Hattie's indecision had saved him from making a fool of himself. He was back in the driver's seat.

He wondered what Hattie was doing right now. Was she at a restaurant, where available men were hitting on her? He slammed his fist on the railing and welcomed the pain. Maybe it would clear his head.

In business, he knew that the key to success was always, always keeping the upper hand. Last night had been a bad mistake. He'd allowed Hattie to see how much he still wanted her. And that knowledge was power.

She was supposed to beg *him* for sex, not the other way around. He wasn't in love with her. This gnawing ache in his gut was simple male lust. His last relationship had ended several months ago, and since then work had been all-consuming.

When Hattie showed up on his doorstep, it made sense that he would respond to her strongly, given their past and his recent stretch of celibacy. And it made sense for them to enjoy each other physically as long as they were legally man and wife. But when Deedee's situation was secure, Luc would make it clear that it was time for the two females to go.

Hattie fell into an exhausted slumber somewhere around two in the morning. So she was peeved when Marcel knocked at her suite before nine. But when she opened the door, the man standing there was not Marcel. It was Leo Cavallo. Her brand-new brother-in-law.

She ran a hand through her hair, ruefully aware that she looked a mess. "What are you doing here?"

He seemed unusually somber. "May I come in?"

Her knees went weak. "Oh, God. Is it Luc?" She grabbed his shirt. "Tell me. Is he okay?" Little yellow dots danced in front of her eyes and the world went black.

When she came to, she was lying flat on her back on the sofa with Leo hovering nearby. He patted her hand. "I'm sorry

I scared you. Luc is fine." His gaze was accusatory. "You still love him."

She sat up carefully. "Of course I don't."

"Are you pregnant? Is that why you fainted?"

"Leo. For God's sake. I didn't eat dinner and I haven't had breakfast. I got woozy. End of story."

She stood up carefully and went to the minibar for a Coke. She needed caffeine badly, and she wasn't prepared to wait for coffee to brew. "You still haven't told me why you're here." She shot him a bewildered look.

He shrugged, dwarfing the armchair in which he sat. "When you told me Luc had gone to Miami, it got me to thinking. At the wedding, only a blind man could have missed the fact that Luc still has strong feelings for you…and vice versa. I wasn't the only one who noticed."

"Your imagination is impressive."

"Deny it if you want. But regardless, it's a crappy thing to do to you…abandoning you on your honeymoon."

"And you've come to tell him that?"

"No. I'm here to get him to sign some papers. They're important, but I wouldn't have bothered him on his honeymoon except for the fact that he apparently doesn't see anything wrong with mixing business with pleasure." He held up his hands. "I'll hang out with you until he gets back."

She shook her head, smiling. "I thought I was the villainess of the piece."

"I've been known to be wrong on occasion." He shrugged, his boyish grin equally as appealing as her husband's. But Leo's smile didn't stir her heartbeat in the least.

"That's sweet of you, but not necessary. I can entertain myself."

"Quit arguing. Go put your swimsuit on. I'll do a quick change myself and get Marcel to roust us up some brunch."

Leo was as good as his word. When Hattie made her

way down to the pool in silver slides and an emerald-green maillot, her brother-in-law was already stretched out on a chaise lounge, apparently content to while away a few hours.

As she sat down beside him, she heard a quiet snore. He must have taken the red-eye. Poor guy. She'd let him sleep.

When the sun warmed her through and through, she slipped into the pool with a sigh of pleasure. Being rich definitely had its advantages. She did some laps and then floated lazily, feeling the hot rays beating down on her.

It was nice of Leo to keep her company, but Hattie wanted her husband…stripped down to nothing but his swim trunks so she could ogle his body to her heart's content.

If Marcel thought it odd that a new bride was frolicking poolside with a man who wasn't her husband, he made no sign. He was polite and unobtrusive when he brought out a tray laden with everything from scrambled eggs and bacon to fresh mangoes and homemade croissants filled with dark chocolate.

Leo roused in time to devour his share of the repast. "I was hungry," he said sheepishly as he snitched a lone strawberry.

Hattie lay back, her cup and saucer balanced on her tummy. "This coffee is to die for. I'll have to find out what brand it is." She finished her drink and turned on her stomach…drifting, half-awake, listening to birdsong and the gentle sough of the wind in the palm fronds.

Leo poked her knee. "You're turning pink, princess. Better put some sunscreen on."

Without opening her eyes, she reached for the bottle of lotion under her chair. "Will you do my back, please? I'll throw a towel over my legs, so don't bother with that."

Luc parked the car in front of the B and B and sat for ten seconds, giving himself a lecture. He was calm. He was in control. Hattie would dance to his tune.

He had a plan. One that would satisfy the hunger riding him and at the same time make it clear to his new wife that nothing had changed. Their marriage was still temporary.

It was an unpleasant shock to find their suite empty. But then he took a deep breath. Hattie was shopping, that was all. Women loved to shop. The tourist district of Key West wasn't all that big. Maybe he would take the car and drive around for a bit, see if he spotted her.

As he hurried back down the stairs, keys in hand, Marcel intercepted him. "Welcome back, Mr. Cavallo. I hope your business was transacted successfully."

"Yeah," Luc muttered, unaccountably embarrassed. "Do you happen to know if Hattie has gone to town?"

Marcel shook his head. "Your wife is out by the pool with her friend. I served them a meal not long ago. Shall I bring more food?"

"No thanks. Not hungry."

Luc's hackles rose. *Her friend?* No doubt, some handsome surfer type had taken advantage of Luc's short absence to make a move.

Well, not for long, buddy.

Luc walked outside, keeping behind the bushes until he got a clear shot of the pool. Hattie was stretched out, facedown, in a suit that made his mouth water. But the sight that took his breath away was the large man rubbing lotion into Hattie's shoulders.

Damn and double damn. The guy had his back to Luc, and at this distance, Luc couldn't really tell much about him… except that he was getting way too chummy with Luc's wife.

The man murmured something to Hattie that made her laugh. Luc's vision blurred with rage and indignation.

He burst through the shrubbery and advanced on the couple by the pool. "What in the hell is going on?"

The man turned his head and smiled…a wicked, *look what*

I'm up to smile. Leo stood up. "Well, hello, Luc. It's about damn time you got here."

Though he was stunned, Luc didn't let on. "Why are you here, Leo? If you're dying for a honeymoon, find your own damn wife."

Leo mocked him deliberately. "When I heard that you were willing to transact business this week, I brought some contracts that need your John Hancock ASAP."

By this time, Hattie had scrambled to her feet. Her sweat-sheened breasts revealed by the relatively modest décolletage of her suit gave Luc pause for a second or two, but he dragged his eyes away from his wife's erotic body and faced off with his sibling.

Luc looked pointedly at Leo's casual attire. "But nothing so urgent that you couldn't chill out by the pool," he said, irritated beyond belief. It had been years since he and Leo had tangled in a fistfight, but Luc was spoiling for a rematch.

Hattie grabbed his arm. "Sit down, Luc. You're being rude."

Leo egged him on. "It's your fault, little bro. I wouldn't be here if you hadn't been such a Type A jerk."

That was it. Luc lunged at Leo, determined to pummel him into the ground. Their bodies collided and the fight was on.

But Luc hadn't counted on Hattie.

She grabbed his shirt and clung to him. "Stop this. Right now. You're both insane."

He shrugged her off. "Get out of the way." He rammed his shoulder into Leo's chest. Leo fired back with a punch to Luc's solar plexus.

Hattie jumped on Luc's back this time, her arms around his neck in a stranglehold. "I mean it," she pleaded, her voice shaking. "He's your brother."

A second time Luc shook her off. "He's a pain in the ass."

Leo was momentarily distracted by Hattie's distress. Luc

used the brief advantage to land another right to Leo's chin, this time splitting his own knuckles.

Hattie tried a third intervention, grabbing Luc's belt with two hands. But both men were in motion and when she lost her grasp, she slipped on the wet surface of the pool deck and fell sideways, her cheek raking the edge of the glass-topped table as she went down.

Luc and Leo froze. Luc was down on his knees in seconds, scooping her into his arms. "Oh, God, Hattie. Are you okay?"

She struggled to a sitting position and said, "Yes."

But she was lying. Blood oozed down her cheek from a nasty gash.

Leo crouched with them, cursing beneath his breath. "Is it bad?"

"I can't tell," Luc said, his hands shaky. "We need to get her checked out."

Hattie waved a hand. "Hellooo. I'm right here. If you two doofuses would kiss and make up, I'll be fine."

Luc eyes his brother sheepishly. "Sorry, man."

Leo grinned. "I deserved it."

Hattie rolled her eyes. "Morons." Luc heard rueful affection in the two syllables.

He motioned to his brother. "Grab one of those cloth napkins."

Leo complied, wetting the fabric in a water glass.

When Luc pressed gently at the wound, Hattie winced. "That hurts. Let me do it."

He surrendered the makeshift swab reluctantly, watching in dismay as Hattie removed more of the blood. It was an odd cut, and one that stitches wouldn't necessarily help.

The unflappable Marcel appeared, handing over a first aid kit. He glanced quickly at Hattie's cheek. "A butterfly bandage should do the trick, I think."

Luc applied antibiotic ointment and pressed the plaster

in place as tenderly as he could. He and Leo helped her to her feet.

Now that the immediate crisis was over, Hattie was clearly flustered. She reached for her sheer cover-up and slid her arms into it. "I'm going upstairs to take a shower," she said, her eyes daring him to protest. "I suggest you two get your act together while I'm gone."

She turned with dignity to Marcel. "Thank you for your help. It's nice to know that someone around here has good sense."

As she flounced her way into the house, Leo shook his head and smiled. "Your wife is one tough cookie."

Luc nodded, sobered by what might have been. "For once, I agree with you completely."

Eleven

When Hattie stepped into the sitting room, she saw Luc ensconced on the sofa, elbows on his knees, waiting for her.

He stood and faced her. "You look nice."

She picked up her purse, fiddling with the contents. "Thanks." She was wearing a gauzy ankle-length dress in shades of taupe and gold. It was sleeveless, and the V neck dipped low front and back. A necklace and bracelet in chunky amber stones complemented the outfit.

The small bandage on her cheekbone made her self-conscious, but that was mostly vanity talking. Her ensemble was dressy but comfortable. After the last few days, relaxation was high on Hattie's list.

She bit her lip, not wanting to resurrect any bad feelings. "Where's Leo?"

Luc made a face. "Don't worry. I signed the damn papers. He's changing downstairs to give us some privacy. I thought we'd go out for a late lunch somewhere nice, and afterward, he'll head home."

Leaving us all alone on our "it-has-to-get-better-than-

this" honeymoon. The thought swept through Hattie's brain like wildfire, singeing neurons and making her legs weak. "Sounds good."

But when they got downstairs, Leo was gone. Marcel handed over a note. Luc read it, his expression blank and then passed it over to Hattie.

Don't want to intrude. Have a good week. See you in Hotlanta.

Hattie tossed the little piece of paper in a nearby trash can, her palms damp. "I guess it's just us."

Luc's gaze was hooded. "Guess so."

He ushered her out to the car, and they drove the short distance to the historic district. After squeezing into a tiny parking space on a street curb, Luc shut off the engine and came around to open Hattie's door. His hand on her elbow did amazing things to her heart rate.

She told herself not to expect too much. Nothing had changed. They weren't a normal couple by any means.

But it was hard to remember such mundane considerations amidst the tropical atmosphere of Key West. Everyone was in a good mood, it seemed. And no wonder. The view from Mallory Square was filled with cerulean seas, colorful watercraft and white, billowing triangles atop sailboats that zigged and zagged across the open waves.

Just offshore lay a palm-fringed island that looked so perfect Hattie wondered if the Chamber of Commerce had painted it against the sky to frame the sunsets.

When she said as much, Luc responded. "One of the large hotel chains owns it. You can rent one-, two- or three-bedroom cottages, and they even have their own man-made beach."

Hattie had already realized that Key West was not a typical "beach" destination. The coastline was rocky or coral-built.

The Conch Republic, as it was called, was literally the last stop before Cuba, a mere ninety miles southwest.

At a marina adjacent to one of the fabulous hotels, Luc took Hattie's hand and helped her down into a sleek speedboat. Moments later, they were cutting across the waves, bound for the island.

In minutes, they pulled up to a well-kept dock and stepped out of the boat. A uniformed attendant directed them to the restaurant. It was open air on three sides, with huge rattan ceiling fans rotating overhead as an adjunct to the natural sea breezes. Delicate potted orchids bloomed on each table. China, silver and crystal gleamed.

The food was amazing…fresh shrimp gumbo and homemade corn bread. Hattie chewed automatically.

She was ready for a showdown, but if she initiated what might turn out to be a shouting match, would it be worth it? Hattie's mother had made a life's work out of tiptoeing around Hattie's stepfather. She always acted as if he might desert her at any moment.

The truth was that the guy loved Hattie's mother and would have given her anything. But early lessons are hard to unlearn. Hattie wasn't proficient at confrontation, but then again, she was no pushover. Luc was doing her a favor, yes. But that didn't mean he could dominate her.

She waited until the server put a piece of key lime pie in front of each of them before she fired the first shot. "How was your business trip?"

Luc choked on a bite of dessert. "Fine," he muttered. "This pie is great."

She wouldn't be deterred. If she had been clearer about her feelings a decade ago, she and Luc might possibly have worked things out. Her jaw tightened. "There was no excuse for you to leave on the first day of our honeymoon. Not only was it disrespectful to me, it also endangered our pretense of a happy marriage. I think you were trying to teach me a lesson, but it backfired."

Luc set down his fork and leaned back in his chair, his face sober. He exhaled slowly, his lips twisted. "You're right, of course. And I do apologize."

She cocked her head, studying him, trying to see inside his brain. "I've never said this, but my leaving you wasn't really about money. It was about control."

Luc jerked as if she had slapped him. "I don't understand."

"As a young woman, my mother had an affair with her boss, a wealthy, powerful man. When she told him she was pregnant, he cast her off without a second thought. That shining example of a man was my father. My biological father."

Shock creased his face. "I wasn't your boss, Hattie. What does that have to do with anything? I feel sorry for your mother, but you're certainly not the kind to do something so reckless."

"You're missing the point. My whole childhood revolved around this missing mystery man. This terrible person who didn't want me. And to hear my mother tell it, money was what gave him all the power. Leaving her power*less* and alone. From the time I was old enough to understand, she drilled into me the importance of making my own way in the world and not letting any man control my destiny."

"And you thought I would do something like that to you?" He looked haunted.

"Of course not. But I was so head over heels in love with you, I was afraid I'd lose myself in your life. It's very easy to be taken care of, very addictive. And I wasn't brave enough to stick with you. In hindsight, I believe I was stronger than I realized at the time. But as a kid of twenty, all I could see was that you had the money and power to do anything you wanted. And I felt lost in your shadow."

"Despite the fact that I wanted you so badly I followed you around like a puppy."

"You were a young man at the mercy of his hormones. Sex makes men do crazy things."

They were sitting at adjoining corners of a table for four. Beneath the linen cloth, Luc took her hand and deliberately pushed it against his erection. "I'm not so young now," he growled, releasing her fingers and eating his pie as if nothing had happened.

The imprint of his rigid flesh was burned into Hattie's palm. She took a reckless swallow of wine. "Don't be crass."

He shrugged, his eyes a dangerous flash of obsidian. "What do you want from me, Hattie?"

She hesitated, torn between fascinated curiosity about his response to her and a healthy sense of caution. "Do you really think we can be intimate and then walk away?"

Luc shrugged again. "I can if you can."

Hattie frowned, licking whipped cream from her spoon. His nonchalance could be an act. Her heart beat faster.

She cocked her head and stared at him, trying to read his mind. He was as inscrutable as the great and powerful wizard of Oz. If Hattie could click her heels in ruby slippers, she'd be able to go back to that innocent time in college.

Did she want to? Or did she want to move ahead as an adult woman with adult needs? She'd be taking an enormous risk. What if she fell in love with Luc again? What if she never had really *stopped* loving him? What if they had sex and it was ho-hum?

Not likely.

She scraped one last bite of topping from her plate and ate it absently. Luc's hungry gaze followed every motion she made. Her throat dried. It was now or never.

When the waiter moved to a safe distance, Hattie rested her arms on the table and moved in close to Luc. She put her hand over his. “You said I had to be the one to say yes or no. But you have to know that my answer has nothing to do with protecting a baby…nothing to do with mistakes we made in the past. No feelings of obligation. This is about us…you and me. And I say—”

Luc put his hand over her mouth, his expression violent. “Not another word.”

Luc was burning up. The tropical heat and Hattie’s proximity made him sweat. Her gaze seemed to dissect him like a bug. To burrow inside his brain and discern his secrets. He lifted an impatient hand for the check, deliberately breaking their physical connection. He was too close to the edge. Hearing Hattie acquiesce to their mutual desire for sexual intimacy could push him over. And it wouldn’t be smart to let her realize how desperate he was to have her. Talking about sex in a public venue had not helped in the least when it came to controlling his baser urges.

After he shoved two large bills into the folio, he took Hattie by the wrist, dragging her toward the exit. “We’re going back to the house,” he said. “I think you have sunstroke.”

She laughed softly. They reached the dock, and it was all he could do not to crush her against one of the wooden posts and ravage her mouth with his. He damned the surroundings that forced him to act like a gentleman. He’d never felt less civilized in his life.

Other tourists joined them beneath the awning, and soon the return boat arrived. Hattie’s hip and thigh were glued to Luc’s in the small, crowded craft. Back on dry land, she followed him meekly to the car. Her honey-blond hair gleamed in the unforgiving sun.

Seeing her pink shoulders made him think of Leo again.

Which made him think of doing the lotion thing for Hattie, covering every inch of her creamy skin with fragrant moisture.

He knew what she was going to say, and his body said a resounding *"hell, yeah!"* But in addition to his need to remain in control, it occurred to him that he owed her some romance…to make up for his less than stellar behavior as a new groom. They had eight or nine hours to kill before bedtime. It was far too hot to walk the streets in the midday heat.

Fortunately, their rental was parked beneath a huge shade tree. Luc leaned his elbows on the top of the car and faced Hattie with the vehicle between them. "What would you like to do now?" he asked, wishing he could supply the answer.

She lifted the hair from the back of her neck and sighed. "I love the pool," she said. "Do you mind too much if we go back and swim? We can play tourist tomorrow."

"Whatever you want," he croaked, his mind racing ahead. Swimming as foreplay made as much sense as anything else to his testosterone fuddled brain.

In the bedroom there was an awkward moment when they both reached into suitcases with plans to change clothes. Luc held up his hands, gripping a pair of black swim trunks. "I'll use the other bathroom."

He was ready in four minutes. It took Hattie an extra twenty. But when she reappeared, he wasn't about to complain. Her hair was swept up on top of her head, leaving recalcitrant tendrils to cling to her damp neck. The white terry robe she wore covered her from throat to knee, but it molded to her breasts and hips with just enough cling to encourage his imagination.

He thought he had himself under control. But all bets were off when they reached the pool and Hattie ditched the cover-up. She wore a different suit this time, and he was damned glad Leo hadn't been around to see this one.

It was a neon-blue bikini. Luc was stunned. She was a sexual goddess, even more lovely than she had been in college. The bikini bottom fastened at the hips with a large gold circlet on either side. The two tiny triangles of fabric that made up the top barely met decency standards.

Luc looked around suspiciously to see if anyone else was enjoying the show, but their privacy was absolute. Nothing but flowers and water and a mermaid just for his entertainment. If there were other guests at the small inn, they were not around at the moment.

Luc made a show of selecting a chaise lounge and flipping out his towel. "I'm going to nap."

Hattie gazed at him over her shoulder, her eyes hidden behind tortoiseshell sunglasses. "Will you do me first?"

His body went rigid in shock until he saw the bottle of sunscreen she held out. "Sure."

When she was situated, he perched on his hip beside her and unscrewed the lid. Immediately, the scent of coconut assailed his nostrils. Hattie pillowed her head on her arms, a small smile tilting her lips.

Luc groaned inwardly. Giving her a taste of romance before the main event might drive him mad.

When his hands touched her back, she flinched. "It's cold."

He ran his fingers across her shoulder blades. "It won't be. Relax."

Too bad he couldn't take his own advice. Every one of his muscles was tight enough to snap. He exhaled slowly and concentrated on Hattie. His fingertips still remembered the hills and valleys of her body. His thumbs pressed on either side of her spine.

Hattie moaned.

Dear Lord.

When he hesitated, she lifted a hand and waved it lazily, her eyes closed. "Don't stop."

He smoothed one final spot of lotion into her skin and capped the bottle. "All done."

Hattie didn't answer. She was so still he suspected she had drifted off. Which irked him, because sleep was the furthest thing from his mind. He stood up and went to the deep end of the pool. After one last glance at Hattie, he dove in and started a series of punishing laps. Harder and faster, pushing his body to exhaustion.

He swam until his legs began to feel like spaghetti. And then he swam some more. When spots of light began to dance behind his eyelids, he dragged himself out of the pool and collapsed onto his lounger facedown. Hattie lay where he had left her, her almost naked body lax and limp, her skin glistening with a dewy sheen of lotion and perspiration.

Luc closed his eyes, his heart pounding in his chest. He had a painful erection. His body was clenched with desire, despite the brutal workout. He was a man, not a eunuch. He might not be in love with Hattie like he'd been as a stupid kid of twenty, but he had normal male needs. If she didn't come to him soon, he'd never be able to keep up the pretense that he was in control of the situation.

It was a shock to feel hands on his back. He'd been so caught up in his own turmoil, he never heard Hattie move. She mimicked his earlier position and was now preparing to rub sunscreen into his burning skin. Thankfully, his Italian heritage made him able to endure the sun without painful consequences, but he knew he needed the protection.

The question was—who or what would protect him from Hattie?

Her hands were small, but strong. Despite the ostensible point of the exercise, this was foreplay. And Luc was strung so tightly, he wasn't sure he could bear it.

Five minutes later, his body aching with the need to roll

over and pull Hattie down into his arms, she finished. He felt her touch on his hair, her fingers ruffling the wet strands.

She leaned in closer, her breast brushing his side. "I'm getting in the water. Why don't you join me?"

It was a dare. He recognized it as such and knew that this game of cat and mouse had only one possible conclusion. But it was up to him to write the script and make sure Hattie knew who was in control.

He swung to a sitting position. Now they were so close, he could have leaned forward a scant two inches and kissed her. But he didn't. Not yet.

He smiled grimly, cursing his body's weakness. "After you."

She didn't try to dive in, but instead used the ladder to lower herself into the pool. The water was only chest high where she stood. He executed a show-off dive from the opposite direction and came up beside her, shoving the hair from his face. Her eyes were wide.

He touched her shoulder. "Want a ride in the deep end?"

Hattie nodded, not speaking.

He took her hand. "Get on my back."

When she complied, her legs wrapping around his waist and her arms encircling his shoulders, he shuddered. "Hang on."

He walked forward, feeling the bottom of the pool fall away beneath his feet. When he could barely touch bottom, he tugged her off his back and around until she faced him. The slightly surprised look in her eyes when she realized she was out of her depth made him smile inwardly.

Her hands clenched his shoulders, her fingernails leaving marks in his skin. Their legs drifted together and apart. He knew she felt the evidence of what she did to him.

Hattie nibbled her bottom lip. "The water feels great."

She was nervous. He liked that. "A lot of things feel great," he said, deliberately taunting her.

"You didn't let me give you my answer earlier," she said, her eyes alight with mischief.

He kissed her softly, a bare brush of mouth to mouth. She tasted like warm summer fruit. "It will keep," he muttered. "No need to rush."

Need swam between them. His. Hers. It might have been a decade, but some pleasures the body never forgets.

Her eyes drifted shut.

"No. Look at me." He cupped one breast.

Hattie's eyelids fluttered open, her gaze unfocused, her cheeks flushed despite the cool water. Her soft cry went straight to his gut.

He kicked his legs rhythmically, keeping them afloat. Now he took the other breast. Two handfuls…warm, seductive, feminine bounty. He massaged gently, moving the barely-there bikini top aside to find naked flesh.

The pleasure flooding him from touching her so intimately blurred his vision. His hands settled at her waist as he took her mouth in a ravaging kiss. They were in danger of losing all rational thought. And he was sinking fast.

As fact matched thought, they slipped beneath the surface of the water. He kissed her again, and this time, he slid his hand into the bottom of her bikini and cupped her, pressing a finger into her tight passage and probing…stroking.

It lasted no more than a few seconds. He dragged them both back up for air. Hattie wrapped her legs around his waist, her ragged breathing matching his. She had a death grip on his shoulders, her breasts mashed to his chest.

She initiated the kiss this time, her small teeth nipping his bottom lip, her tongue sliding between his teeth, dazing him with an ache so intense, his head hurt. Hunger raged like a wild animal, one that hadn't been fed in a decade.

She whimpered when he cupped her bottom, pulling her closer. "Luc…Luc."

Hearing his name on her lips almost unmanned him. "What, Hattie?"

"Please," she groaned. "My answer is yes. Please, please, please make love to me."

Exultation filled his chest. That was what he needed to hear. "Ask me again," he demanded.

Her gaze filled with frustration. "No games. Take me. Now."

Twelve

Hattie stumbled as Luc dragged her toward the house, their few belongings left behind in his haste. His grip on her wrist allowed no protest. But then why would she…protest, that is?

She wanted Luc—the sooner the better.

If she had expected awkwardness in the bedroom, she was wrong. Luc was smooth, determined. He stripped off his trunks, grinning tightly when she looked her fill.

His erection was magnificent. Thick, long and ready for her…only her. His broad chest and strong arms rippled with muscles. He cupped her face in his hands. "Take it off."

His adamant tone brooked no refusal.

She trembled inside and out as she unfastened the knot at the back of her neck and reached behind to undo the clasp. For seconds, the bikini top clung damply to her breasts as she clutched it in sudden, belated hesitation.

The corner of Luc's beautiful mouth quirked in a half smile. "Don't go all shy on me now, Hattie."

She gulped inwardly and let the scraps of fabric fall. Luc inhaled sharply. The look in his eyes made her weak. In college, he had been her first love, her first lover. Now he was a mature man in his sexual prime. She felt the heat of his desire, not as quiet warmth, but as a flashpoint poised to explode.

There was the problem of what to do with her hands. She wanted to cover her breasts instinctively. But she knew Luc would have none of that. So her arms hung at her sides as she shifted from one foot to the other.

He lifted an eyebrow. "You're not finished."

She might have taken umbrage at his arrogant tone had she not been as eager as he was for the next act. Removing her last barrier of modesty proved harder than she expected.

Luc lost patience. He gripped her hips. "Too slow," he growled. He kissed her wildly, his mouth everywhere…her lips, her throat, and finally, her bare breasts. The sensation was an electric shock. Her entire body melted into him, closer and closer still.

His hard shaft bruised her hipbone. The soft, wiry hair on his chest tickled her sensitive skin. Breath by gasping breath they relearned the taste of each other—the touch, the sound, the smell. It was a smorgasbord of sensual delight. A cornucopia of excess.

He tangled his fingers in the rings at her hips and jerked hard, ripping the thin fabric from the metal. The remnants that he tossed aside represented Hattie's last resistance, if indeed she had any.

She was drunk on memories laced with present passion.

A nanosecond later he lifted her. Her legs wrapped around his waist instinctively. The intimate position made her limp with longing. He backed her up to the nearest wall and buried his face in her neck. Tremors shook his large frame. His chest heaved.

Slowly, as if giving her time to protest, he aligned their bodies and entered her with one forceful upward thrust. He was big, but she was ready for him. When he was buried inside her, he went still.

"Hattie?" His voice was hoarse.

"Hmmm?" She bit his earlobe and heard him curse.

"You okay?"

The four-letter word didn't come close to describing what she was. "Don't stop."

"Whatever the lady wants."

The last words were barely audible as he directed all his energy toward driving them both insane. Her bare butt slapped against the door as Luc pounded into her over and over.

A searing heat built inside her, coalesced at the spot where their bodies were joined. Higher. Stronger. The world ceased to exist. Her arms tightened around his neck as she felt the storm begin to break. "Luc..." Stars cartwheeled inside her head and tumbled downward to reignite when Luc's own release sent him rigid and straining against her.

When it was over at last, Luc staggered into their bedroom, still carrying her, and dropped her onto the mattress. He came down beside her and rested his head on her chest.

Her heart stopped. A perfect cocoon of intimacy enveloped them.

She might have slept for a few minutes—she wasn't sure. Luc was out, his body a heavy weight half on top of her. She wanted so badly to stroke his hair, but she resisted. A black hole of self-destruction yawned at her feet. She was far too close to the edge.

Awkwardly, she slid from beneath him and tiptoed to the bathroom. After quickly freshening up, she put on one of the soft luxurious robes that hung on the back of the door. Belting it tightly, she peeked out into the bedroom.

Luc's speculative gaze met hers. "You won't need the robe."

Five simple words. That's all he needed to make the

moisture bloom between her legs. She grasped the door frame to steady herself. "I won't?" All the starch had left her legs. She was melting, body and soul.

He crooked a finger. "Come back to bed."

Removing the robe was even more difficult than shedding her swimsuit. In the heat of the moment, her inhibitions had gone on vacation. But now they were back.

As she padded into the room, shivering, she noticed for the first time that the AC had been kicked up a notch. Luc held a string of condom packets in his hand. "We skipped a step. I'm sorry, Hattie. That was my fault."

She shrugged with what she hoped was blasé sophistication. "It's the wrong part of the month. I'm not worried."

His grin was tight. "Then let's not waste any more time."

The robe fell at her feet. Luc's amusement faded visibly to be replaced by sheer male determination. When she shivered now, it had nothing to do with the temperature in the room and everything to do with the man stretched out on his back like a sleek, not-quite-satisfied predator.

Nothing this older, more experienced Luc did was predictable. Instead of covering her with his aroused body, he pulled her on top. It was a position she had never really liked, because it made her feel too vulnerable. But when she tried to protest, Luc took care of that by lightly touching the small bud of nerves at her center.

She braced her hands on her thighs and tried not to flinch as he explored her most private recesses. In an embarrassingly short amount of time, she moaned and climaxed, the second event no less powerful than the first.

He held her close and stroked her hair, though she could feel the strength of his unappeased desire. Tears clogged her throat. "Luc, I..." *love you.* No, she didn't. It was just the sex talking. Shades of auld lang syne. An overabundance of postcoital hormones.

He kissed her cheek. "You what?"

"I wonder if we made a mistake." She felt him go still.

"Regrets already?"

Something in his tone made her cringe. She shouldn't have introduced reality into their bed. Not now. But she was compelled to answer. "This makes things complicated. When we go our separate ways."

His hands moved from her hair, her shoulders. He shifted her until they lay side by side. Already she missed his warmth.

His tone was perfectly calm when he answered. "You're making too much of nothing. There's no harm in enjoying each other. Divorces are simple nowadays. We'll deal with any complications when we have to. It's nothing to worry about."

She winced inwardly, her lovely moment shattered by her own bad timing and Luc's carelessly callous comment. No more pretending. This wasn't a honeymoon. This was sex for the sake of scratching an itch. No use dressing it up with romantic frills.

No reason for tears to sting her eyes and a painful lump to clog her throat.

She swallowed, her mouth dry. "I want to take a shower."

Luc pounced verbally. "No, Hattie. I don't think so."

He hardly noticed that she didn't answer. He'd been kicked in the gut and was left reeling. The sweat was barely dry on their bodies and she was already talking about leaving him. Damn it to hell. *He* would be the one to end this relationship… not Hattie.

He was hard as a pike, his erection painfully stiff. With jerky motions, he ripped open a packet and rolled on a rubber. A split second later he groaned aloud as he penetrated Hattie's tight, wet warmth. She lay passive beneath him, and it pissed him off.

He took her chin in his hand. "Look at me, Mrs. Cavallo." She obeyed. He had to grit his teeth to keep from coming right then. "What we do in the privacy of our bed is our own business. We're good together. Don't fight it. Don't fight me. Let yourself go, Hattie."

Big brown eyes looked up at him with a mixture of emotions he couldn't decipher even if he wasn't being driven by his baser needs. She whispered the single word. "Okay."

It was enough. He felt her hands touch his hips, recognized the moment when she arched her back and matched her rhythm to his. A red haze clouded his vision. His hips pistoned in agonized yearning for release. It was good…so good.

Hattie gave a small shocked cry as he felt her inner muscles squeeze him. Her release triggered his, and he bore down, losing himself in her welcome embrace and finding momentary oblivion.

Sometime later, sanity returned. He could hear his own jerky breathing in the silence of the room. Hattie was still and quiet again. Had he hurt her? He moved aside with a muttered apology, relieving her of his considerable weight.

Sweet mother of God. He hadn't had sex that good in he didn't know when. *Oh, yes, you do. It was back in college when Hattie was warm and willing and you were both blissfully happy.*

He shook off the memories. No need for those when he had the real thing in his arms. What was she thinking? He was too tired to pry it out of her. He'd barely slept the night before.

His eyes closed involuntarily.

Aeons later it seemed, he felt her try to escape. His fingers closed around her wrist. "Stay."

"I need a shower."

He scrubbed his hands over his face, yawning, his head muzzy. "I'll join you."

The look on her face made him laugh as he got to his feet. "Don't be so modest. It's the green thing to do."

After turning the water to a comfortable temperature, he dragged a clearly reluctant Hattie into the luxurious shower enclosure. His lovely new wife huddled in a tiled corner, her arms wrapped around her waist.

Everything about her screamed innocent seduction…from her long slender legs to her hourglass waist, to her plump, shapely breasts. If he could paint, he'd commit her to canvas exactly like this.

He picked up a bar of soap shaped like a shell. "Turn around."

Hattie was drowning in her own need. In her wildest imagination she had never invented a scenario like this. "Why?" she muttered.

His grin was lethal. "I thought you wanted to get clean."

"You're a dirty old man."

"Not old," he deadpanned.

She gave him her back reluctantly, hyperaware that she was at his sexual mercy. The first touch of the washcloth made her jump. But it was Luc's chuckle that made her blush.

As he washed from her neck down her spine, she braced her hands on the wall and hung her head. Luc had turned the spray so that it cascaded between them. The water was cool on Hattie's hot skin.

Luc moved the rag slowly, more of a massage than a simple exercise in cleanliness. He reached her bottom and squeezed. "Turn around."

She obeyed instinctively, their gazes colliding amidst the steamy air. "I can do the rest," she said.

He shook his head. "Why bother? I'm off to a hell of a

good start." He took her hands and tucked them behind her butt. "Don't move."

The hot water was enervating, draining Hattie of any will to challenge Luc's control. This time he made no pretense of using the washcloth. He took the bar of soap and ran it in circles around her breasts. Then he pressed gently over her nipples, decorating them with tiny bubbles.

When he was satisfied, he paused to kiss her…slow and deep. With one hand, he manacled her wrists behind her back with a firm grip. Now their bodies were touching chest to chest. She felt his erection throbbing between them.

He nuzzled her nose with his and ground his hips into hers. "More work to do," he muttered.

His hand holding the soap found its way south to the middle of her thighs. Her legs parted instinctively to give him access.

When the soap glided over a certain sensitive spot, Hattie cried out and struggled. But Luc kept his tight hold on her wrists as he moved the soap between her legs.

Hattie rested her forehead on his chest, panting. "Enough," she whispered. "I'm clean." She was close to the edge, but she didn't want to make the journey alone. She wanted Luc inside her, filling her, making her his.

Without warning, he dropped the soap and released her wrists. The shower boasted a roomy stone seat. Luc reached for the condom he'd tucked on a ledge, sheathed himself, and then pulled Hattie down to sit astride his lap.

Their bodies were slick and wet, and the moment when they joined was seamless…easy. Hattie threw back her head, the water still streaming over them. Her eyes were closed, intensifying the sensation of having Luc inside her.

He was strong. He lifted her up and down in a gentle rhythm, teasing them both.

Longing crescendoed, hunger peaked. Luc's hands bruised

her bare butt as he gave a muffled shout and found his release. Hattie still lingered on the knife edge of pleasure. She could stay there forever.

Luc bit her neck, ran his tongue over her tightly furled nipples. It was enough. It was too much. She arched her back and gave a choked sob as everything inside her splintered and fanned out through her veins in cascading ripples of pure joy.

Afterward, she was weak as a baby. Luc dried her tenderly and scooped her up in his arms to carry her to their bed. Hattie had lost all sense of time. And didn't really care.

Luc muttered an apology as he slid beneath the covers and moved over her and into her. She had nothing left, but this coupling was warm and lazy. He rode her forever, it seemed, pausing each time he came close to the end and making himself wait, stretching out the incredible connection, the deep, undulating eroticism.

He enveloped her, overwhelmed her. His scent, his touch, his powerful domination.

Somewhere in the deep recesses of her consciousness lingered the knowledge that she would have to pay for this day. That down the line her heart would face pain equal to the present elation.

But she refused to let such maudlin considerations ruin the present.

She put a hand to his cheek, loving him with her eyes. "You're amazing," she whispered. "I haven't felt like this in a very long time."

His cheeks were ruddy, his eyes hooded, his chin shadowed with late-day stubble. Everything about him reeked of uncivilized, ravenous male. Little was left of the suave businessman, the wealthy CEO.

And Hattie loved it…loved him. God help her, she did. This was a man she could live with…share a life with.

But the other Luc still existed outside this room. And that was the problem. Just as it had always been.

He groaned and his whole body shook as his mighty control finally snapped. “Hattie…” He climaxed in a series of long, rapid thrusts.

Despite her exhaustion, echoes of pleasure teased her once again.

In the aftermath, they slept. And as the tropical sun sank low in the sky, coaxing the stars out to play in the gathering dusk, Mr. and Mrs. Luc Cavallo were in perfect accord for one fleeting moment.

Thirteen

Luc rolled over and looked at the clock sometime around 9:00 p.m. His stomach was growling, and no wonder. Their late brunch was the last meal he had eaten.

He slung an arm above his head and yawned, his somber gaze noting that Hattie slept peacefully. Too bad he wasn't as relaxed. The sex had been nothing short of spectacular, but now that his head was in control and not his libido, he was able to think clearly. And the conclusions he drew were unsettling.

He was in danger of falling in love with Hattie all over again. Perhaps in some ways he had never fallen *out* of love… which might explain why the many women he had dated in the last ten years never quite seemed to measure up to some unknown standard. His grandfather had accused him of being too picky…of expecting a paragon of a woman to fill his bed and his life.

Turned out…his grandfather was right.

And that woman was Hattie Parker.

He watched her sleep for a long time, mulling over his

options. Right now she needed him because of the baby. Which gave him an advantage for the moment. But what happened when the kid's father was no longer a threat? What then?

Would Hattie try to bid Luc a pleasant goodbye and walk away? The possibility made his chest tight. He was no longer a naive and vulnerable kid. He'd learned his lesson well. Loving someone too much only opened the way for hurt.

Losing both of his parents at the same time had sent him and Leo into a tailspin. Only their grandfather's gruff, tough affection had rescued them. Perhaps way back in college Luc had fallen hard for Hattie because he needed so badly to fill a void in his life.

He was more self-sufficient now, able to enjoy a physical relationship without involving messy emotions. And besides, the barrier between Hattie and him remained the same: his need for control. He had let her too close once upon a time and suffered the consequences. And if his money gave him power, did she expect him to give it all away and live in a shack?

Perhaps since his embarrassment of riches was currently saving her niece, she might decide that being with a wealthy man wasn't exactly a ticket to purgatory.

He touched her arm…he couldn't help himself. The need to keep her close was all-consuming. She had come to him for help…for protection. He would keep Hattie and Deedee safe at all costs. It was the honorable thing to do. And he'd given his word.

Hattie was grateful to him…and she was attracted to him. But that wasn't enough. He wanted her to need him, to depend on him, to beg him to let her stay. How or why she initially came to him didn't really matter in the end. She was vulnerable now. And God help him, he liked it. His course was clear: enjoy the physical side of their marriage as long as it lasted, maintain his emotional distance…and then…

He refused to contemplate the future. Not now when life was close to perfect. He would keep her as long as it suited him.

The next time he awoke, it was morning; dawn to be exact. Clear, liquid light filtered into the bedroom. He stroked his wife's shoulder. She was sleeping on her stomach, her face turned away from him. "Wake up, sleepyhead. I'm starving."

She blinked her eyes and struggled up onto her elbows. One brief glance at her warm, pink breasts was all he got before she rolled onto her back and clutched the sheet to her chest.

Her eyes were wide, her honey-blond hair tousled. "What time is it?"

"Early. We slept through the night. But missing dinner was definitely worth it."

A deep blush painted her face crimson.

He took pity on her. "I'll use the other bathroom to get ready."

"Ready?"

"I thought we'd go snorkeling this morning. Out to the reef. Are you game?"

She frowned. "I've never done it. Is it difficult?"

He patted her leg. "Not really. You'll love it, I promise." Her expression was unconvinced, so he grinned at her. "Or… we could stay in bed all day."

Hattie stumbled to her feet, almost tripping over her bedsheet toga. "Snorkeling sounds great," she said, the words breathless as she struggled to maintain her modesty. "If you'll order breakfast, I'll be dressed in a jiff." She disappeared into the bathroom.

He chuckled aloud at her discomfiture. Teasing Hattie had

always been fun. Too bad she agreed to the snorkeling. He could have been persuaded to follow option two.

Just thinking about the night before made him hard. With an inward groan, he picked up the phone and called for sustenance. It was going to be a long day, and he needed some serious calories.

Hattie dressed in a modest coral one-piece and covered it with a crisp, white poplin top and khaki walking shorts. A new pair of taupe leather sandals completed the outfit.

When she looked in the mirror, she winced. Going to bed with damp hair meant that she looked like a wild woman. It took a hairbrush and patient determination to tame the mess. Finally, she tucked it up into a ponytail, donned an Atlanta Braves cap and smoothed sheer sunscreen onto her face, neck and arms.

In addition to her new wardrobe, Luc had gifted her with an array of expensive cosmetics. Though most of it was products she would only use for fancy occasions, she had already come to appreciate the many wonderful skin-care creams and lotions.

Breakfast was just arriving when she stepped out of the bathroom. Luc, freshly shaven, his hair damp, tipped the young woman who brought up the largesse.

He spread a hand. “Let’s eat.”

They consumed an embarrassingly large amount of food in record time. Hattie hadn’t realized how hungry she was.

Luc watched her bite into a huge strawberry. “You’ve got juice all over your chin. Let me…” He dabbed her sticky skin with a cloth napkin, his face close to hers. His expression was shuttered, and she wanted badly to know what he was thinking.

Her head was filled with memories of last night… experiences that were life-changing.

But men were far more cavalier about sex and intimacy. When it was over it was over. Luc might want to be with her again, but that didn't mean he'd be doodling a heart with both their names on scrap paper.

Sex was only physical as far as Luc was concerned. She'd do well to keep that fact firmly planted in the front of her brain. And that meant staying out of this suite as much as possible.

She scooted back from the table. "Let's go. I'm excited about this."

Luc had not chartered a private boat. And for that Hattie was glad. Having other people around diffused the natural awkwardness she was experiencing. She couldn't even look at Luc without remembering how his powerful body had joined with hers, how their skin had been damp with exertion, their muscles lax with pleasure.

If she let herself, she could imagine that they were like any normal newlyweds. Deeply in love, and ravenous for each other.

Luc didn't help her resolve to be sensible. He was in turns tender, affectionate and teasing. More and more she saw glimpses of the young man she had fallen in love with. Away from the pressure of business and responsibilities, Luc laughed often, was more relaxed and carefree.

He handed her a pair of flippers. "Put these on, and I'll help you with your mask." All around them, fellow passengers were doing the same thing. The large catamaran had cut its engines and was bobbing in clear blue-green water over the reef below.

Hattie and Luc had already shed their outer clothing and tucked all of it into a big raffia tote bag. She tried not to drool over her new husband. His black swim trunks were plain, but it was his sculpted torso and powerful arms that drew attention. Hattie didn't miss the fact that she wasn't the only one eyeing Luc's masculine beauty.

He wore expensive, reflective sunglasses that made him look like a movie star. It didn't seem fair for one man to have everything—looks, character and money to burn.

She sighed inwardly as he handed her a mask and snorkel tube. "What happens if I swallow water?"

"You'll be fine. I'll be right beside you."

The boat captain gave some basic instructions, including a warning to listen for the whistle that signaled time to return to the boat. Hattie was very glad she had a reliable partner.

She had assumed they would jump over the side like in the movies, but the catamaran had a ladder that could be lowered into the water between the two large hulls. Backing down the steps was a little claustrophobic, but Luc went first and was waiting for her as she descended. He took her arm, his face almost unrecognizable behind his mask. "Come on, little mermaid. We don't want to waste any time."

Hattie was not a superconfident swimmer. And learning to breathe through the tube was challenging. But Luc's patience and support, along with a life vest, erased much of her fear, and soon she was moving through the water, head down, discovering the wonders of the reef.

The colors were muted and not as dramatic as Discovery Channel specials she had seen about the Great Barrier Reef, but the experience was enchanting nevertheless. Corals bobbed and swayed in eerie dances. Multicolored fish, large and small, moved with unconcern in and around the landlubber visitors.

Much of the necessary communication involved pointing and arm touches. But when Hattie spotted a familiar shape, she gasped, swallowed water, and had to come up to catch her breath. "It was a shark," she cried, coughing as she cleared her throat.

Luc shoved his mask on top of his head and laughed. "I've never seen anyone's eyes get that big. I thought you were going to faint dead in the water."

She shuddered. "Don't say dead. I wanted to take some pictures, but he was too fast." The snorkeling package included disposable waterproof cameras. "He wasn't very big though."

Luc tugged her ponytail. "You were hoping for *Jaws?*"

She giggled, feeling happier than she had been in a long time. "Well, not really, but it would have made a great Facebook post."

He glanced at his diver's watch. "We'd better get back to it. Time's almost up."

By the time the whistle sounded, Hattie was ready to quit. The experience was amazing, but the unaccustomed exercise, combined with learning how to manipulate the equipment, had exhausted her.

Back onboard everyone dried off and deposited their gear in large barrels for cleaning. Young crew members passed out lemonade and cookies. Luc and Hattie sat side by side, the wind in their faces as the boat cut rapidly through the waves on the home journey. Their swimsuits dried rapidly in the heat.

Luc put his arm around her back. "Was it what you expected?"

She glanced up at him, controlling a shiver at the delicious feel of his warm skin on hers. "Even better," she said. The sun was making her drowsy. Her head lolled against his shoulder, and she let herself lean into his body.

As they docked in Key West, she roused. It was the work of minutes to slip back into shorts, shoes and top. Luc followed suit, and soon they disembarked with the other passengers.

They lingered at the dock for a few minutes watching

parasail enthusiasts go airborne. Hattie shaded her eyes with a hand. "That looks fun, too."

Luc took her arm. "Maybe tomorrow. Let's find a restaurant."

She punched him softly. "Is that all you ever want to do?"

He paused in the middle of the road and kissed her—hard. He brushed a stray hair from her cheek. "Actually, it's way down on the list, but I'm trying to be a considerate husband."

That shut her up. What would Luc say if she demanded to go back to the guesthouse and spend the afternoon and evening as they had the day before?

Sadly, she didn't have the guts to propose what she really wanted to do. Instead, she pretended interest in the fried plantains at the Cuban restaurant they found near the harbor. She ate mechanically. Every moment that passed brought them closer to the evening hours. When they would go to bed…together?

The uncertainty made her crazy. Was last night a one-time faux pas on their parts, or was Luc assuming they would continue to have sex for the duration of the marriage?

Hattie hated the idea of divorce, but what choice did they have? They had allowed sexual hunger and curiosity to lead them down a dangerous path, and she knew what happened to that proverbial cat.

Luc nudged her elbow. "I thought you'd be hungry. Swimming always gives me an appetite."

She shrugged. "I think it's the heat getting to me. Do you mind if we go back to our place? I'd love to take a shower and wash the seawater off my skin."

His fork stilled in midair, and his cheekbones went dark. He cleared his throat. "Of course. Whatever you want."

Hattie cursed her own artless stupidity. Did that sound like an open invitation for sex? She hadn't meant it that way.

Or had she?

Luc finished his meal and summoned the waiter for their check. Shortly after, they made their way through the crowded streets. Apparently, many tourists had arrived early to celebrate the Memorial Day holiday. Hattie barely noticed the commotion. All she could think about was how to handle the return to their luxurious bridal quarters.

The leather seats in the car were hot…no shade trees this time. She wriggled uncomfortably, and rolled down her window to let the steamy air escape. Luc was silent, his face impossible to read.

The ride was brief and silent. They exited the car. Marcel welcomed them as they strolled through the courtyard. "Are you enjoying your stay in Key West?"

Luc shook his hand, but Hattie answered. "It's lovely. So vibrant and colorful. You're lucky to live here year-round."

Marcel nodded as he trimmed an overgrown bougainvillea. "The only time I rethink my address is during hurricane season, but we are lucky here in the Keys…very few major hits."

Luc frowned. "Have you heard a forecast for tonight and tomorrow?"

"Nothing but calm, clear skies. Perfect vacation weather."

Hattie preceded Luc up the stairs, wondering what was up. Luc seemed focused on some unknown objective. And once in their room, instead of throwing her on the bed as she had hoped or expected, he seemed to be preoccupied…or at least avoiding sex at the moment. "Why were you concerned about the weather?" she asked him.

He tossed the car keys and his sunglasses on the dresser. "I have an idea."

"Uh-oh," she teased. "Should I be worried?"

He sprawled on the sofa. "Do you remember those camping trips we took in college?"

"Of course." They had journeyed to the north Georgia

mountains a number of times, spending several chilly spring and autumn nights curled together in a double sleeping bag… just the two of them. Those had been magical times, and Hattie had loved them even more because the outings were inexpensive.

His arms stretched along the back of the couch, his fingers drumming restlessly. "I thought it might be fun to do that again."

In this heat? Was Luc so spooked by the intense emotion of the night before that he was going to keep them busy, nonstop? "Umm, well…"

"There's an island with an old fort. We can camp there. It would be an adventure. What do you say?"

The boyish eagerness on his face was irresistible. Despite her better judgment, she managed an enthusiastic smile. "Sounds like fun."

Fourteen

While Luc was on the phone making arrangements for their impromptu trip, Hattie showered and then checked in with Ana.

The baby is fine. No problem. Enjoy yourselves.

Hattie ended her call and surveyed the room. Luc was paying who knew how much money for this wonderful suite, and yet he wanted to abandon it for parts unknown. Men… She found him in the sitting room, still on the phone, but now she could tell it was business. Knowing what she did of his work ethic and his drive and determination, it really surprised her that he had been willing and able to get away for a honeymoon, pretend or otherwise.

He hung up and turned to face her, jubilation on his face. "I got us two spots. They only allow a small number of campers each night. But there's one catch."

"Oh?"

He winced, gauging her reaction. "We have to leave right now."

"Seriously?"

"Yeah. Everything for the week was full except for tonight."

Gulp. "Okay. What do I need to pack?"

"Anything that's comfortable and cool. Plus a swimsuit. We'll be able to snorkel in the shallow water around the fort."

And at night? What would happen then?

Hattie pondered that question. And how did one prepare for possible seduction on a remote, uninhabited island? After dithering in the bedroom for several minutes, she dumped out her carry-on bag and began filling it methodically. One set of clean clothes and underwear. Swimsuit. A long T-shirt to sleep in. Sunscreen.

She picked up a lilac silk nightgown and held it to her cheek for a wistful moment. Not exactly camping attire. But what the heck. This was her honeymoon. She stuffed it in.

It was easy to see why Luc was so successful. In barely an hour, he had secured bags of food, all sorts of camping gear, two coolers and transportation. They found parking near the dock and unloaded. Hattie was stunned to see Luc walk toward a stylish, powerful speedboat.

He held out a hand. "Come aboard, my lady."

The vessel must have been wickedly expensive, even as a rental. Everything about it gleamed, from the hardwood deck to the shiny chrome trim. Luc stowed their supplies and tossed Hattie a yellow life jacket.

She wrinkled her nose. "Do I have to?"

He slid his arms into a navy one. "Captain's orders."

"How far are we going?"

"About seventy miles."

Her apprehension must have shown on her face, because he sobered. "It's perfectly safe, Hattie. Leo and I learned to pilot boats before we could drive cars. Grandfather's villa is on the shores of Lake Como, and as teenage boys, we spent all the time we could in and on the water. I'll take care of you, I promise."

He was as good as his word, and in his competent hands, the sleek craft ate up the miles effortlessly. Hattie had donned her baseball cap back at the dock, and she was glad, because the wind whipped and slapped them in joyous abandon.

At times, dolphins leaped beside the boat, gamboling playfully, their beautiful skin glistening in the sun. Hattie laughed in delight and sat back finally, her eyes closed, her face tilted toward the sun. If she and Luc could keep going forever into the next sunset, life would be perfect.

Or almost. She couldn't bear the thought of giving up her niece. Deedee wasn't a burden. The baby was a joy.

Hattie shook off reality with a deliberate toss of her head. She took advantage of Luc's concentration to watch him unobserved. He controlled the boat with a relaxed stance that gave testament to his comfort being on the water. When several dark shapes began growing ahead of them, she scooted up beside him. "Is that it?"

He gave her a sideways grin. "Yep. We're in Dry Tortugas National Park."

"Never heard of it."

"Well it's only been a national park since 1992, so that's not so surprising."

"Why the name?"

"*Tortugas* because they look like a group of turtles, and *Dry* because there's no fresh water on any of them."

As they neared their destination, she stared, incredulous. She and Luc were miles from civilization, literally in the middle of nowhere. Yet perched on a handkerchief-size piece of land sat a sturdy brick fort, its hexagonal walls enclosing a large grassy area, and its perimeter surrounded by a water-filled moat. Even at a distance, the evidence of crumbling decay was visible.

Luc waved a hand as he throttled back the engine. "Fort Jefferson."

Hattie leaned her hands on the railing and absorbed it all. "I can't believe this."

"You know the expression 'Your name is mud'?"

She nodded as Luc tied up to the dock. "Of course."

"Some people attribute that remark to Dr. Samuel Mudd who was incarcerated here in the 1860s."

"What did he do that was so terrible?"

"He had the misfortune to set the broken leg of John Wilkes Booth after Booth assassinated President Lincoln."

"Wow."

"Exactly. Mudd was convicted of treason and sent here to serve a life sentence."

Hattie shuddered. Knowing there was no possibility of escape must have been mentally anguishing. "How dreadful."

"The story does have a bit of a happy ending," Luc said. "As you can imagine, disease was rampant in the fort. Dysentery, malaria, smallpox…and, at one time, a terrible outbreak of yellow fever. It was so bad, the entire medical staff died."

"And that's where Dr. Mudd comes to the rescue?"

"Right. Even knowing as he did that the disease was a killer, he stepped in and began caring for the soldiers, saving dozens of lives. For his heroism, he ultimately received a full pardon and was allowed to return home."

Hattie pondered the sad story. She wasn't a superstitious person, but the island, beautiful though it was, carried an aura of past suffering. Dr. Mudd had earned a second chance. Would Hattie and Luc be as lucky?

Luc had arranged for one of the park ranger's sons to unload all their supplies and set up camp. Luc lent a hand, but even so, it took several loads to carry everything to the designated camping area, a small sandy strip of land lightly dotted with grass and shrubs. At the far end, a young family with two kids had already erected a red-and-white tent.

Luc handled the minimal paperwork with the ranger on duty and then turned to Hattie. "You ready for a swim?"

Disappointment colored her words. "I thought we were going to explore the fort."

He held up his hands and laughed. "Okay. Fine. Maybe it will be a little cooler in there."

They grabbed cameras and water bottles and headed out. The empty silent rooms in the fort almost reeked of despair. The thick walls blocked out some of the afternoon heat, but at the same time contributed to the oppressive dungeonlike atmosphere. There were no furnishings. The stark, barren chambers seemed to echo with the voices of long-ago inmates.

After wandering through several sections of the fort, Luc pointed out the entrance to Dr. Mudd's cell. Hattie read aloud the inscription over the arch. "*Whoso entereth here leaveth all hopes behind.*" She shuddered. "Gruesome. But it sounds familiar."

Luc nodded. "It's from Dante's *Inferno.*"

"I need to see the sky," she muttered. She stepped back out into the sunshine, noting again the way the bricks were slowly disintegrating as time took its toll. "Can we climb the lighthouse?"

Luc took her arm. "It's about a thousand degrees today. The lighthouse is inactive. And I need a swim."

"Wimp," she teased. But she allowed herself to be persuaded. Back at the tent, there was an awkward moment.

Luc avoided her gaze. "Not much room in there," he said gruffly. "You go first."

It didn't take her long. Later, while she waited for Luc to change, she shaded her eyes and watched the numerous boats anchored offshore. Divers were taking advantage of the opportunity to explore the reef and other items of interest on the ocean floor.

When Luc emerged from the tent, she swallowed. He was wearing black nylon racing trunks that left little to the imagination. She smiled weakly, her temples perspiring, as he tossed her a towel.

Luc slung an arm around her shoulders, his own towel around his neck. "Let's go."

The water felt blissfully cool. Hattie paddled happily in the shallow water near the fort, finding it a lot easier than her first experience, since she could occasionally stand up. Some of the boaters were snorkeling as well, but they stayed mostly to the back of the fort.

She noticed that the family with the two children was also taking advantage of an afternoon swim. It suddenly occurred to her to wonder how far sound carried on the night air. Her breathing hitched, and she shivered despite the blazing sun. Anticipation and anxiety mingled in her stomach, making her feel slightly faint. If she got in over her head tonight, she'd have no one to blame but herself.

Luc had been swimming in deeper water, but he reappeared suddenly by her side, tugging off his mask and running a hand through his hair, flinging drops of water everywhere.

He smiled lazily. "Having fun?"

She nodded. "It's amazing."

He glanced at his high tech waterproof watch. "I thought I'd go on back and set up the grill, get the fire started. Will you be okay?"

She motioned him away. "By all means. I'm working up an appetite."

Without warning, he lifted her against his wet chest, her feet dangling in the water. His head lowered. "So am I, Hattie. So am I."

His mouth found hers, and the raw sensuality of his

kiss made her dizzy. She closed her eyes, her other senses intensifying. He tasted salty, with a hint of coconut from the sunscreen he'd used. She pulled his lower lip between her teeth and bit gently.

His entire body quaked. He released her slowly, allowing her to slide the length of his virtually nude form. By the time her feet touched the sandy bottom once again, she could barely stand.

He laughed shakily. "Well, hell. I don't know if I have the strength to climb out of the water." He rested his chin on the top of her head, his arms wrapped around her waist. "You know what's going to happen tonight."

She nodded, mute, her face pressed to the muscular flesh just above his nipple.

He released her and stepped back. "Okay, then."

An hour later, they ate dinner in style. Hattie should have known that a Cavallo wouldn't prepare anything as plebian as hamburgers or hot dogs. Luc grilled T-bones and fresh shrimp over mesquite charcoal and then produced corn on the cob and potato salad to go with it.

She looked at him wryly over her heaping plate. "This isn't how I remember camping."

He shrugged. "My tastes have matured."

They lingered over their al fresco meal. Hattie was relaxed and yet keenly aware of the tension humming between them. Luc offered fresh chocolate-dipped strawberries for dessert. She bit into one carefully, licking the sweet juice from her lower lip.

He watched her constantly until she swatted his arm. "Stop it."

His wide, rakish grin was all innocence. "I don't know what you mean."

Moments later, the teenager showed up to do KP. He would

be leaving soon when his father went off duty. There was no official presence at the fort overnight.

Luc suggested a boat ride. The sun was beginning its slow decline. Hattie prepared her camera. Luc steered the boat to a perfect vantage point to get shots of the fort washed in the beautiful evening light.

Afterward they anchored in deep water and dropped the ladder over the side. Hattie climbed over the rail, but Luc made a neat dive off the rear of the boat.

They swam and played for a long time, until the light began to fade. Back on the boat, they dried off and Hattie put on a T-shirt over her suit. As they picked up speed, the stiff breeze raised goose bumps on her arms and legs.

While they were tying up once again at the boat dock, the young father from the family across the way approached them.

He shook Luc's hand and smiled ruefully. "Our youngest son has developed an earache, and we know from past experience that we'll need medicine, so we're going back to Key West. We wanted to tell someone, because the park service occasionally does a head count out here."

Luc grimaced. "That's too bad. It's going to be a beautiful night. But I'll help you load up."

Hattie walked back to the tent and stretched out on a sleeping bag. Daylight was fading fast. It was a half hour before Luc returned. Out the tent flap she could see the family pull away from the dock. The other boats she had watched offshore earlier in the day had long since lifted anchor and sailed or motored away.

For the first time since their arrival, she and Luc were completely, irrevocably alone.

He crouched and held out a hand. "Let's take a walk."

While she stretched her arms over her head and then donned a windbreaker, Luc retrieved a flashlight from his pack and zipped up the tent. They approached the fort and skirted the edge until they could step onto the sea wall. For most of the perimeter of the fort, the barrier separated the moat from the sea.

Hattie didn't need Luc's warning to watch her step. Although the wall wasn't particularly narrow, the thought of falling into the mysterious ocean was daunting.

On the far side of the fort they sat down, cross-legged, and surveyed the vast expanse of sky and sea. A tiny sliver of new moon did little to illuminate the night. As their eyes became accustomed to the dark, they could just make out the faint line of demarcation separating the silvery pewter of the ocean from the midnight-blue of the sky. Several miles away, a working lighthouse flashed a periodic caution to boats, warning of the reefs and small rocky islands.

They sat in silence for several minutes. Hattie finally whispered, "It's like we're the only two people in the entire world. I'm not sure I like the feeling."

He took her hand and squeezed it. "Do you want to go back?"

"No." She leaned her head on his shoulder. "It's beautiful and awe-inspiring, and a little frightening to be honest, but I wouldn't have missed this for anything. Can you imagine what it must be like here during a hurricane?"

Luc chuckled. "I don't even want to think about it."

They sat hand in hand for a long time, wrapped in a cocoon of darkness and the intimacy of complete isolation. Far out across the waves, traces of phosphorescence lent a ghostly aura to the night.

Eventually, by unspoken consent, they made their way back around to the campsite. After a quick visit to the Spartan toilet facilities near the dock, they met back at the tent and stood facing each other.

Luc lifted a hand and traced her chin with his thumb. "It's

not too late to change your mind. We have a perfectly good king-size bed back at the hotel. I can wait if you'd rather."

She took a step closer, leaning into his chest. "I want you, Luc…tonight."

Fifteen

She felt his chest lift and fall as a shuddering breath escaped his lungs. He wrapped his arms around her. "Do you need a few minutes in the tent to get ready?"

"Yes," she muttered, her throat tight with nervousness. He handed her the small flashlight. She unzipped the tent and knelt to climb in, carefully removing her shoes and leaving them in a corner so no sand would find its way into their comfy sleeping space.

Luc had spread thick, soft sleeping bags on top of a single, large, cushiony air mattress. Since it was too hot to sleep inside the bags, he had also procured crisp cotton sheets complete with small pillows tucked inside lace-edged cases. The resulting effect was one part *Out of Africa* and two parts *Pretty Woman,* a stage unmistakably set for seduction.

Earlier, Hattie had regarded the tent as pleasantly roomy. Now, with Luc standing somewhere outside, it felt surprisingly claustrophobic, especially when she imagined Luc's large frame dominating the enclosed space.

She picked up her overnight case and found her toiletry

bag. After quickly cleaning her face, she stripped off her clothes, thankful that the evening swim had left her skin feeling cool, if a bit salty. Luc had thought to bring a small container of fresh water, so she dampened a cloth and used it to further freshen up.

At Luc's murmured request, she passed the water container and a clean towel out to him. While he was presumably taking care of his ablutions, she found a tube of scented lotion and applied it to her elbows and legs and one or two other interesting spots.

She pulled out the lilac gown and slipped it over her head, relishing the feel of the silk against her bare skin. When she was done, she tucked the flashlight under Luc's pillow, leaving only the smallest beam of light to illuminate the tent.

Taking a deep breath and smoothing her hair, she called out. "I'm ready."

The tent flap peeled back instantly, and she saw him place his shoes and the water canister inside at the foot of the tent before he crawled in, immediately dwarfing the tiny space. He had already undressed.

Hattie's heart stopped for a split second, and then lurched back into service with an unsteady beat. Even her ploy with the flashlight didn't disguise his impressive attributes. She put a hand against her breastbone, feeling a bit like a Regency virgin in need of smelling salts.

Luc zipped the tent flap shut, tossed a few foil packets beside his pillow, and then stretched out with a sigh onto the comfortable bedding. He lay on his side facing her, leaning on his elbow with one leg propped up, looking like a centerfold.

Only, he was real. Here. In the flesh.

Hattie remained seated, her spine stiff as a poker, her legs paralyzed in a pretzel position. He patted the space beside him, and she saw him smile. "You're too far away," he complained.

She uncurled her legs and scooted closer, still leaving a healthy distance between them.

He reached out and smoothed a hand over her thigh covered in lilac silk. "I'm betting you didn't order this little number from L.L. Bean," he said, the words laced with amusement.

Suddenly, he reached behind him and picked up the flashlight, momentarily blinding her when he pointed it in her direction. He focused the tiny beam of light on her left shoulder.

His voice came out of the darkness. "Ditch the gown, Hattie, starting with that strap."

She couldn't see his face, only the outline of his body. Her fingers went to the slim strap he'd indicated, and she lowered it, slipping her arm free, but keeping her breast covered.

The beam of light moved to her other shoulder. "Now that one."

The second strap fell. She put a hand against her chest to hold the gown in place.

The light slipped down to her abdomen. He spoke again, his tone hoarse and rough. "Now all of it."

She rose to her knees, trembling, and let the fabric fall to her hips, and then, with a little shimmy, to the sleeping bag. Luc's indrawn breath was audible. The beam of light rose slowly to circle one breast and then the other. Her nipples tightened painfully. The light slid over the taut plane of her stomach to rest in the shadowed valley between her thighs.

His voice this time was barely a whisper. "Hand me the gown."

She lifted her knees, an awkward maneuver given the situation, and pulled the silk free, tossing it to him.

He buried his face in the cloth momentarily. Then the light went out. He called her name. "Hattie…come here."

She tumbled forward, her eagerness assisted by his firm grasp on her forearm. She landed half-sprawled across his chest, and one of her hands lodged in an interesting position between his legs. She found the hot, smooth length of him and stroked gently.

Luc groaned, covering her lips with his, the kiss ravenous and demanding. His tongue plundered the recesses of her mouth, exploring every crevice, nibbling and biting until she was breathless and whimpering with need.

Seconds later she sensed him trying to slow things down, but it was too late. While he fumbled for a condom, she rubbed her breasts against his chest, savoring the delicious friction. She felt his hands settle on her bottom. He lifted her until she sat astride him, and she tensed.

On and off during the last decade she had dreamed about being with him. But those fleeting fantasies didn't come close to approximating the reality of Luc Cavallo, naked, nudging with barely concealed impatience at the heart of her feminine passage.

She arched her back and felt him enter her, stretching her to an almost painful fullness. "Oh, Luc…" The sensation was incredible.

He froze, not moving an inch, his body taut and trembling. "Am I hurting you?"

She choked out a laugh, wriggling, forcing him centimeters deeper. "No." It was all she could manage. She raked his nipples with her fingernails. He heaved beneath her, burying himself to the hilt. The connection was stunning—her, adjusting to the sensation of his possession, him, clearly struggling for control.

He lifted his hands to cup her sensitive breasts. She cried out, nearing a peak so intense, she could feel it hovering just out of reach. He withdrew almost completely, but before she could voice a protest, he thrust even deeper, initiating a rhythm that sent them both tumbling into a fiery release. Somewhere in the fringes of her consciousness, she heard him shout as he emptied himself into her body, but her orgasm washed over her with such power, she was unable to focus on anything but her own pleasure.

Luc lay perfectly still, trying to recover from the effects of Hurricane Hattie. Her slender body lay draped over his in sensual abandon that filled him with a fierce masculine satisfaction overlaid by the terrifying realization that he had fallen in love with her…again. Far away from the familiar trappings of his daily life, it was all so clear. He didn't need *things* to be happy…not money or electronic toys or even the adrenaline-producing challenge of his job.

His arms tightened around her. A time machine couldn't have taken him back any more successfully than this sham marriage and this ill-conceived honeymoon. Hattie filled his life with an exhilaration he had experienced only once before. She brought *fun* into his days, joy into his home, passion into his bed.

But nothing had changed. He was still rich, and she was still wary about ceding power and control to a man like him.

The baby was the fragile glue holding this house of cards together. Unless he could convince Hattie that great sex covered a multitude of sins, it was only a matter of time until she left him.

He sighed as he felt her tongue trace his collarbone. The slightly rough caress sent trickles of heat down his torso straight to his groin. He smoothed his fingers over her bottom, guiltily aware that he might have bruised her pale skin.

She leaned on her elbow and kissed him briefly. "I think I've developed a whole new appreciation for roughing it…if I can say that with a straight face while lying on 800 thread count sheets."

He chuckled. "I never knew you liked it rough."

She punched his arm. "You're so bad. But I like that about you…" Her head found its way to his shoulder.

As her voice trailed off, he shifted her to one side. Not that he didn't enjoy having her body glued to his like wallpaper, but her proximity made it difficult to form a coherent thought. He hoped that if he handled this interlude correctly, he might be able to bind Hattie to him in such a way that she couldn't escape.

Women, unlike most men, had a hard time separating sex from emotional ties. All he had to do was convince Hattie that the compatibility they experienced in bed could carry over to life in general. That the incredible sex was only a sign of their overall rightness for each other…that they had more in common than she realized.

When Hattie slipped a hand across his thigh, he lost all interest in thinking. Her curious fingers found his partially erect shaft and began exploring. He shuddered, giving himself up to the heady pleasure of having Hattie map his body with an eagerness that was as flattering as it was arousing.

Her questing hands feathered over him like butterfly wings, brushing, touching. He clenched his teeth against a surge of lust as she found a particularly sensitive spot. "Hattie…"

She nipped his hipbone with her teeth. "Hmmm?"

His hands tangled in her hair, and he pulled her up for a hard kiss. This time, it was her tongue that demanded entrance, taunting his mouth with sweet little licks and strokes that made him groan with hunger.

Almost…almost he lifted her astride him as he had earlier, craving the sensation of filling her with one swift thrust. But at the last second, he broke the kiss and pushed her to her back, determined this time to give her the tenderness and attention she deserved.

She reached for him, but he eluded her, sliding down

the length of her body to concentrate on the source of her pleasure. His hands glided over her skin, skin softer than any silk nightgown. He traced her navel and abdomen with his tongue. She twisted restlessly.

Gripping her hips and holding her down, he bent his head lower, ignoring her incoherent protests. She stiffened at the first touch of his lips, her back arching off the sleeping bag. A panting cry escaped her. He licked gently, and seconds later she shattered in a moaning climax.

He scooped her into his arms, holding her tightly as the last tremors racked her body. She was his. He was familiar with sexual satisfaction, but this need to claim, to possess, was something he had experienced only one other time in his life.

When she stirred in his embrace, he stroked the hair from her face with an unsteady hand. He kissed her softly, tenderly, trying to tell her with his touch what he knew she wasn't ready to hear in words.

The kiss lengthened. Deepened. His own unappeased arousal clawed to the surface, reminding him that making Hattie fly moments ago was only a prelude. He rose over her, trapping both her hands in one of his and raising them above her head. His maneuver lifted her breasts in silent invitation. With his free hand, he caressed them, stroking the petal-soft curves, avoiding her nipples, deliberately building her need once again.

When her pleading whispers and writhing hips told him she was ready for his possession, he abandoned her breasts and slid his hand between her legs, testing her heat and dampness with one finger.

She turned her head and bit the tender flesh of his inner arm, silently demanding. He released her hands, scarcely noticing when they grasped his shoulders. His need had become a roaring torrent, a driving urgency toward completion. Damning the necessity, he sheathed his rock-hard erection in a condom.

With one knee, he spread her legs and settled between her thighs, positioning himself. He looked down at her, inwardly cursing the darkness, needing desperately to see her face. "Tell me you want me, Hattie," he said huskily. "Beg me."

She spread her legs even wider, seeking to join their bodies, but he held back, driven by some Neanderthal impulse. "Say it, Hattie."

Her voice, a rasping, air-starved whisper reached his ear. "Please Luc. Take me…please."

He surged forward, shuddering as her body gripped him. She was tight and hot, and her long, slender legs wrapped around his waist. He knew in an instant that once more there would be no slow, sweet loving. He drove into her again and again until the tide swept over him, pulled him under, erasing every thought but one. Hattie was his.

He tried to hold back, to prolong the exquisite sensations for a few moments more, but it was hopeless. With a hoarse shout, he came inside her for long, agonizing seconds, conscious of nothing but searing pleasure and blinding release.

In the aftermath, they clung together, breathing fractured, skin damp, hearts pounding in unison. With his last ounce of energy, he reached for the top sheet, pulled it over them. Hattie's limp body curled spoon fashion against his, her bare bottom pressed to the cradle of his thighs.

Luc surrendered to the oblivion of sleep.

Sixteen

Hattie slipped from Luc's arms and donned a long T-shirt and panties before quietly exiting the tent. Her body was stiff and sore in some interesting places, and she felt at once exhausted and exhilarated.

After a necessary trip to the bathroom, she stood in the eerie gray light of predawn, her arms clasped around her middle. Just a few hundred feet offshore, a tiny strip of land, hardly big enough to merit the designation *island,* was covered with a teeming mass of flapping, squawking birds.

Their raucous calls and noisy confusion mirrored the turmoil in her heart. What in the heck was she going to do? There was no longer any doubt about her feelings for Luc. Having sex with him last night in such an erotic and abandoned way had been at once the most perfect and the most stupid thing she had ever done in her life.

She might one day find another man as intelligent as Luc. As kind, as handsome, as funny…perhaps. But there was no doubt in her mind that the lovemaking they had shared was unique. He'd been a good lover in college, no question. But this time around, the sex was even better. She hadn't expected the intensity, the shattering intimacy, the feeling that she had bound herself to him body and soul.

He was also better at reading her. Some internal radar seemed to pick up her moods, to see inside her head and know what she was thinking. Which made him very dangerous to her peace of mind.

And his empathy was a huge problem given that this relationship was temporary and supposedly pragmatic. She didn't want to feel so connected to him. What a mess. As much as she longed to enjoy this surprising honeymoon all the way to its conclusion, another smarter Hattie said, *Go home.*

She looked over her shoulder at the small blue tent, its outline shrouded in the misty morning fog. In a short while, the cozy housing would be dismantled, much like her short-lived marriage. The campsite would be cleared, leaving no trace of the spot where Hattie Parker had given her heart to Luc Cavallo.

But hearts healed, didn't they? And life went on. She would go back to her job perhaps, settle into a new place, learn to play the role of single mom. And perhaps this ending wouldn't be as painful as the one ten years ago. Maybe Deedee's chortling smiles would be a distraction.

Hattie and Luc might remain friends…or, if not, she'd have memories.… And if she was lucky, someday a lover who didn't know that he was second best.

Luc knew the instant Hattie stirred from his embrace and left the tent. Even in his sleep he'd been aware of her warmth and softness twined in his arms, their legs tangled, her head tucked beneath his chin. Twice more during the night they had come together in exquisite lovemaking, the first a slow gentle mating, the second a hard, fast, almost desperate race to the finish.

But Hattie's recent stealthy departure said louder than words that she needed some time alone. That she hadn't wanted to face him. He understood her motivation. He just didn't like it.

The warm pillows still retained a remnant of her fragrance. He climbed out and put on his shorts. As he ran a hand over the stubble on his chin, he grimaced. Perhaps spending the night on a deserted island wasn't the greatest way to win over a woman. But Hattie had been a good sport about it all, and something about the isolation had deepened the intimacy of their lovemaking.

He exited the tent and walked over to where she stood looking out to sea. Looping his arms around her waist from behind, he rested his chin on the top of her head. "Good morning."

She turned slightly, enough for him to see that she was smiling. "Good morning, Luc."

He squeezed her gently. "You ready for some breakfast?"

She nodded. "At the risk of sounding unladylike, I could eat the proverbial horse."

They fixed the meal together, Hattie cutting up fresh fruit while he toasted bread on the grill. He had hoped to make love to her once more before they left, but it wasn't going to happen. Hattie had retreated to some distant place, and the invisible line in the sand was one he couldn't cross.

By ten o'clock everything was packed up and loaded in the boat. He suggested climbing the lighthouse, but Hattie shook her head, saying she was tired and ready to go back. He wanted to tease her about her fatigue. Lord knew neither of them had gotten much sleep, but his courage failed him. He had just experienced one of the most incredible nights of his life, but the lady involved was treating him like a favorite brother.

It was hell on a man's self-esteem.

They made the return trip to Key West mostly in silence. Hattie sat in the back of the boat on a bench seat wearing her baseball cap pulled low over her eyes and with her arms curled around her knees. Clouds had rolled in during the morning, making the sky sullen and angry. He had to keep both hands on the wheel to handle the choppy waves.

Docking, unloading and getting back to the hotel were interminable chores. He was determined to have his say, strangely afraid that if he didn't mend some unknown rift, she would slip away from him altogether.

Hattie unlocked the door to their room. He followed her in. She dumped her things on the sofa and turned to face him, a forced smile on her lips. "Thanks for taking me to the fort. It was wonderful."

His jaw clenched. "And what about us? Were we wonderful, too?"

He watched as shock followed by what could only be described as a flash of pain crossed her face.

As she took off her cap and ran her hands through her hair, she glanced at him. "What do *you* think?"

He jammed his hands in his pockets to keep from reaching for her. "I think we were pretty damn fabulous.... Wouldn't you agree?"

A rosy flush climbed from her throat to her cheeks. She nodded slowly. "We never had trouble in that department."

He laughed softly. "Hell, no." He sensed a softening in her, so he pressed his advantage. "Imagine what we could do in that big bed with wine and clean sheets and candles."

Her blush deepened. He stepped toward her, smiling inwardly as she backed up until her legs hit the sofa and she fell backward. He leaned over her, bracing his hands on the back of the couch, bracketing her with his arms. "Kiss me, Hattie."

Her dark eyes looking up at him were filled with secrets. "Do you really think we'll stop with a kiss?"

He bent to nuzzle her neck. "Does it matter?"

"We're both pretty grungy." She twisted her lips. "I could use a shower."

He nibbled the skin behind her ear, coming down beside her and scooping her into his lap. "I hadn't noticed."

She sighed as he kissed his way around to her collarbone, pushing aside the neckline of her T-shirt to gain easier access. He slid a hand beneath the hem and stroked her breast through her bra, lightly pinching the nipple. She groaned. "Luc…"

The flush on her cheeks deepened when he slipped a hand inside her shorts, finding the soft fluff between her legs. She arched into his caress, her breathing ragged.

He'd been teasing earlier. He had every intention of giving her a quick kiss and then getting some business done while she was in the shower. But Hattie was smarter than he was. Clearly a kiss wasn't enough.

He ripped at the zipper on her shorts, jerking it down and removing those and her panties in one quick maneuver. Seconds later, he had her beneath him as he settled between her legs. Hearing her chant his name in soft whispers went straight to his gut. Somewhere deep in the recesses of his brain he realized this was dangerous. This mindless, desperate urge to take her. But he couldn't stop. Didn't want to.

He entered her a bare inch and hesitated, his body racked with tremors. Her eyes fluttered shut. He touched her cheek. "Look at me, Hattie."

She complied, her eyes cloudy and unfocused. He went an inch deeper, and they groaned in unison. She panted, her chest rising and falling rapidly, but she held his gaze.

Struggling for almost nonexistent control, he stroked her cheekbone. "We have to deal with this."

Her head moved slowly in a gesture that could have been agreement or denial. "You talk too much." She grabbed a handful of his hair, pulling his head down for a kiss. "Just get on with it."

The breathless demand snapped his feeble efforts to maintain any kind of sanity. If she wanted it, he'd give it to her. No questions asked. He drove deeper into the hot, tight warmth of her, wanting desperately to make it last longer, but realizing with a sort of incredulous despair that he was losing the battle.

He gritted his teeth, holding back the scalding rush of pleasure. But Hattie's sudden cry and his own body defeated him. He surged harder, blindly emptying himself until he felt blackness close in around him.

A long time later he rolled off of her and flopped onto his back on the plush carpet, staring at the ceiling fan rotating overhead. He felt Hattie's fingers twine with his, and heard her voice, filled with unmistakable amusement. "Now I *really* need a shower."

He laughed, stung by chagrin at his emotionally reckless behavior but filled with a deep, boneless contentment. He glanced at his watch and swore. "I have to make two quick calls. But I won't be long, I promise."

She leaned over to kiss him. "It's okay, Luc. Really."

"And was it okay that I took you like a wild man?"

"You *were* pretty intense."

Remorse rode him for not even fully undressing her. "What can I say? You're a temptress."

She looked down at her rumpled clothes and rolled her eyes. "Oh, yeah…that's it."

He stood up, and she followed suit as they each adjusted

their clothing. Though he wanted nothing more than to drag her into the bedroom, he resisted the urge. Unless he knew for sure that Hattie was falling for him, he'd be well-advised to rein in his sexual enthusiasm.

But he couldn't resist the urge to woo her. "Why don't we go somewhere fancy for dinner? We can talk about your situation, maybe dance a little..."

Her expression was difficult to read. "That would be nice."

"And we can relax by the pool this afternoon. I'll get Marcel to serve us lunch out there."

"Sure."

He watched her turn toward the bedroom. "I could join you in the shower," he said, consigning his phone calls to the devil.

Hattie shook her head. "Do what you have to do. We've got plenty of time."

Luc let her go for the moment. She was his, body and soul. Perhaps she didn't know it yet, but he would fight dirty if he had to. He wouldn't lose her.... Not again.

Hattie stepped under the strong, stinging spray of the shower and luxuriated in the hot, steamy flow of water. It was amazing what twenty-four hours of deprivation could accomplish. She would never have made it on that TV survivor show. Never mind eating bugs; she would have begged to be voted off after the second day just so she could be clean again.

She dried off with one of the inn's sinfully thick towels. A nap sounded appealing, but she wasn't prepared to give up a day of sunbathing. Donning a robe, she returned to the bedroom and rummaged in her suitcase for the only swimsuit she had not yet worn. It wasn't at all skimpy by today's standards, but the shiny gold fabric clung to her body like a second skin. When Luc appeared in the doorway, his jaw actually dropped. "Tell me you're not wearing that thing outside our room."

She grinned, and then summoned a pout. "I thought you would love it."

He strode toward her. "Love it, hell. When a suit looks like that on a woman, the designer's only motivation is to drive men insane." He skimmed his hands over her body. "Good Lord. It feels like you're naked." He smoothed her bottom. "Are you sure you want to go to the pool? It's nice and quiet and cool up here in our room."

Though the coaxing note in his voice made her knees weak, Hattie held him at arm's length. "I want to go home with at least a semblance of a tan. So I refuse to be distracted by your masculine charms."

He lifted an eyebrow. "You think I'm charming?"

"I think I've made that pretty obvious this week."

He laughed, and for a brief second, she wondered if he felt anything more for her than lust. His actions seemed to indicate affection, but nothing he had said in any context contradicted his earlier plan to make their marriage temporary.

She wanted so badly to say the words swelling in her heart, but she chickened out. It was still too soon.

When Luc's cell phone rang she headed for the door. "You get that if you want to. I'll be out at the pool."

The concern in his words when he spoke with the caller stopped Hattie dead in her tracks.

The conversation was brief. Luc hung up, his expression serious.

Her skin chilled. "What's wrong?"

"The baby's running a temperature."

Hattie sank onto the sofa. "How bad?"

"A hundred and three. It's probably just a virus. They're on the way to a pediatrician right now. Ana wasn't unduly concerned, but she was sure you'd want to know."

"I do. Of course."

Luc eyed her. "What are you thinking?"

She winced, feeling ungrateful for all he had done. "Do you mind if we go home? I need to be with her…to make sure she's okay."

He nodded. "I thought as much. Start packing, and I'll see what kind of flights I can find."

Seventeen

It was almost midnight when they made it back to Atlanta and drove from the airport to the house. Leo was on hand to pick them up since they didn't have a car. He and Luc sat in the front. Hattie in the back.

Leo looked over his shoulder. "How was Key West?"

"Very nice," she replied, refusing to be baited.

The two brothers chuckled in unison. Hattie pretended a sudden interest in the passing scenery.

Leo helped unload the luggage into the foyer, shook Luc's hand and kissed Hattie on the cheek. "Let me know how Deedee is. I'll be at the office in the morning."

As he drove off, Hattie yawned. Ana met them in the hallway, not waiting to be asked for an update. "She's sleeping. The doctor says it's a bad ear infection. She may need surgery to have tubes put in."

Tears sprang to Hattie's eyes, a reaction to fatigue and the thought of having her small baby put to sleep.

Luc put his arm around her. "We'll deal with that when the

time comes. Thank you, Ana. Hattie and I will take it from here. You go get some rest."

"If you're sure. I wrote down her medication schedule on the nightstand in her room and the two bottles are there, too." In the nursery, Hattie approached the crib on tiptoe. But Deedee was sleeping peacefully, her bottom in the air as she crouched in a ball on the mattress.

Luc touched Hattie's arm. "I'll bring our bags up. Why don't you get ready for bed?"

Hattie couldn't resist stroking the baby's back. "She still feels so hot."

"The antibiotic will take a while to kick in. We can set the alarm and give her ibuprofen during the night. Go on," he urged. "You're weaving on your feet."

"Okay." Hattie took a quick shower and changed into a nightgown that was pretty but not overtly sexy. Now that they were home, her thoughts were in turmoil. She hated that she felt like an insecure teenager again, wondering if a boy liked her. Everything had seemed so simple, so natural out on the island.

But now…back on Luc's home turf, all her earlier reservations returned. Would Luc expect to share her room? Was she supposed to go to his?

The nursery was adjacent to Hattie's suite. Ana and Sherman had slept in a nearby guest room while Luc and Hattie were gone.

When Hattie returned to the baby's room, her steps faltered. She hung back in the hall, her heart wrenching painfully. In the room decorated with nursery rhyme murals, a night-light cast a soft, pink glow. Sitting in the maple rocker, his head leaned back, eyes half-closed, was Luc. And in his arms lay a sleeping baby.

Deedee was nestled against Luc's chest, one tiny hand clutching a fold of his shirt. The contrast between the big strong male and the tiny helpless baby twisted something deep in Hattie's chest. This was what Leo had feared. That Luc would fall in love with Deedee.

Luc himself had alluded to the fact that he understood the bond between parent and child. Clearly Hattie's niece had wormed her way into his heart. Seeing the two people Hattie loved most in the world…seeing them like this made her realize that she had backed herself into a difficult, if not impossible, corner.

Luc didn't believe in romantic love anymore. And Hattie alone was responsible for his cynicism. But if he loved Deedee, how could she take the baby away when the time came? How could she break Luc's heart a second time?

In the dimly lit room, Luc crooned a soft lullaby, his pleasing baritone singing of diamond rings and mockingbirds. The tender way he held the baby was poignant.

Hattie made herself step into the room. "I'll take her now so you can get cleaned up."

Luc's eyes, sleepy lidded, surveyed his wife. "Are you coming to my room to sleep?"

Wow. Trust Luc to cut straight to the chase. She steadied herself with a hand on the dresser. His meaning was crystal clear. But she had no clue how to respond. "Well, uh…"

His expression went blank, no trace of anything revealed on his classically sculpted features. "Don't sweat it, Hattie. We're both tired. But I'll be more than happy to help with the baby during the night if you need a hand."

Before Hattie could come up with words to explain the confusion in her heart, Luc gently placed Deedee in the crib, brushed by Hattie, and was gone.

Hattie rubbed her eyes with the heels of her hands, inhaling deeply. *Damn it.* Had she hurt his feelings? His male pride? She hadn't intended to say no to sleeping with him, but his artless question caught her off guard. This was uncharted territory.

They could no longer use a pretend honeymoon as an excuse to indulge in passionate sex. They were once again smack-dab in the throes of reality. Luc had married Hattie because she asked him to help protect an innocent baby. And perhaps because he could make Hattie dance to his tune and prove that she meant nothing to him. Did he also expect their physical intimacy to continue?

The baby was sleeping peacefully. Hattie made sure the volume on the monitor was adjusted and slipped out of the room, pulling the door shut as she left. Her big bed, which had seemed so luxurious and comfortable last week, was now a torture device. She tossed and turned, flipping the covers back in an effort to get cool.

She missed Luc, missed his big strong body snuggling with hers. What did he want from her? He'd seemed completely calm during their earlier conversation…not that it was much of a conversation. He'd taken her momentary confusion as a "no," and Hattie hadn't meant that at all, at least not completely.

Her befuddled brain had been scrambling to process all the pros and cons of maintaining a sexual relationship now that they were home. Ana and Sherman would know…and Leo, probably. Something like that was difficult to keep a secret.

So when the situation with Eddie was resolved and Hattie had to go, what then?

The next morning, Deedee was noticeably improved. Luc played with her for a half hour before announcing he was going to the office.

Hattie handed the baby off to Ana and frowned as she followed Luc down to the foyer. "You're still supposed to be on your honeymoon. They won't be expecting you…"

He shrugged into an immaculately tailored navy suit jacket, his expression impassive. "I'm back. Work will have piled up. I might as well get a jump start on things."

Hattie couldn't think of a thing to say to stop him from walking out the door.

As she stood at the window watching her husband's car move down the driveway, her cell phone rang. After ascertaining that it was an unknown number, she answered. "Hello."

"Mrs. Cavallo?"

"Yes."

"This is Harvey Sharpton. I work for your husband, and I have good news."

Hattie's chest tightened. "What is it? Tell me, please."

"Little Deedee's father has screwed up royally this time. Another DUI. A hit-and-run again, this time involving pedestrians. Fortunately, no one was fatally injured, but the judge threw the book at him. And when we came forward with the nurse's testimony, the one who heard Angela's request, the judge granted you sole custody."

Hattie could barely speak. "Thank you so much," she croaked.

"There are some papers you need to sign."

"I'll call you and make an appointment soon. I appreciate your calling me."

She sank down on the bottom step of the grand, sweeping staircase and put her face in her hands. The relief was overwhelming. She wanted to tell Luc immediately…needed to share her joy with the one person who would understand more than anyone else. But he was gone.

All day she rehearsed what she would say. Forty-eight hours ago, it would have been much easier. The Luc she had made love to on her honeymoon was far more approachable than the stern businessman he had reverted to upon their return.

When he didn't make it home in time for dinner, her stomach sank. Maybe she was foolishly naive. Building castles in the air instead of planning for a future without Luc.

Finally, at eleven o'clock, she went to bed and fell into a fitful sleep. Something awoke her in the wee hours—a muffled thud, perhaps a door closing. She glanced at the clock on the bedside table. It was already time to give the baby a dose of medicine. Without bothering to put on a robe, she stole down the hall in her bare feet and opened the nursery door. For the second time, she found Luc with Deedee in his arms. He was standing beside the bed, the infant on his shoulder, patting her softly on the back.

Luc was wearing nothing but thin cotton boxers. Despite the hour and her fatigue, Hattie's body responded. It was conditioned now to expect searing pleasure, and Luc's scent, his masculine beauty, triggered all sorts of dancing hormones.

He turned to face her, speaking softly. "I've already given her the medicine. I thought you were asleep."

She shrugged. "I had a lot on my mind."

Ignoring Hattie's conversational gambit, Luc kissed Deedee's head before laying her back in the bed. He yawned and stretched, the corded muscles in his arms and chest flexing and rippling. "I checked her temp. It's almost normal. You don't need to worry."

Deedee wasn't Hattie's greatest concern at the moment. Instead, it was the way Luc was acting…aloof, unconcerned—about Hattie, that is. She took a step closer to him. "I never meant to imply that I wasn't going to sleep with you. You caught me by surprise, that's all. Do you want me to come with you now? I'm glad you're home."

He stilled, his dark eyes opaque, impossible to read. His shrug spoke volumes. "The baby needs you."

And I don't.

The unspoken words hovered between them. They might as well have been an aerial banner tugged through the sky by a plane.

Hattie didn't know what to say. It seemed as if he was trying purposefully to hurt her. And he was succeeding.

But she had learned a lot about him in the last week. Deep inside the coldly confident, unemotional man was a younger Luc. One who had been hurt repeatedly. One who had learned to shield his softer side. One who built walls. She took a courageous step in his direction. "The reason I wasn't able to sleep is because you weren't beside me."

Luc teetered on the edge of his own personal hell. Hattie was offering herself to him, coming to him of her own free will.

He was almost positive she was falling in love with him. Women couldn't hide things like that. Hattie didn't sleep around. And even though he was her husband, she wouldn't have shared his bed just for sex.

So why was he hesitating?

The dark knot of remembered pain inside him said, *Do it. Tell her to go to hell. Tell her you don't need a wife who's been bought and paid for. Tell her you don't want her.*

Would she see through the lie?

Could he instead reach for the rosy future that seemed almost within his grasp? A wife, a baby, a happily-ever-after?

People he loved left him. His parents. Hattie. If he brought her and the baby into his heart and home and then lost them, he wasn't sure he'd survive.

He clenched his fists, fighting the urge to grab her and pull her close. Instead, he shrugged. "We should probably reevaluate our relationship. See where things stand with the custody situation. I have a hell of a lot to catch up on at work…and you'll be spending time with the baby."

Hattie's face went white, her expression agonized. "So you were just using me in Key West because I was convenient?"

"Don't cast me as the villain in this drama," he said roughly. Sexual desire and searing regret choked him. "If anything, we used each other. You were wet and willing."

"You're a selfish ass," she said, tears choking her voice and welling in her beautiful eyes.

"I gave you what you wanted. You and the baby are safe. Don't ask for the moon, Hattie."

Eighteen

Don't ask for the moon, Hattie. The careless words jangled in her head. She barely slept at all, and when dawn broke, she knew what she had to do. It would have to be a covert operation. Ana and Sherman couldn't be caught in the middle.

Breakfast was miserable. Despite Deedee's chortling happiness, Luc and Hattie barely spoke, concentrating on brief exchanges of information that left her grieving and heartsick.

By ten o'clock the house was empty. Ana and Sherman had gone to the market. Patti was back at school. Luc was at the office. As soon as Deedee went down for her morning nap, Hattie started packing. She walked the hallways back and forth, barely able to concentrate, her skin cold as ice. The pain was crushing. When the suitcases were in the car, she fled. Out the door, down the steps, the baby clasped to her chest.

Luc had sent Hattie's clunker car into the shop for an overhaul. The stylish new minivan that she was still learning to drive was backed into the garage. She snapped Deedee into the car seat, hands shaking, jumped into the driver's seat, put the car in gear and tore out of the driveway.

She drove on autopilot, her heart bleeding. Luc would never love her again. She had killed those feelings in him. He wanted her body, but with his iron control, he was clearly able to deny them even that.

If she stayed in his house an hour more, she might be reduced to begging. And Luc didn't deserve that. He had helped her when she needed it most, but that reason no longer existed. She and Deedee were on their own.

The miles flashed by as she cruised the interstate. Where would she go? What was the next step? She had credit cards galore, but what if Luc disabled them in order to force her home?

Hastily, she did a mental accounting of the cash in her purse...maybe four hundred dollars at the most. That wouldn't last long. But she had to go someplace where no one could find her. At least until she figured out what she was going to do.

Luc leaned back in his office chair and rubbed his neck. He had a killer headache. Thank God Leo was coming over for dinner tonight. His company would be a welcome diversion from the stilted, overly polite conversation to which he and Hattie had been reduced.

For the first time since the honeymoon, Luc arrived home at five-thirty. Leo was not far behind him.

Luc's brother wore a rumpled suit and offered a rueful apology. "Sorry for arriving unfashionably early. But I had a meeting in this part of town, and it didn't seem worth driving back to the office at rush hour."

Luc led him into the library and poured them each a finger of whiskey. "No worries. Deedee is starting to pull up on things, so Ana says she thinks Hattie and the baby went shoe shopping. They're not even back yet. We've got time to relax before dinner."

Leo settled his large frame into a spacious easy chair. After downing his drink in one gulp, he sighed, closed his eyes and spoke. "How are the two of you getting along?"

"No problems." Luc paced restlessly.

"Do you love her?"

"Who are you? Dr. Ruth? I'm not sure what love is."

"Then why did you marry her? Our lawyers have the ability to make mincemeat out of old Eddie. Tying the knot was totally unnecessary. So why did you do it?"

Luc had asked himself that same question a hundred times. The answer was clear, but it was too soon to tell his brother. Leo's propensity for mischief shouldn't be underestimated.

"It was the right thing to do. Protecting the baby."

"I'll give you that. You always did love playing the hero. But there's got to be more."

Sherman appeared in the door. "Excuse me, Mr. Luc. Ana found this note with your name on it. It was on the desk in the kitchen."

Luc ripped open the envelope and stared at the words without comprehension.

Leo came to stand beside him. "What is it? What's wrong?"

Luc had never been as scared as he was at this moment. "She's gone. She has custody, and she's gone."

His brother snatched the piece of paper and scanned it rapidly, cursing beneath his breath. "We'll find her. She can't have gone far."

But they didn't. One day passed. Then two. Then three. Hattie's cell phone was turned off, so the GPS locator was useless. None of her credit cards showed any sign of activity. It was as if she and Deedee had vanished off the face of the earth.

Luc was surviving on black coffee and three hours of sleep a night. His frustration with the police was enormous, but even he had to admit that there was no indication of foul play.

Hattie had left of her own free will. And she had taken his heart with her, dragging it in the wake of the speeding car, shredding it as the miles passed.

Leo was a rock. He moved in, and between the two of them, they hired the best detectives their considerable fortune could buy. But the P.I. reports were little comfort. When a person wanted to disappear, it could take weeks, months to track them down.

Luc lay in bed, night after night, dry-eyed, his body ice-cold. Pride. Injured pride had caused this debacle. All he'd had to do was tell Hattie he loved her more than life. Assure her that he had no plans to ever be parted from her or from Deedee.

If the lawyer had managed to give the news to Luc first instead of Hattie, Luc could have been prepared. But Luc had been too damn busy to listen to his voice mails.

On the fourth day, he caught a break. In her haste, Hattie had left behind the baby's antibiotic. Since Deedee had only been taking it a few days, there was a good chance the child's infection would return without the whole course of treatment.

Once Luc realized the omission, the detectives started monitoring the pediatrician's office with the cooperation of the doctor who was a friend of Luc's. At two-thirty in the afternoon of the fifth miserable day, a call came in requesting a replacement refill.

Luc practically grabbed the detective by the throat. "Tell me you got some information."

The grizzled sixtysomething veteran nodded, his gaze sympathetic. "The call originated from a Motel 6 in Marietta. Here's the address."

* * *

Hattie walked the floor, trying to soothe the cranky infant. Based on the last time she'd started the medicine, Deedee might not feel any better until at least forty-eight hours had passed.

Right after the honeymoon when the baby was ill, Hattie had been backed up with Luc's help and support. Now she was completely alone. The feelings of desolation and heartbreak were too much to bear. Her psyche adapted by shutting down all of Hattie's emotional pain sensors.

She was calm, too calm, but the unnatural state enabled her to function.

She had finally gotten Deedee to sleep late in the afternoon and had slumped onto the adjoining bed, craving a nap, when a loud knock hammered on the door of Room 106. Thankfully, the baby was dead asleep and didn't even stir.

Hattie peered through the peephole. *Dear God. Luc.* She wrung her hands, her brain paralyzed.

His distinctive voice sounded through the thin wood. "I see the car. I know you're in there. Open up, damn it."

Like a robot, she twisted the lock and turned the knob. As she stepped back into the room, Luc blew in with a barrage of rain and wind. A storm was brewing, the skies dark and boiling with clouds.

They faced off in the boxlike room.

He was haggard and pale, his shirt wrinkled, his hair a mess. Nothing about him suggested a successful entrepreneur.

Her heart iced over as the recollection of his deliberate cruelty flooded back.

"What do you want, Luc?" Fatigue enveloped her. She turned her back on him deliberately, sitting on the nearest bed and scooting back against the headboard. She pulled her knees to her chest, arms wrapped protectively around them.

His eyes were dark with misery. "I want *you*."

"Liar." She said it without inflection, but she saw him flinch as the insult found its mark.

He shrugged out of his jacket and swiped a hand through his wet hair. Thunder boomed, and the lights flickered. "I made a mistake. I was afraid to tell you how I felt. I never meant to drive you away."

Her fingernails dug into her legs. "I'm not stupid, Luc. I realized early on that one reason you agreed to help me was so that you could control things. You wanted the power this time. Lucky you. It worked."

He took a step toward the bed, but she stopped him with an outstretched arm.

Frustration carved grooves into his handsome face. "That idea lasted for about ten minutes. I told myself I wanted to hurt you…like you had hurt me. But I was kidding myself. I didn't want you to leave, Hattie."

"The lawyer called me. Eddie's not a threat anymore."

"I know. I read your note. It's wonderful news, but I'd rather have heard it from you face-to-face."

"You can give me part of that settlement now," she said calmly, her heart coming to life so that it could shatter into a million painful pieces. "We don't need your help anymore. We don't need you."

The look in his eyes made her ashamed. Spitefulness was not in her nature, but the need to lash out was inescapable.

He sat down at the foot of the bed, close enough for her to smell his aftershave and his natural, masculine scent. His eyes were dark, but no darker than the shadows beneath them. And he hadn't shaved. The anomaly disturbed her.

He touched her knee. A brief flash of heat tried to warm her, but he took his hand away. "What if *I* need *you?*" he asked hoarsely.

Hope flared in her chest. She smashed it ruthlessly. "You can buy anything you need."

The tired, wry twist of his lips was painful to watch. "I'm pretty sure you believed that ten years ago. It wasn't true then, and it isn't true now. My money doesn't give me control over you, Hattie. You're the one with all the power in this relationship."

"I'm a single, homeless mom with no job."

Again he winced. "You have a home," he said quietly. "And a husband who loves you more than life."

A single tear found its way down her cheek. "You never told me. Not once. We had sex a dozen times, maybe more... but you treated it like recreation. Not at all like love. And I know that's my fault. I'm sorry, Luc. Sorry I treated your love so callously back then."

He bowed his head briefly. "I should have said the words you needed to hear. But I was scared," he said. "You had the power to destroy me, Hattie. You still do."

Her lips trembled. "You've played games with my feelings. You hate me for what I did to you."

"I *tried* to hate you," he said softly. "For years. But it didn't work. When you showed up in my office that day, it was as if life had given me another chance. For a very short while, I told myself it was revenge I wanted. But I lied even to myself, Hattie. I loved you. I love you. I don't think I ever really stopped loving you. You have to believe me."

"Or what?"

"Or I'm going to buy this motel and lock you in this room until you come to your senses and admit you love me, too."

Hattie was shaking so hard, she was afraid she might fly apart. She wanted so badly to be certain he was telling the truth. "I don't want a relationship where both of us are jockeying for control. I don't want to play mind games. I need to be in an equal partnership. If I decide to go back to my career when Deedee starts school, I don't want any flack about that just because you're too rich for your own good. I'll dress up for parties and I'll hostess for you, but I may still clip the occasional coupon…" She ran out of breath.

"Is that all?"

"Isn't that enough?"

"I'll let you make all the decisions from now on."

"Liar." This time she said it with rueful humor.

He leaned forward and found her mouth in a kiss so exquisitely tender it thawed the block of ice in her chest. Tears trickled down her cheeks, but he kissed them away. He took her face in his hands, his expression grave. "I love you, Hattie Parker."

Her lips trembled. Her arms went around his neck in a stranglehold. "I love you, Luc Cavallo. And remember…my name isn't Parker anymore. I belong to you."

She felt the mighty shudder that racked his body, struggled to breathe as his arms crushed her in an unbreakable grip.

"Have you forgiven me?" she asked quietly, still feeling the sting of regret. "I cost us so much time."

He pulled back to look her in the eyes, his own deadly serious. "Maybe we both needed to grow up. Maybe we needed to be the people we are now so we could love Deedee as our own."

She sniffled, having a hard time with the juxtaposition of soaring happiness and recent despair. "Take me home, Luc. Take *us* home."

He tucked her head beneath his chin, their heartbeats thudding in unison. "I thought you'd never ask."

Epilogue

Five months later, in a small villa in the south of France, Hattie caught her breath as her husband's rigid length entered her slowly. The sensation was exquisite.

His breathing was labored, his face flushed. He loved her gently, as he had in recent weeks.

She wrapped her legs around his waist and squeezed. "I won't break," she complained.

Late-afternoon shadows painted their nude bodies with warm light. In a nearby cheval mirror, she watched as he penetrated her with a lazy rhythm. The tantalizing pace sent her soaring. He waited until her peak receded slowly and then found his own release.

Afterward, Luc ran his hand over the small bump where her flat stomach used to be. They had made a baby that very first time in Key West. A fact that Luc continually referred to with pride.

He nuzzled her belly. "I think he's a boy." Their ultrasound was scheduled soon.

She sighed, feeling sated and content. "We're going to have our hands full with two little ones so close together."

"We have Ana and Sherman to help. We'll be fine."

She brushed a lock of dark hair from his forehead. "You're my knight in shining armor. You rescued Deedee and me. I'll never forget it."

Luc rolled to his back, taking her with him to sprawl on his chest. His eyes were alight with happiness. "You've got it all wrong, my love. The two of you rescued me."

* * * * *

Book of the Month

We love this book because...

Rafe St Alban is the most dark-hearted, sinfully attractive rake in London. So get ready for fireworks when he sweeps prim Miss Henrietta Markham off her feet in Marguerite Kaye's compellingly sensual story of redemption!

On sale 4th May

Visit us Online

Find out more at
www.millsandboon.co.uk/BOTM

0412/BOTM

Special Offers

Every month we put together collections and longer reads written by your favourite authors.

Here are some of next month's highlights—and don't miss our fabulous discount online!

On sale 20th April

On sale 20th April

On sale 20th April

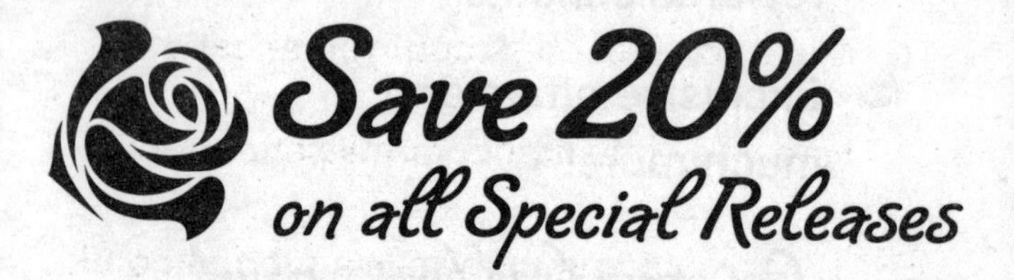

Find out more at
www.millsandboon.co.uk/specialreleases

Visit us Online

0412/ST/MB369